ICON

FREDERICK FORSYTH

ICON

BANTAM BOOKS

NEW YORK   TORONTO   LONDON   SYDNEY   AUCKLAND

ICON

A Bantam Book / November 1996

Library of Congress Cataloging-in-Publication Data
Forsyth, Frederick, 1938–
Icon / Frederick Forsyth.
p.   cm.
ISBN 0-553-09128-X
I. Title.
PR6056.O699I28   1996
823'.914—dc20   96-23434
CIP

Published simultaneously in the United States and Canada

PRINTED IN THE UNITED STATES OF AMERICA

BVG   10 9 8 7 6 5 4 3 2 1

for Sandy

CAST OF CHARACTERS

Appearing Throughout

Jason Monk	Former Agent, Central Intelligence Agency
Sir Nigel Irvine	Former Chief, British Secret Intelligence Service (SIS)
Igor A. Komarov	Leader, Ultraright Wing Russian UPF Party
Colonel Anatoli V. Grishin	Ex-KGB, Chief of Security for UPF
Ivan Markov	Acting President of Russia after July 1999
Umar Gunayev	KGB Officer, Oman; later Mafia boss, Moscow

Appearing in Part One

THE RUSSIANS

Gennadi Zyuganov	Leader, neo-Communist Party, Russia
Josef Cherkassov	President of Russia until July 1999
Boris Kuznetsov	Head of Propaganda, UPF Party
Leonid Zaitsev	Office Cleaner, UPF Party headquarters
Nikita Akopov	Confidential Private Secretary to Igor Komarov

Nikolai Turkin — KGB Officer, recruited by Jason Monk

Colonel Stanislav Androsov — Rezident, KGB, Soviet Embassy, Washington

Oleg Gordievsky — KGB Colonel, recruited by British SIS (1985)

Chief Inspector Vadim Chernov — Senior Investigator, Burglary Squad, Moscow

Mikhail Gorbachev — President of USSR 1985–1991

General Viktor Chebrikov — Chairman KGB in 1985

General Vladimir Kryuchkov — Head of First Chief Directorate, KGB, in 1985

General Vitali Boyarov — Head of Second Chief Directorate, KGB, in 1985

Pyotr Solomin — GRU Officer, recruited by Jason Monk

Professor Georgi Kuzmin — Forensic pathologist, Moscow

Pavel Volsky — Detective Inspector, Homicide, Moscow Militia

Yevgeni Novikov — Detective Inspector, Homicide, Moscow Militia

Colonel Vladimir Mechulayev — KGB Officer, controller of Ames, Rome and after

Valeri Kruglov — Soviet Diplomat, recruited by Jason Monk

Vassili Lopatin — Detective Inspector, Homicide, Moscow Militia

Professor Ivan Blinov — Nuclear Physicist, recruited by Jason Monk

THE BRITISH

Celia Stone — Assistant Press Attaché, British Embassy, Moscow

Hugo Gray — SIS Officer, British Embassy, Moscow

Jock Macdonald — Head of Station, SIS, British Embassy, Moscow

Bruce "Gracie" Fields — SIS Officer, British Embassy, Moscow

Jeffrey Marchbanks — Head of Russia Division, SIS headquarters, London

Sir Henry Coombs — Chief of SIS, London

Margaret Thatcher — British Prime Minister in 1985

Brian Worthing — Editor, *Daily Telegraph*, London

Mark Jefferson — Columnist, *Daily Telegraph*

Lady Penelope Irvine — Wife of Sir Nigel Irvine

Ciaran — Former Special Forces Soldier

Mitch — Former Special Forces Soldier

Sir William Palmer — Permanent Under-Secretary Foreign Office

THE AMERICANS

Carey Jordan — Former Deputy Director Operations, CIA, Langley

Aldrich Ames — Former CIA Officer and Traitor

Ken Mulgrew — Former CIA Official

Harry Gaunt — Former Head of Soviet Division, CIA, Langley

Saul Nathanson — Financier, Washington and Wyoming

Appearing in Part Two

Alexei II — Patriarch of Moscow and All the Russias

Father Maxim Klimovsky — Valet/Butler to the Patriarch

Inspector Dmitri Borodin — Detective, Homicide, Moscow Militia

Brian Vincent, aka Marks — Former Special Forces Soldier

General Nikolai Nikolayev — Retired Soviet Tank Veteran

Dr. Lancelot Probyn — Genealogist of the College of Heralds, London

Father Gregor Rusakov — Itinerant Revivalist Preacher

Aslan, Magomed, Sharif — Chechen Gangsters and Bodyguards

General Yuri Drozdov — Former Spymaster, KGB

Leonid Bernstein — Chairman, Moskovsky Federal Bank

Anton Gurov — Senior Executive, Commercial TV, Moscow

Major General Valentin Petrovsky — Chief, Organized Crime Division, Moscow Militia

Major General Misha Andreev — Commander, Tamanskaya Division

General Vyacheslav Butov — Deputy Defense Minister, Moscow

General Sergei Korin — Commander, Presidential Guard, Kremlin

ICON

PART ONE

CHAPTER 1

IT WAS THE SUMMER WHEN THE PRICE OF A SMALL LOAF OF BREAD topped a million rubles.

It was the summer of the third consecutive year of wheat crop failures and the second of hyperinflation.

It was the summer when in the back alleys of the faraway provincial towns the first Russians began dying of malnutrition.

It was the summer when the president collapsed in his limousine too far from help to be saved, and an old office cleaner stole a document.

After that nothing would ever be the same.

It was the summer of 1999.

•　　•　　•

IT was hot that afternoon, oppressively hot, and it took several blasts on the horn before the gatekeeper scurried from his hut to haul open the great timber doors of the Cabinet building.

The presidential bodyguard dropped his window to call to the man to shape up as the long black Mercedes 600 eased under the arch and out into Staraya Ploshad. The wretched gatekeeper threw what he hoped passed for a salute as the second car, a Russian Chaika with four more bodyguards, followed the limousine. Then they were gone.

In the back of the Mercedes President Cherkassov sat alone,

slumped in thought. In the front were his militia driver and the personal bodyguard assigned to him from the Alpha Group.

As the last drab outskirts of Moscow gave way to the fields and trees of the open countryside, the mood of the president of Russia was one of profound gloom, as well it might be. He had been three years in the office he had won after stepping in to replace the ailing Boris Yeltsin, and as he watched his country crashing into destitution, they had been the three most miserable years of his life.

Back in the winter of 1995 when he had been the prime minister, appointed by Yeltsin himself as a "technocrat" premier to lick the economy into shape, the Russian people had gone to the polls to elect a new Parliament, or Duma.

The Duma elections were important but not vital. In the preceding years more and more power had passed from the Parliament to the presidency, most of this process the work of Boris Yeltsin. By the winter of 1995 the big Siberian, who four years earlier had straddled a tank in the attempted coup of August 1991, earned the admiration of not only Russia but also the West as the great fighter for democracy, and seized the presidency for himself, had become a broken reed.

Recovering from a second heart attack in three months, puffing and bloated by medications, he watched the parliamentary elections from a clinic in the Sparrow Hills, formerly the Lenin Hills, northeast of Moscow, and saw his own political protégés hammered into third place among the delegates. That this was not as crucial as it might have been in a western democracy was largely due to the fact that because of Yeltsin, the great majority of actual power lay in the hands of the president himself. Like the United States, Russia had an executive presidency, but unlike the United States, the web of checks and balances that the Congress can impose upon the White House did not exist. Yeltsin could in effect rule by decree, and did.

But the parliamentary elections did at least show which way the wind was blowing and give an indication of the trend for the much more important presidential elections slated for June 1996.

The new force on the political horizon in the winter of 1995 was, ironically enough, the Communists. After seventy years of Communist tyranny, five years of Gorbachev reforms, and five years of Yeltsin, the Russian people began to look back with nostalgia to the old days.

The Communists, under their leader Gennadi Zyuganov, painted a rosy picture of the way things used to be: guaranteed jobs, assured salaries, affordable food, and law and order. No mention was made of the despotism of the KGB, the Gulag archipelago of slave labor camps, the suppression of all freedom of movement and expression.

The Russian voters were already in a state of profound disillusion with the two once-heralded saviors: capitalism and democracy. The second word was uttered with contempt. For many Russians, looking around at the all-embracing corruption and pandemic crime, it had all been a big lie. When the parliamentary votes were counted, the crypto-Communists had the biggest single bloc of deputies in the Duma and the right to appoint the speaker.

At the other extreme were their apparently diametric opposites, the neo-Fascists of Vladimir Zhirinovsky, leading the ironically named Liberal Democratic Party. In the 1991 elections this crude demagogue with his taste for bizarre behavior and scatological expressions had done amazingly well, but his star was falling. Nevertheless it had not fallen enough to rob him of the second largest bloc of deputies.

In the middle were the political center parties, clinging to the economic and social reforms they had introduced. They came in third.

But the real effect of those elections was to prepare the ground for the presidential race of 1996. There had been forty-three separate parties contesting the Duma elections and most of the leaders of the main parties realized that they would be best served by a program of coalescence.

Before the summer the crypto-Communists allied with their natural friends, the Agrarian or Peasants' Party, to form the Socialist Union, a clever title inasmuch as it employed two of the initials of the old USSR. The leader remained Zyuganov.

In the ultraright wing moves for unification were also afoot, but were fiercely resisted by Zhirinovsky. Vlad the Mad reckoned he could win the presidency without help from the other right-wing factions.

Russian presidential elections, like the French, are held in two parts. In the first round all candidates compete against one another. Only those candidates coming in first and second qualify for the runoff vote of the second round. Coming in third is no use. Zhirinovsky came in third. The smarter political thinkers on the extreme right were furious with him.

The dozen parties of the center united, more or less, into the Democratic Alliance, with the key question throughout the spring of 1996 whether Boris Yeltsin would be fit enough to stand for, and win, the presidency again.

His downfall would later be ascribed by historians to a single word—Chechnya.

Exasperated to the breaking point twelve months earlier, Yeltsin had launched the full might of the Russian army and air force against a small, warlike mountain tribe whose self-appointed leader was insisting on complete independence from Moscow. There was nothing new about trouble from the Chechens—their resistance went back to the days of the czars and beyond. They had somehow survived pogroms launched against them by several czars, and by the cruelest tyrant of them all, Josef Stalin. Somehow they had survived the repeated devastation of their tiny homeland, the deportations and genocide, and continued to fight back.

Launching the full might of the Russian armed forces against the Chechens was an impetuous decision that led not to a quick and glorious victory but to the utter destruction—on camera and in glorious Technicolor—of the Chechen capital of Grozny and to the endless train of Russian soldiers in body bags coming back from the campaign.

With their capital reduced to rubble, but still armed to the teeth with weapons largely sold to them by corrupt Russian generals, the Chechens took to the hills they know so well and refused to be flushed out. The same Russian army that had met its inglorious Vietnam in attempting to invade and hold Afghanistan had now created a second one in the wild foothills of the Caucasus Range.

If Boris Yeltsin had launched his Chechen campaign to prove he was a strong man in the traditional Russian mold, it became a gesture that had failed. All through 1995 he lusted for his final victory, and always it eluded him. As they saw their young sons coming back from the Caucasus in sacks, the Russian people turned viciously anti-Chechen. They also turned against the man who could not deliver them a victory.

By early summer, after grueling personal effort, Yeltsin rewon his presidency after a runoff. But a year later he was gone. The mantle passed to the technocrat Josef Cherkassov, leader of the Russian Homeland Party, by then part of the broad Democratic Alliance.

Cherkassov seemed to have started well. He had the benign good wishes of the West and, more important, its financial credits to keep the Russian economy in some kind of shape. Heeding Western advice, he negotiated at last a peace deal with Chechnya, and although the vengeful Russians hated the idea of the Chechens getting away with their rebellion, bringing the soldiers home was popular.

But things began to go wrong within eighteen months. The causes for this were twofold: first, the depredations of the Russian mafia simply became too burdensome at last for the Russian economy to bear, and second, there was yet another foolish military adventure. In late 1997 Siberia, home of ninety percent of Russian wealth, threatened to secede.

Siberia was the least tamed of all Russia's provinces. Yet under her permafrost, barely even exploited, were oil and gas deposits that made even Saudi Arabia look deprived. Added to that were gold, diamonds, bauxite, manganese, tungsten, nickel, and platinum. By the late nineties, Siberia was still the last frontier on the planet.

The problem began with reports reaching Moscow that some Japanese but mainly South Korean underworld emissaries were circulating in Siberia urging secession. President Cherkassov, illadvised by his circle of sycophants and seemingly oblivious of his own predecessor's mistakes in Chechnya, sent the army east. The move provoked a double catastrophe. After twelve months without a military solution he had to negotiate a deal granting the Siberians far more autonomy and control over the proceeds of their own wealth than they had ever had. Second, the adventure triggered hyperinflation.

The government tried to print its way out of trouble. By the summer of 1999 the days of five thousand rubles to the dollar of the mid-nineties were a memory. The wheat crop from the black earth country of the Kuban had failed twice, in 1997 and 1998, and the crop from Siberia was delayed until it rotted because the partisans blew away the railroad tracks. In the cities bread prices spiraled. President Cherkassov clung to office but was clearly no longer in power.

In the countryside, which should at the least have been growing enough food to feed itself, the conditions were at their worst. Underfunded, undermanned, their infrastructure collapsing, the farms stood idle, their rich soil producing weeds. Trains stopping at wayside halts were besieged by peasants, mainly elderly, offering furniture, clothes, and bric-a-brac to the carriage windows for money or, even better, food. There were few takers.

In Moscow, the capital and showcase of the nation, the destitute slept out on the quays along the Moskva and in the back alleys. The police—called the militia in Russia—having virtually abandoned the struggle against crime, tried to pick them up and hustle them onto trains heading back where they came from. But more kept arriving, seeking work, food, relief. Many of them would be reduced to begging and dying on the streets of Moscow.

In the early spring of 1999 the West finally gave up pouring subsidies into the bottomless pit, and the foreign investors, even those in partnership with the mafia, pulled out. The Russian economy, like a war refugee raped too many times, lay down by the side of the road and died of despair.

This was the gloomy prospect that President Cherkassov contemplated as he drove that hot summer's day out to his weekend retreat.

The driver knew the road to the country dacha, out beyond Usovo on the banks of the Moskva River, where the air was cooler under the trees. Years ago the fat cats of the Soviet Politburo had had their dachas in the woods along this bend of the river. Much had changed in Russia, but not that much.

Traffic was light because gasoline was expensive and the trucks they passed belched great plumes of pure black smoke. After Archangelskoye they crossed the bridge and turned along the road beside the river, which flowed quietly in the summer haze toward the city behind them.

Five minutes later President Cherkassov felt himself to be short of breath. Although the air conditioning was at full blast he pushed the button to open the rear window next to his face and let nature's air blow over him. It was hotter, and made his breathing little better. Behind the partition screen neither driver nor bodyguard had noticed. The turnoff to Peredelkino came up on the right. As they passed it, the president of Russia leaned to his left and fell sideways across his seat.

The first thing the driver noticed was that the president's head had disappeared from his rearview mirror. He muttered something to the bodyguard, who turned his torso around to look. In a second the Mercedes slewed into the side of the road.

Behind, the Chaika did the same. The head of the security detail, a former colonel of Spetsnaz, leaped from the front passenger seat and ran forward. Others came out from their seats, guns drawn, and formed a protective ring. They did not know what had happened.

The colonel reached the Mercedes, where the bodyguard had the rear door open and was leaning in. The colonel yanked him backward to see better. The president was half on his back, half on his side, both hands clutching at his chest, eyes closed, breathing in short grunts.

The nearest hospital with top-of-the-line intensive care facilities was the Number One State Clinic miles away in the Sparrow Hills. The colonel got into the rear seat beside the stricken Cherkassov and ordered the driver to hang a U-turn and head back for the Orbital Beltway. White-faced, the driver did so. From his portable phone the colonel raised the clinic and ordered an ambulance to meet them halfway.

The rendezvous was half an hour later in the middle of the divided highway. Paramedics transferred the unconscious man from the limousine to the ambulance and went to work as the three-vehicle convoy raced to the clinic.

Once there the president came under the care of the senior cardiac specialist on duty and was rushed to the ICU. They used what they had, the latest and the best, but they were still too late. The line across the screen of the monitor refused to budge, maintaining a long straight line and a high-pitched buzz. At ten minutes past four the senior physician straightened up and shook his head. The man with the defibrillator stood back.

The colonel punched some numbers into his mobile phone. Someone answered at the third ring. The colonel said: "Get me the office of the prime minister."

•   •   •

SIX hours later, far out on the rolling surface of the Caribbean, the *Foxy Lady* turned for home. Down on the afterdeck Julius the boatman hauled in the lines, detached the wire traces, and stowed the rods. It had been a full-day charter and a good one.

While Julius wound the traces and their brilliant plastic lures into neat circles for storing in the tackle box, the American couple popped a couple of cans of beer and sat contentedly under the awning to slake their thirst.

In the fish locker were two huge wahoo close to forty pounds each and half a dozen big dorado that a few hours earlier had been lurking under a weed patch ten miles away.

The skipper on the upper bridge checked his course for the islands and eased the throttles forward from trolling speed to fast cruise. He reckoned he would be sliding into Turtle Cove in less than an hour.

The *Foxy Lady* seemed to know her work was almost over and her berth in the sheltered harbor up the quay from the Tiki Hut was waiting for her. She tucked in her tail, lifted her nose, and the deep-V hull began to slice through the blue water. Julius dunked a bucket in the passing water and sluiced the afterdeck yet again.

•   •   •

WHEN Zhirinovsky had been leader of the Liberal Democrats the party headquarters were in a shabby slum of a building in Fish Alley, just off Sretenka Street. Visitors not aware of the strange ways of Vlad the Mad had been amazed to discover how tawdry it was. The plaster peeling, the windows displaying two flyblown posters of the demagogue, the place had not seen a wet mop in a decade. Inside the chipped black door, visitors found a gloomy lobby with a booth selling T-shirts with the leader's portrait on the front and racks of the requisite black leather jackets worn by his supporters.

Up the uncarpeted stairs, clothed in gloomy brown paint, was the first half-landing, with a grilled window where a surly guard asked the caller's business. Only if this was satisfactory could he then ascend to the tacky rooms above where Zhirinovsky held court when he was in town. Hard rock boomed throughout the building. This was the way the eccentric fascist had preferred to keep the headquarters, on the grounds that the image spoke of a man of the people rather than one of the fat cats. But Zhirinovsky was long gone now, and the Liberal Democratic Party had been amalgamated with the other ultraright and neofascist parties into the Union of Patriotic Forces.

Its undisputed leader was Igor Komarov, and he was a completely

different kind of man. Nevertheless, seeing the basic logic of showing the poor and dispossessed whose votes he sought that the Union
of Patriotic Forces permitted itself no expensive indulgences, he
kept the Fish Alley building, but maintained his own private offices
elsewhere.

Trained as an engineer, Komarov had worked under Communism but not for it, until halfway through the Yeltsin period he had
decided to enter politics. He had chosen the Liberal Democratic
Party, and though he privately despised Zhirinovsky for his
drunken excesses and constant sexual innuendo, his quiet work in
the background had brought him to the Politburo, the inner council
of the party. From here, in a series of covert meetings with leaders
of other ultraright parties, he had stitched together the alliance of all
the right-wing elements in Russia into the UPF. Presented with an
accomplished fact, Zhirinovsky grudgingly accepted its existence
and fell into the trap of chairing its first plenum.

The plenum passed a resolution requiring his resignation and
ditched him. Komarov declined to take the leadership but ensured
that it went to a nonentity, a man with no charisma and little
organizational talent. A year later it was easy to play upon the sense
of disappointment in the Union's governing council, ease out the
stopgap, and take the leadership himself. The career of Vladimir
Zhirinovsky had ended.

Within two years after the 1996 elections the crypto-Communists
began to fade. Their supporters had always been predominantly
middle-aged and elderly and they had trouble raising funds. Without
big-banker support the membership fees were no longer enough. The
Socialist Union's money and its appeal dwindled.

By 1998 Komarov was undisputed leader of the ultraright and in
prime position to play upon the growing despair of the Russian
people, of which there was plenty.

Yet along with all this poverty and destitution there was also
ostentatious wealth to make the eyes blink. Those who had money
had mountains of it, much of it in foreign currency. They swept
through the streets in long stretch limousines, American or German, for the Zil factory had gone out of production, often accompanied by motorcycle outriders to clear a path and usually with a
second car of bodyguards racing along behind.

In the lobby of the Bolshoi, in the bars and banquet halls of the

Metropol and the National, they could be seen each evening, accompanied by their hookers trailing sable, mink, the aroma of Parisian scent, and glittering with diamonds. These were the fat cats, fatter than ever.

In the Duma the delegates shouted and waved order papers and passed resolutions. "It reminds me," said an English foreign correspondent, "of all I ever heard of the last days of the Weimar Republic."

The one man who seemed to offer a possible ray of hope was Igor Komarov.

In the two years since he had taken power in the party of the right, Komarov had surprised most observers, both inside and outside Russia. If he had been content to remain simply a superb political organizer, he would have been just another apparatchik. But he changed. Or so observers thought. More probably he had a talent he had been content to keep hidden.

Komarov made his mark as a passionate and charismatic popular orator. When he was on the podium those who recalled the quiet, soft-spoken, fastidious private man were amazed. He seemed transformed. His voice increased and deepened to a rolling baritone, using all the many expressions and inflections of the Russian language to great effect. He could drop his tone almost to a whisper so that even with microphones the audience had to strain to catch the words, then rise to a ringing peroration that brought the crowds to their feet and had even the skeptics cheering.

He quickly mastered the area of his own specialty, the living crowd. He avoided the televised fireside chat or television interview, aware that though these might work in the West, they were not for Russia. Russians rarely invited people into their homes, let alone the entire nation.

Nor was he interested in being trapped by hostile questions. Every speech he made was stage-managed, but the technique worked. He addressed only rallies of the party faithful, with the cameras under the control of his own filmmaking team commanded by the brilliant young director Litvinov. Cut and edited, these films were released for nationwide television viewing on his own terms, to be aired complete and unabridged. This he could achieve by buying TV time instead of relying upon the vagaries of newscasters.

His theme was always the same and always popular—Russia, Russia, and again Russia. He inveighed against the foreigners whose international conspiracies had brought Russia to her knees. He clamored for the expulsion of all the "blacks," the popular Russian way of referring to Armenians, Georgians, Azeris, and others from the south, many of whom were known to be among the richest of the criminal profiteers. He cried out for justice for the poor, down-trodden Russian people who would one day rise with him to re-store the glories of the past and sweep away the filth that clogged the streets of the motherland.

He promised all things to all men. For the out-of-work there would be employment, a fair day's wage for a good day's work, with food on the table and dignity again. For those with obliterated life savings there would be honest currency again and something to put by for a comfortable old age. For those who wore the uniform of the Rodina, the ancient motherland, there would be pride again to wipe out the humiliations visited upon them by cravens elevated to high office by foreign capital.

And they heard him. By radio and television they heard him across the wide steppes. The soldiers of the once-great Russian army heard him, huddled under canvas, expelled from Afghanistan, East Germany, Czechoslovakia, Hungary, Poland, Latvia, Lithuania, and Estonia in an endless series of retreats from empire.

The peasants heard him in their cottages and izbas, scattered across the vast landscape. The ruined middle classes heard him among the bits of furniture they had not pawned for food on the table and a few coals in the hearth. Even the industrial bosses heard him and dreamed that their furnaces might one day roar again. And when he promised them that the angel of death would walk among the crooks and gangsters who had raped their beloved Mother Rus-sia, they loved him.

In the spring of 1999, at the suggestion of his PR adviser, a very clever young man who had graduated from an American Ivy League college, Igor Komarov granted a series of private interviews. Young Boris Kuznetsov picked the candidates well, mainly legisla-tors and journalists of the conservative wing across America and Western Europe. The purpose of the reception was to calm their fears.

As a campaign, it worked brilliantly. Most arrived expecting to find what they had been told they would find: a wild-eyed ultraright demagogue, variously dubbed racist or neo-Fascist or both.

They found themselves talking to a thoughtful, well-mannered man in a sober suit. As Komarov spoke no English, it was his PR aide who sat by his side, both guiding the interview and interpreting. Whenever his adored leader said something he knew might be ill-interpreted in the West, Kuznetsov simply translated it into something much more acceptable in English. No one noticed, for he had ensured that none of the visitors understood Russian.

Thus Komarov could explain that, as practicing politicians, we all have constituencies and we cannot needlessly offend them if we wish to be elected. Thus we may on occasion have to say what we know they want to hear, even though to achieve it may be much harder than we pretend. And the senators nodded understandingly.

He explained that in the older western democracies people broadly understood that social discipline began with oneself, so that externally imposed discipline, by the state, might be the lighter. But where all forms of self-discipline had broken down, the state might have to be firmer than would be acceptable in the West. And the MPs nodded understandingly.

To the conservative journalists he explained that the restoration of a sound currency could simply not be achieved without some draconian measures against crime and corruption in the short term. The journalists wrote that Igor Komarov was a man who would listen to reason on matters economic and political, such as cooperation with the West. He might be too far right for acceptance in a European or American democracy, and his powerful demagoguery too frightening for western palates, but he might well be the man for Russia in her present straits. In any case, he would almost certainly win the presidential election in June 2000. The polls showed that. The farsighted would be wise to support him.

In chancelleries, embassies, ministries, and boardrooms across the West, the cigar smoke rose to the ceilings and heads nodded.

•   •   •

IN the northern sector of the central area of Moscow, just inside the Boulevard Ring road and halfway down Kiselny Boulevard, is a side street. Midway along the west side of the street there is a small park, about half an acre in size, surrounded on three sides by windowless buildings and protected at the front by ten-foot-high green steel sheets, over the top of which the tips of a line of conifers can just be seen. Set in the steel wall is a double gate, also steel.

The small park is in fact the garden of a superb prerevolutionary town house or mansion, exquisitely restored in the mid-1980s. Although the interior is modern and functional, the classic facade is painted in pastel shades, the plasterwork over doors and windows picked out in white. This was the real headquarters of Igor Komarov.

A visitor at the front gate would be in full view of a camera atop the wall and would announce himself via an intercom. He would be talking to a guard in a hut just within the gate, who would check with the security office inside the dacha.

If the gates opened, a car could roll forward for ten yards before stopping at a row of spikes. The steel gates, sliding sideways on rollers, would close automatically behind it. The guard would then emerge to check identification papers. If these were in order, he would retire to his hut and press an electric control. The spikes would recede and the car could go forward to the gravel forecourt where more guards would be waiting.

From either side of the dacha chain-link fencing ran to the edges of the compound, bolted firmly to the surrounding walls. Behind the chain-link were the dogs. There were two teams, and each responded only to one dog handler.' The handlers worked alternate nights. After dark, gates in the fencing were opened and the dogs had the run of the whole compound, front and back. Thereafter the gate guard stayed inside his hut, and in the event of a late visitor he would have to contact the handler to call off the dogs.

In order to avoid losing too many of the staff to the dogs, there was an underground passage at the rear of the building, leading to a narrow alley which itself led to Kiselny Boulevard. This passage had three keypad doors: one inside the dacha, one at the street, and one midway. This was the access and egress for deliveries and staff.

At night, when the political staff had left and the dogs prowled the grounds, two security men remained on duty inside the dacha. They had a room of their own, with a TV and facilities for snacks, but no beds because they were not supposed to sleep. Alternately, they prowled the three floors of the dacha until relieved by the day shift arriving at the breakfast hour. Mr. Komarov came later.

But dust and cobwebs are no respecters of high office, and every night except Sunday, when the buzzer from the rear alley sounded, one of the guards would let in the cleaner.

In Moscow most cleaners are women but Komarov preferred an all-male environment around him, including the cleaner, a harmless old soldier called Leonid Zaitsev. The surname means "rabbit" in Russian, and because of his helpless manner, threadbare ex-army greatcoat worn winter and summer, and the three stainless steel teeth that gleamed at the front of his mouth—Red Army dentistry used to be pretty basic—the guards at the dacha just called him Rabbit. The night the president died they let him in as usual at 10:00 P.M.

It was one in the morning when, with bucket and duster in hand, dragging the vacuum cleaner behind him, he reached the office of N. I. Akopov, the personal private secretary of Mr. Komarov. He had only met the man once, a year ago, when he had arrived to find some of the senior staff working very late. The man had been extremely rude to him, ordering him out with a stream of invective. Sometimes, since then, he had got his own back by sitting in Mr. Akopov's comfortable leather swivel chair.

Because he knew the guards were downstairs, the Rabbit sat in the swivel chair and reveled in the lush comfort of the leather. He had never had a chair like that and never would. There was a document on the desk blotter, about forty pages of typescript bound at the edge with a spiral binding and covered front and back with heavy black paper.

The Rabbit wondered why it had been left out. Normally Mr. Akopov put everything away in his wall safe. He must have, for the Rabbit had never seen a document before and all the desk drawers were always locked. He flicked open the black cover and looked at the title. Then he opened the file at random.

He was not a good reader, but he could do it. His foster mother had taught him long ago, and then the teachers at the state school and finally a kindly officer in the army.

What he saw troubled him. He read one passage several times; some of the words were too long and complex, but he understood the meanings. His arthritic hands trembled as he turned the pages. Why should Mr. Komarov say such things? And about people like his foster mother whom he had loved? He did not fully understand, but it worried him. Perhaps he should consult the guards downstairs? But they would just hit him about the head and tell him to get on with his work.

An hour went by. The guards should have patrolled but they were glued to their television where the extended news program had informed the nation that the prime minister, in accordance with Article Fifty-nine of the Russian constitution, had taken over the duties of president, per interim, for the prescribed three months.

The Rabbit read the same few passages over and over until he understood their meaning. But he could not grasp the meaning behind the meaning. Mr. Komarov was a great man. He was going to become the next president of Russia, was he not? So why should he be saying such things about the Rabbit's foster mother and people like her, for she was long dead?

At two in the morning the Rabbit stuffed the file inside his shirt, finished his work, and asked to be let out. The guards reluctantly left their TV screen to open the doors and the Rabbit wandered off into the night. He was a bit earlier than usual, but the guards did not mind.

Zaitsev thought of going home, but decided he had better not. It was too early. The buses, trams, and subways were all shut down as usual. He always had to walk home, sometimes in the rain, but he needed the job. The walk took an hour. If he went now he would wake his daughter and her two children. She would not like that. So he wandered through the streets wondering what to do.

By half past three he found himself on the Kremlevskaya Quay, beneath the southern walls of the Kremlin. There were tramps and derelicts sleeping along the quay, but he found a bench with some space, sat down, and stared out across the river.

•   •   •

THE sea had calmed down as they approached the island, as it always did in the afternoon, as if telling the fisherman and the mariners that the contest for the day was over and the ocean would call a truce till tomorrow. To right and left the skipper could see several other boats heading for the Wheeland Cut, the northwestern gap in the reef that gave access from the open sea to the flat lagoon.

To starboard Arthur Dean in his open *Silver Deep* raced past, making eight knots better than the *Foxy Lady*. The islander waved a greeting and the American skipper waved back. He saw two divers in the back of the *Silver Deep* and reckoned they had been exploring the coral off Northwest Point. There would be lobster in the Dean household tonight.

He slowed the *Foxy Lady* to navigate the cut, for on either side the razor-tipped coral was barely inches below the surface, and once through they settled down for the easy ten minutes down the coast to Turtle Cove.

The skipper loved his boat, his livelihood and mistress all in one. She was a ten-year-old thirty-one-foot Bertram Moppie—originally so named after designer Dick Bertram's wife—and though not the biggest nor the most luxurious charter fishing vessel in Turtle Cove, her owner and skipper would match her against any sea and any fish. He had bought her five years earlier when he moved to the islands, secondhand from a yard in South Florida via a small ad in the *Boat Trader,* then worked on her himself night and day until she was the sassiest girl in all the islands. He had not regretted a dollar of her, even though he was still paying off the finance company.

Inside the harbor he eased the Bertram into her slot two down from fellow American Bob Collins on the *Sakitumi,* switched off, and came down to ask his clients if they had had a good day. They had indeed, they assured him, and paid his fee with a generous gratuity for himself and Julius. When they had gone he winked at Julius, let him keep the entire tip and the fish, took off his cap, and ran his fingers through his tousled blond hair.

Then he left the grinning islander to finish cleaning off the boat, fresh-water rinsing all the rods and reels and leaving *Foxy Lady* shipshape for the night. He would come back to close her up before going home. In the meantime he felt a straight lime daiquiri coming on, so he strolled down the boardwalk to the Banana Boat, greeting all he met as they greeted him.

CHAPTER 2

TWO HOURS AFTER SITTING ON HIS RIVERSIDE BENCH, LEONID Zaitsev still had not worked out his problem. He wished now he had not taken the document. He did not really know why he had. If they found out, he would be punished. But then, life always seemed to have punished him and he could not really understand why.

The Rabbit had been born in a small and poor village west of Smolensk in 1936. It was not much of a place, but one like tens of thousands scattered across the land—a single rutted street, dusty in summer, a river of mud in ·autumn, and rock-hard with frost in winter. Thirty or so houses, some barns, and the former peasants now herded into a Stalinist collective farm. His father was a farm worker and they lived in a hovel just off the main road.

Down the road, with a small shop and a flat above it, lived the village baker. His father told him he should not have anything to do with the baker, because he was *"yevrey."* He did not know what that meant, but clearly it was not a good thing to be. But he noticed his mother bought her bread there, and very good bread it was.

He was puzzled that he should not talk to the baker, for he was a jolly man who would sometimes stand in the doorway of his shop, wink at Leonid, and toss him a *bulochka,* a warm sticky bun fresh from the oven. Because of what his father said, he would run behind the cattle shed to eat the bun. The baker lived with his wife and two daughters, whom he could sometimes see peeping out from the shop, though they never seemed to come out and play.

On a day in late July 1941 death came to the village. The little boy did not know it was death at the time. He heard the rumbling and growling and ran out of the barn. There were huge iron monsters coming from the main road up to the village. The first one came to a halt right in the middle of the houses. Leonid stood in the street to have a better look.

It seemed enormous, as big as a house itself, but it rolled on tracks and had a long gun sticking out in front. At the very top, above the gun, a man was standing with his upper half in the open. He took off a thick padded helmet and laid it beside him. It was very hot that day. Then he turned and looked down at Leonid.

The child saw that the man had almost white-blond hair and eyes of a blue so pale that it was as if the summer sky was shining straight through the skull from the back. There was no expression in the eyes, neither love nor hatred, just a sort of blank boredom. Quite slowly the man reached to his side and pulled a handgun from a pouch.

Something told Leonid all was not well. He heard the whump of grenades thrown through windows, and screams. He was frightened, turned and ran. There was a crack and something fanned through his hair. He got behind the cattle shed, began to cry, and kept running. There was a steady chattering sound behind him and the smell of burning timber as the houses flamed. He saw the forest ahead of him and kept running.

Inside the forest he did not know what to do. He was still crying and calling for his mommy and his daddy. But they never came. They never came again.

He came upon a woman, screaming about her husband and her daughters, and recognized the baker's wife, Mrs. Davidova. She seized him and hugged him to her bosom, and he could not understand why she should do that, and what would his father think, because she was *yevrey*!

The village had ceased to exist and the SS–Panzer unit had turned and gone. There were a few other survivors in the forest. Later they met some partisans, hard, bearded men with guns who lived there. With a partisan guide a column of them set off, eastward, always eastward.

When he became tired, Mrs. Davidova carried him, until at last, weeks later, they reached Moscow. She seemed to know some people there, who gave them shelter, food, and warmth. They were nice to him and looked like Mr. Davidov, with ringlets from their temples to their chins and broad-brimmed hats. Although he was not *yevrey*, Mrs. Davidova insisted she adopt him and she looked after him for years.

After the war the authorities discovered he was not her real son and separated them, sending him to an orphanage. He cried very much when they parted and so did she, but he never saw her again. At the orphanage they taught him that *yevrey* meant Jewish.

The Rabbit sat on his bench and wondered about the document under his shirt. He did not fully comprehend the meaning of phrases like "total extermination" or "utter annihilation." The words were too long for him, but he did not think they were good words. He could not understand why Mr. Komarov should want to do that to people like Mrs. Davidova.

There was a hint of pink in the east. In a big mansion across the river on Sofiskaya Quay a Royal Marine took a flag and began to climb the stairs toward the roof.

·   ·   ·

THE skipper took his daiquiri, rose from the table, and wandered to the wood rail. He looked down at the water, then up across the darkening harbor.

Forty-nine, he thought, forty-nine and still in hock to the company store. Jason Monk, you're getting old and past it.

He took a swig and felt the lime and rum hit the spot.

What the hell, it's been a pretty good life. Eventful, anyway.

It had not started that way. It started in a humble timber-frame house in the tiny town of Crozet in south-central Virginia, just east of the Shenandoah, five miles off the highway from Waynesboro to Charlottesville.

Albemarle County is farming country, steeped in memorials of the War Between the States, for eighty percent of that war was fought in Virginia and no Virginian ever forgets it. At the local county grade school most of his schoolmates had fathers who raised tobacco, soybeans, or hogs, or all three.

Jason Monk's father, by contrast, was a forest ranger working in the Shenandoah National Park. No one ever became a millionaire working for the Forestry Service, but it was a good life for a boy, even if dollars were short. Vacations were not for lazing around but for finding opportunities to do extra work to make some money and help out in the home.

He recalled how his father would take him as a child up into the park that covered the Blue Ridge Mountains to show him the difference between spruce, birch, fir, oak, and loblolly pine. Sometimes they would meet the game wardens and he would listen round-eyed to their tales of black bear and deer, and their hunts for turkey, grouse, and wild pheasant.

Later he learned to use a gun with unerring accuracy, to track and trail, make camp and hide all traces in the morning, and when he was big and strong enough he got vacation work in the logging camps.

He attended the county grade school from age five until twelve, and just after his thirteenth birthday enrolled at County High in Charlottesville, rising every morning before dawn to commute from Crozet to the city. It was at the high school that something was to happen that would change his life.

Back in 1944 a certain GI sergeant had, with thousands of others, hauled himself off Omaha Beach and struck into the hinterland of Normandy. Somewhere outside Saint-Lo, separated from his unit, he had come into the sights of a German sniper. He was lucky; the bullet grazed his upper arm. The twenty-three-year-old American crawled into a nearby farmhouse where the family tended his wound and gave him shelter. When the sixteen-year-old daughter of the house put the cold compress on his wound and he looked into her eyes, he knew he had been struck harder than any German bullet would ever do.

A year later he returned from Berlin to Normandy, proposed, and married her in the orchard of her father's farm with a U.S. Army chaplain officiating. Later, because the French do not marry in orchards, the local Catholic priest did the same in the village church. Then he brought his bride back to Virginia.

Twenty years later he was deputy principal of Charlottesville County High, and his wife, with their children off their hands, suggested she might teach French there. Mrs. Josephine Brady was pretty and glamorous and French, so her classes quickly became very sought after.

In the fall of 1965 there was a newcomer in her first-year class, a rather shy youth with an untidy shock of blond hair and a fetching grin, called Jason Monk. Within a year she could avow she had never heard a foreigner speak French like him. The talent had to be natural; it could not be inherited. But it was there, not just a mastery of the grammar and the syntax, but an ability to copy the accent to perfection.

In his last year at County High, he would visit her house and they would read Malraux, Proust, Gide, and Sartre (who was incredibly erotic for those days) but their mutual favorites were the older romantic poets, Rimbaud, Mallarmé, Verlaine, and De Vigny. It was not intended to happen but it did. Perhaps the poets were to blame, but despite the age gap, which worried neither of them, they had a brief affair.

By the time he was eighteen Jason Monk could do two things unusual in teenagers of Southern Virginia; he could speak French and make love, each with considerable skill. At eighteen he joined the army.

In 1968 the Vietnam War was very much in full flow. Many young Americans were trying to avoid serving there. Those who presented themselves as volunteers, signing on for three years, were welcomed with open arms.

Monk did his basic training and somewhere along the line he filled in his résumé. Under the question "foreign languages" he filled in "French." He was summoned to the office of the Camp Adjutant.

"You really speak French?" asked the officer. Monk explained. The adjutant called Charlottesville High and spoke with the school secretary. She contacted Mrs. Brady. Then she rang back. This took a day. Monk was told to report again. This time there was a major from G2, Army Intelligence, present.

Apart from speaking Vietnamese, most people of a certain age in this former French colony spoke French. Monk was flown to Saigon. He did two tours, with a gap in between back in the States.

On the day of his release, the C.O. ordered him to report to his office. There were two civilians present. The colonel left.

"Please, sergeant, take a seat," said the older and more genial of the two men. He toyed with a briar pipe while the more earnest one broke into a torrent of French. Monk replied in like vein. This went on for ten minutes. Then the French speaker gave a grin and turned to his colleague.

"He's good, Carey, he's damn good." Then he too left.

"So, what do you think of Vietnam?" asked the remaining man. He was then about forty, with a lined, amused face. It was 1971.

"It's a house of cards, sir," said Monk. "And it's falling down. Two more years and we'll have to get out of there."

Carey seemed to agree. He nodded several times.

"You're right, but don't tell the army. What are you going to do now?"

"I haven't made up my mind, sir."

"Well, I can't make it up for you. But you have a gift. I don't even have it myself. My friend out there is as American as you and me, but he was raised in France for twenty years. If he says you're good, that's enough for me. So why not continue?"

"You mean college, sir?"

"I do. The G.I. Bill will pick up most of the tab. Uncle Sam feels you've earned it. Take advantage."

During his years in the army Monk had sent most of his spare cash home to his mother to help raise the other children.

"Even the G.I. Bill requires a thousand dollars in cash," he said.

Carey shrugged. "I guess a thousand dollars can be raised. If you'll major in Russian."

"And if I do?"

"Then give me a call. The outfit I work for might be able to offer you something."

"It could take four years, sir."

"Oh, we're patient folk where I work."

"How did you know about me, sir?"

"Down in Vietnam, some of our people in the Phoenix Program spotted you and your work. You got some good tips on the VC. They liked that."

"It's Langley, isn't it, sir? You're the CIA."

"Oh, not all of it. Just a small cog."

Carey Jordan was actually much more than a small cog. He

would go on to become Deputy Director (Operations), that is, head of the whole espionage arm.

Monk took the advice and enrolled at the University of Virginia, right back in Charlottesville. He drank tea with Mrs. Brady again, but just as friends. He studied Slavonic languages and majored in Russian at a level his senior adviser, himself a Russian, termed "bilingual." He graduated at the age of twenty-five in 1975 and just after his next birthday was accepted into the CIA. After the usual basic training at Fort Peary, known in the agency simply as "the Farm," he was assigned to Langley, then New York, and back to Langley.

It would be five years, and many, many courses later, before he would get his first posting abroad, and then it was to Nairobi, Kenya.

•   •   •

CORPORAL Meadows of the Royal Marines did his duty that bright morning of July 16. He snap-locked the reinforced edge of the flag to the hoisting cord and ran the banner up the pole to the top. There it fluttered open in the dawn breeze to tell all the world who dwelt beneath it.

The British government had actually bought the handsome old mansion on Sofia Quay from its previous owner, a sugar magnate, just before the revolution, turned it into the embassy, and had stayed there through thick and thin ever since.

Josef Stalin, the last dictator to live in the State Apartments of the Kremlin, used to rise each morning, throw back his curtains, and see the British flag fluttering right across the river. It made him extremely angry. Repeated pressure was brought to persuade the British to move. They refused.

Over the years the mansion became too small to house all the departments required by the mission to Moscow, so that subsections were scattered all over the city. But despite repeated offers to house all the sections in one compound, London politely replied that it would prefer to stay on Sofia Quay. As the building was sovereign British territory, there it stayed.

Leonid Zaitsev sat across the river and watched the flag flutter open as the first rays of dawn tipped the hills to the east. The sight brought back a distant memory.

At eighteen the Rabbit had been called up for the Red Army and after the usual minimal basic training he had been posted with the tanks to East Germany. He was a private, tagged by his instructors as not even corporal material.

One day in 1955, on a routine march outside Potsdam, he had become separated from his company in dense forest. Lost and afraid, he blundered through the woods until he stumbled out on a sandy track. There he halted, rooted to the spot, paralyzed with fear. Ten yards away was an open jeep containing four soldiers. They had evidently paused for a break while on patrol.

Two were still in the vehicle, two were standing beside it, smoking cigarettes. They had bottles of beer in their hands. He knew at once they were not Russians. They were foreigners, Westerners, from the Allied Mission at Potsdam, set up under the Four-Power Agreement of 1945, of which he knew nothing. He knew only, because he had been told, that they were the enemy, come to destroy Socialism and, if they could, to kill him.

They stopped talking when they saw him and stared at him. One of them said: " 'Ello, 'ello. What have we got 'ere? A bleeding Russky. Allo, Ivan."

He did not understand a word. He had a tommy gun slung over his shoulder but they did not seem afraid of him. It was the other way around. Two of them wore black berets, with shining brass cap badges and behind the emblems a cluster of white-and-red feathers. He did not know it, but he was looking at the regimental hackle of the Royal Fusiliers.

One of the soldiers next to the vehicle peeled himself away and sauntered toward him. He thought he was going to wet himself. The man was also young, with red hair and a freckled face. He grinned at Zaitsev and held out a bottle.

"Come on, mate. 'Ave a beer."

Leonid felt the chill of the cold glass in his hand. The foreign soldier nodded encouragingly. It would be poisoned of course. He put the neck of the bottle to his lips and tilted. The cold liquid hit the back of his throat. It was strong, better than Russian beer, and good, but it made him cough. Carrot-hair laughed.

"Go on, then. 'Ave a beer," he said. To Zaitsev it was just a voice making sounds. To his amazement the foreign soldier turned his back and sauntered the few feet to his vehicle. The man was not even afraid of him. He was armed, he was the Red Army, and the foreigners were grinning and joking.

He stood by the trees, drinking the cold beer and wondered what Colonel Nikolayev would think. The colonel commanded his squadron. He was only about thirty, but he was a decorated war hero. Once he had stopped and asked Zaitsev about his background, where he came from. The private had told him: an orphanage. The colonel had patted him on the back and told him that now he had a home. He adored Colonel Nikolayev.

He was too frightened to throw their beer back at them, and anyway it tasted very good, even if it was poisoned. So he drank it. After ten minutes the two soldiers on the ground climbed into the rear and pulled on their berets. The driver started up and they drove away. No hurry, no fear of him. The one with red hair turned and waved. They were the enemy, they were preparing to invade Russia, but they waved at him.

When they had gone he threw the empty bottle as far into the woods as he could, and ran through the trees until eventually he saw a Russian truck, which brought him back to camp. The sergeant gave him a week's kitchen duty for getting lost, but he never told anyone about the foreigners or the beer.

Before the foreign vehicle drove off he noticed that it had some sort of regimental insignia on the front right wing and a wasp aerial high above the back. On the aerial was a flag, about a foot square. It had crosses: one upright in red and two diagonal, red and white. All on a blue background. A funny flag in red, white, and blue.

Forty-four years later, there it was again, fluttering above a building across the river. The Rabbit had solved his problem. He knew he should not have stolen the file from Mr. Akopov, but he could not take it back now. Perhaps no one would notice it was missing. So he would give it to the people with the funny flag who gave him beer. They would know what to do with it.

He rose from his bench and began to walk down the riverbank toward the Stone Bridge across the Moskva to the Sofia Quay.

Nairobi, 1983

WHEN the little boy developed a headache and a slight temperature his mother thought at first it was a summer chill. But by nightfall the five-year-old was screaming that his head hurt and he kept both parents awake all night. In the morning their neighbors in the Soviet diplomatic compound, who had not slept too well either because the walls were thin and the windows open in the heat, asked what was wrong.

That morning the mother took her son to the doctor. None of the Soviet Bloc embassies merited a doctor all to themselves, but they shared one. Dr. Svoboda was at the Czech Embassy but he ministered to the whole Communist community. He was a good and conscientious man and it took him only a few moments to assure the Russian mother that her boy had a touch of malaria. He administered the appropriate dose of one of the niviquine/paludrine variants used by Russian medicine at that time, with further tablets to be taken daily.

There was no response. In two days the child's condition worsened. The temperature and the shivers increased, and he screamed from his headache. The ambassador had no hesitation in granting permission for a visit to Nairobi General Hospital. Because the mother could speak no English, her husband, Second Secretary (Trade) Nikolai Ilyich Turkin, went with her.

Dr. Winston Moi was also a fine physician and he probably knew the tropical diseases better than the Czech doctor. He did a thorough diagnosis and straightened up with a smile.

"Plasmodium falciparum," he decreed. The father leaned forward with a puzzled frown. His English was good, but not that good. "It is a variant of malaria, but alas resistant to all the chloroquine-based drugs such as those prescribed by my good colleague Dr. Svoboda."

Dr. Moi administered an intravenous injection of a strong broad-spectrum antibiotic. It seemed to work. At first. After a week, when the drug course ceased, the condition returned. By now the mother was hysterical. Denouncing all forms of foreign medicine, she insisted she and her son be flown back to Moscow and the ambassador agreed.

Once there, the boy was admitted to the exclusive KGB clinic.

This was possible because Second Secretary (Trade) Nikolai Turkin was in fact Major Turkin of the First Chief Directorate of the KGB.

The clinic was good, and it had a fine tropical medicine department, because KGB men can be posted all over the world. Because of the intractable nature of the small boy's case, it went right to the departmental head, Professor Glazunov. He read both the files from Nairobi and ordered a series of CT and ultrasound scans, then the last word in technology, unavailable just about anywhere else in the USSR.

The scans worried him badly. They revealed a series of developing internal abscesses on various organs inside the boy. When he asked Mrs. Turkin into his office his face was grave.

"I know what it is, at least I am sure I do, but it cannot be treated. With heavy use of antibiotics, your boy may survive a month. More, unlikely. I am very sorry."

The weeping mother was escorted out. A sympathetic assistant explained to her what had been found. It was a rare disease called melioidosis, very uncommon indeed in Africa but more common in Southeast Asia. It was the Americans who had identified it, during the Vietnam war.

U.S. helicopter pilots had been the first to produce symptoms of a new and usually fatal illness. Research discovered that their rotor blades, hovering over the rice paddies, whipped up a fine aerosol spray of paddy water that some of them had breathed in. The bacillus, resistant to all known antibiotics, was in the water. The Russians knew this because although they shared none of their own discoveries at that time, they were like a sponge when it came to absorbing Western knowledge. Professor Glazunov would automatically receive every single Western technical publication in his field.

In a long telephone call punctuated by sobbing, Mrs. Turkin told her husband their son was going to die. From melioidosis. Major Turkin wrote it down. Then he went to see his superior, the KGB Head of Station, Colonel Kuliev. He was sympathetic but adamant.

"Intervene with the Americans? Are you crazy?"

"Comrade Colonel, if the Yanks have identified it, and seven years ago at that, they may have something for it."

"But we can't ask them that," protested the colonel. "There is a question of national prestige here."

"There is a question of my son's life here," shouted the major.

"That is enough. Consider yourself dismissed."

Taking his career in his hands Turkin went to the ambassador. The diplomat was not a cruel man but he too could not be moved.

"Interventions between our Ministry of Foreign Affairs and the State Department are rare and confined to matters of state," he told the young officer. "By the way, does Colonel Kuliev know you are here?"

"No, Comrade Ambassador."

"Then for the sake of your future prospects, I shall not tell him. And neither will you. But the answer is no."

"If I were a member of the Politburo . . ." Turkin began.

"But you are not. You are a junior major of thirty-two serving his country in the middle of Kenya. I am sorry for your boy, but there is nothing that can be done."

As he went down the stairs Nikolai Turkin reflected bitterly that First Secretary Yuri Andropov was daily being kept alive by medications flown in from London. Then he went out to get drunk.

•   •   •

GETTING into the British Embassy was not that easy. Standing on the pavement across the quay Zaitsev could see the big ocher-colored mansion and even the top of the pillared portico that shielded the giant carved-timber doors. But there was no way of just wandering in.

Along the frontage of the still-shuttered building ran a wall of steel, penetrated by two wide gates for cars, one for "in" and one for "out." Also made of corrugated steel, they were electrically operated and firmly closed.

To the right-hand side was an entrance for pedestrians, but there were two barred grilles. At pavement level two Russian militiamen were posted to check on anyone trying to walk in. The Rabbit had no intention of presenting himself to *them*. Even past the first grille there was a passage and a second barred gate. Between the two was the hut of the embassy security, itself manned by two British-employed Russian guards. Their business was to ask entrants what they wanted, and then check inside the embassy. Too many seeking visas had tried to wangle their way into the building via that gate.

Zaitsev wandered aimlessly around to the back where, in a narrow street, was the entrance to the visa section. It was seven in the morning and the door would not open for another three hours, but already there was a queue a hundred meters long. Clearly many had waited all night. To join the line now would mean almost two days of waiting. He ambled back to the front. This time the militiamen gave him a long and searching look. Frightened, Zaitsev shuffled off down the quay to wait until the embassy opened for business and the diplomats arrived.

Just before ten, the first of the British began to appear. They came in cars. The vehicles paused at the "in" gate but clearly each one was expected and the gate rumbled open to let the car in before sliding closed again. Zaitsev, watching down the quay, thought of trying to approach a car, but they all had the windows closed and the militiamen were only feet away. The people in the cars would think he was a petitioner of some kind and would keep their windows closed. Then he would be arrested. The police would find out what he had done and tell Mr. Akopov.

Leonid Zaitsev was not accustomed to complex problems. He was puzzled but he was also fixated. He just wanted to give his pieces of paper to the people with the funny flag. So through that long hot morning he watched and he waited.

Nairobi, 1983

LIKE all Soviet diplomats Nikolai Turkin had a limited resource of foreign exchange and that included Kenyan currency. The Ibis Grill, Alan Bobbe's Bistro, and the Carnivore were a mite expensive for his pocket. He went to the open-air Thorn Tree Café at the New Stanley Hotel on Kimathi Street, took a table in the garden not far from the big old acacia tree, ordered a vodka and a beer chaser, and sat sunk in despair.

Thirty minutes later a man of about his own age who had sipped half a beer at the bar eased himself off his stool and walked over. Turkin heard a voice say in English:

"Hey, lighten up, old pal, it may never happen."

The Russian looked up. He recognized the American vaguely. Someone from their embassy. Turkin worked in Directorate K of the First Chief Directorate, the counterintelligence wing. His job was not only to monitor all the Soviet diplomats and protect the local KGB operation from penetration, but also to keep a sharp eye open for a vulnerable Westerner who might be recruited. As such he had the freedom to mix with other diplomats, including Westerners, a freedom denied to any ordinary Russian on the staff.

The CIA suspected, precisely from his freedom of movement and contact, what Turkin really did, and had a slim file on him. But there was no handle to grip. The man was a copper-bottomed child of the Soviet regime.

For his part Turkin suspected the American was probably CIA, but he had been taught that *all* American diplomats were probably CIA; a fond illusion but an error on the side of caution.

The American sat down and held out a hand.

"Jason Monk. You're Nik Turkin, right? Saw you at the British garden party last week. You look like you just got posted to Greenland."

Turkin studied the American. He had a shock of corn-colored hair that fell over his forehead and an engaging grin. There seemed to be no guile in his face; perhaps he was not CIA after all. He seemed the sort of man one could talk to. On another day Nikolai Turkin would have leaned back on all those years of training and remained polite but noncommittal. This was not another day. He needed to talk to someone. He started, and poured his heart out. The American was concerned and sympathetic. He noted the word melioidosis on a beer coaster. They parted long after dark. The Russian went back to the guarded compound and Monk to his apartment off Harry Thuku Road.

•   •   •

CELIA Stone was twenty-six, slim, dark, and pretty. She was also Assistant Press Attaché at the British Embassy, Moscow, on her first foreign posting since being accepted into the Foreign Office two years earlier after graduating in Russian from Girton College, Oxford. She was also enjoying life.

That July 16 she came out of the embassy's big front doors and glanced down at the parking area where her small but functional Rover was parked.

From inside the embassy compound she could see what Zaitsev could not, because of the steel wall. She stood at the top of the five steps leading down to the blacktop parking area, punctured by tonsured lawns, small trees, bushes, and a blaze of flower beds. Looking over the steel wall, she could see across the river the towering bulk of the Kremlin, pastel lime, ocher, cream, and white with the gleaming golden onion domes of the various cathedrals jutting above the crenellated red stone wall that encircled the fortress. It was a magnificent sight.

On either side of her the raised entrance was reached by two ramps, up which only the ambassador was allowed to drive. Lesser mortals parked below and walked. Once a young diplomat had done his career a power of no good by driving his VW Beetle up the ramp in sheeting rain and parking beneath the portico. Minutes later the ambassador, arriving to find his access blocked, had to get out of his Rolls-Royce at the bottom, and walk the rest of the way. He was soaked and not amused.

Celia Stone tripped down the steps, nodded at the gate man, got into the bright red Rover, and started up. By the time she had pulled to the "out" gate the steel sheets were sliding back. She rolled out onto Sofia Embankment and turned left toward the Stone Bridge, heading for her lunch date with a reporter from *Sevodnya*. She did not notice a scruffy old man shuffling frantically after her. Nor did she realize hers was the first car to leave the embassy that morning.

The Kamenny Most, or Stone Bridge, is the oldest permanent bridge across the river. In olden days pontoon bridges were used, erected in spring and dismantled in winter when the ice became hard enough to ride over.

Because of its bulk, it not only spans the river but jumps over Sofia Quay as well. To gain access from the quay by road, a driver has to turn left again for a hundred yards until the bridge returns to ground level, then hang a U-turn and drive up the slope of the bridge. But a walker can run up the steps direct from the quay below to the bridge above. That is what the Rabbit did.

He was on the pavement of the Stone Bridge when the red Rover came by. He waved his arms. The woman inside gave a startled look and drove on. Zaitsev set off in hopeless pursuit. But he had noted the Russian number plate, and saw that on the northern side of the bridge the Rover pulled half left into the traffic maelstrom of Borovitskaya Square.

Celia Stone's destination was Rosy O'Grady's Pub on Znamenka

Street. This unlikely Muscovite tavern is actually Irish, and the watering hole where the Irish ambassador is likely to be found on New Year's Eve if he can get away from the stuffier parties of the diplomatic circuit. It also serves lunch. Celia Stone had chosen to meet her Russian reporter there.

She found a parking space without difficulty just round the corner, for fewer and fewer Russians could afford cars or the petrol to run them, and began to walk back. As always when an obvious foreigner approached a restaurant the derelicts and beggars hauled themselves out of their doorways and off the pavement to intercept and ask for food.

As a young diplomat, she had been briefed at the Foreign Office in London before her posting, but the reality always shocked her. She had seen beggars in the Underground of London and in the alleys of New York, the bag people who had somehow slid down the ladder of society to take up residence on its bottom rung. But in Moscow, the capital of a country experiencing the onset of real famine, the wretches with their hands out for money or food had once, and not long ago, been farmers, soldiers, clerks, and shopkeepers. She was reminded of TV documentaries of the Third World.

Vadim, the giant doorman of the Rosy O'Grady, saw her several yards away and ran forward, clouting several begging fellow Russians out of the way in order to secure safe passage for a vital hard-currency patron of his employers' restaurant.

Offended by the spectacle of the supplicants' humiliation at the hands of another Russian, Celia protested feebly, but Vadim swept a long, muscular arm between her and the row of extended hands, swept open the restaurant door, and ushered her inside.

The contrast was immediate, from the dusty street and the hungry beggars to the convivial chatter of fifty people who could afford meat and fish for lunch. Being a good-hearted young woman, she always had trouble when lunching or dining out, trying to reconcile the food on her own plate with the hunger outside. The genial Russian reporter who waved to her from a corner table had no such problem. He was studying the list of *zakuski* starters and settled for Archangel prawns.

Zaitsev the Rabbit, still plodding on his quest, scoured Borovitskaya Square for the red Rover, but it had gone. He checked all the streets leading off to the left and right for a flash of red paintwork, but there was none. Finally he chose the main boulevard on the far side of the square. To his amazement and joy he saw it two hundred yards further on, just round a corner from the pub.

Indistinguishable from the others waiting with the patience of the utterly cowed, Zaitsev took up position near the Rover and started to wait again.

Nairobi, 1983

IT had been ten years since Jason Monk had been a sophomore at the University of Virginia and he had lost touch with many of the students he had known. But he still recalled Norman Stein. Theirs had been an odd friendship, the medium-height but hard-muscled football player from the farm country and the unathletic son of a Jewish doctor from Fredericksburg. It was a shared and mocking sense of humor that had made them friends. If Monk had had the talent for languages, Stein was the near genius in the Biology Department.

He had graduated summa cum laude one year before Monk and gone straight to medical school. They had kept in touch the usual way, by Christmas cards. Crossing a restaurant lobby in Washington two years earlier, just before his Kenyan posting came through, Monk had seen his friend lunching alone. They had had half an hour together before Stein's lunch partner had showed. That had enabled them to catch up on each other's news, though Monk had had to lie and say he worked for the State Department.

Stein had become a doctor, then taken a Ph.D. in tropical medicine, and was even then rejoicing in his new appointment to the research facility at Walter Reed Army Hospital. From his apartment in Nairobi, Jason Monk checked his address book and made a call. A blurred voice answered at the tenth ring.

"Yeah."

"Hi, Norm. It's Jason Monk." Pause.

"Great. Where are you?"

"In Nairobi."

"Great. Nairobi. Of course. And what time is it there?"

Monk told him. Midday.

"Well it's five in the fucking morning here and my alarm is set for seven. I was up half the night with the baby. It's teething, for God's sake. Thanks a lot, pal."

"Calm down, Norm. Tell me something. You ever heard of something called melioidosis?"

There was a pause. The voice that came back had lost all trace of sleep.

"Why do you ask?"

Monk spun him a story. Not about a Russian diplomat. He said there was a kid of five, son of a guy he knew. Seemed the boy was likely to die. He had heard vaguely that Uncle Sam had had some experience with that particular illness.

"Give me your number," said Stein. "I have to make some calls. I'll get back to you."

It was five in the afternoon when Monk's phone rang.

"There is—may be—something," said the physician. "Now listen, it's completely revolutionary, prototype stage. We've done some tests, they seem good. So far. But it hasn't even been submitted to the FDA yet. Let alone cleared. We're not through testing yet."

What Stein was describing was a very early cephalosporin antibiotic with no name in 1983. It would later be marketed in the late eighties as ceftazidime. Then it was just called CZ-1. Today it is the standard treatment for melioidosis.

"It may have side effects," said Stein. "We don't know."

"How long to develop these side effects?" asked Monk.

"No idea."

"Well, if the kid's going to be dead in three weeks, what's to lose?"

Stein sighed heavily.

"I don't know. It's against all the regulations."

"I swear, no one will ever know. C'mon, Norm, for all those chicks I used to pull for you."

He heard the roar of laughter coming all the way from Chevy Chase, Maryland.

"You ever tell Becky and I'll kill you," said Stein, and the line went dead.

Forty-eight hours later a package arrived for Monk at the embassy. It came via an international freight express company. It contained a vacuum flask with dry ice. A short, unsigned note said the ice contained two vials. Monk made a call to the Soviet embassy and left a message with the Trade Section for Second Secretary Turkin. Don't forget our beer at six tonight, he said. The message was reported to Colonel Kuliev.

"Who is this Monk?" he asked Turkin.

"He's an American diplomat. He seems disillusioned with U.S. foreign policy in Africa. I am trying to develop him as a source."

Kuliev nodded heavily. That was good work, the sort of thing that went well on the report to Yazenevo.

At the Thorn Tree Café Monk handed over his package. Turkin looked apprehensive in case anyone from his own side had seen them. The package could contain money.

"What is it?" he asked.

Monk told him.

"It might not work, but it can do no harm. It's all we have."

The Russian went stiff, his eyes cold.

"And what do you want for this . . . gift?" It was obvious there would be a payback.

"You were on the level about your kid? Or just acting?"

"No acting. Not this time. Always we act, people like you and me. But not this time."

In fact Monk had already checked with the Nairobi General Hospital. Dr. Winston Moi had confirmed the basic facts. Tough, but this is a tough world, he thought. He rose from the table. According to the rules he should twist this man into passing something over, something secret. But he knew the story of the small son was not a con, not this time. If he had to behave that way he might as well be a street sweeper in the Bronx.

"Take it, pal. Hope it works. No charge."

He walked away. Halfway to the door a voice called him.

"Mr. Monk, you understand Russian?"

Monk nodded. "A bit."

"I thought you would. Then you will understand the word *spassibo*."

• • •

SHE came out of Rosy O'Grady's just after two and approached the driver's side of her car. The Rover has central locking. As she unlocked the driver's door, the passenger door also unlocked. She was in her seat belt, engine started and ready to go, when the passenger door opened. She looked up, startled. He was standing there, stooping to the open door. Threadbare old army coat, four soiled medals clinging to the lapel, stubbled chin. When he opened his mouth three steel teeth glinted at the front. He tossed a file into her lap. She easily understood enough Russian to repeat later what he said.

"Please, give to Mister Ambassador. For the beer."

The sight of him frightened her. He was clearly mad, perhaps schizophrenic. People like that can be dangerous. White-faced, Celia Stone pulled out into the street, the open door flailing until it was closed by the car's momentum. She tossed the ridiculous petition, or whatever it was, onto the floor of the front passenger area and drove back to the embassy.

CHAPTER 3

IT WAS JUST BEFORE NOON ON THE SAME DAY, JULY 16, THAT IGOR Komarov, sitting in his office on the first floor of the dacha off Kiselny Boulevard, contacted his chief personal assistant by intercom.

"The document I lent you yesterday, you have had a chance to read it?" he asked.

"I have indeed, Mr. President. Quite brilliant, if I may say so," Akopov replied. All of Komarov's staff referred to him as Mr. President, meaning president of the executive committee of the Union of Patriotic Forces. They were in any case convinced that within twelve months he would still be Mr. President but for a different reason.

"Thank you," said Komarov. "Then please return it to me."

The intercom went dead. Akopov rose and went to his wall safe. He knew the combination by heart and spun the central dial the required six times. When the door swung open he looked inside for the black-bound file. It was not there.

Puzzled, he emptied the safe, paper by paper and file by file. A cold fear, part panic and part disbelief, gripped him. Taking a hold on himself, he began again. The files on the carpet around his knees were sorted out and examined, sheet by sheet and one by one. No black file. A light sweat beaded his forehead. He had worked contentedly in the office all morning, convinced that before leaving the

previous evening he had put every confidential document safely
away. He always did; he was a creature of habit.

After the safe, he began on the drawers of his desk. Nothing. He
searched the floor under the desk, then every cupboard and closet.
Just before one he knocked on Igor Komarov's door, was admitted,
and confessed he could not find it.

The man who most of the world presumed would be the next
president of Russia was a highly complex personality who, behind
his public persona, preferred to keep much of himself intensely private. He could not have been a greater contrast to his predecessor,
the ousted Zhirinovsky, whom he now openly referred to as a buf-
foon.

Komarov was of medium height and build, clean-shaven. with
neatly trimmed iron-gray hair. Among his two most evident fetishes
were an absorption with personal cleanliness and a deep dislike of
physical contact. Unlike most Russian politicians, with their back-
slapping, vodka-toasting, arms-around-the-shoulders bonhomie,
Komarov insisted on formal dress and manner of speech in his personal entourage. He rarely if ever donned the uniform of the Black
Guard and was usually to be found in a double-breasted gray suit
with collar and tie.

After years in politics none but a very few could claim to be on
close personal terms with him, and no one dared pretend to be an
intimate. Nikita Ivanovich Akopov had been his confidential private
secretary for a decade but the relationship was still one of master and
slavishly devoted servant.

Unlike Yeltsin, who had raised staff members to the rank of
drinking and tennis-playing buddies, Komarov would, so far as was
known, only permit one man to refer to him by first name and
patronymic. That was his Head of Security, Colonel Anatoli
Grishin.

But like all successful politicians, Komarov could play the chame-
leon when he had to. To the media, on the rare occasions when he
deigned to meet them personally, he could become the grave statesman. Before his own rallies, he became transformed in a manner
that never ceased to evoke Akopov's utter admiration. On the podium the precise former engineer vanished as if he had never been.
In his place appeared the orator, a pillar of passion, a sorcerer of
words, a man of all the people enunciating their hopes, fears, and

desires, their rage and their bigotry, with unerring accuracy. To them and only them would he play the figure of geniality with the common touch.

Beneath both personae there was a third, the one that frightened Akopov. Even the rumor of the existence of the third man beneath the veneer was enough to keep those around him—staff, colleagues, and guards—in a permanent state of the deference he demanded.

Only twice in ten years had Nikita Akopov seen the demonic rage inside the man well up and spew out of control. On another dozen occasions he had seen the struggle to control that rage, and witnessed the effort succeed. On the two occasions when the control had failed, Akopov had seen the man who dominated, fascinated, and controlled him, the man he followed and worshipped, turn into a screaming, raging demon.

He had hurled telephones, vases, and ink-stands at the trembling servant who had offended him, reducing one senior Black Guard officer to a blubbering wreck. He had used language more foul than Akopov had ever heard, broken furniture, and once had to be restrained as he belabored a victim with a heavy ebony ruler lest he actually kill the man.

Akopov knew the sign that one of these rages in the president of the UPF was coming to the surface. Komarov's face went deathly pale, his manner became even more formal and courteous, and two bright red spots burned high on each cheekbone.

"Are you saying you have lost it, Nikita Ivanovich?"

"Not lost, Mr. President. Apparently mislaid."

"That document is of a more confidential nature than anything you have ever handled. You have read it. You can understand why."

"I do indeed, Mr. President."

"There are only three copies in existence, Nikita. Two are in my own safe. No more than a tiny group of those closest to me will ever be allowed to see it. I even wrote it and typed it myself. I, Igor Komarov, actually typed all the pages myself rather than entrust it to a secretary. It is that confidential."

"Very wise, Mr. President."

"And because I count . . . counted you as one of that tiny group, I permitted you to see it. Now you tell me it is lost."

"Mislaid, temporarily mislaid, I assure you, Mr. President."

Komarov was staring at him with those mesmeric eyes that could charm skeptics into collaboration or terrify backsliders. On each cheekbone the red spot burned bright in the pale face.

"When did you last see it?"

"Last night, Mr. President. I stayed late in order to read it in privacy. I left at eight o'clock."

Komarov nodded. The night-duty guards' register would confirm or deny that.

"You took it with you. Despite my orders, you permitted the file to leave the building."

"No, Mr. President, I swear it. I locked it in the safe. I would never leave a confidential document lying around, or take it with me."

"It is not in the safe now?"

Akopov swallowed, but he had no saliva.

"How many times have you been to the safe before my call?"

"None, Mr. President. When you called, that was the first time I went to the safe."

"It was locked?"

"Yes, as usual."

"It had been broken into?"

"Apparently not, Mr. President."

"You have searched the room?"

"From top to bottom and end to end. I cannot understand it."

Komarov thought for several minutes. Behind his blank face he felt a rising panic. Finally he called the security office on the ground floor.

"Seal the building. No one enters, no one leaves. Contact Colonel Grishin. Tell him to report to my office. Immediately. Wherever he is, whatever he is doing, I want him here within the hour."

He lifted his forefinger from the intercom and gazed at his white-faced and trembling assistant.

"Return to your office. Communicate with nobody. Wait there until further notice."

•   •   •

AS an intelligent, single, and thoroughly modern young woman, Celia Stone had long decided that she had the right to take her pleasures whenever and with whomsoever she fancied. At the moment she fancied the hard young muscles of Hugo Gray, who had arrived from London barely two months earlier and six months after herself. He was Assistant Cultural Attaché and the same grade as she, but two years older and also single.

Each had a small but functional apartment in a residential block assigned to British Embassy staff off Kutuzovsky Prospekt, a square building with a central courtyard useful for parking, and with Russian militiamen posted at the entrance barrier. Even in modern Russia everyone presumed that goings in and out were noted, but at least the cars remained unvandalized.

After lunch she drove back inside the protective screen of the embassy on Sofia Quay and wrote up her report of lunch with the journalist. Much of their talk had been about the death of President Cherkassov the previous day and what was likely to happen now. She had assured the journalist of the continuing deep interest of the British people in Russian events, and hoped he believed her. She would know when his article appeared.

At five she drove back to her apartment for a bath and a short rest. She had a dinner date with Hugo Gray at eight, after which she intended they both return to her own flat. She did not wish to do much sleeping during the night.

•   •   •

BY four in the afternoon Colonel Anatoli Grishin had convinced himself the missing document was not within the building. He sat in Igor Komarov's office and told him so.

In four years the two men had become interdependent. It had been in 1994 that Grishin had resigned his career with the Second Chief Directorate of the KGB with the rank of full colonel. He had become thoroughly disillusioned. Since the formal ending of Communist rule in 1991 the former KGB had become in his view a whited sepulchre. Even before then, in September 1991, Mikhail Gorbachev had broken up the world's biggest security apparatus and farmed out its various wings into different commands.

The external intelligence arm, the First Chief Directorate, had remained at its old headquarters at Yazenevo, out beyond the ring road, but had been renamed the Foreign Intelligence Service, or SVR. That was bad enough.

What was worse was that Grishin's own division, the Second Chief Directorate, hitherto responsible for all internal security, the exposure of spies, and the suppression of dissent, had been emasculated, renamed the FSB, and ordered to reduce its own powers to a travesty of what they had once been.

Grishin regarded this with contempt. The Russian people needed discipline, and firm and occasionally harsh discipline, and it was the Second Chief Directorate that had provided it. He stuck with the reforms for three years, hoping to make major general, then quit. A year later he had been engaged as personal security chief by Igor Komarov, then still just one of the Politburo of the old Liberal Democratic Party.

The two men had risen to prominence and power together, and there was more, much more, to come. Over the years Grishin had created for Komarov his own utterly loyal close-protection squad, the Black Guards, now numbering six thousand fit young men whom he personally commanded.

Supporting the Guard was the League of Young Combatants, twenty thousand of them, the teenage wing of the UPF, all imbued with the correct ideology and fanatically loyal, which he also commanded. He was one of the few men who called Komarov by his first name and patronymic. The humblest street shouter could yell "Igor Alexeivitch" at Komarov, but that was part of the man-of-the-people camaraderie expected in Russia. In his private entourage Komarov demanded the formality of "Mr. President" from all but a few intimates.

"You are sure the file is no longer in this building?" asked Komarov.

"It cannot be, Igor Alexeivitch. In two hours we have practically taken the place apart. Every cupboard, every locker, every drawer, every safe. Every window and windowsill has been examined, every yard of the grounds. There was no break-in.

"The expert from the safe manufacturers has just finished. The safe was not forced. Either it was opened by someone who knew the combination, or the file was never in it. The garbage of last night has been impounded and searched. Nothing.

"The dogs were running free from seven P.M. No one entered the building after that—the night guards had relieved the day shift at six and the day shift left ten minutes later. Akopov was in his office until eight. The dog handler for last night has been brought back. He swears he restrained the dogs three times yesterday evening, to allow three late-working staff to leave by car, and Akopov was the last. The night log confirms that."

"So?" asked Komarov.

"Human error or human malice. The two night guards have been collected from their barracks. I expect them any moment. They had the run of the building from Akopov's departure at eight until the arrival of the day shift at six this morning. Then the day shift was here alone until the office staff arrived around eight. Two hours. But the day guards swear that on their first patrol all office doors on this floor were locked. Everyone working on this floor, including Akopov, confirms that."

"Your theory, Anatoli?"

"Either Akopov took it with him, by accident or design, or he never locked it up and one of the night shift took it. They had master keys to the office doors."

"So, it is Akopov?"

"First suspect, certainly. His private apartment has been ransacked. In his presence. Nothing. I thought he might have taken it with him, then lost his attaché case. That happened once at the Ministry of Defense. I was in charge of the investigation. It turned out not to be espionage but criminal negligence. The person responsible went to the camps. But Akopov's briefcase is the same he always uses. It has been identified by three people."

"So, he did it deliberately?"

"Possibly. But I have a problem with that. Why did he come in this morning and wait around to be caught? He had twelve hours to disappear. I may wish to . . . um . . . interrogate him at greater length. To establish elimination or confession."

"Permission granted."

"And after that?"

Igor Komarov turned in his swivel chair to face the window. He mused for a while.

"Akopov has been a very good personal secretary," he said at length. "But after this, a replacement will be required. My problem is, he has seen the document. Its contents are extremely confidential. If he is retained in a diminished capacity, or dismissed, he might feel a sense of resentment, even be tempted to divulge what he knows. That would be a pity, a great pity."

"I understand completely," said Colonel Grishin.

At that point the two bewildered night guards arrived and Grishin went downstairs to question them.

By 9:00 P.M. the night guards' quarters at the Black Guard barracks outside the city had been searched, revealing nothing more than the expected toiletries and porn magazines.

Inside the dacha the two men were separated and interviewed in different rooms. Grishin questioned them personally. They were clearly terrified of him, as well they might be. His reputation preceded him.

Occasionally he shouted obscenities in their ears, but for the two sweating men the worst ordeal was when he sat close and whispered the details of what awaited those caught lying to him. By eight he had a complete picture of what had happened during their shift the previous night. He knew their patrols had been erratic and irregular, that they had been glued to the TV screen for details of the president's death. And he learned for the first time of the presence of the cleaner.

The man had been let in at ten. As usual. Via the underground passage. No one had accompanied him. Both guards had been needed to open the three doors, because one had the keypad combination to the street door, the other to the innermost door, and both to the middle door.

He knew the guards had seen the old man start on the top floor. As usual. He knew the guards had then broken from their TV watching to open the offices of the middle floor, the vital executive suite. He knew that one had stood in the doorway while the cleaning of Mr. Komarov's personal office had been accomplished and the door then relocked, but that both men had been downstairs when the cleaner completed the remainder of the middle floor. As usual. So . . . the cleaner had been alone in Akopov's office. And he had left earlier than usual, in the small hours.

At nine Mr. Akopov, extremely pale, was escorted from the building. His own car was used but one of the Black Guard drove. Another sat beside the disgraced secretary in the rear. The car did not drive to Akopov's apartment. It headed out of the city to one of the sprawling camps housing the Young Combatants.

By nine Colonel Grishin had finished reading the file from the staff and personnel office containing the employment details of one

Zaitsev, Leonid, aged sixty-three, office cleaner. There was a private address, but the man would have left. He was due at the dacha at ten.

He did not appear. At midnight Colonel Grishin and three Black Guards left to visit the old man's residence.

•   •   •

AT that hour Celia Stone rolled off her young lover with a happy smile and reached for a cigarette. She smoked little, but this was one of those moments. Hugo Gray, on his back in her bed, continued to pant. He was a fit young man who kept himself in shape with squash and swimming, but the previous two hours had required most of his stamina.

Not for the first time he wondered why God had so arranged things that the appetites of a love-hungry woman would always exceed the capacities of a male. It was extremely unfair.

In the darkness Celia Stone took a long pull, felt the nicotine hit the spot, leaned over her lover, and tousled his dark brown curls.

"How on earth did you get to be a cultural attaché?" she teased. "You wouldn't know Turgenev from Lermontov."

"I'm not supposed to," grumbled Gray. "I'm supposed to tell the Russkies about our culture—Shakespeare, Brontë, that sort of thing."

"And is that why you have to keep going into conference with the Head of Station?"

Gray came off the pillow fast, gripped an upper arm, and hissed into her ear:

"Shut up, Celia. This place could be bugged."

In a huff Celia Stone left to make coffee. She didn't see why Hugo should be so picky about a little tease. Anyway, what he did in the embassy was a pretty open secret.

She was right, of course. For the previous month Hugo Gray had been the third and junior member of the Moscow Station of the Secret Intelligence Service. Once it had been much bigger, in the good old days, at the height of the Cold War. But times change and budgets diminish. In its collapsing state Russia was seen as a small enough threat.

More important, ninety percent of things that had once been

secret were openly available or of minimal interest. Even the former KGB had a press officer, and across the city in the U.S. Embassy the CIA was down to a football team.

But Hugo Gray was young and keen, and convinced most diplomatic apartments were still bugged. Communism might have gone, but Russian paranoia was doing fine. He was correct, of course, but the FSB agents had already tagged him for what he was and were quite happy.

•   •   •

THE weirdly named Enthusiasts' Boulevard is probably the most decrepit, shabbiest, and meanest quarter in the city of Moscow. In a triumph of Communist planning it was situated downwind of the chemical warfare research establishment, which had filters like tennis nets. The only enthusiasm ever noted among its inhabitants was possessed by those slated to move out.

According to the records Leonid Zaitsev lived with his daughter, her truck-driver husband, and their child in a flat just off the main street. It was half-past twelve and still a warm summer's night when the sleek black Chaika, its driver's head stuck out of the window to read the grimy street names, pulled up outside.

The son-in-law's name was different of course, and they had to check with a roused and drowsy neighbor on the ground floor to establish that the family lived on the fourth. There was no elevator. The four men clumped up the stairs and hammered on the peeling door.

The woman who answered, sleepy and bleary-eyed, must have been in her mid-thirties but looked a decade older. Grishin was polite but insistent. His men pushed past and fanned out to search the flat. There was not much to search; it was tiny. Two rooms in fact, with a fetid lavatory and a curtained cooking alcove.

The woman had been sleeping with her six-year-old in the one family-sized bed in one of the rooms. The child now woke and began to whimper, the whine rising to a cry when the bed was turned over to see if anyone hid beneath it. The two miserable plywood cupboards were opened and ransacked.

In the other room Zaitsev's daughter pointed helplessly at the cot along one wall where her father slept, and explained that her husband was miles away on a trip to Minsk and had been for two days.

By now weeping helplessly, a cue taken up by the child, she swore her father had not returned the previous morning. She was worried but had taken no steps to report him missing. He must have fallen asleep on a park bench, she thought.

In ten minutes the Black Guards had established that no one was hidden in the flat, and Grishin was convinced the woman was too terrified and ignorant to lie. Within thirty minutes they were gone.

Grishin directed the Chaika not back into central Moscow but to the camp forty miles away where Akopov was being held. For the rest of the night he questioned the hapless secretary himself. Before dawn the sobbing man admitted that he must have left the vital document consigned to his care lying on his desk. He had never done such a thing before. He could not understand how he had forgotten to lock it up. He begged for forgiveness. Grishin nodded and patted him on the back.

Outside the barracks block he summoned one of his inner-core deputies.

"It is going to be a stinking hot day. Our friend in there is distressed. I think a predawn swim is in order."

Then he drove back to the city. If the vital file had been left lying on Akopov's desk, he reasoned, it had either been wrongly thrown out, or the cleaner had taken it. The former theory did not work. Trash from party headquarters was always retained for several days, then incinerated under supervision. The paper trash of the previous night had been sifted sheet by sheet. Nothing. So, the cleaner. Why a semiliterate old man should want to do such a thing, or what he had done with it, Grishin could not fathom. Only the old man could explain. And explain he would.

Before the normal hour of breakfast he had put two thousand of his own men, all in civilian clothes, onto the streets of Moscow to search for an old man in a threadbare ex-army greatcoat. He had no photograph, but the description was precise, even down to the three steel teeth at the front of the mouth.

However, the job was not that easy, even with two thousand searchers. There were ten times that number of derelicts crowding the back alleys and parks, of all ages and sizes, and all shabbily dressed. If, as he suspected, Zaitsev was now living on the streets, everyone would have to be examined. One of them would have three steel teeth and a black-covered file. Grishin wanted both and without delay. His bewildered but obedient Black Guards, in ordinary pants and shirts for the day was hot, fanned out through Moscow.

Langley, December 1983

JASON Monk rose from his desk, stretched, and decided to go down to the commissary. A month back from Nairobi, he had been told his performance reports were good and in some cases extremely so. Promotion was in the pipeline and the head of the Africa Division was pleased but would be sorry to lose him.

Monk had arrived back to find himself assigned to the Spanish language course on which he would begin just after the Christmas and New Year break. Spanish would constitute his third foreign language, but more, it would open up the whole Latin American Division to him.

South America was a big territory and an important one, for not only was it within the American backyard, as prescribed by the Monroe Doctrine, it was also a prime target for the Soviet bloc, which had targeted it for insurrection, subversion, and Communist revolution. As a result the KGB had a big operation south of the Rio Grande, one the CIA was determined to head off. For Monk at thirty-three South America was a good career move.

He was stirring his coffee when he felt someone standing in front of his table.

"Great suntan," said a voice. He looked up. Monk recognized the man who was smiling down at him. He rose, but the man gestured him to stay seated, one of the aristocracy being nice to the peasants.

Monk was surprised. He knew the speaker was one of the key men in the Ops Directorate, for someone had pointed him out in the corridor, the newly appointed head of the Soviet Branch, Counterintelligence Group of the Soviet/East European Division.

What surprised Monk was how nondescript the man appeared. They were much the same height, two inches under six feet, but the other man, though nine years older, was well out of condition. Monk noticed the greasy hair slicked back straight from the forehead, the thick moustache covering the upper section of a weak and vain mouth, the owlish myopic eyes.

"Three years in Kenya," he said to explain the tan.

"Back to wintry Washington, eh?" said the man. Monk's antennae were giving him bad vibes. Behind the eyes there was a mockery. I'm a lot smarter than you, they seemed to be saying, I'm extremely smart indeed.

"Yes, sir," replied Monk. A heavily nicotine-stained hand came out. Monk noticed this and the maze of tiny capillaries round the base of the nose that often betrayed the heavy boozer. He rose and flashed a grin, the one the girls in the typing pool called among themselves the Redwood Special.

"And you must be . . . ?" said the man.

"Monk. Jason Monk."

"Good to know you, Jason. I'm Aldrich Ames."

•   •   •

NORMALLY, the embassy staff would not have been working on a Saturday—least of all, on a hot summer Saturday when they could have been off on a sylvan weekend—but the president's death had produced a welter of extra work and weekend labors were required.

If Hugo Gray's car had started that morning, many men who later died would have stayed alive and the world would have taken a different course. But ignition solenoids are a law unto themselves. After frantically trying to get a reaction, Gray ran after the red Rover as it neared the barrier of the enclave and tapped on the window. Celia Stone gave him a lift.

He sat beside her as she swerved out into Kutuzovsky Prospekt and headed past the Ukraina Hotel toward the Arbat and the Kremlin. His heels scuffed something on the floor. He stooped and retrieved it.

"Your takeover bid for *Izvestia*?" he asked. She looked sideways and recognized the file he was holding.

"Oh, God, I was going to trash it yesterday. Some old lunatic threw it into the car. Nearly frightened the life out of me."

"Another petition," said Gray. "They never stop. Usually it's for visas, of course." He flicked open the black cover and glanced at the title page. "No, it's more political."

"Great. I'm Mister Bonkers and here is my master plan to save the world. Just give it to the ambassador."

"Is that what he said? Give it to the ambassador?"

"Yep. That, and thanks for the beer."

"What beer?"

"How should I know? He was a nutcase."

Gray read the title page and turned over several more. He grew quiet.

"It *is* political," he said. "It's some kind of manifesto."

"You want it, you have it," said Celia. They left the Alexandrovsky Gardens behind and turned toward the Stone Bridge.

Hugo Gray was going to give the unwanted gift a quick skim and then ease it into the wastepaper basket. But he read ten pages, rose, and sought an interview with the Head of Station, a shrewd Scot with a mordant wit.

The Head's office was swept daily for bugs, but really secret conferences were always held in the "bubble." This strange confection is usually a conference chamber suspended from reinforced beams so that it is surrounded on all sides by an air-filled gap when the doors are closed. Regularly swept inside and out, the bubble is deemed unbuggable by hostile intelligence. Gray did not feel confident enough to ask they adjourn to the bubble.

"Yes, laddie?" said the Head.

"Look, Jock, I don't know whether I'm wasting your time. Probably am. Sorry. But something odd happened yesterday. An old man threw this into the car of Celia Stone. You know? That press attaché girl. It may be nothing . . ."

He petered out. The Head regarded him over the top of his half-moons.

"Threw it into her car?" he asked gently.

"She says. Just tore the door open, threw it into the car, asked her to give it to the ambassador, and was gone."

The Head of Station put out his hand for the black-covered file with Gray's two footprints on it.

"What kind of man?" he asked.

"Old, shabby, stubbled. Like a tramp. Frightened the hell out of her."

"A petition, perhaps."

"That's what she thought. She was going to throw it away. But she gave me a lift in this morning. I read some of it on the way. It seems more political. The inside title page has the stamp of the logo of the UPF. It reads as if written by Igor Komarov."

"Our president-to-be. Odd. All right, laddie, leave it with me."

"Thanks, Jock," said Gray, and rose. The intimacy of first names even between juniors and senior mandarins is encouraged inside the British Secret Intelligence Service. It is deemed to encourage a sense of camaraderie, of family, underlining the us-and-them psychology common to all services in this strange trade. Only the chief himself is referred to as Chief or Sir.

Gray had reached the door when his boss caused him to pause, his hand on the doorknob.

"One thing, laddie. Apartments in the Soviet era were shoddily built and the walls were thin. They remain thin. Our Third Trade Secretary this morning is red-eyed with lack of sleep. Fortunately his lady wife is in England. Next time, could you and the delightful Miss Stone be just a wee bit quieter?"

Hugo Gray went as red as the Kremlin walls and left. The Head of Station put the black document to one side. He faced a busy day and the ambassador wanted to see him at eleven. His Excellency was a busy man and would not wish to be troubled with objects thrown into staff cars by tramps. It would not be until that night, working late in his office, that the spymaster would read what would later come to be known as the Black Manifesto.

Madrid, August 1984

BEFORE it moved to a new address in November 1986, the Indian Embassy in Madrid was situated in an ornate turn-of-the-century building at 93 Calle Velasquez. On Independence Day 1984 the Indian ambassador held, as customary, a large reception for leading members of the Spanish government and for the diplomatic corps. As always, it was on August 15.

Because of the extreme heat of Madrid in that month, and the fact that August is usually chosen for governmental, parliamentary, and diplomatic vacations, many senior figures were away from the capital and were represented by more junior officers.

From the ambassador's point of view it was regrettable, but the

Indians can hardly rewrite history and change their Independence Day.

The Americans were represented by their chargé d'affaires, supported by the second trade secretary, one Jason Monk. The chief of the CIA station within the embassy was also away, and Monk, elevated to the number-two slot in the station, was standing in for him.

It had been a good year for Monk. He had passed the six-month Spanish course with flying colors, and earned a promotion from GS-12 to GS-13. The Government Schedule (GS) tag might mean little to those in the private sector because it is the pay scale for federal civil servants, but within the CIA it indicated not only salary but rank, prestige, and the progress of a career.

More to the point, in a shuffle of top officers, CIA Director William Casey had just appointed a new Deputy Director (Operations) to replace John Stein. The DD(O) is the head of the entire intelligence-gathering arm of the agency and therefore in charge of every agent in the field. The new man was Monk's original spotter and recruiter, Carey Jordan.

Finally, on completing the Spanish course, Monk had been assigned not to the Latin America Division but to Western Europe, which had only one Spanish-speaking country, Spain itself.

Not that Spain was a hostile territory—quite the contrary. But for a single thirty-four-year-old CIA officer the glamorous Spanish capital beat the hell out of Tegucigalpa.

Because of the good relations between the United States and her Spanish ally, much of the CIA work was not spying on Spain but collaborating with the Spanish counterintelligence people and keeping an eye on the large Soviet and East European community, which was riddled with hostile agents. Even in two months, Monk had created some good relationships with the Spanish domestic agency, most of whose senior officers dated back to the days of Franco and were intensely anti-Communist. Having a problem pronouncing "Jason," which comes out in Spanish as "Xhasson," they had dubbed the young American El Rubio, Blondie, and liked him. Monk had that effect on people.

The reception was hot and typical; groups of people circulating slowly, sipping the Indian government's champagne, which became warm in the fist in ten seconds, and making polite but desultory conversation that they did not mean. Monk, having estimated he had done his bit for Uncle Sam, was about to leave when he spotted a face he knew.

Sliding through the throng he came up behind the man and waited until the dark gray suit had finished talking to a lady in a sari and was alone for a second. From behind, he said in Russian:

"So, my friend, what happened with your son?"

The man stiffened and turned. Then he gave a smile.

"Thank you," said Nikolai Turkin, "he recovered. He is fit and well."

"I'm glad," said Monk, "and by the look of it your career survived as well."

Turkin nodded. Taking a gift from the enemy was a serious offense and had he been reported he would never have left the USSR again. But he had been forced to throw himself on the mercy of Professor Glazunov. The old physician had a son of his own and privately believed his country should cooperate with the best research establishments in the world on matters medical. He had decided not to report the young officer and had modestly accepted his colleagues' plaudits for the remarkable recovery.

"Thankfully, yes, but it was close," he replied.

"Let's have dinner," said Monk. The Soviet looked startled. Monk held up his hands in mock surrender. "No pitch, I promise."

Turkin relaxed. Both men knew what the other did. The fact that Monk spoke such perfect Russian indicated he could not possibly be in the Trade Section at the U.S. Embassy. Monk knew that Turkin had to be KGB, probably in Line KR, the counterintelligence branch, because of his liberty to be seen talking to Americans.

The word Monk had used gave the game away, and the fact that he would use it in a joking fashion indicated he was suggesting a brief truce in the Cold War. A "pitch" or "cold pitch" is a term used when one intelligence officer simply proposes to someone from the other side that they change teams.

Three nights later the two men came separately to a small back street in the old quarter of Madrid called Calle de los Cuchilleros, the street of the knife grinders. Halfway down what is hardly more than an alley is an old wooden door leading to steps into a basement of brick arches, formerly an old wine store dating back to the Middle Ages. For many years it has served traditional Spanish dishes under the name Sobrinos de Botin. The old arches form booths with a table in the center, and Monk and his guest had one to themselves.

The meal was good. Monk ordered a Marquès de Riscal. They stayed off shop talk out of courtesy, but talked of wives and children—Monk admitted he still had neither. Little Yuri was now at school but staying with his grandparents during the summer vacation. The wine flowed, a second bottle came.

Monk failed to realize at first that behind Turkin's affable facade he entertained a seething rage: not at the Americans, but at the system that had so nearly killed his son. The second bottle of the Marquès was nearly gone when he suddenly asked:

"Are you happy, working for the CIA?"

Is this a pitch? Monk wondered. Is the idiot trying to recruit *me*?

"Pretty good," he said lightly. He was pouring wine, watching the bottle, not the Russian.

"If you have problems, do they support you, your people?"

Monk kept his eyes on the falling wine, the hand steady.

"Sure. My people will always go to the wire for you, if you need help. It's part of the code."

"It must be good to work for people who live in such freedom," said Turkin. Finally Monk put down the bottle and looked across the table. He had promised no pitch, but it was the Russian who had made it—to himself.

"Why not? Look, my friend, the system you work for is going to change. Soon now. We could help it change faster. Yuri will grow up to live as a free man."

Andropov had died, despite the medications from London. He had been succeeded by another geriatric, Konstantin Chernenko, who had to be held up under the armpits. But there was talk of a fresh wind blowing in the Kremlin, a younger man called Gorbachev. By the coffee Turkin was recruited; from henceforth he would stay "in place" at the heart of the KGB but work for the CIA.

Monk's luck was in that his superior, the Chief of Station, was away on vacation. Had he been in place Monk would have had to hand Turkin over to others to handle. Instead it fell to him to encode the top secret cable to Langley describing the recruitment.

Of course there was initial skepticism. A major of Line KR right in the heart of the KGB was a top prize. In a series of covert meetings throughout Madrid for the rest of the summer, Monk learned about his Soviet contemporary.

Born in Omsk, western Siberia, in 1951, the son of an engineer in the military industry, Turkin had not been able to get into the university he wanted at the age of eighteen and had gone into the army. He was assigned to Border Guards, nominally under the control of the KGB. There he was spotted and posted to the Dservinsky High School, counterintelligence department, where he learned English. He shone.

With a small group he was transferred to the KGB foreign intelligence training center, the prestigious Andropov Institute. Like Monk, on the other side of the world, he had been tagged as a high-flier. On graduating with distinction Turkin was permitted to join Directorate K of the First Chief Directorate—counterintelligence within the intelligence-gathering arm.

Still only twenty-seven, Turkin also married in 1978 and had a son, Yuri, the same year. In 1982 he got his first foreign posting, to Nairobi; his primary task was to try to penetrate the CIA Station in Kenya and recruit agents either there or throughout the Kenyan establishment. It was a posting to be cut short prematurely by his son's illness.

Turkin delivered his first package to the CIA in October. Knowing that a complete covert communications system had been set up, Monk took the package back to Langley personally. It turned out to be dynamite. Turkin blew away just about the entire KGB operation in Spain. To protect their source, the Americans would release what they had bit by bit to the Spanish, ensuring that each roundup of Spaniards spying for Moscow would appear as a fluke, or good detection by the Spanish. In each case the KGB was permitted to learn (via Turkin) that the agent himself had made a silly mistake leading to his own capture. Moscow suspected nothing, but lost its whole Iberian operation.

In his three years in Madrid Turkin rose to become deputy *Rezident,* which gave him access to just about everything. In 1987 he would transfer back to Moscow and after a year became head of the entire Directorate K Branch within the KGB's huge *apparat* in East Germany until the final pullout after the collapse of the Berlin Wall and then of Communism and the reunification with West Germany in 1990. In all that time, although he passed hundreds of messages and packages of intelligence through dead drops and cutouts, he insisted that he be handled by only one man, his friend-across-the-Wall, Jason Monk. It was an unusual arrangement. Most spies have several handlers, or "controllers," in a six-year career, but Turkin insisted and Langley had to put up with it.

When Monk got back to Langley that fall of 1986 he was summoned to the office of Carey Jordan.

"I've seen the stuff," said the new DDO. "It's good. We thought he might be a double, but the Spanish agents he has blown away are Grade A. Your man's on the level. Well done."

Monk nodded his appreciation.

"There is just one thing," said Jordan. "I didn't get into this game five minutes ago. Your report on the recruitment strategy is adequate, but there's something else, isn't there? What were his real reasons for volunteering?"

Monk told the DDO what he had not put in the report, the illness of the son in Nairobi and the medications from the Walter Reed.

"I ought to can your ass," said Jordan at length. He rose and walked to the window. The forest of birch and beech running down to the Potomac was a blaze of red and gold, the leaves just about to fall.

"Jesus," he said after a while. "I don't know any guy in the agency who would have let him get away without a favor for those drugs. You might never have seen him again. Madrid was a fluke. You know what Napoleon said about generals?"

"No, sir."

"He said I don't care if they're good; I want 'em lucky. You're weird, but you're lucky. You know we'll have to transfer your man to SE Division?"

At the very top of the CIA was always the Director. Under him came the two main Directorates, Intelligence and Operations. The first, headed by the Deputy Director (Intel), or DDI, had the task of collating and analyzing the great mass of raw information pouring in, and to produce from it the intelligence digests that would go out to the White House, the National Security Council, the State Department, Pentagon, et al.

The actual gathering was done by Operations, headed by the

DDO. Ops Directorate subdivided into divisions according to a global map—Latin American Division, Middle East, Southeast Asia, and so forth. But for forty years of the Cold War, from 1950 to 1990 and the collapse of Communism, the key division was Soviet/East European, known as SE.

Officers in other divisions were often resentful that even though they might cultivate and recruit a valuable Soviet asset in Bogotà or Djakarta, he would after recruitment be transferred to the control of SE Division, which would handle him from then on. The logic was that the recruit would be transferred one day from Bogotà or Djakarta anyway, probably back to the USSR.

Because the Soviet Union was the main enemy, SE Division became the star unit in Ops Directorate. Places were sought after. Even though Monk had majored in Russian at college, and spent years perusing Soviet publications in a back room, he had still served a tour in African Division and was even then assigned to Western Europe.

"Yes, sir," he said.

"You want to go with him?"

Monk's spirits leaped.

"Yes, sir. Please."

"Okay, you found him, you recruited him, you run him."

Monk was transferred to SE Division within a week. He was tasked to run Major Nikolai Ilyich Turkin, of the KGB. He never returned to Madrid to reside, but he visited, meeting Turkin covertly at picnic sites high in the Sierra de Guadarrama, where they would talk of a thousand things as Gorbachev came to power and the twin programs of perestroika and glasnost began to relax the rules. Monk was glad, because apart from an asset he regarded Turkin as a friend.

Even by 1984 the CIA was becoming, and some would say had already become, a vast and creaking bureaucracy, dedicated more to paperwork than pure intelligence gathering. Monk loathed bureaucracy and despised paperwork, convinced that what was written down could be stolen or copied. At the ultrasecret heart of the paperwork of the SE Division were the 301 files, which listed the details of every Soviet agent working for Uncle Sam. That fall Monk "forgot" to list all the details of Major Turkin, code-named GT Lysander, in the 301 files.

•   •   •

JOCK Macdonald, Head of Station for the British SIS in Moscow, had a dinner he could not avoid on the night of July 17. He returned briefly to his office to deposit some notes he had made during dinner—he never trusted his apartment not to be burgled—and his eye fell on the black-covered file. Idly he flicked it open and began to read. It was in Russian, of course, and typed, but he was bilingual.

In fact he never went home that night. Just after midnight he called his wife to explain, then returned to the file. There were some forty pages, divided into twenty subject headings.

He read the passages concerning the reestablishment of a one-party state and the reactivation of the chain of slave-labor camps for dissidents and other undesirables.

He perused the tracts dealing with the final solution of the Jewish community and the treatment of the Chechens in particular, plus all the other racial minorities.

He studied the pages concerning the nonaggression pact with Poland to buffer the western border, and the reconquest of Belarus, the Baltic States, and the southern republics of the former USSR, Ukraine, Georgia, Armenia, and Moldova.

He ingested the paragraphs dealing with the reestablishment of the nuclear arsenal and the targeting of the surrounding enemies.

He pored over the pages describing the destiny of the Russian Orthodox Church and all other religious denominations.

According to the manifesto the shamed and humiliated armed forces, now brooding sullenly in tents, would be rearmed and reequipped, not as a force for defense but for reconquest. The populations of the reacquired territories would work as serfs to produce food for the Russian masters. Control over them would reside in the ethnic Russian populations in the outer territories, under the aegis of an imperial governor from Moscow. National discipline would be assured by the Black Guard, increased to a force of 200,000 men. They would also handle the special treatment of the antisocials—liberals, journalists, priests, gays, and Jews.

The document also purported to reveal the answer to one enigma that had already puzzled Macdonald and others: the source of the Union of Patriotic Forces' limitless campaign wealth.

In the aftermath of 1990, the criminal underworld of Russia had been a vast patchwork of gangs who, in the early days, conducted vicious turf wars, leaving scores of their own dead on the streets. Since 1995, a policy of unification had been in progress. By 1999, all Russia from the western border to the Urals was the fiefdom of four great consortia of criminals, chief among them the Dolgoruki, based in Moscow. If the document before him was true, it was they who were funding the UPF, to earn their reward in the future, the elimination of all other gangs and the supremacy of their own.

It was five in the morning when, after the fifth rereading, Jock Macdonald closed the Black Manifesto. He sat back and stared at the ceiling. He had long ago given up smoking, but now he longed for a drag.

Finally he rose, locked the document in his safe, and let himself out of the embassy. On the pavement, in the half light, he gazed across the river at the walls of the Kremlin beneath whose shadow an old man in a threadbare greatcoat had sat forty-eight hours earlier and stared at the embassy.

Spymasters are not generally conceived to be religious people, but appearances and professions can be misleading. In the Highlands of Scotland there is a long tradition among the aristocracy of devout adherence to the Roman Catholic faith. These were the earls and barons who rallied with their clansmen to the banner of the Catholic Bonnie Prince Charlie in 1745, to be wiped out a year later at the field of Culloden.

The Head of Station came from the heart of that tradition. His father was a Macdonald of Fassifern, but his mother had been a scion of the house of Fraser of Lovat and had brought him up in the faith. He began to walk. Down the embankment to the next bridge, the Bolshoi Most, then across toward the Orthodox St. Basil's Cathedral. He skirted the onion-domed edifice and wended his way through the waking city center toward New Square.

It was as he was leaving New Square that he saw the first early-morning queues for the soup kitchens beginning to form. There was one just behind the square, where once the Central Committee of the Communist Party of the USSR had held sway.

A number of foreign charitable organizations were involved in the relief aid to Russia, as was the United Nations on a more official basis; the West had donated as generously as earlier to Romanian orphanages and Bosnian refugees. But the task was formidable, for the destitute from the countryside poured toward the capital, were rounded up and expelled by the militia, and reappeared again either as the same people or their replacements.

They stood in the predawn half light, the old and ragged, the women with babies at their breasts, the peasantry of Russia unchanged since Potemkin in their oxlike passivity and patience. In late July the weather was warm enough to keep all alive. But when the cold came, that bitter cutting cold of the Russian winter. . . . The previous January had been bad, but as for the next . . . Jock Macdonald shook his head at the thought and marched on.

His path brought him to Lubyanskaya Square, formerly known as Dzerzhinski. Here for decades had stood the statue of Iron Feliks, Lenin's founder of the original terror machine, the Cheka. At the back of the square stood the great gray and ocher block known simply as Moscow Center, headquarters of the KGB.

Behind the old KGB building lies the infamous Lubyanka jail where confessions too numerous to count had been extracted and executions carried out. Behind the jail are two streets, Big Lubyanka and Little Lubyanka. He chose the second. Halfway up Lubyanka Malaya is the Church of St. Louis, where many of the diplomatic community and some of the few Russian Catholics go to worship.

Two hundred yards behind him and out of his vision because of the KGB building, a number of tramps were sleeping in the broad doorway of the giant toy shop, Detskiy Mir, or Children's World.

Two burly men in jeans and black leather jackets walked into the shop doorway and began to turn the sleeping bodies over. One wore an old army greatcoat with a few soiled medals clinging to the lapel. The men stiffened, then bent over him again, shaking him out of his slumber.

"Is your name Zaitsev?" snapped one of them. The old man nodded. The other man whipped a portable phone out of his blouse pocket, punched in some numbers, and spoke. Within five minutes a Moskvitch swerved to the curb. The two men hustled the figure between them and threw him into the rear, piling in on top of him. The old man tried to say something before he went in, and there was a glint of stainless steel at the front of his mouth.

The car raced around the square, drove behind the great building that once housed the All-Russian Insurance Corporation before becoming a house of terror, and roared up Lubyanka Malaya, passing the figure of a British diplomat on the pavement.

Macdonald let himself into the church with the aid of a drowsy sacristan, walked to the end of the aisle, and knelt in front of the altar. He looked up and the figure of the crucified Christ looked down. And he prayed.

A man's prayers are a very private thing, but what he prayed was: "Dear God, I beg you, let it be a forgery. For if it is not, a great and dark evil is going to descend upon us."

CHAPTER 4

BEFORE ANY OF THE REGULAR STAFF ARRIVED FOR WORK JOCK Macdonald was back at his desk. He had not slept, but no one would know it. A fastidious man, he had washed and shaved in the staff bathroom on the ground floor and changed into the clean shirt he kept in his desk.

His deputy, Bruce "Gracie" Fields, was awakened at his apartment and asked to be in by nine. Hugo Gray, now back in his own bed, received a similar call. At eight Macdonald asked the security staff, both senior ex-NCOs from the army, to prepare the bubble for a conference at 9:15.

"The point is," explained Macdonald to his two colleagues just after that time, "yesterday I came into possession of a document. No need to tell you its contents. Suffice to say, if it is a forgery or a hoax, we are wasting our time. If it is genuine, and I don't know that yet, it could be a significant input. Hugo, tell Gracie the background, will you?"

Gray filled in what he knew, what Celia Stone had told him.

"In a perfect world," said Macdonald, using one of his favorite phrases and causing the younger men to cover their grins, "I'd like to know who the old man was, the manner by which he came into possession of what might be a seriously classified file, and why he chose that car in that place to deposit it. Did he know Celia Stone? Did he know it was an embassy car? And if so, why us? In the meantime, is there anyone in the embassy who can draw?"

"Draw?" asked Fields.

"As in create a picture, a portrait."

"I think one of the wives runs an art class," said Fields. "Used to be an illustrator of children's books in London. Married to some fellow in Chancery."

"Check it out. If she can, put her together with Celia Stone. Meanwhile I'm going to have a chat with Celia myself. Two other things. Chummy may show up again, try to approach us, hang around the building. I'm going to ask Corporal Meadows and Sergeant Reynolds to keep an eye on the main gate. If they spot him, they'll report to either of you. Try and get him inside for a cup of tea. Second, he may try other tricks elsewhere and get himself arrested. Gracie, don't you have somebody in the police?"

Fields nodded. He was the longest-serving in Moscow of the three, inheriting when he arrived a range of low-level sources around Moscow and creating several of his own.

"Inspector Novikov. He's with Homicide at the Petrovka headquarters building. Occasionally useful."

"Have a word," said Macdonald. "Nothing to do with documents thrown into cars. Just say there's an old codger been pestering our staff out on the street, demanding a private interview with the ambassador. We're not fussed about it, but we'd like to ask him to leave us alone. Show him the picture, if we get a picture, but don't let him keep it. When's your next meet?"

"Nothing scheduled," said Fields. "I call him from phone booths."

"Okay, see if he can help. Meanwhile, I'm going to go over to London for a couple of days. Gracie, you hold the fort."

Celia Stone was intercepted in the lobby when she arrived and, somewhat startled, was asked to join Macdonald, not in his office but in Conference Room A. She did not know this room was the bug-proof one.

Macdonald was very kind and talked with her for almost an hour. He noted every detail and she accepted his story that the old man had pestered other staff members with his demands to see the ambassador. Would she agree to help draw up a portrait of the old tramp? Of course she would; anything to help.

Attended by Hugo Gray, she spent the lunch hour with the wife of the Deputy Head of Chancery who, with her guidance, produced a charcoal and crayon sketch of the tramp. A silver marking pen highlighted the three steel teeth. When it was finished Celia nodded and said: "That's him."

After lunch Jock Macdonald asked Corporal Meadows to draw a sidearm and escort him to Sheremetyevo Airport. He did not expect to be intercepted, but he did not know whether the rightful owners of the document in his briefcase might wish to recover their property. As an added precaution he chained the case to his left wrist, covering the metal with a light summer raincoat.

When the embassy Jaguar rolled out of the gates, all this was invisible anyway. He noticed a black Chaika parked down Sofia Quay, but it made no move to follow the Jaguar, so he thought no more of it. In fact the Chaika was waiting for a small red Rover to emerge.

At the airport Corporal Meadows escorted him to the barrier, where his diplomatic passport eliminated all controls. After a short wait in Departures he boarded the British Airways flight for Heathrow and after takeoff breathed a slow sigh and ordered a gin and tonic.

Washington, April 1985

IF the Archangel Gabriel had descended on Washington to ask the Rezident of the KGB team in the Soviet Embassy which of all the officers in the CIA he would like to turn traitor and spy for Russia, Colonel Stanislav Androsov would not have hesitated long.

He would have replied: I'd like the head of the Counterintelligence Group attached to the Soviet Division of Ops Directorate.

All intelligence agencies have a counterintelligence arm working inside the apparatus with them. The job of the counterintelligence people, which does not always make them popular with their colleagues, is to check up on everyone else. It is a job that breaks down into three functions.

Counterintelligence will attend and play a leading role in the debriefing of defectors from the other side, simply to try to discover whether the defector is genuine or a cunning plant. A false defector may bring some real information with him, but his primary task is to spread disinformation: either to convince his new hosts they do not have a traitor in their own midst when they do, or in some other way to lead their hosts down a maze of cul-de-sacs and blind alleys. Years of wasted time and effort can result from a skillful plant.

Counterintelligence also checks out those from the opposition who, while not actually crossing over in person, have allowed themselves to be recruited as spies but may in fact be double agents. A double is one who pretends to be recruited while in fact remaining loyal to his own team and acting on its orders. He will provide some granules of genuine information to establish his authenticity and then spring the real sting, which is entirely false and can create havoc among the people he is supposed to be working for.

Finally, counterintelligence has to ensure that its own side has not been penetrated, is not harboring a traitor at its own breast.

To accomplish these tasks, counterintelligence has to have total access. It can call up all the files on all the defectors and their debriefings, going back over years. It can examine the careers and recruitment of all current assets working for the agency deep in the heart of opponent territory and exposed to every conceivable danger of betrayal. And counterintelligence can demand the personnel file of every officer on its own side. All in the name of checking loyalty and genuineness.

Because of rigorous compartmentalization and the need-to-know principle, an intelligence officer acting as controller of one or two operations can betray those operations, but will normally have no idea what his colleagues are working on. Only counterintelligence has access to the lot. That is why Colonel Androsov, had he been asked by the archangel, would have chosen the head of counterintelligence for the Soviet Division. Counterintelligence people have to be the most loyal of the loyal.

In July 1983, Aldrich Hazen Ames was appointed to head the Soviet Counterintelligence Group of the SE Division. As such he had complete access to its two subbranches: the USSR Desk handling all Soviet assets working for the United States but posted inside the USSR, and the External Ops Desk handling all assets then posted outside the USSR.

On April 16, 1985, short of money, he walked into the Soviet Embassy on Washington's Sixteenth Street, asked to see Colonel Androsov, and volunteered to spy for Russia. For fifty thousand dollars.

He brought with him some small bona fides. He gave away the names of three Russians who had approached the CIA offering to work for it. Later he would say he thought they were probably double agents, i.e., not genuine. Whatever, those three gentlemen were never heard from again. He also brought an internal CIA personnel list with his own name highlighted to prove he was who he said he was. Then he left, walking for the second time right past the FBI cameras filming the front forecourt. The tapes were never played back.

Two days later he got his fifty thousand dollars. It was just the start. The most damaging traitor in America's history, back to and probably including Benedict Arnold, had just started work.

Later analysts would puzzle over two enigmas. The first was how such a grossly inadequate, underperforming, alcohol-abusing loser could ever have risen through the ranks to such an amazing position of trust. The second was how, when the senior hierarchs knew by that December in their secret hearts that they had a traitor among them somewhere, he could have remained unexposed for a further—and for the CIA catastrophic—eight years.

The answer to the second has a dozen facets. Incompetence, lethargy, and complacency within the CIA, luck for the traitor, a skillful disinformation campaign by the KGB to protect its mole, more lethargy, squeamishness, and indolence at Langley, red herrings, more luck for the traitor, and, finally, the memory of James Angleton.

Angleton had once been head of counterintelligence at the agency, rising to become a legend and ending deranged by paranoia. This strange man, without private life or humor, became convinced there was a KGB mole, code-named Sasha, inside Langley. In fanatic pursuit of this nonexistent traitor, he crippled the careers of loyal officer after loyal officer until he finally brought the Operations Directorate to its knees. Those who survived him, risen by 1985 to high office, were desolated at the thought of doing what had to be done—searching with rigor for the real mole.

As for the first question, the answer can be given in two words: Ken Mulgrew.

In twenty years with the agency before he turned traitor, Ames had had three postings outside Langley. In Turkey his Chief of Station deemed him to be a complete waste of space; the veteran Dewey Clarridge loathed and despised him from the start.

In the New York office he had a lucky break that brought him kudos. Although the Under-Secretary General of the United Nations, Arkady Shevchenko, had been working for the CIA before Ames arrived, and his final defection to the States in April 1978 was masterminded by another officer, Ames handled the Ukrainian in between. He was by then already becoming a very serious drinker.

His third posting, in Mexico, was a fiasco. He was consistently drunk, insulted colleagues and foreigners, fell down and was helped home by the Mexican police, broke every standing operating procedure imaginable, and recruited nobody.

On both the overseas postings Ames's performance reports were appalling. In one wide-spectrum performance assessment he came 198th out of 200 officers.

Normally such a career would go nowhere near the top. By the early eighties all the senior hierarchs—Carey Jordan, Dewey Clarridge, Milton Bearden, Gus Hathaway, and Paul Redmond— thought he was a useless article. But not Ken Mulgrew, who became his friend and protector.

It was he who sanitized the dreadful performance and assessment reports, smoothed the path, and procured the promotions. As Ames's senior he overrode the objections and, while heading up Personnel Allocations, slipped Ames into the Counterintelligence Group.

Basically, they were drinking buddies, both serial boozers who with the self-pity of the alcoholic agreed with each other that the agency was grossly unfair to both of them. It was a judgmental error that would soon cost a lot of lives.

•　　•　　•

LEONID Zaitsev the Rabbit was dying but he did not know it. He was in great pain. This he knew.

Colonel Grishin believed in pain. He believed in pain as persuasion, pain as example to the witnesses, and pain as punishment. Zaitsev had sinned and the colonel's orders were that he should fully comprehend the meaning of pain before he died.

The interrogation had lasted all day and there had been no call to use violence because he had told everything that was asked of him. Grishin had been alone with him most of the time, because he did not wish the guards to hear what had been stolen.

The colonel had asked him, quite gently, to start at the beginning, so he had. He had been required to repeat the story over and over again until Grishin was satisfied no detail had been left out. There was not really much to tell.

Only when he explained why he had done it was the colonel's face masked in disbelief.

"A beer? The English gave you a *beer?*"

By midday Grishin was convinced he had it all. The chances were, he reckoned, that confronted with this scarecrow the young Englishwoman would throw the file away, but he could not be sure. He dispatched a car with four trusted men to stake out the embassy and wait for the small red car, then follow it to wherever she lived and report back.

Just after three he gave final orders to his Guards and left. As he drove out of the compound, an A-300 Airbus with British Airways livery on its tailfin turned toward northern Moscow and headed west. He did not notice. He ordered his driver to take him back to the dacha off Kiselny Boulevard.

There were four of them. The Rabbit's legs would have buckled, but they knew that so two of them held him up, fingers digging hard into his upper arms. The other two were one front, one back. They worked slowly and placed their punches diligently.

The big fists were wrapped in heavy knobbed brass knuckles. The punches crushed his kidneys, tore his liver, and ruptured his spleen. A kick pulped his old testicles. The man at the front drove into the belly, then moved up to the chest. He fainted twice but a bucket of cold water brought him around and the pain returned. His legs ceased to function so they held his light frame on tiptoe.

Toward the end the ribs in the skinny chest cracked and sprung, two driving deep into the lungs. Something warm and sweet and sticky rose in his throat so that he could not breathe.

His vision narrowed to a tunnel and he saw not the gray concrete blocks of the room behind the camp armory, but a bright sunny day with a sandy road and pine trees. He could not see the speaker, but a voice was saying to him:

"Come on, mate, 'ave a beer . . . 'ave a beer."

The light faded to gray but he could still hear the voice repeating words he could not understand. " 'Ave a beer, 'ave a beer . . ." Then the lights went out forever.

Washington, June 1985

TWO months almost to the day after he got his first cash payment of $50,000, Aldrich Ames, in a single afternoon, destroyed almost the entire SE Division of the Ops Directorate of the CIA.

Just before lunch, having raided the top secret 301 files, he swept seven pounds of classified documents and cable traffic off his desk and into two plastic shopping bags. With these he walked down the labyrinthine corridors to the elevators, rode to the ground floor, and let himself out through the turnstiles with his laminated ID card. No guard paused to ask what was in the bags. Climbing into his car in the huge parking lot, he drove the twenty minutes to Georgetown, the elegant section of Washington renowned for its European-style restaurants.

He arrived at Chadwick's, a bar and restaurant under the K Street Freeway on the waterfront, and met the contact designated for him by Colonel Androsov, who as the KGB Rezident knew he himself would probably have been tailed by the FBI watchers. The contact was an ordinary Soviet diplomat called Chuvakhin.

To the Russian Ames handed over what he had. He never even demanded a price. When it came it would be enormous, the first of many that would make him a millionaire. The Russians, normally stingy with valuable hard-currency dollars, never even haggled after that. They knew they had hit the mother lode.

From Chadwick's the bags went to the embassy and thence to the Yazenevo headquarters of the First Chief Directorate. There the analysts could not believe their eyes.

The coup made Androsov an instant star and Ames the most vital asset in the firmament. The FCD's commanding general, Vladimir Kryuchkov, originally a snoop put into the FCD by the ever-suspicious Andropov but since risen to higher things, at once ordered the formation of a top-secret group to be detached from all other tasks and assigned only to handle the Ames product. Ames was code-named Kolokol, meaning Bell, and the task force became the Kolokol Group.

In those shopping bags were descriptions of fourteen agents, almost the SE Division's entire array of assets within the USSR. The actual names were not included, but they did not need to be.

Any counterintelligence detective, told that there is a mole inside his own network and told that the man was recruited in Bogotà, then worked in Moscow, and is now in service in Lagos, would work it out pretty fast. Only one career will match those postings. A check of the records usually suffices.

A senior CIA officer later calculated that forty-five anti-KGB operations, virtually the CIA's entire menu, collapsed after the summer of 1985. Not a single top agent working for the CIA whose name had been on the 301 files continued to function after the spring of 1986.

• • •

JOCK Macdonald's first port of call on arriving in the late afternoon at Heathrow was the headquarters building of the SIS at Vauxhall Cross. He was tired, although he had dared to take a catnap on the plane, and the notion of going to his club for a bath and a real sleep was tempting. The flat he and his wife, still in Moscow, retained in Chelsea was not available, being let to others.

But he wanted the file in the briefcase still attached to his wrist under lock and key inside the HQ building before he could relax. The Service car that had met him at Heathrow dropped him in front of the green-glass and sandstone monster on the south bank of the Thames that now housed the Service since its move from shabby old Century House seven years earlier.

He penetrated the security systems at the entrance, assisted by the eager young probationer who had accompanied him from the airport, and finally lodged the file in the safe of the head of Russia Division. His colleague had welcomed him warmly but with some curiosity.

"Drink?" asked Jeffrey Marchbanks, indicating what appeared to be a wood-paneled filing cabinet but which both men knew contained a bar.

"Good idea. Been a long day, and a rough one. Scotch."

Marchbanks opened the cabinet door and contemplated his repertoire. Macdonald was a Scot and took the brew of his ancestors neat. The divisional head poured a double tot of the Macallan, with no ice, and handed it over.

"Knew you were coming of course, but not why. Tell me."

Macdonald narrated his story from the beginning.

"It must be a hoax, of course," said Marchbanks at last.

"On the face of it, yes," agreed Macdonald. "But it must be the most unsubtle bloody hoax I've ever heard of. Who's the hoaxer?"

"Komarov's political enemies, one supposes."

"He's got enough of them," said Macdonald. "But what a way to present it. Damn well asking for it to be thrown away unread. It was only a fluke young Gray found it."

"Well, the next step is to read it. You've read it, I suppose?"

"All last night. As a political manifesto, it's . . . unpleasant."

"In Russian, of course?"

"Yes."

"Mmmm. I suspect my Russian won't be up to it. We'll need a translation."

"I'd prefer to do that myself," said Macdonald. "Just in case it's not a hoax. You'll see why when you read it."

"All right, Jock. Your call. What do you want?"

"Club first. Bath, shave, dinner, and a sleep. Then come back here about midnight and work on it till opening hours. See you again then."

Marchbanks nodded.

"All right. You'd better borrow this office. I'll notify Security."

By the time Jeffrey Marchbanks returned to his office just before ten the following morning, it was to find Jock Macdonald full-length on his sofa with his shoes and jacket off and tie loosened. The black file was on his desk with a pile of unbound white sheets beside it.

"That's it," he said. "In the language of Shakespeare. By the way, the disk is still in the machine but it should be got out and logged safely."

Marchbanks nodded, ordered coffee, pulled on his glasses, and began to read. He looked up after a while.

"The man's mad, of course."

"If it is Komarov writing, then yes. Or very bad. Or both. Either way, potentially dangerous. Read on."

Marchbanks did so. When he had finished he puffed out his cheeks and exhaled.

"It has to be a hoax. No one who meant it would ever write it down."

"Unless he thought it was confined to his own inner core of fellow fanatics," suggested Macdonald.

"Stolen then?"

"Possibly. Forged, possibly. But who was the tramp, and how did *he* get hold of it? We don't know."

Marchbanks pondered. He knew that if the manifesto was a forgery and a hoax, there would be nothing but grief for the SIS if they took it seriously. If it turned out to be genuine, there would be even more grief if they did not.

"I think," he said at length, "I want to run this past the Controller, maybe even the Chief."

The Controller, Eastern Hemisphere, David Brownlow, saw them at twelve and the Chief offered the three of them lunch in his paneled top-floor dining room with its panoramic views of the Thames and Vauxhall Bridge at 1:15.

Sir Henry Coombs was just short of sixty and in his final year as chief of the SIS. Like his predecessors he had come up through the ranks and honed his skills in the Cold War that had ended a decade earlier. Unlike the CIA, whose directors were political appointments and not always skillful ones, the SIS for thirty years had persuaded prime ministers to give them a chief who had been through the mill.

And it worked. After 1985 three successive directors of the CIA had admitted they were told hardly anything of the true awfulness of the Ames affair until they read the newspapers. Henry Coombs had the trust of his subordinates and knew all the details he needed to know. And they knew that he knew.

He read the file while sipping his vichyssoise. But he read fast and he took it all in.

"This must be very tiresome for you, Jock, but tell it again."

He listened attentively, asking two brief questions, then nodded.

"Your views, Jeffrey?"

After the Head of Russia Division, he asked Brownlow, the Controller East. Both said much the same. Is it true? We need to know.

"What intrigues me," said Brownlow, "is simply this: If all this is Komarov's true political agenda, why did he write it down? We all know even the most top-secret documents can be stolen."

Sir Henry Coombs's deceptively mild eyes turned to his Moscow Head of Station.

"Any ideas, Jock?"

Macdonald shrugged.

"Why does anyone write down their innermost thoughts and plans? Why do people confess the unconfessable to their private diaries? Why do people keep impossibly intimate journals? Why do major services like ours store hypersensitive material? Perhaps it was intended as a very private briefing document for his own inner circle, or just as therapy for himself. Or perhaps it is a forgery designed to damage the man. I don't know."

"Ah, there you have it," said Sir Henry. "We don't know. But, having read it, I think we agree we must know. So many questions. How the hell did this come to be written? Is it really the work of Igor Komarov? Is this appalling torrent of madness what he intends to fulfill if, or more likely, when he comes to power? If so, how was it stolen, who stole it, and why throw it at us? Or is it all a farrago of lies?"

He stirred his coffee and stared at the documents, both the original and Macdonald's copy, with profound distaste.

"Sorry, Jock, but we've got to have those answers. I can't take this up the river until we do. Possibly not then. It's back to Moscow, Jock. I don't know how you are going to do it; that's your business. But we need to know."

The Chief of the SIS, like all his predecessors, had two tasks. One was professional, to run the best covert intelligence service for the nation that he could. The other was political, to liaise with the Joint Intelligence Committee, the mandarins of the SIS's principal customers, the Foreign Office, who were not always easy, to fight for budget with the Cabinet Office, and to cultivate friends among the politicians who made up the government. It was a multifaceted task and not for the squeamish or the foolish.

The last thing he needed was to produce some harum-scarum

story of a tramp throwing into the car of an extremely junior diplomat some file that now had footprints on it and described a program of deranged cruelty that might or might not be genuine. He would be shot down in flames and he knew it.

"I'll fly back this afternoon, Chief."

"Nonsense, Jock, you've had two miserable nights in a row. Take in a show, get eight hours in a bed. Grab tomorrow's first schedule back to the land of the Cossacks." He glanced at his watch. "And now, if you'll excuse me . . ."

The three filed out. Macdonald never made the theater or the eight hours in bed. There was a message in Marchbanks's office, fresh from the cipher room. Celia Stone's apartment had been raided and torn apart. She had come home from dinner and disturbed two masked men who clubbed her with a chair leg. She was in the hospital but not in danger.

Silently Marchbanks handed the slip to Macdonald who read it also.

"Oh shit," he said.

Washington, July 1985

THE tip, when it came, was as so often in the world of espionage oblique, third-hand, and possibly a complete waste of time.

An American volunteer, working with a UNICEF aid program in the unlovely Marxist-Leninist republic of South Yemen, was back in New York on furlough and had dinner with a former classmate who was with the FBI.

Discussing the enormous Soviet military aid program being offered to South Yemen by Moscow, the United Nations worker described an evening at the bar of the Rock Hotel in Aden when he had fallen into conversation with a Russian army major.

Like most of the Russians there, the man spoke virtually no Arabic, but communicated with the Yemenis, citizens of a former British colony until 1976, in English. The American, aware of the unpopularity of the United States in South Yemen, customarily told people he was Swiss. He told the Russian this.

The Russian, becoming increasingly more drunk and out of earshot of any of his fellow countrymen, launched into a violent denunciation of the leadership of his own country. He accused them of massive corruption, criminal waste, and not giving a damn about their own people in their efforts to subsidize the Third World.

Having delivered himself of his dinner-table anecdote, the aid worker would have passed out of the story, if the FBI man had not mentioned the matter to a friend in the CIA's New York office.

The CIA man, having consulted his bureau chief, set up a second dinner with the aid worker at which the wine flowed copiously. To be provocative, the CIA man lamented how the Russians were making great strides in cementing friendships with the nations of the Third World, especially in the Middle East.

Eager to show off his superior knowledge, the UNICEF worker broke in that this was simply not so; he had personal knowledge that the Russians tended to loathe the Arabs and to become quickly exasperated at their inability to master simple technology and their ability to break or crash anything they were given to play with.

"I mean, take where I just came back from . . ." he said.

By the end of the meal the CIA man had a picture of a huge military advisory group whose members were at their wits' end with frustration and could see no point in their presence in the People's Democratic Republic of Yemen. He also had a description of a seriously fed-up major: tall, muscular, rather Oriental face. And a name: Solomin.

The report went back to Langley, where it came to the desk of the head of SE Division who discussed it with Carey Jordan.

"It may be nothing and it may be dangerous," said the DDO to Jason Monk three days later. "But do you think you could get into South Yemen and have a talk with this Major Solomin?"

Monk consulted lengthily with the backroom experts on the Middle East and soon realized South Yemen was a tough nut. The United States was in deep disfavor with the Communist government there, which was being ardently courted by Moscow. Despite that, there was a surprisingly large foreign community, apart from the Russians. This included the United Nations, with three operations: FAO was helping with agriculture, UNICEF with the street children, and WHO with health projects.

However well one speaks a foreign language, it is a daunting prospect to pose as a member of that nation and then run into the real article. Monk decided to avoid pretending to be British because the Brits would spot the difference in two minutes. The same with the French.

But the United States was the principal paymaster of the United Nations and had influence, overt and covert, in a number of the agencies. Research revealed there was no Spaniard in the Food and Agriculture Organization mission to Aden. A new persona was created and it was quietly agreed that Monk would travel to Aden in October on a one-month visa as a visiting inspector from FAO headquarters in Rome to check on progress. He would be, according to his papers, Esteban Martinez Llorca. In Madrid, the still-grateful Spanish government provided genuine paperwork.

•   •   •

JOCK Macdonald arrived in Moscow too late to visit Celia Stone in the hospital but was there the next morning. The Assistant Press Attaché was bandaged and woozy, but able to talk. She had gone home at the normal hour, she had noticed no one following. But then, she was not trained for that.

After three hours in her flat, she had gone out for dinner with a girlfriend from the Canadian Embassy. She had returned about 11:30. The thieves must have heard her key in the lock because all was quiet when she entered. She put on the light in the foyer and noticed the door to the living room was open and the room was dark. That was odd, because she had left a lamp on. The living room windows faced the central courtyard, and the light behind the curtains would indicate someone was at home. She thought the bulb must have blown.

She reached the door of the room and two figures came at her out of the darkness. One swung something and hit her on the side of the head. As she went down she half-heard, half-felt two men jumping over her and heading for the front door. She passed out. When she came to—she did not know how much later—she crawled to her telephone and rang a neighbor. Then she fainted again and woke up in the hospital. There was nothing more she could tell.

Macdonald went to the flat. The Ambassador had protested to the Foreign Ministry, which had hit the roof and complained to Interior. They had ordered the Moscow Prosecutor's office to send their best investigator. A full report would be on its way as soon as possible. In Moscow that meant: Don't hold your breath.

The message to London had been wrong in one respect. Celia Stone had not been hit by a chair leg, but by a small china figurine. It had shattered. Had it been metal she could have been dead.

There were Russian detectives in the flat and they happily answered the British diplomat's questions. The two militiamen stationed at the entry to the courtyard had admitted no Russian car, so the men must have come on foot. The militiamen had seen no one pass them. They would say that anyway, thought Macdonald.

The door had not been forced so it must have been picked unless the burglars had had a key, which was unlikely. They were probably looking for hard currency in these difficult times. It was very regrettable. Macdonald nodded.

Privately he thought the intruders might have been from the Black Guards, but more likely it was a contract job by the local underworld. Or ex-KGB hirelings—there were enough about. Moscow burglars hardly ever touched diplomatic residences; too much fall-out. Cars on the open street were fair game, but not guarded apartments. The search had been thorough and professional, but nothing had been taken, not even some costume jewelry in the bedroom. A pro job and for a single item, not found. Macdonald feared the worst.

Back at the embassy he had an idea, rang the Prosecutor's office, and asked if the detective assigned to the case would be kind enough to call on him. Inspector Chernov came to visit at three P.M.

"I may be able to help you," said Macdonald.

The detective raised an eyebrow.

"I would be most grateful," he said.

"Our young lady, Miss Stone, was feeling better this morning. Much better."

"Deeply gratified," said the inspector.

"So much so that she was able to give a reasonable description of one of her attackers. She saw him in the light coming from the hall just before the blow struck."

"Her first statement indicated she saw neither of them," said Chernov.

"Memory sometimes returns in cases like these. You saw her yesterday afternoon, Inspector?"

"Yes, at four P.M. She was awake."

"But still dizzy, I expect. This morning she was in a clearer state of mind. Now, one of the wives of our staff here is something of an artist. With Miss Stone's help she was able to create a picture."

He handed over his desk a portrait in charcoal and crayon. The inspector's face lit up.

"This is extraordinarily useful," he said. "I will circulate it among the Burglary Squad. A man of this age must have a record." He rose to go. Macdonald arose.

"Just pleased to be helpful," he said. They shook hands and the detective left.

During the lunch hour both Celia Stone and the artist had been briefed on the new story. Neither understood why, but agreed to confirm it if Inspector Chernov ever interviewed them. In fact he never did.

Nor did his burglary teams, scattered across Moscow, recognize the face. But they put it on the walls of their squad rooms anyway.

Moscow, July 1985

IN the wake of the windfall harvest just arrived from Aldrich Ames, the KGB did something quite extraordinary.

It is an unbreakable rule in the Great Game that if an agency suddenly acquires a priceless asset deep in the heart of the enemy, that asset must be protected. Thus, when the asset reveals a host of turncoats, the newly enlightened agency will pick up those turncoats very slowly and carefully, in each case creating a seemingly different reason for his capture.

Only when their asset has escaped from danger and is safely behind the lines may the agents he has betrayed be picked up all at once. To do otherwise would be the equivalent of taking a full-page advertisement in *The New York Times* to say: "We have just acquired a major mole right inside your outfit, and look what he has given us."

As Ames was still very much at the heart of the CIA, with many years of good service to come, the First Chief Directorate would have liked to abide by the rules and pick up the fourteen blown turncoats slowly and carefully. In this they were completely over-ruled, against their almost tearful protests, by Mikhail Gorbachev.

Sorting through the harvest from Washington, the Kolokol Group realized that some of the descriptions were immediately identifiable while others would need careful checking to track down. Of the immediates, some were still posted abroad and would have to be carefully lured back home in a manner so skillful they would not smell a rat. It might take months.

One of the fourteen was actually a longtime agent of the British. The Americans never knew his name, but as London had given Langley his product, the CIA knew a bit about him and could deduce a bit more. He was actually a colonel of the KGB who had been recruited in Denmark in the early seventies and had been a British asset for twelve years. Already under some suspicion, he had nevertheless returned to Moscow from his post as Rezident at the Soviet Embassy in London for one last visit. Ames's betrayal simply confirmed the Russian suspicions.

But Colonel Oleg Gordievsky was lucky. Seeing by July that he was under total surveillance, with the net closing and arrest imminent, he used a prearranged distress signal. The British SIS mounted a very fast extraction operation, plucked the wiry colonel off the street while he was jogging, and smuggled him out to Finland. He survived, later to be debriefed in a CIA safe house by Aldrich Ames.

•   •   •

JEFFREY Marchbanks thought there might be a way he could help his colleague in Moscow in his search for the authenticity, or lack of it, of the Black Manifesto.

One of Macdonald's problems was that he had no reasonable means of gaining access to the person of Igor Komarov. Marchbanks calculated that a personal in-depth interview with the leader of the Union of Patriotic Forces might give some clue about whether the man who portrayed himself as an admittedly right-wing Conserva-tive and Nationalist hid beneath his veneer the ambitions of a raging Nazi.

He thought he might know someone who could get that inter-view. The previous winter he had been on a pheasant shoot and among the guests had been the newly appointed editor of Britain's leading Conservative daily newspaper. On July 21 Marchbanks called the editor, reminded him of the pheasant shoot, and set up a lunch date for the following day at his club in St. James's.

Moscow, July 1985

THE escape of Gordievsky caused a blazing row in Moscow. It took place on the last day of the month in the personal office on the third floor of the KGB headquarters on Dzerzhinski Square of the chairman of the KGB himself.

It was a gloomy office that had in its time been the den of some of the bloodiest monsters the planet has known. Orders had been signed at the T-shaped desk that caused men to shriek under torture, to die of hypothermia in the wastelands of Siberia or kneeling in a bleak courtyard with a pistol bullet in the brain.

General Viktor Chebrikov did not quite have those powers anymore. Things were changing and execution orders had to be approved by the president himself. But for traitors they would still be signed, and the conference of that day would ensure that more were yet to come.

Very much on the defensive in front of the chairman's desk was the head of the First Chief Directorate, Vladimir Kryuchkov. It was his men who had fouled up so badly. On the attack was the head of the Second Chief Directorate, the short, chunky, bull-shouldered General Vitali Boyarov, and he was spitting angry.

"The whole thing has been a complete . . . *razebaistvo*," he stormed. Even among the generals, the use of locker-room language was very much the thing, a proof of soldierly crudeness and working-class origins. The word means "fuckup."

"It won't happen again," muttered Kryuchkov defensively.

"Let us agree then," said the Chairman, "on a structure from which we do not deviate. On the sovereign territory of the USSR traitors will be arrested and interrogated by the Second Chief Directorate. If there are ever any more traitors identified, that is what will happen. Understood?"

"There will be more," muttered Kryuchkov. "Thirteen more."

There was silence in the room for several seconds.

"Are you trying to tell us something, Vladimir Aleksandrovitch?" asked the Chairman quietly.

That was when Kryuchkov revealed what had happened at Chadwick's in Washington six weeks earlier. Boyarov let out a long whistle.

Within a week General Chebrikov, flushed with his agency's success, revealed all to Mikhail Gorbachev.

Meanwhile, General Boyarov was preparing his Ratcatcher Commission, the team who would interrogate the traitors as and when they were identified and arrested. To head the team he wanted someone special. The file was on his desk, a colonel, only forty but experienced, an interrogator who never failed.

Born 1945 in Molotov, formerly Perm and now called Perm again since Stalin's henchman Molotov fell into disgrace in 1957. Son of a decorated soldier who had survived and returned home to sire a son.

Little Tolya grew up under strict official indoctrination in the gray northern city. The notes recalled that his fanatical father loathed Khrushchev for criticizing the hero Stalin and that the boy had inherited and abided by all his father's attitudes.

In 1963 he had been called up at eighteen and seconded to the Interior Troops of the Interior Ministry, the MVD. These troops were assigned to protect prisons, labor camps, and detention centers and were used as antiriot troops. The young soldier had taken to the work as a duck to water.

In those units the spirit of repression and mass control prevailed. So well did the boy do that he received a rare reward, a transfer to the Leningrad Military Institute of Foreign Languages. This was a cover for the KGB training academy, known in the agency as "the manger" because it turned out constant fodder for the ranks. Graduates of the Kormushka were famous for their ruthlessness, dedication, and loyalty. The young man shone again, and was again rewarded.

This time it was a posting to the Moscow Oblast (city and region) branch of the Second Chief Directorate where he spent four years earning a fine reputation as a clever desk officer, thorough investigator, and tough interrogator. Indeed he so specialized in the latter that he wrote a highly regarded paper on it, which gained him a transfer to the national headquarters of the Second Chief Directorate.

Since then he had never left Moscow, working out of headquarters mainly against the hated Americans, covering their embassy and tailing their diplomatic personnel. At one point he spent a year in the Investigative Service, before returning to the Second CD. Superior officers and instructors had taken the time to note in the files his passionate hatred of Anglo-Americans, Jews, spies, and traitors, and an unexplained but acceptable level of sadism in his interrogations.

General Boyarov closed the dossier with a smile. He had his man. If quick results were wanted and no messing about, Colonel Anatoli Grishin was the man for him.

•   •   •

OF the remaining thirteen, one was lucky, or smart. Sergei Bokhan was an officer of Soviet military intelligence, posted in Athens. He was abruptly ordered back to Moscow on the grounds that his son was having exam problems at his military academy. He happened to know the boy was doing fine. Having deliberately missed the booked plane home, he contacted the CIA station in Athens and was brought out of there in a hurry.

The other twelve were caught. Some were inside the USSR, others abroad. Those abroad were ordered home on a variety of pretexts, all false. All were arrested on arrival.

Boyarov had chosen well. All twelve were intensively interrogated and all twelve confessed. The alternative was even more intensive interrogation. Two escaped with years in slave labor camps and now live in America. The other ten were tortured and shot.

CHAPTER 5

HALFWAY UP ST. JAMES'S STREET, HEADING NORTH WITH THE ONE-way traffic, is an anonymous gray stone building with a blue door and some potted green shrubs outside. It bears no name. Those who know what and where it is will have no trouble finding it; those who do not will be those who have no invitation to enter, and will pass on by. Brooks's Club does not advertise.

It is however a favorite watering hole of civil servants from Whitehall not far away. It was here that Jeffrey Marchbanks met the editor of the *Daily Telegraph* for lunch on July 22.

Brian Worthing was forty-eight and had been a journalist for over twenty years when, two years earlier, the Canadian proprietor Conrad Black had headhunted him from the *Times* to take over the vacant editorship. Worthing's background was as a foreign and war correspondent. He had covered the Falklands War as a young man, his first real war, and later the Gulf in 1990–1991.

The table Marchbanks had secured for himself was a small one in a corner, far enough from the others not to be overheard. Not that anyone would dream of attempting such a thing. In Brooks's a chap would never dream of eavesdropping another chap's conversation, but old habits die hard.

"I think I probably mentioned at Spurnal that I was with the Foreign Office," said Marchbanks over the potted shrimp.

"I recall that you did," said Worthing. He had been of two minds about whether to accept the lunch invitation at all. His day would as always last from ten in the morning until after sundown and taking two hours out for lunch—three if you counted the haul from Canary Wharf up to the West End and back—had better be worth it.

"Well, actually I work at another building further down the river from King Charles Street and on the other side," said Marchbanks.

"Ah," said the editor. He knew all about Vauxhall Cross though he had never been in it. Perhaps the lunch was going to produce something after all.

"My particular concern is Russia."

"I don't envy you," said Worthing, demolishing the last shrimp with a slice of thin brown bread. He was a big man with a notable appetite. "Going to hell in a handbasket, I would have thought."

"Something like that. Since the death of Cherkassov the next prospect seems to be the forthcoming presidential elections."

The two men fell silent as a young waitress brought the lamb chops and vegetables with a carafe of the house claret. Marchbanks poured.

"Bit of a foregone conclusion," said Worthing.

"Our view precisely. The Communist revival has fizzled over the years and the reformers are at sixes and sevens. There seems to be nothing to stop Igor Komarov from taking the presidency."

"Is that bad?" asked the editor. "The last piece I saw about him, he appeared to be talking some sense. Get the currency back in shape, halt the slide to chaos, give the mafia a hard time. That sort of thing."

Worthing prided himself on being a man of direct speech and tended to talk in staccato.

"Exactly, sounds wonderful. But he's still a bit of an enigma. What does he really intend to do? How, specifically does he intend to do it? He says he despises foreign credits, but how can he get by without them? More to the point, will he try to negate Russia's debts by paying them off in worthless rubles?"

"He wouldn't dare," said Worthing. He knew the *Telegraph* had a resident correspondent in Moscow but he had not filed a piece on Komarov for some time. Perhaps this lunch was not a waste after all.

"Wouldn't he now?" countered Marchbanks. "We don't know. Some of his speeches are pretty extreme, but then in private conversation he persuades visitors he's not such an ogre after all. Which is the real man?"

"I could ask our Moscow man to seek an interview."

"Unlikely to be granted, I'm afraid," suggested the spymaster. "I believe just about every resident correspondent in Moscow does the same regularly. He only grants interviews with exceptional rarity and purports to loathe the foreign press."

"I say, there's treacle tart," said Worthing. "I'll take it."

The British in middle age are seldom more content than when being offered the sort of food they were fed in nursery school. The waitress brought treacle tart for both.

"So, how to get at the man?" asked Worthing.

"He has a young publicity adviser whose advice he seems to listen to. Boris Kuznetsov. Very bright, educated at one of the American Ivy League colleges. If there's a key, he's it. We understand he reads the western press every day and particularly likes the articles by your man Jefferson."

Mark Jefferson was a staffer and regular contributor to the main feature page of the *Telegraph*. He dealt with politics, domestic and foreign, was a fine polemicist and a trenchant conservative. Worthing chewed on his treacle tart.

"It's an idea," he said at length.

"You see," said Marchbanks, warming to his ploy, "resident correspondents in Moscow are two a penny. But a star feature writer coming to do a major portrait of the coming leader, man-of-tomorrow sort of thing—that might appeal."

Worthing thought it over.

"Perhaps we should think of pen-portraits of all three candidates. Keep a sort of balance."

"Good idea," said Marchbanks, who did not think so. "But Komarov is the one who seems to fascinate people, one way or the other. The other two are ciphers. Shall we go upstairs for coffee?"

"Yes, it's not a bad idea," agreed Worthing when they were seated in the upstairs drawing room beneath the portrait of the Dilettantes. "Touched as I am by your concern for our circulation figures, what do you want him asked?"

Marchbanks grinned at the directness of the editor.

"All right. Yes, we would like to know a few things that we can feed to our masters. Preferably something not in the article itself. They can also read the *Telegraph,* and do. What does the man *really* intend? What about the minority ethnic groups? There are ten million of them in Russia, and Komarov is a Russian supremacist. How does he really intend to produce the rebirth to glory of the Russian nation? In a word, the man's a mask. What lies behind the mask? Is there a secret agenda?"

"If there is," mused Worthing, "why should he reveal all to Jefferson?"

"One never knows. Men get carried away."

"How does one get to this Kuznetsov?"

"Your man in Moscow will know him. A personal letter from Jefferson would probably be well received."

"All right," said Worthing as they descended the wide staircase to the lower hall. "I can see a center-page spread in my mind's eye. Not bad. If the man has something to say. I'll get on to our Moscow office."

"If it works, I'd like to have a word with Jefferson afterward."

"Debriefing? Huh. He's pretty prickly, you know."

"I shall be all olive oil," said Marchbanks.

They parted on the pavement. Worthing's driver spotted him and glided up from his illegal parking spot opposite the Suntory to carry him back to Canary Wharf in Dockland. The spymaster decided to walk off the treacle tart and the wine.

Washington, September 1985

BEFORE he even began spying, back in 1984, Ames had applied for the post of Soviet Branch chief at the CIA's big station in Rome. In September 1985 he learned he had the job.

This put him in a quandary. He did not know then that the KGB was unwillingly going to put him in extreme danger by picking up all the men he had betrayed with such speed.

The Rome slot would remove him from Langley and access to the 301 files and the Soviet Branch of the Counterintelligence Group attached to the SE Division. On the other hand, Rome was considered an attractive place to live and a prime assignment. He consulted the Russians.

Their attitude was approving. For one thing they had months of investigations, arrests, and interrogations ahead of them. So vast was the harvest that Ames had brought them and, for security reasons, so small the Kolokol Group working on that material in Moscow, that the full analysis could take years.

For in the interim Ames had provided much more. Among his secondary and tertiary deliveries to his cutout, Chuvakhin, was background material on just about every case officer of any note in Langley. There were not only full résumés of each of these officers, with their postings and achievements, but photos as well. Fore-warned by this, the KGB would be able to spot these CIA officers whenever and wherever they showed up.

Also, the Russians estimated that in Rome, one of the key cen-ters in the SE Division, Ames would have access to all CIA opera-tions and collaborations with its allies along the Mediterranean from Spain to Greece, an area of vital interest to Moscow.

Finally, they knew they could have much easier access to Ames in Rome than in Washington where there was always the danger of the FBI spotting them meeting. They urged him to take the posting.

So that same September Ames went off to language school to learn Italian.

At Langley the full import of the catastrophe about to hit the agency had not started to impinge. Two or three of their best agents in Russia had seemingly gone out of contact, which was worrying but not yet disastrous.

Among the personal dossiers Ames had passed to the KGB was that of one young man just transferred to the SE Division whom Ames referred to, because word had run like wildfire through the office, as a rising star. His name was Jason Monk.

•   •   •

OLD Gennadi had been picking mushrooms in those woods for years. In retirement he used nature's cost-free crop as a supplement to his pension, either taking them fresh to the best restaurants of Moscow or drying them in bunches for the few delicatessens that remained.

The thing about mushrooms is, you have to be out early in the morning, before dawn if possible. They grow in the night and after dawn the voles and squirrels get at them or, even worse, other mushroom pickers. Russians love mushrooms.

On the morning of July 24 Gennadi took his bicycle and his dog and rode from the small village where he lived to a forest he knew where they tended to grow thickly on summer nights. Before the dew was gone, he expected to have a good basketful.

The forest he chose was just off the great Minsk Highway where the trucks rolled and growled west toward the capital of Belarus. He rode into the wood, parked his bicycle by a tree, took his rush basket, and set off through the wood.

It was half an hour, with his basket half full and the sun just rising, that his dog whined and headed into a clump of shrubs. He had trained the mutt to sniff out mushrooms, so clearly he had found something good.

As he neared the spot he caught the sweet sickly odor. He knew that smell. Had he not smelt it enough, years before as a teenage soldier all the way from the Vistula to Berlin?

The body had been dumped, or had crawled there and died. It was a scrawny old man, massively discolored, eyes and mouth open. The birds had had the eyes. Three steel teeth glinted with dew. The body was stripped to the waist but an old overcoat was in a heap nearby. Gennadi sniffed again. In that heat, it told him, several days.

He pondered for a while. He was of the generation that recalled civic duty, but mushrooms were still mushrooms, and there was nothing he could do for the fellow. A hundred yards away through the forest he could hear the rumble of the trucks on the road from Moscow to Minsk.

He finished filling his mushroom basket and pedaled back to his village. There he put his crop out to dry in the sun and reported to the small and ramshackle *selsovet,* the local council office. It was not much, but it had a phone.

He dialed 02 and the call was taken by the police central control office.

"I've found a body," he said.

"Name?" said the voice.

"How the hell should I know? He's dead."

"Not his, idiot, yours."

"Do you want me to hang up?" said Gennadi.

There was a sigh.

"No, don't hang up. Just give me your name and your location."

Gennadi did so. The control office quickly checked the place on the map. It was just inside the Moscow City Region—Oblast—in the extreme west but still in Moscow's jurisdiction.

"Wait at the *selsovet*. An officer will come out to see you."

Gennadi waited. It took half an hour. When he came he was a young inspector from the uniformed branch. There were two other militiamen and they came in the usual yellow-and-blue Uzhgorod jeep-type vehicle.

"You the one who found the body?" asked the lieutenant.

"Yes," said Gennadi.

"All right, let's go. Where is it?"

"In the woods."

Gennadi felt quite important riding along in a police jeep. They dismounted where Gennadi suggested and set off in single file through the trees. The mushroom picker recognized the birch where he had left his bicycle, and his trail from there on. Soon they smelled the odor.

"He's in there," said Gennadi, pointing to the clump. "He doesn't half stink. Been there awhile."

The three policemen approached the body and examined it visually.

"See if there's anything in the trouser pockets," said the officer to one of his men. To the other, "Check out the greatcoat."

The one who had drawn the short straw held his nose and ran his spare hand through both trouser pockets. Nothing. With his toecap he turned the body over. There were maggots underneath. He checked the rear trouser pockets and stood back. He shook his head. The other threw down the overcoat and did the same.

"Nothing? No ID at all?" asked the lieutenant.

"Nothing. No coins, handkerchief, keys, papers."

"Hit and run?" suggested one of the policemen.

They listened to the rumble from the highway.

"How far to the road?" asked the officer.

"About a hundred meters," said Gennadi.

"Hit-and-run drivers move on fast. They don't lug the victim a hundred yards. Anyway, ten yards would do in all these trees." To one of his men the lieutenant said:

"Walk up to the highway. Check the shoulder for a smashed-up bicycle or a wrecked car. He might have been in a pile-up and crawled here. Then stay there and flag down the ambulance."

The officer used his mobile phone to call for an investigator, photographer, and medical expert. What he saw could not be a natural causes. He also asked for an ambulance but confirmed that life was extinct. One of the policemen set off through the trees for the road. The others waited, moving away from the stench.

The plainclothes trio came first, in a plain buff Uzhgorod. They were waved down on the highway, parked on the shoulder, and walked the rest of the way. The investigator nodded at the lieutenant.

"What have we got?"

"He's over there. I called you because I can't see how it could be natural causes. Badly knocked about and a hundred yards from the road."

"Who found him?"

"The mushroom picker over there."

The detective walked over to Gennadi.

"Tell me. From the beginning."

The photographer took pictures, then the doctor pulled on a gauze mask and made a quick examination. He straightened up and pulled off his rubber gloves.

"Ten kopecks to a good bottle of Moskovskaya, it's a homicide. The lab will tell us more, but someone knocked the shit out of him before he died. Probably not here. Congratulations, Volodya, you just got your first *zhmurik* of the day."

He used the Russian police and underworld slang for a "stiff." Two orderlies from the ambulance came through the wood with a stretcher. The doctor nodded and they zipped the corpse into a body bag before taking it back to the road.

"Are you finished with me?" asked Gennadi.

"No chance," said the detective. "I need a statement, at the station."

The policemen took Gennadi back to their precinct house, the headquarters of the Western District three miles down the road toward Moscow. The body went further, into the heart of the city, to the morgue of the Second Medical Institute. There it was put in a cold chest. Forensic pathologists were few and far between and their workload was overwhelming.

Yemen, October 1985

JASON Monk infiltrated South Yemen in mid-October. Though small and poor, the People's Republic had a first-class airport, formerly the military base of the Royal Air Force. Big jets could and did land there.

Monk's Spanish passport and supporting United Nations travel documents excited thorough but finally unsuspicious attention at Immigration, and after half an hour, clutching his all-purpose suitcase, he was through.

Rome had indeed informed the head of the Food and Agriculture Organization program that Señor Martinez was coming, but gave him a date which postdated Monk's actual arrival by a week. The Yemeni officers at the airport did not know that. So there was no car to receive him. He took a taxi and checked in at the new French hotel, the Frontel, on the spit of land joining the rock of Aden to the mainland.

Even though his papers were good and he expected to run into no real Spaniards, he knew the mission was dangerous. It was black, very black.

The great majority of espionage is carried out by officers inside an embassy and technically posing as embassy staff. They thus benefit from diplomatic status if anything goes wrong. Some are "declared," meaning they make no bones about what they do, and the local counterintelligence people know and accept this, though the real job remains tactfully unmentioned. A big station in hostile territory will always try to maintain a few "undeclared" officers whose cover jobs in the trade, culture, chancery, or press section remain unblown. The reason is simple.

Undeclared officers have a better chance of not being tailed out on the street, and therefore being freer to service dead drops or attend covert meetings than those always being followed.

But a spy working outside diplomatic cover cannot benefit from the Vienna Accords. If a diplomat is exposed he can be declared persona non grata and expelled. His country will then protest its innocence and expel one of the other nation's diplomats. The tit-for-tat dance having been gone through, the game resumes as before.

But a spy going in "on the black" is an illegal. For him, depending on the nature of the place where he has been caught, exposure can mean terrible torture, a long spell in a labor camp, or a lonely death. Even the people who sent him in can rarely help him.

In the democracies there will be a fair trial and a humane jail. In the dictatorships there are no civil rights. Some have never even heard of them. South Yemen was like that, and the United States did not even have an embassy there in 1985.

In October the heat is still fierce and Friday is the day of rest when no work is done. What, thought Monk, will a fit Russian officer do on a blazing hot day off? Have a swim was a reasonable idea.

For security's sake the original source who had had that dinner in New York with his FBI ex-classmate had not been recontacted. He might have given a better description of Major Solomin, even helped compose a portrait. He could even be back in Yemen, in a position to point the man out. But the assessment had been that he was also a braggart who talked too much.

Finding the Russians was no problem. They were all over the place, and evidently allowed to mix pretty freely with the West European community, something that would have been unheard of back home. Maybe it was the heat or the sheer impossibility of keeping the Soviet military advisory group pinned into their compounds day and night.

Two hotels, the Rock and the new Frontel, had inviting pools. Then there was the great sweep of sand with its foaming breakers, Abyan Beach where the expatriates of all nationalities were wont to swim either after work or on their day off. Finally there was a big Russian PX-style commissary up in the town where non-Russians were allowed to shop—the USSR needed the foreign currency.

It was quickly clear that the Russians on display were almost all officers. Very few Russians speak a word of Arabic, and not many more know English. Those that do would have attended a special school, i.e., be officers or officer material. Private soldiers and NCOs would be unlikely to have either language and therefore could not communicate with their Yemeni pupils. Thus, noncommissioned ranks would likely be confined to mechanics and cooks. Orderlies would be locally recruited Yemenis. Russian noncoms could not afford the prices of the Aden watering holes. Officers had a hard currency allowance.

Another possibility was that the American from the U.N. had found the Russian drinking alone at the bar of the Rock. Russians like to drink, but they also prefer company, and the ones around the pool at the Frontel were definitely in an impenetrable group. Why did Solomin drink alone? Just a fluke that night? Or was he a solitary who preferred his own company?

There was a possible clue here. The American had said he was tall and muscular with black hair but almond-shaped eyes. Like an Oriental, but without the flat nose. The language experts at Langley put the name somewhere in the Soviet Far East. Monk knew Russians are irretrievably racist, with an open contempt for *chorni*—blacks—meaning anyone not pure Russian. Perhaps Solomin was tired of jibes about his Asiatic features.

Monk haunted the commissary—the Russian officers were all living as bachelors—the pools, and the bars after dark. It was on the third day, strolling along Abyan Beach in boxer shorts with a towel over his shoulder, that he saw a man come out of the sea.

He was about six feet tall with heavily muscled arms and shoulders; not a youth, but a very fit fortyish. The hair was black as a raven's wing, but there was no body hair save beneath the armpits when he raised his hands to squeeze the water from his hair. Orientals have very little body hair; black-haired Caucasians usually a lot.

The man strolled up the sand, found his towel, and plonked himself down facing the sea. He pulled on a pair of dark glasses and was soon lost in thought.

Monk slipped off his shirt and walked toward the sea like a bather coming for his first swim. The beach was reasonably crowded. It was natural enough to choose a vacant spot a yard from the Russian. He took his wallet and wrapped his shirt around it. Then his towel. He kicked off his sandals and made a mound of them all. Then he looked around in apprehension. Finally he glanced at the Russian.

"Please," he said. The Russian glanced at him. "You stay for a few more minutes?" The man nodded.

"The Arabs do not steal my things, okay?"

The Russian nodded again and went back to staring at the ocean. Monk ran down the beach and swam for ten minutes. When he came back, dripping, he smiled at the black-haired man.

"Thanks." The man nodded for a third time. Monk toweled off and sat down.

"Nice sea. Nice beach. Pity about the people who own it."

The Russian spoke for the first time, in English.

"What people?"

"The Arabs. The Yemenis. I haven't been here long, but already I can't stand them. Useless people."

Behind the black glasses the Russian was looking at him but Monk could read no expression through the lenses. After two minutes he resumed.

"I mean, I'm trying to teach them to use basic tools and tractors. To increase their food, to feed themselves. No chance. Everything they break or smash up. I'm just wasting my time and the United Nations' money."

Monk was speaking good English but with a Spanish accent.

"You are English?" asked the Russian at last. It was his first contribution.

"No. Spanish. With the Food and Agriculture program, United Nations. And you? Also United Nations?"

The Russian grunted a negative.

"From USSR," he said.

"Ah, well, it will be hotter here than back home, for you. For me? About the same. And I can't wait to get back home."

"Me too," said the Russian. "I prefer the cold."

"You been here long?"

"Two years. And one to go."

Monk laughed. "Good God, we have to do one year, and I'll never stay that long. It's a job with no point. Well, I must be going. Tell me, after two years you must know, is there any good place to have a drink after dinner around here? Any nightclubs?"

The Russian laughed sardonically.

"No. No diskoteki. The bar at the Rock Hotel is quiet."

"Thanks. Oh, by the way, I am Esteban. Esteban Martinez."

He held out his hand. The Russian hesitated, then shook.

"Pyotr," he said. "Or Peter. Peter Solomin."

It was on the second night that the Russian major returned to the bar of the Rock Hotel. This former colonial hostelry is built literally into and on a rock, with steps up from the street to the small reception area and, on the top floor, a bar with panoramic views of the harbor. Monk had taken a window table and was staring out.

He could see Solomin enter by the reflection in the plate glass, but he waited until the man had his drink before turning.

"Ah, Señor Solomin, we meet again. Join me?"

He gestured to the other chair at his table. The Russian hesitated and then sat down. He lifted his beer.

"*Za vashe zdorovye.*"

Monk did the same.

"*Pesetas, faena, y amor.*" Solomin frowned. Monk grinned. "Money, work, and love—in any order you like." The Russian smiled for the first time. It was a good smile.

They talked. About this and that. About the impossibility of working with the Yemenis, of the frustration of seeing their machinery smashed up, of doing a task neither of them had any faith in. And they talked, as men far away will, of home.

Monk told him of his native Andalusia where he could ski in the high peaks of the Sierra Nevada and swim in the warm waters off Sotogrande on the same day. Solomin told of the deep forests in the snow, where the Siberian tigers still roam, where fox, wolf, and deer are there for the skilled hunter.

They met on four consecutive nights, enjoying each other's company. On the third day Monk had to present himself to the Dutchman who headed the FAO program and be taken on a tour of inspection. The CIA's Rome Station had procured a detailed briefing of that program from the FAO in the same city, and Monk had memorized it. His own farming background helped him understand the problems, and he was unstinting in his praise. The Dutchman was quite impressed.

During the evenings and late into the night, he learned about Major Pyotr Vasilyevitch Solomin, and what he heard he liked.

The man had been born in 1945 in that tongue of Soviet land lying between northeastern Manchuria and the sea, with the North Korean border to the south. It is called Primorskiy Krai and the town of his birth was Ussuriysk.

His father had come from the countryside to the city to seek work, but he raised his son to speak the language of their tribe, the Udegey people. He also took the growing boy back to the forests whenever he could, so the lad grew to have a deep affinity with the elements of his land: forest, mountains, water, and animals.

In the nineteenth century, before the final conquest of the Udegey by the Russians, the writer Arsenyev had visited the enclave and written a book still famous in Russia about these people. He called it *Far Eastern Tigers*.

Unlike the short, flat-featured Asiatics to the west and south, the Udegey were tall and hawk faced. Many centuries before, some of their ancestors had moved north, crossed the Bering Straits into what is Alaska today, and then turned south, spreading through Canada to become the Sioux and the Cheyenne.

Looking at the big Siberian soldier across the table, Monk could envisage the faces of the long dead buffalo hunters of the Platte and Powder Rivers.

For the young Solomin it was the factory or the army. He took the train north and enlisted at Khabarovsk. All youths had to do three years military service anyway and after two the best were picked for sergeant rank. With his skills out on maneuver, he was then chosen for officer school, and after two further years was commissioned as a lieutenant.

He served for seven years as lieutenant and senior lieutenant before making major at the age of thirty-three. In that time he married and had two children. He made his way without patronage or influence, surviving the racist taunts of *churka*, a Russian insult meaning "log" or "thick as a plank." Several times he had used his fists to settle the argument.

The assignment to Yemen in 1983 had been his first foreign posting. He knew most of his colleagues enjoyed it. Despite the harsh conditions of the land, with its heat, blistering rocks, and lack of entertainment, they had roomy quarters, very different from the USSR, in the old British barracks. There was plenty of food, with lamb and fish barbecues on the beach. They could swim and, using catalogues, order clothes, videos, and music tapes from Europe.

All of this, especially the sudden exposure to the new delights of Western consumer culture, Peter Solomin appreciated. But there was something that had made him bitter and disillusioned with the regime he served. Monk could smell it, but feared to push too hard.

It came out on the fifth evening of drinking and talking. The inner anger just came bubbling over.

In 1982, a year before the Yemen posting and with Andropov still in the presidency, Solomin had been assigned to the Administration Department, Ministry of Defense, Moscow.

There he had caught the eye of a deputy defense minister and was assigned to a confidential task. Using money skimmed from the defense budget, the minister was building a sumptuous dacha for himself out along the river by Peredelkino.

Against party rules, Soviet law, and all basic morality the minister assigned over a hundred soldiers to build his luxurious mansion in the woods. Solomin was in charge. He saw the built-in kitchen units that any army wife would have given her right arm for rolling in from Finland, bought with foreign currency. He saw the Japanese hi-fi system installed in every room, the gilt bathroom fittings from Stockholm, and the bar with its aged-in-oak scotch whiskies. The experience turned him against the party and the regime. He was by far not the first loyal Soviet officer to rebel against the sheer, blind corruption of the Soviet dictatorship.

At night he taught himself English, then tuned in to the BBC World Service and the Voice of America. Both also broadcast in Russian, but he wanted to understand them directly. He learned, contrary to what he had always been taught, that the West did not want war with Russia.

If there was anything more needed to tip him over the edge, it was Yemen.

"Back home our people huddle in tiny apartments, but the *nachalstvo* live in mansions. They treat themselves like princes on our money. My wife cannot get a good hair dryer or shoes that do not fall apart, yet billions are wasted on crazy foreign missions to impress . . . who? *These* people?"

"Things are changing," said Monk helpfully. The Siberian shook his head.

Gorbachev had been in power since March, but the reforms he unwillingly, and in most cases unwittingly, introduced did not begin to bite until late 1987. Moreover, Solomin had not seen his native land for two years.

"Not changing. Those shits at the top . . . I tell you, Esteban, since I moved to Moscow I have seen waste and profligacy you would not believe."

"But the new man, Gorbachev, maybe he will change things,"

said Monk. "I am not so pessimistic. One day the Russian people will be free of this dictatorship. They will have votes, real votes. Not so long now . . ."

"Too long. Not fast enough."

Monk took a deep breath. A cold pitch is a dangerous ploy. In a Western democracy a loyal Soviet officer receiving a pitch can complain to his ambassador. It can lead to a diplomatic incident. In an obscure tyranny it can lead to a long and lonely death. Without any warning, Monk dropped into flawless Russian.

"You could help it change, my friend. Together, we could help it all to change. The way you want it to be."

Solomin stared at him intently for a good thirty seconds. Monk stared back. Finally the Russian said in his own language:

"Who the hell *are* you?"

"I think you know that already, Pyotr Vasilyevitch. The question now is whether you will betray me, knowing what these people will do to me before I die. And then live with yourself."

Solomin continued to stare at him. Then he said:

"I wouldn't betray my worst enemy to these monkeys. But you have a hell of a nerve. What you ask is crazy. Madness. I should tell you to go fuck yourself."

"Perhaps you should. And I would go. Fast, for my own sake. But to sit on your thumbs—to watch, hate and do nothing. Is that not also crazy?"

The Russian rose, his beer undrunk.

"I must think," he said.

"Tomorrow night," said Monk, still in Russian. "Here. You come alone, we talk. You come with guards, I am dead. You do not come, I leave on the next plane."

Major Solomin stalked out.

All Standard Operating Procedures would have told Monk to get out of Yemen, and fast. He had not had a total rebuff, but he had not made a score either. A man with his mind in turmoil can change that mind, and the cellars of the Yemeni secret police are fearsome places.

Monk waited twenty-four hours. The major returned, alone. It took two days more. Concealed in his toiletries Monk had brought the basics for a communications package: the secret inks, the safe addresses, the harmless phrases that contained their hidden meanings. There was not much Solomin could divulge from Yemen, but in a year he would be back in Moscow. If he still wished, he could communicate.

When they parted, their handshake lasted several seconds.

"Good luck, my friend," said Monk.

"Good hunting, as we say back home," replied the Siberian.

In case they might be seen leaving the Rock together, Monk sat on. His new recruit would need a code name. Far above, the stars glittered with that amazing brightness only seen in the tropics.

Among them Monk picked out the belt of the Great Hunter. Agent GT Orion was born.

•   •   •

ON the second of August Boris Kuznetsov received a personal letter from the British journalist Mark Jefferson. It was on the letterhead of the *Daily Telegraph* in London, and although faxed to the newspaper's Moscow bureau, it had been hand-delivered at the headquarters of the UPF Party.

Jefferson made plain his personal admiration of the stance taken by Igor Komarov against chaos, corruption, and crime, and his own study of the party leader's speeches over recent months.

With the recent death of the Russian president, he went on, the whole question of the future of the world's largest country was once again a matter of focal interest. He personally wished to visit Moscow in the first half of August. For the sake of tact, he would no doubt have to interview both the candidates for the future presidency of the left and the center. This however would only be a matter of form.

Clearly the outer world's only real interest would be in the foregone victor of that contest, Igor Komarov. He, Jefferson, would be deeply grateful if Kuznetsov could see his way clear to recommending that Mr. Komarov receive him. He could promise a major, center-page spread in the *Daily Telegraph,* with certain syndication across Europe and North America.

Although Kuznetsov, whose father had been a diplomat with the United Nations for years and had used his position to see his son graduate from Cornell, knew the United States better than Europe, he certainly knew London.

He also knew that much of the American press tended to be

liberal and had been generally hostile to his employer on the occasions when interviews had been granted. The last had been a year ago, and the questioning had been adversarial. Komarov had forbidden further exposures to the American press.

But London was different. Several major newspapers and two national magazines were firmly conservative, though not as far to the right as Igor Komarov in his public pronouncements.

"I would recommend that an exception be made for Mark Jefferson, Mr. President," he told Igor Komarov at their weekly meeting the next day.

"Who is this man?" asked Komarov, who disliked all journalists, Russian included. They asked questions he saw no reason he should answer.

"I have prepared a file on him here, Mr. President," said Kuznetsov, handing over a slim folder. "As you will see, he supports the restoration of capital punishment for murder in his own country. Also vigorous opposition to Britain's membership in the collapsing European Union. A staunch conservative. The last time he mentioned yourself, it was to say you were the sort of Russian leader London should support and do business with."

Komarov grunted, and then agreed. His reply went to the *Telegraph*'s Moscow office by courier the same day. It said Mr. Jefferson should be in Moscow for the interview on August 9.

Yemen, January 1986

NEITHER Solomin nor Monk could have predicted that the major's tour in Aden would end nine months prematurely. But on January 13 a violent civil war broke out between two rival factions within the governing caucus. So fierce was the fighting that the decision was made to evacuate all foreign nationals, Russians included. This took place over six days, starting January 15. Peter Solomin was among those who took to the boats.

The airport was being raked with fire, so the sea was the only way out. By a fluke the British royal yacht *Britannia* had just emerged from the southern end of the Red Sea, heading for Australia to prepare for Queen Elizabeth to tour.

On a message from the British Embassy in Aden, the Admiralty in London was alerted and consulted the queen's private secretary. He checked with the monarch and Queen Elizabeth ordered that the *Britannia* should do all it could to help.

Two days later Major Solomin, with a group of other Russian officers, made a dash from cover to the sea at Abyan Beach where the gigs from *Britannia* were rolling in the surf. British sailors hauled them out of the waist-deep water and within an hour the bemused Russians were spreading their borrowed bedrolls along the cleared floor of the queen's private sitting room.

On her first mission *Britannia* filled up with 431 refugees, and on subsequent runs to the beach finally pulled 1,068 people from fifty-five nations off the sand. Between evacuations, she ran across to Djibouti on the Horn of Africa to discharge her human cargo. Solomin and his fellow Russians were flown home via Damascus to Moscow.

What no one knew then was that if Solomin still entertained any doubts about what he was going to do, the balance was tipped by the contrast between the easy camaraderie of the British, French, and Italians with the Royal Navy sailors and the bleak paranoia of the debriefings in Moscow.

All the CIA knew was that a man they thought one of their own had recruited three months earlier had disappeared back into the all-consuming maw of the USSR. Either he would communicate or he would not.

Throughout that winter the Soviet Division's operational arm literally disintegrated piece by piece. One by one the Russian assets working for the CIA on foreign stations were quietly recalled on a variety of plausible excuses: your mother is ill, your son is doing badly at college and needs his father, there is a promotions board being convened. One by one they fell for the ruse and returned to the USSR. On arrival they were at once arrested and taken to Colonel Grishin's new base, an entire wing partitioned off from the rest of the grim fortress of Lefortovo jail. Langley knew nothing of the arrests, simply that the men were disappearing one by one.

As for those stationed inside the USSR, they simply ceased to give routine "signs of life."

Inside the USSR there was no question of giving a man a call at the office to say "Let's have coffee." All phones were tapped, all diplomats tailed. Foreigners, by their dress alone, stood out a mile. Contacts had to be extremely delicate and were usually rare.

When made, they were usually by dead drop. This very basic ruse sounds crude but still works. Aldrich Ames used drops right up to the end. The drop is simply a small receptacle or hiding place somewhere—a hollow drainpipe, a culvert, a hole in a tree.

The agent can put a letter or consignment of microfilm in the drop, then alert his employers that he has done so by a chalk mark on a wall or lamppost. The position of the mark means: Drop so-and-so has something in it for you. An embassy car, cruising by, even with native counterintelligence coming up behind, can spot the chalk mark through the windows and drive on.

Later, an undeclared officer will try to slip his surveillance and recover the package, possibly leaving money in its place. Or further instructions. Then *he* will make a chalk mark somewhere. The asset driving by will spot it and know his delivery has been received but something awaits him. By dead of night, he will recover the consignment.

In this manner a spy can stay in touch with a spymaster for months, even years, without a face-to-face meet.

If the spy is way outside the capital where the diplomats cannot go, or even in the city but has nothing to deposit, the rule is that he will give a sign of life at regular intervals. In the capital, where the diplomats can cruise by, these may be more chalk marks, which by their shape and location mean: I'm fine but I have nothing for you. Or: I am worried, I think I am under surveillance.

Where distance prevents these secret messages, and the provinces in the USSR were always out of bounds to U.S. diplomats, small ads in the main newspapers are a favorite for a sign of life. "Boris has charming Labrador puppy for sale. Ring . . ." might innocently appear among all the others. Inside the embassy, the controlling agents scan them. The wording is all. Labrador might mean "I'm fine" while spaniel could mean "I'm in trouble." "Charming" might say "I'll be in Moscow next week and will service the usual drop." "Delightful" could mean "I can't make Moscow for at least another month."

The point is, the sign of life messages must happen. When they stop, there could be a problem. Maybe a heart attack or a highway crash and the asset is in the hospital. When they *all* stop, there is a very major problem.

That was what happened through the fall and winter of 1985 into 1986. They all stopped. Gordievsky made his desperate "I'm in deep trouble" call and was pulled out by the British. Major Bokhan in Athens smelled a rat and made a run for safety in the United States. The other twelve just vaporized.

Each individual control officer at Langley or abroad would know about his own missing asset and would report back. But Carey Jordan and the head of SE Division had the overview. They knew there was something badly wrong.

Ironically it was the very weirdness of what the KGB was doing that saved Ames. The CIA calculated that no one would dream of carrying out such a blitz of agents so quickly if the betrayer were still in the heart of Langley. Thus they were able to persuade themselves of what they wanted to believe anyway: they, the elite of the elite, could not be entertaining a traitor in their midst. Nevertheless, a frantic search had to be made, and it was, but elsewhere.

The first suspect was Edward Lee Howard, the linchpin of an earlier fiasco, by then safely tucked away in Moscow. Howard had been a CIA man, working in the SE Division and being briefed to take a posting to the Moscow embassy. He was even told operational details. Just before his posting it was discovered his finances were crooked and he took drugs.

Forgetting the golden rule of Machiavelli, the CIA fired him but left him running around for two years. Finally the CIA told the FBI, which hit the roof, put Howard under their own surveillance, then screwed up. They lost him, but he had seen them. Within two days, in September 1985, Howard was with the Soviet Embassy in Mexico City, which passed him via Havana to Moscow.

A check revealed Howard could have betrayed three of the missing agents, maybe even six. In fact he did betray the only three he knew about, but they had already been given away by Ames the previous June. All three were double betrayed.

Another lead came from the Russians themselves. Desperate to protect their mole, the KGB was mounting a huge diversion and disinformation campaign; anything to turn the CIA in the wrong direction. They succeeded. An apparently genuine leak in East Berlin revealed that some codes had been broken and signal traffic intercepted.

The codes were used by a major CIA covert transmitter at Warrenton, Virginia. For a year Warrenton and its staff were gone through with a fine-tooth comb. Nothing, no hint of a code break. If there had been a code break, the KGB would clearly have learned of yet other things, but on these they had taken no action. Therefore, the codes were intact.

The third seed the KGB sedulously planted was that they had done some brilliant detective work. This was met by amazing complacency at Langley where one report suggested that "every operation has within it the seeds of its own destruction." In other words, fourteen agents had all suddenly decided to behave like idiots.

Some in Langley did not fall for the complacency. One was Carey Jordan, another was Gus Hathaway. At a lower level, learning through the internal grapevine of the problems tearing his division apart, was Jason Monk.

A check was made of the 301 files where all the details were stored. The findings were horrific. In all, 198 people had access to the 301 files. It was a terrifying figure. If you are deep inside the USSR with your life on the line, the last thing you need is for 198 complete strangers to have access to your file.

CHAPTER 6

PROFESSOR KUZMIN SCRUBBED UP IN THE EXAMINATION ROOM OF the mortuary below the Second Medical Institute, facing with little pleasure his third postmortem of the day.

"Who's next?" he called to his assistant as he dried off with an inadequate paper towel.

"Number one-five-eight," said his helper.

"Details."

"White Caucasian male, late middle age. Cause of death unknown, identity unknown."

Kuzmin groaned. Why do I bother, he asked himself. Another tramp, another hobo, another derelict whose bits, when he had finished, would perhaps assist the medical students in the academy three floors up to understand what protracted abuse could do to human organs, whose skeleton might even end up in an anatomy class.

Moscow, like any major city, produced its nightly, weekly, and monthly harvest of cadavers but fortunately only a minority required a postmortem or the professor and all his colleagues in forensic pathology would have ceased to cope.

The majority in any city are the "natural causes," all those who die at home or in the hospital of old age or any one of a hundred terminal and predicted causes. The infirmaries and the local doctors could sign the certificates for those.

Then came the "natural causes, unforeseen," usually fatal heart attacks, and again the hospitals to which the unfortunates were taken could cope with the basic, and usually very basic, bureaucratic formalities.

After these unfortunates came the accidents: domestic, industrial, and automobile. Moscow had two more categories that had grown massively over the years: freezing to death (in winter) and suicides. The numbers ran into thousands.

Bodies recovered from the river, identified or not, went into three categories. Fully clothed, no alcohol in the system: suicide; clothed, hugely drunk: accident; swim shorts: accidentally drowned while swimming.

Then came the homicides. These went to the police, detective branch, which turned to Professor Kuzmin. Even these postmortems were usually a formality. The great majority, as in all cities, were the "domestics." Eighty percent happened inside the home or the perpetrator was a family member. The police usually had them within hours, and the postmortem simply confirmed what was already known—Ivan had stabbed his wife—and helped the courts bring in a quick verdict.

After these came the bar brawls and gangland killings; in the latter case he knew the police conviction rate was a miserable three percent. Cause of death, however, was no problem; a bullet in the brain is a bullet in the brain. Whether the investigators ever found the hitman (probably not) was not the professor's problem.

In all the above, thousands and thousands a year, one thing was certain. The authorities knew who the dead man was. Occasionally they had a John Doe. Cadaver 158 was a John Doe. Professor Kuzmin drew on his gauze mask, flexed his fingers inside the rubber gloves, and approached with a flicker of interest as his assistant drew back the sheet.

Ah, he thought, odd. Even interesting. The stench that would have caused a layman to gag at once left him unmoved. He was used to it. Scalpel in hand he circled the long table, staring at the damaged corpse. Very odd.

The head seemed intact apart from the empty eye sockets, but he could see that this damage was the work of birds. The man had lain for about six days undiscovered in the woods near the Minsk Highway. Below the pelvis the legs seemed discolored, as with age and putrefaction, but undamaged. Between thorax and genitals there was hardly a square inch not black with massive bruising.

Putting down the scalpel, he turned the body over. Same at the back. Rolling the corpse back again, he took his scalpel and began to cut, giving his running commentary into the turning tape recorder. Later this tape would enable him to write up his report for the goons in Homicide down at Petrovka. He began with the date: August 2, 1999.

Washington, February 1986

IN the middle of the month, to the joy of Jason Monk and the considerable surprise of his superiors in SE Division, Major Pyotr Solomin made contact. He wrote a letter.

Wisely, he did not even attempt to contact any Westerner in Moscow and certainly not the American Embassy. He wrote to the address Monk had given him in East Berlin.

The giving of the address at all was a risk but a calculated one. If Solomin had gone to the KGB to betray the safe house, he would have had some impossible questions to answer. The interrogators would have known he would never have been given such an address unless he had agreed to work for the CIA. If he protested that he had only been pretending to work for the CIA, that would have been worse.

Why, he would have been asked, did you not report the approach immediately, on first contact, to the commanding colonel of the GRU in Aden, and why did you allow the American who contacted you to escape? Those questions were unanswerable.

So Solomin was either going to stay mum about the whole thing, or he was on the team. The letter indicated the latter.

In the USSR all mail coming in from or heading out to abroad was intercepted and read. Ditto all phone calls, cables, faxes, and telexes. But internal Soviet mail, by its sheer volume, could not be unless sender or recipient were under suspicion. The same applied to mail within the Soviet bloc, and that included East Germany.

The East Berlin address belonged to a subway driver who worked as a postman for the agency and was well paid for it. Letters arriving at his apartment in a run-down building in the Friedrichshain district were always addressed to Franz Weber.

Weber had actually been the previous tenant of the flat and was conveniently dead. If the subway driver had ever been challenged, he could plausibly have sworn that there had been two letters already, he could not understand a word of Russian, they were addressed to Weber, Weber was dead so he had thrown them away. An innocent man.

The letters never had a return address or surname. The text was banal and boring: Hope this finds you well, things here are fine, how are your studies in Russian coming along, I hope we shall renew our acquaintance one day, all best wishes, your pen pal Ivan.

Even the East German secret police, the Stasis, could have deduced from the text only that Weber had met a Russian on some kind of cultural exchange fest and they had become pen pals. This sort of thing was encouraged anyway.

Even if the Stasis had deciphered the hidden message in invisible ink between the lines, it would have indicated only that Weber, deceased, had been a rat who had got away with it.

At the Moscow end, once the missive had been dropped in a mailbox, the sender became untraceable.

Once he had received a letter from Russia, the subway motorman, Heinrich, sent it over the Wall into the West. How he did it sounds weird, but much stranger things happened in the divided city of Berlin during the Cold War. In fact his method was so simple that he was never caught. The Cold War ended, Germany was reunited, and Heinrich retired to a very comfortable old age.

Before Berlin was divided by the Wall in 1961 to prevent the East Germans escaping, it shared an all-city subway system. After the Wall, many tunnels between East and West were blocked off. But there was one stretch where the East German section of the system became an elevated rail and rattled across a stretch of West Berlin.

For this transit from East across a bit of the West and back into the East, all windows and doors were sealed. East Berlin passengers could sit and look down on a piece of West Berlin, but they could not get there.

Up in the cab, all alone, Heinrich would ease down his window and at a certain point, using a catapult, shoot a projectile like a small golf ball out into a derelict bomb site. Knowing Heinrich's work roster, a middle-aged man would be walking his dog there. When the train had rattled out of sight, he would pick up the golf ball and bring it to his colleagues at the CIA's enormous West Berlin Station. Unscrewed, the ball revealed the tightly furled onionskin letter inside.

Solomin had news, and it was all good. After repatriation there had been intensive debriefing and then a week's leave. He had reported back to the Ministry of Defense for reassignment. In the lobby he had been spotted by the deputy defense minister for whom he had built the dacha three years earlier. The man had been promoted to First Deputy Minister.

Although he wore the uniform of a Colonel General, with enough medals to sink a gunboat, the man was really a creature of the apparat who had come up the political ladder. It pleased him to have a rugged combat soldier from Siberia in his entourage. He was delighted with his dacha, completed under schedule, and his aide-de-camp had just retired on health (consumption of vodka) grounds. He raised Solomin to Lieutenant-Colonel and gave him the post.

Finally Solomin, at considerable risk, gave his own residential address in Moscow and asked for instructions. Had the KGB intercepted and deciphered the letter he would have been done for. But as he could not approach the U.S. Embassy, Langley had to be told how to approach him. He should have been supplied with a much more sophisticated communications package before leaving Yemen, but the civil war intervened.

Ten days later he got a traffic violation final-notice demand. The envelope bore the logo of the Central Traffic Office. It was posted in Moscow. No one intercepted it. The demand and the envelope were so well forged that he nearly rang the Traffic Office to protest he had never gone through a red light. Then he saw the sand trickling out of the envelope.

He kissed his wife as she left to take the children to school, and when he was alone painted the demand notice with the enhancer from the small flask he had smuggled back from Aden in his shaving kit. The message was simple. The following Sunday. Midmorning. A café on Leninsky Prospekt.

He was on his second coffee when an anonymous figure passed by, struggling into an overcoat against the chill blast outside. From the empty sleeve a single pack of Russian Marlboros dropped onto Solomin's table. He covered it with his newspaper. The overcoat left the café without looking back.

The pack appeared to be full of cigarettes, but the twenty filters were a block, glued together and with nothing smokable beneath them. In the cavity were a tiny camera, ten rolls of film, a sheet of rice paper describing three dead drops with directions for how to find them, and six types of chalk mark, with their locations, to indicate when the drops were empty or needed servicing. Also a warm personal letter from Monk beginning, "So, my hunter friend, we are going to change the world."

A month later Orion made his first delivery and picked up more rolls of film. His information came from the deepest heart of the Soviet arms-industrial complex, and it was priceless.

•   •   •

PROFESSOR Kuzmin checked over the transcript of his notes on the postmortem of Cadaver 158 and made a few annotations in his own hand. He was not even going to ask his overworked secretary to do a retype; let the mutton-heads down at Homicide work it out for themselves.

He had no doubt that Homicide was where the file would have to go. He tried to be merciful to the detectives, and where there was some doubt he would sign off the deceased as an "accidental" or "natural causes" if he could. Then the relatives could collect and do what they wished, or, in the event of an unidentified body, it would remain in the morgue for the statutory time required by law. He would alert Missing Persons, and if they could not come up with an ID, the body would eventually go to a pauper's grave, courtesy of the mayor of Moscow, or to the anatomy classes.

But 158 was a homicide, and there was no way of getting around it. Short of a pedestrian being hit by a truck at full gallop, he had seldom seen such internal damage. One single blow, even by a truck, could not have achieved it all. He supposed being trampled on by a herd of buffalo might produce the same effect, but there were few buffalo in Moscow and in any case they would stamp on head and legs as well. Cadaver 158 had been beaten many times by blunt objects between the neck and hips, both sides.

When he had finished his notes he signed and dated them, August 3, at the bottom and put them in his out tray.

"Homicide?" asked his secretary brightly.

"Homicide, John Doe Desk," he confirmed. She typed out the buff envelope, put the file inside, and placed the package beside her. On her way out that evening she would give it to the porter who lived in a cubbyhole on the ground floor, and he would in due course give it to the van driver who took the files to their various destinations around Moscow.

In the meantime Cadaver 158 lay in the icy darkness minus his eyes and most of his innards.

Langley, March 1986

CAREY Jordan stood at his window and stared out at his favorite view. It was late in the month and the first faint haze of green was coming upon the forest between the CIA main building and the Potomac River. Soon the glint of water, always visible through the leafless woods in winter, would disappear. He loved Washington; it had more woods, trees, parks, and gardens than any city he knew, and spring was his favorite month.

At least, it had been. Spring 1986 was proving a nightmare. Sergei Bokhan, the GRU officer the CIA had been running in Athens, had made clear during his repeated debriefings in America that he believed if he had flown back to Moscow he would have faced a firing squad. He could not prove it, but the excuse his superior officer had given for his recall, his son's bad grades at military academy, were simply a lie. Therefore, he had been blown. He had not made any mistakes himself, so he believed he had been betrayed.

As Bokhan had been among the first three to experience problems, the CIA had been skeptical. Now they were less unbelieving. Five others around the world had been mysteriously recalled in midposting and had vaporized into thin air.

That made six. With the Brits' man Gordievsky, seven. Five

more, based inside the USSR, had also vanished. There was not a single major source, representing years of hard work, patience, and cunning, and a massive investment of tax dollars, now left functioning. Bar two.

Behind him Harry Gaunt, head of the SE Division, which was the principal—nay, at the moment the only—victim of the virus, sat plunged in thought. Gaunt was the same age as the DDO and they had come up through the ranks together, weathering years in foreign outstations, recruiting their sources, and playing the Great Game against the KGB enemy, and they trusted each other like brothers.

That was the trouble; inside the SE Division they all trusted each other. They had to. They were the inner core, the most exclusive club, the cutting edge of the covert war. Yet each man harbored a terrible suspicion. Howard, code breaks, clever detective work by the KGB's Line KR, might account for five, six, even seven blown-away agents. But fourteen? The whole goddam lot?

And yet there could not be a traitor. There *must* not be. Not in the Soviet/East European Division. There was a knock on the door. The mood lightened. The last remaining success story was waiting to come in.

"Sit down, Jason," said the DDO. "Harry and I just wanted a word to say 'Well done.' Your man Orion has come up with real paydirt. The guys in Analysis are having a field day. So we reckon the agent who brought him in is worth a GS-15 tag."

Promotion, from GS-14 to GS-15. He thanked them.

"How is your man Lysander in Madrid?"

"He's fine, sir. He's reporting regularly. Not cosmic stuff, but useful. His tour's nearly up. He'll be going back to Moscow soon."

"He hasn't been recalled prematurely?"

"No, sir. Should he?"

"No reason at all, Jason."

"Could I say something, speak frankly?"

"Fire away."

"There's word out in the Division that we've been having a rough time these past six months."

"Really?" said Gaunt. "Well, people will gossip."

Up to that point the full import of the disaster had been confined to a top ten men at the peak of the agency hierarchy. But though

Ops had six thousand employees, a thousand of them in the SE Division with only a hundred at Monk's level, it was still a village and in a village word spreads. Monk took a breath and plunged on.

"The talk is that we have been losing agents. I even heard a figure of up to ten."

"You know the need-to-know rules, Jason."

"Yes, sir."

"All right, maybe we have had a few problems. It happens in all agencies. Runs of good luck and runs of bad. What's your point?"

"Even if the figure was anything like ten, there is only one place all such information is gathered together in one place. The 301 files."

"I think we know how the agency is run, soldier," growled Gaunt.

"So how come Lysander and Orion are still running free?" asked Monk.

"Look, Jason," said the DDO patiently. "I told you once you were weird. Meaning unconventional, a rule breaker. But that you were lucky. Okay, we have had some losses, but don't forget your two assets were in the 301 files as well."

"No, they weren't."

An observer could have heard a peanut drop on the pile carpet. Harry Gaunt stopped fiddling with his pipe, which he never smoked indoors but used like an actor's prop.

"I just never got around to filing their details with Central Registry. It was an oversight. I'm sorry."

"Just where are the original reports? Your own reports, covering recruitment details, places, times of meetings?" asked Gaunt at last.

"In my safe. They've never left."

"And all ongoing operating procedures?"

"In my head."

There was another even longer pause.

"Thank you, Jason," said the DDO at last. "We'll be in touch."

Two weeks later there was a major strategy campaign at the pinnacle of the Ops Directorate. Carey Jordan, working with only two fellow analysts, had whittled the 198 who theoretically had had access over the previous twelve months to the 301 files down to forty-one. Aldrich Ames, by then still taking his Italian course, was on the smaller list.

Jordan, with Gaunt, Gus Hathaway, and two others argued that to make sure, the forty-one should be subjected, however painful it might be, to serious investigation. That would mean a hostile polygraph test and a check of private finances.

The polygraph was an American invention and great store was set by it. Only research in the late eighties and early nineties revealed how flawed it could be. For one thing, an experienced liar can beat it, and espionage is based on deception, hopefully only of the enemy.

For another, the questioners need to be superbly briefed to ask the right questions. They cannot be so briefed unless the subject has been checked out. To sort out the liar, they need to cause the guilty party to think, Oh my God, they know, they know, and set the pulses racing. If the liar can discern from the questions that they know nothing, he will calm down and stay calm. This is the difference between a friendly and a hostile polygraph test. The friendly version is a waste of paper if the subject is a skilled and prepared dissembler.

Key to the inquiry the DDO wanted would be a check on the subjects' finances. Had they but known it, Aldrich Ames, broke and desperate after a messy divorce and remarriage twelve months earlier, was by then awash with cash, all deposited since April 1985.

Leading the group that opposed the DDO was Ken Mulgrew. He evoked the frightening damage that James Angleton had achieved with his constant checking on loyal officers, pointing out that to check out private finances was a massive invasion of privacy and an assault on civil rights.

Gaunt countered that never in Angleton's day had there been a sudden loss of a dozen agents in a brief six months. Angleton's own investigations had been based on paranoia; the agency in 1986 was gazing at solid evidence that something had gone badly wrong.

The hawks lost. Civil rights won the day. The "hard" check on the forty-one was vetoed.

•   •   •

INSPECTOR Pavel Volsky sighed as another file thumped onto his desk.

A year earlier he had been perfectly happy as a top sergeant in Organized Crime. At least there they had got a chance to raid the warehouses of the underworld and confiscate their ill-gotten gains. A smart sergeant could live well when confiscated luxuries suffered a slight skim-off before being handed over to the state.

But no, his wife had wanted to be the lady of a Detective Inspector so when the chance occurred he took the course, the promotion, and the transfer to Homicide.

He could not foresee that they would give him the John Doe desk. When he gazed at the tide of "who-knows-who cares" files that drifted across his vision, he often wished he was back at Shabolovka Street.

At least most John Does had a motive attached. Robbery, of course. With the wallet gone the victim had lost his money, credit cards, family snapshots, and the all-important *pazport,* the internal Russian ID document, with picture, that carried all the necessary details. Oh, and his life, or he would not be on a slab in a morgue.

In the case of an upstanding citizen with a wallet worth taking there would usually be family. They would complain to Missing Persons, who ran a weekly gallery of family photos over to him, and often a match could be made. Then the weeping family could be told where to identify and collect their missing member.

In the cases where robbery was not the motive, the body would usually still have the pazport somewhere about the pockets, so the file would never come to Volsky anyway.

Nor would all the derelicts who threw their ID away because it revealed where they came from and they did not want the militia to shunt them back there, but who still died of cold or alcohol on the streets, come his way. Volsky only dealt with certain homicides, by a person unknown of a person unknown. It was, he mused, an exclusive but pretty futile occupation.

The file that landed in front of him on August 4 was different. Robbery could hardly be the motive. A glance at the Scene of Discovery report from the Western Division told him the cadaver had been discovered by a mushroom picker in the woods off the Minsk Highway just inside the city limits. A hundred yards off the highway—discount hit-and-run.

The Personal Effects list was gloomy. Victim was wearing (from the bottom up) shoes plastic, cheap, cracked, down-at-heel; socks cheap, store-bought, ingrained with grime; undershorts ditto; trousers, thin, black, greasy; belt, plastic, worn. That was it. No shirt, tie, or jacket. Just a greatcoat found nearby, described as ex-army, fifties vintage, very threadbare.

There was a brief paragraph at the bottom. Contents of pockets nil, repeat nil. No watch, ring, or any item of personal possession.

Volsky glanced at the photo taken at the scene. Someone had kindly closed the eyelids. A thin, unshaven face, mid-sixties perhaps, looking a decade older. Haggard, that was the word, and that would be before he died.

Poor old sod, thought Volsky, I'll bet no one did you in for your Swiss bank account. He turned to the postmortem report. After several paragraphs he stubbed out his cigarette and swore.

"Why can't these characters write in simple Russian?" he asked the wall, not for the first time. It was all talk of lacerations and contusions; if you mean cuts and bruises, say so, he thought.

A number of aspects puzzled him once he had worked his way through the jargon. He checked the official stamp of the mortuary at Second Medical and rang the number. He was lucky. Professor Kuzmin was at his desk.

"Is that Professor Kuzmin?" he asked.

"It is. Who speaks?"

"Inspector Volsky. Homicide. I have your report in front of me."

"Lucky you."

"May I be frank with you, Professor?"

"In our day and age it would be a privilege."

"It's just that some of the language is a bit complex. You mention severe bruising on each upper arm. Can you say what caused that?"

"As a pathologist, no, it's just severe contusion. But between us, those marks were made by human fingers."

"Someone grabbed him?"

"Meaning he was held up, my dear Inspector. Held up, supported, by two strong men while he was being beaten."

"This was all done by humans then? No machinery involved?"

"If his head and legs were in the same condition, I'd say he'd been dropped from a helicopter onto concrete. And not a low-flying helicopter. But no, any form of impact with the ground or a truck would have damaged the head and legs as well. No, he was struck repeatedly between the neck and the hips, front and back, with hard blunt objects."

"Cause of death . . . asphyxia?"

"That's what I said, Inspector."

"Forgive me, he was beaten to pulp but died of asphyxia."

Kuzmin sighed.

"All his ribs were broken, bar one. Some in several places. Two were driven back into his lungs. Pulmonary blood then entered the trachea causing asphyxiation."

"You mean he choked on the blood in his throat?"

"That's what I have been trying to tell you."

"I'm sorry, I'm new here."

"And I'm hungry here," said the professor. "It is the lunch hour. Good day to you, Inspector."

Volsky rechecked the report. So the old boy had been beaten. It all said "gangland." But gangsters were usually younger than that. He must really have offended someone in the mafia. If he hadn't died of asphyxia, he would have croaked from the trauma.

So what did they want, the killers? Information? Surely he'd have given them what they wanted without all this? Punishment? Example? Sadism? A bit of all three perhaps. But what on earth could an old man who looked like a tramp have in his possession that a gang boss would want so badly, or what could he have done to a gang boss to deserve what he got?

Volsky noticed one more thing under "Identifying marks." The professor had written: "None upon the body, but in the mouth two frontal incisors and one canine, all of stainless steel, apparently the inheritance of some crude military dentistry." Meaning the man had three steel teeth at the front.

The forensic pathologist's last remark reminded Volsky of something. It *was* the lunch break and he had agreed to meet a friend, also in Homicide. He got up, locked his shabby office behind him, and left.

Langley, July 1986

THE letter from Colonel Solomin caused quite a problem. He had made three deliveries by dead drop in Moscow but now wanted a remeet with his controller Jason Monk. As he had no opportunity to leave the USSR, it would have to be on Soviet territory.

The first reaction of any agency receiving such a suggestion would be to suspect their man had been caught and was writing under duress.

But Monk was convinced Solomin was neither a fool nor a coward. There was a single word that, if he were writing under duress, he should avoid using at all costs, and another he should try to insert into the message. Even under duress he would probably be able to comply with one or other condition. His letter from Moscow contained the word that should be there and did not contain the one that should not. In other words, it seemed to be genuine.

Harry Gaunt had long agreed with Monk that Moscow, infested with KGB agents and watchers, was too risky. With a short-term diplomatic posting the Soviet Foreign Ministry would still want full details, which they would pass on to the Second Chief Directorate. Even disguised, Monk would be under surveillance throughout his stay and meeting the aide-de-camp of the Deputy Defense Minister in safety would be just about impossible. In any case, Solomin did not propose that.

He said he had a leave break due in late September and had been awarded a prize—a vacation apartment in the Black Sea resort of Gurzuf.

Monk checked it out. A small village on the coast of the Crimean peninsula, a renowned resort for the military and home to a major Defense Ministry hospital where injured or recuperating officers could convalesce in the sun.

Two former Soviet officers residing in the United States were consulted. Both agreed they had not been there but knew of Gurzuf—a beautiful former fishing village where Chekhov had lived and died in his villa by the sea, fifty minutes by bus or twenty-five by taxi up the coast from Yalta.

Monk switched his research to Yalta. The USSR was still virtually a sealed country in many respects, and to fly into the area on a scheduled route was out of the question. The air route would be to Moscow, change for Kiev, change again for Odessa, and then to Yalta. There was no way a foreign tourist was going to make that route, and there was no particular reason why a foreign tourist would want to head for Yalta. It might be a Soviet resort, but a single foreigner would stand out like a sore thumb. He looked at the sea routes and got a break.

Ever hungry for foreign hard currency, the Moscow government allowed the Black Sea Shipping Company to run sea cruises of the Mediterranean. Although all the crews were Soviet, with a sprinkling of KGB agents among them (that went without saying), the passengers were mainly from the West.

Because of the cheapness of such cruises for Westerners, the passenger groups tended to be students, academics, senior citizens. There were three liners doing these cruises in the summer of 1986: the *Litva,* the *Latvia,* and the *Armenia.* The one that fitted September was the *Armenia.*

According to the London agent for the Black Sea Company, the liner would leave Odessa for the Greek port of Piraeus, mainly empty. From Greece she would head due west for Barcelona, then turn back via Marseilles, Naples, Malta, and Istanbul before heading into the Black Sea for Varna on the coast of Bulgaria, then Yalta, and finally back to Odessa. The bulk of her Western passengers would join at Barcelona, Marseilles, or Naples.

At the end of July, with the cooperation of the British Security Service, a very skillful break-in was effected at the offices of the London-based agency of the shipping company. No trace of entry or exit was ever left. The bookings for the *Armenia* that had been made in London were photographed.

A study of these revealed a block booking for six members of the American-Soviet Friendship Society. Back in the States they were checked out. All appeared to be middle-aged, sincere, naïve, and dedicated to the improvement of American-Soviet relations. They also lived in or near the northeastern United States.

In early August Professor Norman Kelson of San Antonio joined the society and applied for its literature. From this he learned of the forthcoming expedition on the *Armenia,* boarding at Marseilles, and applied to join as the seventh member of the group. The Soviet organization Intourist saw no objection and the extra booking was made.

The real Norman Kelson was a former CIA archivist who had retired to San Antonio and bore a passing resemblance to Jason Monk although fifteen years older, a difference that would be made up with gray hair tint and smoked eyeglasses.

In mid-August Monk replied to Solomin that his friend would wait for him at the turnstile to the Yalta Botanical Gardens. The gardens are a famous landmark in Yalta, situated out of town, one-third of the way up the coast to Gurzuf. The friend would be there at noon on September 27 and 28.

•   •   •

INSPECTOR Volsky was late for his lunch date so he strode rapidly through the corridors of the big gray edifice on Petrovka that houses the headquarters of the Moscow militia. His friend was not in his office so he tried the squad room and found him talking to a bunch of colleagues.

"Sorry I'm late," he said.

"No sweat, let's go."

There was no question of two men on their salaries eating out, but the militia provided a very low-budget canteen with a lunch voucher system and the food was adequate. Both men turned toward the door. Just inside it was a bulletin board. Volsky cast a glance at it and stopped dead.

"Come on," said his friend. "There'll be no tables left."

"Tell me," said Volsky when they were seated, each with a plate of stew and half a liter of beer. "The squad room . . ."

"What about it?"

"The bulletin board. Inside the door. There's a picture. Sort of copy of a crayon drawing. Old guy with funny teeth. What's the story?"

"Oh, that," said Inspector Novikov, "our mystery man. Apparently some woman at the British Embassy had a break-in. Two guys. They didn't steal anything but they trashed the place. She disturbed them so they knocked her out. But she caught a look at one of them."

"When was this?"

"About two weeks ago, maybe three. Anyway, the embassy complained to the Foreign Ministry. They hit the roof and complained to Interior. They went ballistic and told Burglary Division to find the man. Someone made up a drawing. You know Chernov? No? Well, he's the big investigator in Burglary; so he's running around with his butt on fire because his career's on the line, and getting nowhere. Even came down to us and stuck up one of his pictures."

"Any leads?" asked Volsky.

"Nope. Chernov doesn't know who he is or where he is. This stew has more fat and less meat every time I come here."

"I don't know who he is, but I know where he is," said Volsky. Novikov paused with his beer glass halfway to his lips.

"Shit, where?"

"He's on a slab in the morgue down at Second Medical. His file came in this morning. He's a John Doe. Found in the woods out in the west about a week ago. Beaten to death. No ID."

"Well, you'd better get on to Chernov. He'll be all over you."

As he chomped on the remainder of his stew, Inspector Novikov was a very thoughtful man.

Rome, August 1986

ALDRICH Ames had arrived with his wife in the Eternal City to take up his new posting on July 22. Even after eight months at language school, his Italian was workaday and passable but not good. Unlike Monk he had no ear for foreign tongues.

With his newfound wealth he was able to live in a far better style than ever before, but no one in the Rome Station spotted the difference because no one had seen his lifestyle before April of the previous year.

Before long it became clear that Ames was a habitual drunk and underachiever. This seemed not to worry his colleagues, and even less the Russians. As at Langley, he began to sweep masses of classified material off his desk and into shopping bags with which he strolled out of the embassy to deliver to the KGB.

In August his new KGB controller came down from Moscow to meet him. Unlike Androsov in Washington, he did not live locally but flew in from Moscow whenever a meet was necessary. In Rome there were far fewer problems than in the States. The new controller, "Vlad," was in fact Colonel Vladimir Mechulayev of Directorate K of the First Chief Directorate.

At their first meeting Ames was going to protest at the inordinate speed with which the KGB had picked up the men he had betrayed, thus putting him in danger. But Vlad got in first, apologizing for the crudity and explaining that Mikhail Gorbachev had personally overruled them all. Then he came down to the business that brought him to Rome.

"We have a problem, my dear Rick," he said. "The volume of

material you have brought us is quite enormous and of inestimable value. High among these documents are the brief pen portraits and photos you supplied of the top control officers for spies being run inside the USSR."

Ames was puzzled, trying to register through a fuzz of alcohol.

"Yes, anything wrong?" he asked.

"Not wrong, just a puzzle," Mechulayev said, and produced a photograph that he laid on the coffee table.

"This one. A certain Jason Monk. Right?"

"Yeah, that's him."

"In your reports you describe his reputation in the SE Division as 'a rising star.' Meaning, we presume, that he controls one, maybe two assets inside the Soviet Union."

"That's the view around the office, or it was when I last looked in. But you must have them."

"Ah, my dear Rick, *that* is the problem. All the traitors you kindly revealed to us have now been identified, arrested, and . . . talked to. And each has been, how shall I put it . . . ." The Russian recalled the shuddering men he had faced in the interrogation room after Grishin had introduced the prisoners to his own personal brand of pressure to cooperate.

"They have all been very frank, very candid, most cooperative. Each has told us who his control officers were, in some cases several of them. But no Jason Monk. Not one. Of course, false names can be used, usually are. But the picture, Rick. Not one recognized the picture. Now, you see my problem? Who does Monk run, and where are they?"

"I don't know. I can't understand it. They must have been on the 301 files."

"My dear Rick, neither can we because they weren't."

Before the meeting ended Ames had been given a vast amount of money and a list of tasks. He stayed in Rome for three years and betrayed everything he could, an enormous haul of secret and top-secret documents. Among these were four more agents, but all non-Russians, nationals of the East European Bloc countries. But task number one was clear and simple: On your return to Washington or hopefully before, find out who Monk runs in the USSR.

•   •   •

WHILE Detective Inspectors Novikov and Volsky had been indulging in their informative lunch in the canteen at militia headquarters, the Duma had been in full session.

It had taken time to recall the Russian parliament from its summer recess, for so large is the territory that many of the delegates had to travel thousands of miles to attend the constitutional debate. Nevertheless, the debate was calculated to be of extraordinary importance because the issue at stake was a change of the constitution.

After the unforeseen death of President Cherkassov, Article Fifty-nine of the constitution required the prime minister to take over the presidency per interim. The period of interregnum was decreed to be three months.

Prime Minister Ivan Markov had indeed taken over the Acting Presidency but, after consulting a number of experts, had been advised that as Russia was due for a fresh presidential election in June 2000, to have set an earlier one for October 1999 could cause serious dislocation, even chaos. The motion before the Duma was therefore in favor of a once-only Amendment Act, extending the acting presidency for three further months and advancing the year 2000 election from June to January.

The word *Duma* comes from the verb *dumat,* meaning to think or contemplate; thus the Duma is "a place of thinking." Many observers felt the Duma more a place of screaming and shouting than of mature contemplation. On that hot summer's day it certainly justified the latter description.

The debate lasted all day, rising to levels of passion such that the Speaker spent much of his time shouting for order, and at one time threatened to suspend the session until further notice.

Two delegates were so abusive that the Speaker ordered their ejection, accompanied by violent scuffles recorded by the television cameras, until the expelled pair were on the pavement outside. There both, who disagreed violently with each other, held impromptu press conferences that degenerated into a pavement brawl until broken up by the police.

Inside the chamber, as the air-conditioning system broke down under the strain and the sweating delegates of what purported to be the world's third most populous democracy screamed and swore at each other, the lineup became clear.

The Fascist Union of Patriotic Forces, under orders from Igor

Komarov, insisted the presidential elections should be decreed for October, three months after the death of Cherkassov and in accordance with Article Fifty-nine. Their tactic was obvious. The UPF was so far ahead in the polls that it could only see its own access to supreme power being advanced by nine months.

The neo-Communists of the Socialist Union and the reformists of the Democratic Alliance for once found themselves in agreement. Both were trailing in the polls and needed all the time they could get to restore their positions. Put another way, neither was ready for an early election.

The debate, or shouting match, raged until sundown when an exhausted and hoarse Speaker finally decreed that enough voices had been heard for a vote to be called. The left wing and the centrists voted together to defeat the ultraright, and the motion was carried. The June 2000 presidential elections were rescheduled for January 16, 2000.

Within an hour the outcome of the vote was carried across the nation by the national TV newscast *Vremlya* as its lead item. Embassies throughout the capital worked late and lights burned as coded cables from ambassadors to their home governments flooded out.

It was because the British Embassy was also still fully staffed that Gracie Fields was at his desk when the call from Inspector Novikov came through.

Yalta, September 1986

THE day was hot and there was no air-conditioning in the taxi that rattled along the coastal highway northeastward out of Yalta. The American wound down the window to let the cooler air from the Black Sea blow over him. Leaning to one side he was also able to see in the rearview mirror above the driver's head. No car from the local Cheka seemed to be following.

The long cruise from Marseilles via Naples, Malta, and Istanbul had been tiresome but tolerable. Monk had played his part in a manner that aroused no suspicion. With gray hair, tinted glasses, and elaborate courtesy he was just another academic retiree taking a summer vacation cruise.

His fellow Americans on board had accepted that he shared their sincere belief that the only hope for world peace was for the peoples of the United States and the Union of Soviet Socialist Republics to get to know one another better. One of them, a spinster teacher from Connecticut, was much taken with the exquisitely mannered Texan who held out her chair and tipped his low-crowned Stetson whenever they met on deck.

At Varna in Bulgaria he had not gone ashore, pleading a touch of the sun. But at all the other ports of call he had accompanied the tourists of five Western nationalities to ruins, ruins, and more ruins.

At Yalta he stepped down for the first time in his life onto the soil of Russia. Exhaustively prepared and briefed as he was, it was easier than he had thought. For one thing, although the *Armenia* was the only cruise liner in port, there were a dozen other cargo freighters from outside the USSR, and their crews had no trouble wandering ashore.

The tourists of the cruise ship, cooped aboard since Varna, went down the gangway like a flock of birds, and two Russian immigration officials at the bottom gave their passports a cursory glance and nodded them through. Professor Kelson attracted several looks because of the way he was dressed, but they were approving and friendly glances.

Rather than try to appear inconspicuous, Monk chose to go the other way, the hide-in-plain-sight routine. He wore a cream shirt with string tie, held by a silver clasp; a tan suit of lightweight pants and jacket, and his Stetson, along with cowboy boots.

"My oh my, Professor, you do look smart," gushed the schoolteacher. "Are you coming with us up the chairlift to the mountaintop?"

"No, ma'am," said Monk, "I guess I'll just stroll along the docks and maybe get me a coffee."

The Intourist guides took their parties off in different directions and left him alone. He walked instead out of the harbor, past the Sea Terminal building and into the town. A number of people glanced at him, but most grinned. A small boy stopped, threw his hands to his side, and did a double fast-draw with imaginary Colt .45s. Monk ruffled his hair.

He had learned that entertainment in the Crimea was rather unvaried. The television was dull as dishwater, and the big treat was the movies. The favorite by miles were the cowboy films permitted by the regime, and here was a real cowboy. Even a militiaman, sleepy in the heat, stared, but when Monk tipped his hat he grinned and threw up a salute. After an hour and a coffee in an open-fronted café, he became convinced he was not being followed, took a taxi from a rank of several, and asked for the Botanical Gardens. With his guidebook, map, and fractured Russian he was so obviously a tourist off one of the ships that the driver nodded and set off. Besides, thousands visited the famous gardens of Yalta.

Monk dismounted in front of the main gate and paid off the taxi driver. He paid in rubles, but added a five-dollar tip and a wink. The driver grinned, nodded, and left.

There was a big crowd in front of the turnstiles, mainly Russian children with their teachers on an educational excursion. Monk waited in line, keeping an eye open for men in shiny suits. There were none. He paid his entrance fee, went through the barrier, and spotted the ice cream booth. Buying a large vanilla cone, he found a secluded park bench, sat down, and started to lick.

A few minutes later a man sat at the other end of the bench, studying a map of the vast gardens. Behind the map, no one could see his lips move. Monk's lips were moving because he was licking an ice cream.

"So, my friend, how are you?" asked Pyotr Solomin.

"The better for seeing you, old pal," muttered Monk. "Tell me, are we under surveillance?"

"No. I have been here for an hour. You were not followed. Nor I."

"My people are very happy with you, Peter. The details you provide will help shorten the Cold War."

"I just want to bring the bastards down," said the Siberian. "Your ice cream is melting. Throw it away, I'll get two more."

Monk threw his dripping stub into the trash can nearby. Solomin strolled over to the booth and bought two cones. When he came back the gesture enabled him to sit closer.

"I have something for you. Film. Inside the cover of my map. I will leave it on the bench."

"Thank you. Why not transmit in Moscow? My people were a bit suspicious," said Monk.

"Because there is more, but it must be spoken."

He began to describe what was happening that summer of 1986

inside the Politburo and the Defense Ministry in Moscow. Monk kept a straight face to prevent himself giving a long, low whistle. Solomin talked for half an hour.

"Is this true, Peter? It is really happening at last?"

"As true as I sit here. I have heard the defense minister himself confirm it."

"It will change many things," said Monk. "Thank you, old hunter. But I must go."

As strangers on a park bench who have talked to each other, Monk held out his hand. Solomin stared in fascination.

"What is that?"

It was a ring. Monk did not usually wear rings, but it went with the persona of a Texan. A Navajo ring of turquoise and raw silver of the sort worn all over Texas and New Mexico. He could see that the Udegey tribesman from the Primorskiy Krai loved it. On a gesture Monk slipped it from his hand and gave it to the Siberian.

"For me?" asked Solomin.

He had never asked for money and Monk had guessed he would give offense if he offered it. From the Siberian's expression the ring was more than recompense, a hundred dollars worth of turquoise and silver hacked from the hills of New Mexico and crafted by Ute or Navajo silversmiths.

Aware that an embrace was impossible in public, Monk turned to go. He looked back. Peter Solomin had slipped the ring onto the small finger of his left hand and was admiring it. It was the last image Monk had of the hunter from the east.

The *Armenia* sailed into Odessa and discharged its human cargo. Customs examined every suitcase but they were only looking for anti-Soviet printed material. Monk had been told they never did a body search of a foreign tourist unless the KGB was in charge, and that would be for a very special reason.

Monk had his rows of tiny transparencies between two layers of plaster tape adhering to one buttock. With the other Americans Monk closed his suitcase and all were hustled by the Intourist guide through the formalities and onto the Moscow train.

In the capital the next day Monk dropped off his consignment at the embassy, whence it would come home to Langley in the diplomatic bag, and flew back to the States. He had a very long report to write.

CHAPTER 7

"GOOD EVENING, BRITISH EMBASSY," SAID THE OPERATOR ON Sofiskaya Quay.

"*Schto?*" said a bewildered voice at the other end of the line.

"*Dobri vecher, Angliyskoye Posolstvo,*" the operator repeated in Russian.

"I want the Bolshoi Theatre ticket office," said the voice.

"I'm afraid you have the wrong number, caller," the operator said, and hung up.

The listeners at the bank of monitors in the headquarters of FAPSI, the Russian electronic eavesdropping agency, heard the call and logged it, but otherwise thought no more of it. Wrong numbers were two a penny.

Inside the embassy the operator ignored the flashing lights of two more incoming calls, consulted a small notebook, and dialed an internal number.

"Mr. Fields?"

"Yes."

"Switchboard here. Someone just called asking for the Bolshoi Theatre ticket office."

"Right, thank you."

Gracie Fields rang Jock Macdonald. Internal extensions were regularly swept by the man from the Security Service and were deemed secure.

"My friend from Moscow's finest just called," he said. "He used the emergency code. He needs a callback."

"Keep me posted," said the Head of Station.

Fields checked his watch. One hour between calls and five minutes gone. At a public phone in the lobby of a bank two blocks from the militia building, Inspector Novikov also checked his watch and decided to take a coffee to fill the intervening fifty minutes. Then he would report to another public phone a block further down and wait.

Fields left the embassy ten minutes later and drove slowly to the Kosmos Hotel on Mira Prospekt. Built in 1979, modern by Moscow standards, the Kosmos has a row of public phone booths close to the lobby.

An hour after the call came to the embassy he checked a notepad from his jacket pocket and dialed. Public booth-to-booth calls are a nightmare for counterintelligence organizations and virtually uncheckable because of the sheer numbers of them.

"Boris?" Novikov was not called Boris. His given name was Yevgeni, but when he heard "Boris" he knew it was Fields on the line.

"Yes. That drawing you gave me. Something has come up. I think we should meet."

"All right. Join me for dinner at the Rossiya."

Neither man had any intention of going to the vast Rossiya Hotel. The reference was to a bar called the Carousel halfway up Tverskaya Street. It was cool and dark enough to be discreet. Again the time lapse was one hour.

•   •   •

LIKE many of the larger British embassies, the Moscow legation contains on its staff a member of the British internal security service known as MI5. This is the sister service of the foreign intelligence-gathering Secret Intelligence Service, wrongly but popularly called MI6.

The task of the MI5 man is not to gather information about the host country, but to guarantee the security of the embassy, its various outstations, and its staff.

The staff do not regard themselves as prisoners and in Moscow during the summer frequent a pretty bathing spot outside the city where the River Moskva curves in a manner that exposes a small sandy beach. For diplomatic staff this is a favored picnicking and bathing spot.

Before he was elevated to the rank of inspector and transferred to Homicide, Yevgeni Novikov had been the officer in charge of that country district, including the resort area known as Serebryani Bor, or Silver Woods.

It was here he had got to know the then British security service officer, who introduced him to the newly arrived Gracie Fields.

Fields cultivated the young policeman and eventually suggested that a small monthly retainer in hard currency could make life easier for a man on a fixed salary in inflationary times. Inspector Novikov became a source, low-level it was true, but occasionally useful. During this week the homicide detective was going to repay all the effort.

"We have a body," he told Fields as they sat in the gloom of the Carousel and sipped chilled beer. "I'm pretty sure it's the man in the drawing you gave me. Old, steel teeth, you know. . . ."

He narrated the events as he had learned them from his colleague Volsky on the John Doe desk.

"Nearly three weeks, that's a long time to be dead in this weather. The face must be ghastly," said Fields. "It might not be the same man."

"He was only in the forest for a week. Then nine days in a cold box. He should be recognizable."

"I'll need a photograph, Boris. Can you get one?"

"I don't know. They're all with Volsky. Do you know of a man called Inspector Chernov?"

"Yes, he's been around to the embassy. I gave him one of the drawings too."

"I know," said Novikov. "Now they're all over the place. Anyway, he'll be back. Volsky will have told him by now. He'll have a real photograph of the corpse's face."

"For himself, not for us."

"It could be difficult."

"Well try, Boris, try. You're in Homicide, aren't you? Say you want to show it around some gangland contacts. Make any excuse. This is a homicide now. That's what you do, isn't it? Solve murders?"

"Supposed to," admitted Novikov gloomily. He wondered if the Englishman knew the cleanup rate for gang killings was three percent.

"There'll be a bonus in it for you," said Fields. "When our staff are attacked we are not ungenerous."

"All right," said Novikov. "I'll try and get one."

As it happened he did not need to bother. The mystery man file came to Homicide of its own accord and two days later he was able to abstract one of the sheaf of photos of the face taken out in the woods by the Minsk Highway.

Langley, November 1986

CAREY Jordan was in an exceptionally good mood. Such moods were brief in late 1986 because the Iran-Contra scandal was raging through Washington, and Jordan more than most others knew how deeply the CIA had been involved.

But he had just been summoned to the office of the director, William Casey, to receive the warmest plaudits. The cause of such unaccustomed benignity from the old director was the reception in the highest quarters of the news brought back from Yalta by Jason Monk.

In the very early eighties, the USSR instituted a series of highly aggressive policies against the West, its last desperate attempt to break the will of the NATO alliance by intimidation. Ronald Reagan was in the White House at the time and Margaret Thatcher in Downing Street. The two Western leaders decided they would not be browbeaten by threats.

President Andropov died, Chernenko came and went, Gorbachev came to power, but still the war of wills and industrial power went on.

Mikhail Gorbachev had become General Secretary of the party in March 1985. He was a dedicated Communist born and raised. The difference was that unlike his predecessors he was pragmatic and refused to accept the lies that they had swallowed. He insisted on knowing the real facts and figures of Soviet industry and the economy. When he saw them he was traumatized.

By the summer of 1986, deep in the heart of the Kremlin and the

Defense Ministry, it was becoming clear that the military–industrial complex and the weapons procurement program were absorbing sixty percent of Soviet gross domestic product, an unsustainable figure. The people were at last becoming restive with their privations.

That summer a major examination was undertaken to see how long the Soviet Union could keep up the pace. The picture in the report could not have been blacker. Industrially, the capitalist West was outperforming the Russian dinosaur at every level. It was this report that Solomin brought on microfilm to the park bench at Yalta.

What it said, and what Solomin confirmed verbally, was that if the West could hang on for two more years, the Soviet economy would come apart at the seams, and the Kremlin would have to concede and dismantle. As in a game of poker, the Siberian had just shown the West the Kremlin's entire hand.

The news went right into the White House and across the Atlantic to Mrs. Thatcher. Both leaders, beset by internal hostility and doubt, took heart. Bill Casey was congratulated by the Oval Office and passed the plaudits on to Carey Jordan. He summoned Jason Monk to share his congratulations. At the end of their talk Jordan brought up a topic he had raised before.

"I have a real problem with those damn files of yours, Jason. You can't just leave them sitting in your safe. If anything happened to you, we wouldn't know where to begin to handle these two assets, Lysander and Orion. You have to log them with the others."

It had been over a year since the first treachery of Aldrich Ames, and six months since the disaster of the missing agents had become apparent. The culprit was by then in Rome. Technically the mole hunt still plodded on, but the urgency had gone out of it.

"If it ain't broke, don't fix it," pleaded Monk. "These guys are putting their lives on the line. They know me and I know them. We trust each other. Let it be."

Jordan had known before of the strange bond that could be forged between asset and handler. It was a relationship the agency officially frowned on for two reasons. The agent runner might have to be moved to a different post, or might retire or die. A too-personal relationship could mean the asset deep in the heart of Russia might decide he could not or would not go on with a new handler. Second, if anything happened to the asset, the agency man could become too depressed to retain his usefulness. In a long career an asset might have several handlers. Monk's one-on-one bond with his two agents worried Jordan. It was . . . irregular.

On the other hand, Monk *was* irregular, one of a kind. If Jordan had but known it, which he did not, Monk made a point of ensuring that each asset inside Moscow (Turkin had left Madrid and was back home, producing amazing material from the very heart of K Directorate of the FCD) received long personal letters from him, along with the usual tasking lists.

Jordan settled for a compromise. The files containing details of the men, where and how they were recruited, how they were "serviced," their different postings—everything but their names and yet quite enough to identify them—would be transferred to the DDO's own personal safe. If anyone wanted to get at them, he would have to go by the DDO himself and explain why. Monk settled for that and the transfer was made.

• • •

INSPECTOR Novikov was right about one thing. Inspector Chernov did indeed reappear at the embassy. He came the next morning, August 5. Jock Macdonald asked him to be escorted to his office where he masqueraded as an attaché of the Chancery section.

"We think we may have found the man who broke into your colleague's apartment," said Chernov.

"My congratulations, Inspector."

"Unfortunately, he is dead."

"Ah, but you have a photograph?"

"I do. Of the body. Of the face. And . . ." he tapped a canvas bag by his side, "I have the overcoat he was probably wearing."

He placed a glossy print on Macdonald's desk. It was fairly gruesome, but a close match to the crayon drawing.

"Let me summon Miss Stone and see if she can identify this unfortunate man."

Celia Stone was escorted in by Fields, who remained. Macdonald warned her what she was about to see was not pretty, but he would be grateful for her advice. She glanced at the photo and put her hand over her mouth. Chernov took out the frayed ex-army greatcoat and held it up. Celia looked desperately at Macdonald and nodded.

"That's him. That was the man who—"

"—you saw running out of your apartment. Of course. Clearly, thieves fall out, Inspector. I am sure it is the same the world over."

Celia Stone was escorted out.

"Let me say on behalf of the British government, Inspector, that you have done a remarkable job. We may never know the man's name, but it matters little now. The wretch is dead. Be assured the most favorable report will be received by the Commanding General of the Moscow militia," Macdonald told the beaming Russian.

As he left the embassy and climbed into his car Chernov was glowing. The moment he got back to Petrovka he passed the whole file from Burglary to Homicide. The fact there was supposed to be a second burglar involved was irrelevant. Without a description or the dead man's testimony, it was a needle in a haystack.

After he had left, Fields returned to Macdonald's office. The Head of Station was pouring himself a cup of coffee.

"What do you reckon?" he asked.

"My source says the man was beaten to death. He has a pal in the John Doe office who spotted the drawing on the wall and made the match. The postmortem report says the old boy had been about a week in the woods before he was found."

"And that was?"

Fields consulted the notes he had written up immediately after the talk in the Carousel Bar.

"July twenty-fourth."

"So, killed about the seventeenth or eighteenth. The day after he threw that file into Celia Stone's car. The day I flew to London. These lads don't waste time."

"Which lads?"

"Well, it's a million quid to a pint of flat beer it was the thugs commanded by that shit Grishin."

"Komarov's chief of personal security?"

"That's one way of putting it," said Macdonald. "Have you ever seen his file?"

"No."

"You should, someday. Ex-Second Chief Directorate interrogator. Deeply nasty."

"If it was a punishment beating, and death, who was the old

man?'' asked Fields. Macdonald stared out of the window, across the river to the Kremlin.

"Probably the thief himself."

"So how did an old tramp like that get hold of it?"

"I can only suppose he was some obscure employee of one kind or another who got lucky. As it happened, extremely unlucky. You know, I really think your policeman friend is going to have to earn himself a very fat bonus."

Buenos Aires, June 1987

IT was a bright young agent in the CIA station in the Argentine capital who first suspected Valeri Yurevitch Kruglov of the Soviet Embassy might have a flaw. The American Chief of Station consulted Langley.

The Latin America Division already had a file on him, dating from a previous Kruglov posting in the mid-seventies in Mexico City. They knew he was a Russian Latin America expert, with three such postings behind him in a twenty-year career in the Soviet Foreign Service. Because he appeared friendly and outgoing, the file even logged his career.

Born in 1944, Valeri Kruglov was the son of a diplomat, another specialist in Latin America. It was the father's influence that got the boy into the prestigious Institute of International Relations, the MGIMO, where he learned Spanish and English. He was there from 1961 to 1966. After that he did two South American postings, in Colombia as a youth, then Mexico a decade later, before reappearing as First Secretary in Buenos Aires.

The CIA was convinced he was not KGB, but a regular diplomat. His biography was of a fairly liberal, possibly pro-Western Russian, not the usual hardline "homo sovieticus." The reason for the alert in the summer of 1987 had been a conversation with an Argentine official, passed on to the Americans, in which Kruglov revealed that he was returning soon to Moscow, never to travel abroad again, and that his lifestyle would plunge.

Because he was a Russian, the alert involved SE Division as well, and Harry Gaunt suggested a new face be put in front of Kruglov.

As he spoke Spanish and Russian, he suggested Jason Monk. Jordan agreed.

It was a simple enough task. Kruglov had only a month to go. In the words of the song, it was now or never.

Five years after the Falklands War, with democracy restored to Argentina, Buenos Aires was a relaxed capital and it was easy for the American "businessman," partnering a girl from the American Embassy, to meet Kruglov at a reception. Monk made sure they got on well and suggested a dinner.

The Russian, who as First Secretary had considerable freedom from his ambassador and the KGB, found the idea of dining with someone outside the diplomatic circuit attractive. Over dinner, Monk borrowed from the real-life story of his former French teacher, Mrs. Brady. He explained that his mother had been an interpreter with the Red Army and after the fall of Berlin had met and fallen in love with a young American officer. Against all the rules, they had slipped away and married in the West. Thus in the parental home, Monk had been brought up to speak English and Russian with equal fluency. After that, they dropped into Russian. Kruglov found it a relief. His Spanish was excellent but his English a strain.

Within two weeks, Kruglov's real problem had emerged. At forty-three, divorced but with two teenage children, he was still sharing an apartment with his parents. If only he had a sum close to $20,000 he could acquire his own small flat in Moscow. As a wealthy polo player, down in Argentina to check out some new ponies, Monk would be happy to lend his new friend the money.

The Chief of Station proposed photographing the handover of the cash but Monk demurred.

"Blackmail won't work. He either comes as a volunteer or he won't come."

Although Monk was junior, the Chief of Station agreed it was his ball game. The "play" Monk used was the enlightened-against-the-warmongers theme. Mikhail Gorbachev, he pointed out, was hugely popular in the States. This Kruglov already knew and it gratified him. He was very much a Gorbachev man.

Gorby, suggested Monk, was genuinely trying to dismantle the war machine and bring peace and trust between their two peoples.

The trouble was, there were still entrenched Cold War warriors on both sides, even right in the heart of the Soviet Foreign Ministry. They would try to sabotage the process. It would be so helpful if Kruglov could alert his new pal to what was really going on inside Moscow's Foreign Ministry. Kruglov must have known by then to whom he was talking, but he evinced no surprise.

To Monk, who had already developed a passion for game fishing, it was like pulling in a tuna that had accepted the inevitable. Kruglov got his dollars, and a communications package. Details of personal plans, position, and access should be sent in secret ink on a harmless letter to a live letter box in East Berlin. Hard intelligence—documents—should be photographed and passed to the CIA Moscow via one of two drops in the city.

They embraced when they parted, Russian-style.

"Don't forget, Valeri," said Monk. "We . . . us . . . we, the good guys, are winning. Soon all this nonsense will be over and we will have helped it happen. If ever you need me, just call and I'll come."

Kruglov flew home to Moscow and Monk returned to Langley.

$$\bullet \qquad \bullet \qquad \bullet$$

"BORIS, here. I've got it!"

"Got what?"

"The photograph. The picture you wanted. The file came back to Homicide. I pinched one of the best prints in the bunch. The eyes are closed so it doesn't look so bad."

"Good, Boris. Now I have in my jacket pocket an envelope with five hundred pounds in it. But there's something else I need you to do. Then that envelope grows fatter. It contains one thousand British pounds."

In his phone booth Inspector Novikov took a deep breath. He could not even work out how many hundreds of millions of rubles that sort of envelope could buy. Over a year's salary anyway.

"Go on."

"I want you to go to see the director in charge of all personnel and staff at the headquarters of the UPF Party and show it to him."

"The what?"

"The Union of Patriotic Forces."

"What the hell have they got to do with it?"

"I don't know. Just an idea. He might have seen the man before."

"Why should he?"

"I don't know, Boris. He might have. It's just an idea."

"What excuse do I give?"

"You're a homicide detective. You're on a case. You're following a lead. The man may have been seen hanging around party headquarters. Perhaps he was trying to break in. Did any of the guards see him lurking about in the street. That sort of thing."

"All right. But these are important people. If I get busted, it's your fault."

"Why should you get busted? You're a humble cop doing his job. This desperado was seen in the neighborhood of Mr. Komarov's dacha off Kiselny Boulevard. It's your duty to bring it to their attention, even if he's dead. He might have been part of a gang. He might have been casing the joint. You're watertight. Just do it, and the thousand pounds is yours."

Yevgeni Novikov grumbled some more and hung up. These Anglichani, he reflected, were bloody mad. The old fool had only broken into one of their flats, after all. But for a thousand pounds, it was was the trouble of asking.

Moscow, October 1987

COLONEL Anatoli Grishin was frustrated, as in the manner of one whose high point of achievement was seemingly over, with nothing more to do.

The last of the interrogations of the agents betrayed by Ames was long over, the last drop of recollection and information squeezed from the trembling men. There had been twelve of them living in the weeping basements below Lefortovo, to be brought up on demand to confront the question masters from the First and Second Chief Directorates, or taken back to Grishin's special room in the event of recalcitrance or loss of memory.

Two, against Grishin's pleading, had received only long terms in labor camps instead of death. This was because they had worked only a very short time for the CIA or been too lowly to have done much damage. The rest had received their death sentences. Nine had been executed, taken to the graveled courtyard behind the sequestered prison wing, forced to kneel and to await the bullet into the back of the brain. Grishin had been present as senior officer on all occasions.

Only one remained alive, on Grishin's insistence, and he was the oldest of them all. General Dmitri Polyakov had worked for America for twenty years before he was betrayed. He had in fact been in retirement after returning to Moscow in 1980 for the last time.

He had never taken money; he did it because he was disgusted by the Soviet regime and the things it did. And he told them so. He sat upright in his chair and told them what he thought of them and what he had done for twenty years. He showed more dignity and courage than all the others. He never pleaded. Because he was so old, nothing he had to say was of current value anyway. He knew of no ongoing operations nor did he have names other than of CIA handlers themselves retired.

When it was over, Grishin hated the old general so much he kept him alive for special treatment. Now the pensioner lay in his excrement on his concrete slab and wept. Now and again Grishin looked in to make sure. It would not be until March 15, 1988, that at General Boyarov's insistence he was finally finished off.

"The point is, my dear colleague," Boyarov told Grishin that month, "there is nothing more to do. The Ratcatcher Commission must be disbanded."

"There is surely still this other man, the one they talk of in the First Chief Directorate, the one who handles traitors here but who has not been caught."

"Ah, the one they cannot find. Always references, but not one of the traitors had ever heard of him."

"And if we catch his people?" asked Grishin.

"Then we catch them, and we make them pay," said Boyarov, "and if that happens, if Yazenevo's man in Washington can give them to us, you can reconvene your people and start again. You can even rename yourselves. You can be called the Monakh Committee."

Grishin did not get the point, but Boyarov did, and laughed uproariously. *Monakh* is the Russian for monk.

• • •

IF Pavel Volsky thought he had heard the last of the forensic pathologist at the morgue, he was wrong. His phone rang the same morning his friend Novikov was talking covertly to an officer of British Intelligence, August 7.

"Kuzmin here," said a voice. Volsky was puzzled.

"Professor Kuzmin, Second Medical Institute. We spoke a few days ago about my postmortem on a John Doe."

"Oh, yes, Professor, how can I help you?"

"I think it's the other way round. I may have something for you."

"Well, thank you, what is it?"

"Last week a body was pulled out of the Moskva at Lytkarino."

"Surely, that's their business, not ours?"

"It would have been, Volsky, but some smartass down there reckoned the body had been in the water for about two weeks—he was right, actually—and that in that time it probably floated down the current from Moscow. So the bastards shipped it back here. I've just finished with it."

Volsky thought. Two weeks in the water in high summer. The professor must have a stomach like a concrete mixer.

"Murdered?" he asked.

"On the contrary. Wearing only undershorts. Almost certainly went for a swim in the heat wave, got into trouble, and drowned."

"But that's an accident. The Civil Authority. I'm Homicide," protested Volsky.

"Listen, young man. Just listen. Normally there would be no identification. But those fools at Lytkarino failed to spot something. The fingers were so swollen they didn't see it. Hidden by the flesh. A wedding band. Solid gold. I removed it—had to take the finger off, actually. Inside are the words: *N. I. Akopov, from Lidia.* Good, eh?"

"Very good, Professor, but if it's not a homicide . . ."

"Listen, do you ever have anything to do with Missing Persons?"

"Of course. They send around a folio of pictures every week to see if I can make a match."

"Well, a man with a big gold wedding band might have family. And if he's been missing for three weeks they might have reported it. I just thought you could benefit from my detective genius by scoring some brownie points with your friends in Missing Persons. I don't know anyone in Missing Persons, so I called you."

Volsky brightened up. He was always asking favors from Missing Persons. Now he might clear up a case for them and earn some kudos. He noted the details, thanked the professor, and hung up.

His usual contact at Missing Persons came on the line after ten minutes.

"Do you have an MP in the name of N. I. Akopov?" asked Volsky. His contact checked the records and came back.

"Certainly do. Why?"

"Give me the details."

"Reported missing July seventeenth. Never came home from work the previous night, not been seen since. Reporting party, Mrs. Akopov, next of kin . . ."

"Mrs. Lidia Akopov?"

"How the hell did you know? She's been in four times asking for news. Where is he?"

"On a slab in the morgue at Second Medical. Went swimming and drowned. Pulled out of the river last week at Lytkarino."

"Great. The old lady will be pleased. I mean, to have the mystery solved. You don't know who he is . . . or rather was?"

"No idea," said Volsky.

"Only the personal private secretary to Igor Komarov."

"The politician?"

"Our next president, no less. Thanks, Pavel, I owe you one."

You certainly do, thought Volsky as he got on with his work.

Oman, November 1987

CAREY Jordan was forced to resign that month. It was not the matter of the missing agents. It was Iran-Contra. Years earlier the CIA had covertly sold arms to Iran to fund the Nicaraguan rebels. The order had come from President Reagan via the late CIA director Bill Casey. Carey Jordan had carried out the demands of his president and his director. Now one had amnesia and the other was dead.

Webster appointed as the new Deputy Director Ops a retired

CIA veteran Richard Stoltz who had been gone for six years. As such, he was clean of any involvement in Iran–Contra. He also knew nothing of the devastation of the SE Division two years earlier. While he was finding his feet, the bureaucrats took over in force. Three files were removed from the departed DDO's safe and relogged with the main body, or what was left of it, in the 301 file. They contained the details of agents code-named Lysander, Orion, and a new one, Delphi.

Jason Monk knew none of this. He was on vacation in Oman. Always hunting the sea-angling magazines for new hot spots to fish, he had read of the great shoals of yellowfin tuna that stream past the coast of Oman just outside the capital, Muscat, in November and December.

As a courtesy he had checked in with the tiny one-man CIA station at the embassy in the heart of Old Muscat close to the Sultan's palace. He never expected to see his CIA colleague again after their friendly drink.

On his third day, having taken too much sun out on the open sea, he elected to stay ashore and do some shopping. He was dating a ravishing blonde from the State Department and went by cab to the souk at Mina Qaboos to see if, among the stalls of incense, spices, fabrics, silver, and antiques he could find something for her.

He settled on an ornate, long-spouted silver coffee pot, forged long ago by some smith high in the Jebel. The antique-shop owner wrapped it and put it in a plastic shopping bag.

Having got himself completely lost in the labyrinth of alleys and courtyards, Monk finally emerged not on the seaward side but somewhere in the back streets. As he came out of an alley no wider than his shoulders, he found himself in a small courtyard with a narrow entrance at one end and an exit at the other. A man was crossing the yard. He looked like a European.

Behind him were two Arabs. As they debouched into the courtyard, each reached to his waist and withdrew a curved dagger. With that they ran past Monk toward their target.

Monk reacted without thinking. He swung the bag with full force, catching one of the assailants full on the side of the head. Several pounds of metal moving at full bore caused him to crash to the ground.

The other knifeman paused, caught between two fires, then swung at Monk. Monk saw the glittering blade high in the air, moved under the arm, blocked it, and slammed a fist into the soiled dishdash robe at solar plexus height.

The man was tough. He grunted, retained his grip on his knife, but decided to run. His companion scrambled to his feet and followed, leaving one knife on the ground.

The European had turned and taken in the action without a word spoken. Clearly he knew he would have been killed but for the intervention of the blond man ten yards away. Monk saw a slim young man with olive skin and dark eyes but not a local Arab, wearing a white shirt and dark suit. He was about to speak when the stranger gave a brief nod of thanks and slipped away.

Monk stooped to pick up the dagger. It was not an Omani kunja at all, and indeed muggings by the Omanis are unheard of. It was a Yemeni gambiah, with its much simpler and straighter hilt. Monk thought he knew the origin of the assailants. They were Audhali or Aulaqi tribesmen from the Yemeni interior. What the hell, he thought, were they doing so far along the coast in Oman and why did they hate the young Westerner so much?

On a hunch he went back to his embassy and sought out the CIA man there.

"Do you by any chance have a rogues' gallery of our friends at the Soviet Embassy?" he asked.

It was common knowledge that since the fiasco of the civil war in Yemen in January 1986 the USSR had pulled out completely, leaving the pro-Moscow Yemeni government impoverished and embittered. Consumed with rage at their humiliation, as they saw it, Aden had to go to the West for trade credits and cash to keep going. From then on a Russian's life in Yemen would hang by a thread. Heaven knows no rage like love to hatred turned. . . .

By the end of 1987 the USSR had opened a full-fledged embassy in the distinctly anti-Communist Oman and were wooing the pro-British sultan.

"I don't," said his colleague, "but I'll bet the Brits will."

It was only a step down the road from the maze of narrow and humid corridors that made up the American Embassy to the more elaborate British one. They penetrated the vast carved wood doors, nodded at the gatekeeper, and headed across the courtyard. The whole complex had once been the mansion of a wealthy trader and was steeped in history.

On one wall of the yard was a plaque left behind by a Roman legion that marched off into the desert and was never seen again. In the center of the space was the British flagpole, which long ago would guarantee a slave his freedom if he could reach it. They turned left toward the embassy building and the senior SIS man was waiting for them. They shook hands.

"What's the prob, old boy?" asked the Englishman.

"The prob," replied Monk, "is that I have just seen a guy in the souk I think may be a Russian."

It was only a small detail, but the man in the souk had worn the collar of his open-necked white shirt outside his jacket, as Russians tended to do but Westerners avoided.

"Well, let's have a look at the mug book," said the Brit.

He led them through the steel filigree security doors, down the cool and pillared hall and up the stairs. The British SIS operation lived on the top floor. From a safe the SIS man took an album and they flicked through it.

The newly arrived Soviet staff were all there, caught at the airport, crossing the street, or at an open café terrace. The young man with the dark eyes was the last, photographed crossing the concourse of the airport on arrival.

"The local chaps are pretty helpful to us about this sort of thing," said the SIS man. "The Russians have to preannounce themselves to the Foreign Ministry here and seek accreditation. We get the details. Then when they come we get a tip-off so we can be handy with a Long Tom lens. This him?"

"Yes. Any details?"

The SIS man consulted a sheaf of cards.

"Here we are. Unless it's all a bunch of lies, he's Third Secretary, aged twenty-eight. Name of Umar Gunayev. Sounds Tartar."

"No," said Monk thoughtfully, "he's a Chechen. And a Moslem."

"You think he's KGB?" asked the Britisher.

"Oh yes, he's a spook all right."

"Well, thanks for that. Want us to do anything about him? Complain to the government?"

"No," said Monk. "We all have to make a living. Better to know who he is. They'd only send a replacement."

As they strolled back, the CIA man asked Monk, "How did you know?"

"Just a hunch."

It was a bit more than that. Gunayev had been sipping an orange juice at the bar of the Frontel in Aden a year earlier. Monk had not been the only one to recognize him that day. The two tribesmen had spotted him and decided to take revenge for the insult to their country.

• • •

MARK Jefferson arrived at Sheremetyevo Airport, Moscow, on the afternoon flight on August 8 and was met by the bureau chief of the *Daily Telegraph*.

The star political feature writer was a slight, dapper, middle-aged man with thinning ginger hair and a short beard of the same hue. His temper, it was reputed, was the same length as his body and beard.

He declined to join his colleague and wife for supper, and asked only to be driven to the prestigious National Hotel on Manege Square.

Once there, he told his colleague he would prefer to interview Mr. Komarov unaccompanied, and if need be would engage a limousine with driver through the good offices of the hotel itself. Well rebuffed, the bureau chief drove off.

Jefferson checked in, and his registration was handled by the manager himself, a tall and courteous Swede. His passport was retained by the reception clerk so that the appropriate details could be copied out and filed with the Ministry of Tourism. Before leaving London, Jefferson had instructed his secretary to inform the National who he was and how important he was.

Once up in his room he called the number he had been given by Boris Kuznetsov in their exchange of faxes.

"Welcome to Moscow, Mr. Jefferson," said Kuznetsov in flawless English with a slight American accent. "Mr. Komarov is much looking forward to your meeting."

It was not true but Jefferson believed it anyway. The appointment was made for seven the following evening, because Komarov would be out of town all day. A car and driver would be sent to the National to collect him.

Satisfied, Mark Jefferson dined alone in the hotel and slept.

On the following morning, after a breakfast of bacon and eggs, Mark Jefferson decided to indulge in what he regarded as the Englishman's inalienable right in any part of the world, to take a stroll.

"A stroll?" queried the Swedish general manager with a perplexed frown. "Where do you want to stroll?"

"Anywhere. Get a breath of air. Stretch the legs. Probably go across to the Kremlin and look around."

"We can provide the hotel limousine," said the manager. "So much more comfortable. And safer."

Jefferson would have none of it. A stroll was what he wanted and a stroll he would have. The manager at least prevailed upon him to leave his watch and all foreign cash behind, but to take a wad of million-ruble notes for the beggars. Enough to satisfy the mendicants but not enough to provoke a mugging. With luck.

The British journalist, who despite his eminence in the features department had spent his career in London-based political journalism and never covered the hot spots of the world as a foreign correspondent, was back two hours later. He seemed somewhat put out.

He had been to Moscow twice before, once under Communism and eight years earlier when Yeltsin was just in power. On each occasion he had confined his experiences to the taxi from the airport, a top hotel, and the British diplomatic circuit. He had always thought Moscow a drab and grubby city, but he had not been expecting his experiences of that morning.

His appearance had been so obviously foreign that even along the river quays and around the Alexandrovsky Gardens he had been besieged by derelicts, who seemed to be camping out everywhere. Twice he thought gangs of youth were following him. The only cars seemed to be military, police, or the limousines of the rich and privileged. Still, he reasoned, he had some powerful points to put to Mr. Komarov that evening.

Taking a drink before lunch—he decided to stay inside the hotel until Mr. Kuznetsov called for him—he found himself alone in the bar except for a world-weary Canadian businessman. In the manner of strangers in a bar, they fell into conversation.

"How long you been in town?" asked the man from Toronto.

"Came in last night," said Jefferson.

"Staying long?"

"Back to London tomorrow."

"Hey, lucky you. I've been here three weeks, trying to do business. And I can tell you, this place is weird."

"No success?"

"Oh, sure, I have the contracts. I have the office. I also have the partners. You know what happened?"

The Canadian seated himself next to Jefferson and explained.

"I get in here with all the introductions in the timber business that I need, or think I need. I rent an office in a new tower building. Two days later there's a knock on the door. There's a guy standing there, neat, smart, suit and tie. 'Good morning, Mr. Wyatt,' he says. 'I'm your new partner.' "

"You knew him?" asked Jefferson.

"Not from hell. He's the representative of the local mafia. And that's the deal. He and his people take fifty percent of everything. In exchange they buy or forge every permit, allocation, franchise, or piece of paper I will ever need. They will square away the bureaucracy with a phone call, ensure deliveries are on schedule, with no labor disputes. For fifty percent."

"You told him to take a running jump," said Jefferson.

"No way. I learned fast. It's called having a 'roof.' Meaning protection. Without a roof you get nowhere, fast. Mainly because, if you turn them down, you have no legs. They blow them off."

Jefferson stared at him in disbelief.

"Good God, I'd heard crime was bad here. But not like that."

"I tell you, it's like nothing you could ever imagine."

One of the phenomena that had amazed Western observers after the fall of Communism was the seemingly lightning rise of the Russian criminal underworld, called for want of a better phrase "the Russian mafia." Even Russians began to refer to the *"maffiya."* Some foreigners thought it was a new entity, born only after Communism ended. This was nonsense.

A vast criminal underworld has existed in Russia for centuries. Unlike the Sicilian Mafia it had no unified hierarchy and never exported itself abroad. But it existed, a great sprawling brotherhood with regional and gang chieftains and members loyal to their gangs unto death and with the appropriate tattoos to prove it.

Stalin attempted to destroy it, sending thousands of its members to the slave camps. The only result was that the *zoks* ended up virtually running the camps with the connivance of the guards, who preferred a quiet life to having their families traced and punished. In many cases the *vori v zakone,* the "thieves by statute" or equivalents of the mafia dons, actually ran their enterprises on the outside from their cabins in the camps.

One of the ironies of the Cold War is that Communism would probably have collapsed ten years earlier but for the underworld. Even the Party bosses finally had to make their covert pact with it.

The reason was simple: It was the only thing in the USSR that ran with any degree of efficiency. A factory manager, producing a vital product, might see his principal machine tool grind to a halt because of the breakdown of a single valve. If he went through the bureaucratic channels he would wait six to twelve months for his valve while his entire plant stood idle.

Or he could have a word with his brother-in-law who knew a man who had contacts. The valve would arrive within a week. Later the factory manager would turn a blind eye to the disappearance of a consignment of his steel plate, which would find its way to another factory whose steel plate had not arrived. Then both factory managers would cook the books to show they had completed their "norms."

In any society where a combination of sclerotic bureaucracy and raw incompetence has caused all the cogs and wheels to seize up, the black market is the only lubricant. The USSR ran on that lubricant throughout its life and depended utterly upon it for the last ten years.

The mafia simply controlled the black market. All it did after 1991 was come out of the closet to prosper and expand. Expand it certainly did, moving rapidly from the usual areas of racketeering—alcohol, drugs, protection, prostitution—into every single facet of life.

What *was* impressive was the speed and ruthlessness with which the virtual takeover of the economy was achieved. Three factors enabled this to happen. The first was the capacity for immediate and massive violence the Russian mafia demonstrated if it was frustrated in any way, a violence that would have made the American Cosa

Nostra look positively squeamish. Anybody, Russian or foreign, objecting to mafia involvement in his enterprise was given one warning—usually a beating or an outbreak of arson—and then executed. This applied right up to heads of major banks.

The second factor was the helplessness of the police, who, underfunded, understaffed, and without any experience or forewarning of the blizzard of crime and violence that was going to overwhelm them in the aftermath of Communism, simply could not cope. The third factor was the pandemic Russian tradition of corruption. The massive inflation that followed 1991 until it steadied around 1995 assisted in this.

Under Communism the exchange rate stood at two U.S. dollars to the ruble, a ridiculous and artificial rate in terms of value and purchasing power, but enforced within the USSR, where not lack of money but lack of goods to buy with it was the problem. Inflation wiped out savings and reduced fixed-salary employees to poverty.

When a street cop's weekly wage is worth less than his socks it is hard to persuade him not to take a banknote enclosed in an evidently forged driving license.

But that was small potatoes. The Russian mafia ran the system right up to the senior civil servants, recruiting almost the entire bureaucracy as their allies. And the bureaucracy runs everything in Russia. Thus permits, licenses, civic real estate, concessions, franchises—all could quickly be bought from the issuing civil servant, enabling the mafia to create astronomical profits.

The other skill of the Russian mafia that impressed observers was the speed with which they moved from conventional racketeering (while keeping a firm hold on it) into legitimate business. It took the American Cosa Nostra a generation to realize that legitimate businesses, acquired from racket profits, served both to increase profits and launder crime money. The Russians did it in five years, and by 1995 owned or controlled forty percent of the national economy. By then they had already gone international, favoring their three specialties of arms, drugs, and embezzlement, backed up by instant violence, and targeting all Western Europe and North America.

The trouble was, by 1998 they had overdone it. The sheer greed had broken the economy off which they lived. By 1996, fifty billion dollars' worth of Russian wealth, mainly in gold, diamonds, precious metals, oil, gas, and timber, was being stolen and illegally exported. The goods were bought with almost worthless rubles, and even then at knockdown prices from the bureaucrats running the state organs, and sold for dollars abroad. Some of the dollars would be reconverted to a blizzard of rubles and brought back to fund more bribes and more crime. The rest were stashed abroad.

"The trouble is," said Wyatt gloomily, as he drained his beer, "the hemorrhage has just become too much. Between the corrupt politicians, the even more corrupt bureaucrats, and the gangsters, they've killed the golden goose that made them all rich. Did you ever read *The Rise of the Third Reich?*"

"Yes, long ago. Why?"

"Do you remember those descriptions of the last days of the Weimar Republic? The unemployment queues, the street crime, the ruined life savings, the soup kitchens, the quarreling midgets in the Reichstag yelling their heads off while the country went bankrupt? Well, that's what you're watching here. All over again. Hell, I must go. Got to meet people downstairs for lunch. Good to talk with you, Mr. . . ."

"Jefferson."

The name didn't ring a bell. Clearly Mr. Wyatt didn't read the London *Daily Telegraph*.

Interesting, thought the London journalist when the Canadian had left. All his briefings from morgue clippings indicated the man he was due to interview that evening might be the man able to save the nation.

The long black Chaika called for Jefferson at half-past six and he was waiting in the doorway. He was invariably punctual and expected others to be the same. He wore dark gray slacks, a blazer, a crisp white cotton shirt, and a Garrick Club tie. He looked smart, neat, fussy, and every inch an Englishman.

The Chaika wended its way through the evening traffic north to Kiselny Boulevard, turning off down the side street just before the Garden Ring Road. As he approached the green steel gates, the driver activated an alert button on a communicator he produced from his jacket pocket.

The cameras atop the wall picked up the approaching car and the gate guard checked the TV monitor, which showed him the car and its license plate. The plate corresponded with the one he was expecting and the gates rolled back.

Once inside, they closed again and the guard approached the driver's window. He checked the ID, glanced in the back, nodded, and lowered the steel spikes.

Mr. Kuznetsov, alerted by the gate, was in the entrance of the dacha to greet his guest. He led the British journalist to a well-appointed reception area on the first floor, a room adjacent to Komarov's own office and on the other side from that once occupied by the late N. I. Akopov.

Igor Komarov permitted neither drinking nor smoking in his presence, something Jefferson did not know and never learned, because it was not mentioned. A nondrinking Russian is a rarity in a country where drinking is almost a sign of manhood. Jefferson, who had screened a number of videos of Komarov in his man-of-the-people mode, had seen him with the obligatory glass in his hand, drinking innumerable toasts in the Russian fashion, and showing no damage for it. He did not know Komarov was always supplied with spring water. That evening, only coffee was offered, and Jefferson declined.

After five minutes Komarov entered, an imposing figure of about fifty, gray-haired, just under six feet, with staring hazel eyes that his fans described as "mesmeric."

Kuznetsov shot to his feet and Jefferson followed a mite more slowly. The PR adviser made the introductions and the two men shook hands. Komarov seated himself first, in a button-back leather chair that was slightly higher than those occupied by the other two.

From his inner breast pocket Jefferson produced a slim tape recorder and asked if there would be no objection. Komarov inclined his head to indicate he understood the inability of most Western journalists to use shorthand. Kuznetsov nodded encouragingly at Jefferson to start.

"Mr. President, the news of the moment is the recent decision by the Duma to extend the interim presidency by three months but to bring forward next year's elections to January. How do you view that decision?"

Kuznetsov translated rapidly and listened while Komarov replied in sonorous Russian. When he had finished, the interpreter turned to Jefferson.

"Clearly I and the Union of Patriotic Forces were disappointed by the decision but as democrats we accept it. It will be no secret to you, Mr. Jefferson, that things in this country, which I love with a deep passion, are not good. For too long incompetent government has tolerated a high level of economic profligacy, corruption, and crime. Our people suffer. The longer this goes on, the worse it will become. Thus the delay is to be regretted. I believe that we could have won the presidency this October, but if January it must be, then we will win in January."

Mark Jefferson was far too experienced an interviewer not to realize that the answer was too pat, too rehearsed, as if delivered by a politician who had been asked the same question many times and could reel off the answer as if by rote. In Britain and America it was customary for politicians to be more relaxed with members of the press, many of whom they knew on first-name terms. Jefferson prided himself on being able to present a portrait in the round, using both the words of the interviewee and his own impressions to create a real newspaper article rather than a litany of political clichés. But this man was like an automaton.

The reporter's experience had already taught him that Western European politicians were accustomed to a far greater degree of deference from the press than British or American ones, but this was different. The Russian was as stiff and formal as a tailor's dummy.

By his third question Jefferson realized why: Komarov clearly hated the media and the whole process of being interviewed. The Londoner tried a lighthearted approach, but there was not a flicker of amusement from the Russian. A politician taking himself very seriously was nothing new, but this man was a fanatic of self-importance. The answers continued to come out as if on cue.

He glanced at Kuznetsov with puzzlement. The young interpreter was clearly American-educated, bilingual, worldly, and sophisticated, yet he treated Igor Komarov with spaniellike devotion. He tried again.

"You will know, sir, that in Russia most of the real power is vested in the office of the President, far more than in the President of the United States or the Prime Minister of Great Britain. If you were to contemplate the first six months of that power in your own hands, what changes would an objective observer see taking place? In other words, the priorities?"

Still the answer came as if from a political tract. Routine mention was made of the need to crush organized crime, reform a burdensome bureaucracy, restore agricultural production, and reform the currency. Further questions about precisely how this could be achieved were met with meaningless clichés. No politician in the West could have got away with this sort of thing, but it was clear Kuznetsov expected Jefferson to be completely satisfied.

Recalling the briefing he had received from his own editor, Jefferson asked Komarov how he intended to bring about the rebirth of the greatness of the Russian nation. For the first time he got a reaction.

Something he said seemed to jolt Komarov as if he had received an electric shock. The Russian sat staring at him with those unblinking hazel eyes, to the point that Jefferson could no longer meet the gaze and glanced at his tape recorder. Neither he nor Kuznetsov noticed that the president of the UPF had gone deathly pale and two small bright red spots burned high on each cheek. Without a word Komarov suddenly rose and left the room, passing into his own office and closing the door behind him. Jefferson raised an inquiring eyebrow at Kuznetsov. The younger man was clearly also puzzled but his natural urbanity took over.

"I am sure the president will not be long. Clearly he had just recalled something urgent that must be done without delay. He will be back as soon as he has finished."

Jefferson reached forward and switched off his recorder. After three minutes and a brief telephone call Komarov returned, sat down, and answered the question in measured tones. As he began, Jefferson put the machine back on.

An hour later Komarov indicated the interview was at an end. He rose, nodded stiffly at Jefferson, and withdrew to his office. In the doorway he beckoned Kuznetsov to follow him.

The adviser emerged two minutes later and was clearly embarrassed.

"I'm afraid we have a problem with the transport," he said as he escorted Jefferson down the stairs to the lobby. "The car you came in is urgently required and all the others belong to staff members working late. Could you take a taxi back to the National?"

"Well, yes, I suppose so," said Jefferson, who now wished he had brought his own transport from the hotel and ordered it to wait for him. "Perhaps you could order one?"

"I'm afraid they don't take phone orders anymore," said Kuznetsov, "but just let me show you how."

He led the mystified feature writer from the main door to the steel gate, which rolled aside to let them pass. In the side street Kuznetsov pointed to Kiselny Boulevard a hundred yards away.

"Right on the boulevard you'll pick up a cruising cab in seconds, and at this hour you'll be back at the hotel in fifteen minutes. I do hope you understand. It's been a pleasure, a real pleasure, to meet you, sir."

With that he was gone. An extremely put-out Mark Jefferson walked up the narrow street to the main road. He was fiddling with his tape recorder as he walked. Finally he slipped the machine back into the inside breast pocket of his blazer as he reached Kiselny Boulevard. He glanced up and down for a cab. Predictably there were none. With an irritable scowl he turned left, toward central Moscow, and began to walk, glancing over his shoulder every now and then for a taxi.

The two men in black leather jackets saw him come out of the side street and walk toward them. One of them opened the rear passenger door of their car and they slid out. When the Englishman was ten yards away each man slipped a hand inside his jacket and produced a silenced automatic. No words were spoken and only two bullets fired. Both hit the journalist in the chest.

The force stopped the walking man, and then he simply sat down as his legs gave way. The torso began to topple but the two killers had covered the ground between them and him. One held him upright and the other flicked a hand inside the jacket, quickly pulling out the tape recorder from one breast pocket and his wallet from the other.

Their car rolled up beside them and they jumped in. After it roared away a woman passerby looked down at the body, thought it was another drunk, saw the trickling blood, and began to scream. No one took the car's license number. It was false anyway.

CHAPTER 8

SOMEONE IN A RESTAURANT DOWN THE STREET FROM THE KILLING
had heard the screaming woman, looked outside, and dialed 03 on
the manager's phone to summon an ambulance.

The crew had thought they might have a cardiac arrest until they
saw the bullet holes in the front of the double-breasted blue blazer
and the mess of blood beneath. They called the police as they raced
toward the nearest hospital.

An hour later Inspector Vassili Lopatin of the Homicide Division
stared moodily at the corpse on the gurney in the trauma unit of the
Botkin Hospital while the night duty surgeon peeled off his rubber
gloves.

"Not a chance," said the surgeon. "A single bullet, straight
through the heart, close range. It's still in there somewhere. The
postmortem will recover it for you."

Lopatin nodded. Big deal. There were enough handguns in Moscow to reequip the army and his chances of finding the gun that fired
the bullet, let alone the owner of the hand on the gun, were about
zero and he knew it. Out on Kiselny Boulevard he had established
that the woman who apparently saw the killing had disappeared. It
seemed she had seen two killers and a car. No descriptions.

On the gurney the ginger beard jutted angrily upward above the
pale freckled body. The expression on the face was of mild surprise.
An orderly pulled a green sheet across the cadaver to blot out the

glare from the overhead lights on to the eyes that could see nothing anyway.

The body was naked now. On a side table lay the clothes and in a steel kidney dish a few personal effects. The detective walked over and took the jacket, looking at the label inside the collar. His heart sank. It was foreign.

"Can you read this?" he asked the surgeon.

The doctor peered at the embroidered tag in the jacket.

"L-a-n-d-a-u," he read slowly, then, underneath the outfitter's name, "Bond Street."

"And this?" Lopatin pointed at the shirt.

"Marks and Spencer," read the surgeon. "That's in London," he added helpfully. "I think Bond Street is, too."

There are over twenty words in Russian for human excrement and parts of the male and female genitalia. Mentally Lopatin ran through them all. A British tourist, oh God. A mugging that went wrong, and it had to be a British tourist.

He went over to the personal effects. There were few of them. No coins of course; Russian coins were long since valueless. A neatly folded white handkerchief, a small clear plastic bag, a signet ring, and a watch. He assumed the screaming woman had prevented the muggers from taking the watch off the left wrist or the ring off the pinkie finger.

But neither had any identification. Worst of all, no wallet. He went back to the clothes. The shoes had the word *Church* inside them; plain black lace-ups. The socks, dark gray, had nothing, and the words *Marks and Spencer* were repeated in the undershorts. The tie, according to the doctor, was from somewhere called Turnbull and Asser in Jermyn Street; London again, no doubt.

More in desperation than in hope, Lopatin returned to the blazer. The medical orderly had missed something. Something hard in the top pocket where some men kept their spectacles. He withdrew it, a card of hard plastic, perforated.

It was a hotel room key, not the old-fashioned type but the computer-fashioned kind. For security it bore no room number— that was the point, to prevent room thieves—but it had the logo of the National Hotel.

"Where is there a phone?" he asked.

Had it not been August Benny Svenson, the manager of the

National, would have been at home. But tourists were many and two of the staff were off with summer colds. He was working late when his own operator came through.

"It's the police, Mr. Svenson."

He depressed the "connect" switch and Lopatin came on the line.

"Yes?"

"Is that the manager?"

"Yes, Svenson here. Who is this?"

"Inspector Lopatin, Homicide, Moscow militia."

Svenson's heart sank. The man had said Homicide.

"Do you have a British tourist staying with you?"

"Of course. Several. A dozen at least. Why?"

"Do you recognize this description? One meter seventy tall, short ginger hair, ginger beard, dark blue double-breasted jacket, tie with horrible stripes."

Svenson closed his eyes and swallowed. Oh no, it could only be Mr. Jefferson. He had come across him in the lobby that very evening, waiting for a car.

"Why do you ask?"

"He's been mugged. He's at the Botkin. You know it? Up near the Hippodrome?"

"Yes, of course. But you mentioned homicide."

"I'm afraid he's dead. His wallet and all identification papers seem to have been stolen, but they left a plastic room key with your logo on it."

"Stay there, Inspector. I'll come at once."

For several minutes Benny Svenson sat at his desk consumed with horror. In twenty years in the hotel business he had never known a guest to be murdered.

His sole off-duty passion was playing bridge, and he recalled that one of his regular partners was on the staff at the British Embassy. Consulting his private address book he found the diplomat's home number and called him. It was ten to midnight and the man had been asleep, but he came awake fast when told the news.

"Good Lord, Benny, the journalist fellow? Writes for the *Telegraph*? Didn't know he was in town. But thanks anyway."

This will cause a hell of a flap, thought the diplomat when he put down the phone. Alive or dead, British citizens in trouble in foreign parts were a matter for the Consular Section of course, but he felt he should tell someone before the morning. He rang Jock Macdonald.

Moscow, June 1988

VALERI Kruglov had been back home for ten months. There was always a risk with an asset recruited abroad that he would change his mind on his return home and make no contact, destroying the codes, inks, and papers he had been given.

There was nothing the recruiting agency could do about it, short of denouncing the man, but that would be pointless and cruel, serving no advantage. It took cool nerve to work against a tyranny from the inside, and some men did not have it.

Like everyone at Langley, Monk would never entertain comparisons between those who worked against the Moscow regime and an American traitor. The latter would be betraying the entire American people and their democratically elected government. If caught, he would get humane treatment, a fair trial, and the best lawyer he could procure.

A Russian was working against a brutal despotism that represented no more than ten percent of the nation and kept the other ninety percent in subjection. If caught he would be beaten and shot without trial, or sent to a slave labor camp.

But Kruglov had kept his word. He had communicated three times via dead drops with interesting and high-level policy documents from inside the Soviet Foreign Ministry. Suitably edited to disguise the source, these enabled the State Department to know the Soviet negotiating position before they even sat at the table. Throughout 1987 and 1988 the East European satellites were moving to open revolt—Poland had already gone, Romania, Hungary, and Czechoslovakia were on the boil—and it was vital to know how Moscow would seek to handle this. To know just how weak and demoralized Moscow felt itself to be was vitally important. Kruglov revealed it.

But in May agent Delphi indicated he needed a meeting. He had something important, he wanted to see his friend Jason. Harry Gaunt was distraught.

"Yalta was bad enough. No one here slept much. You got away with it. It could have been a trap. So could this. Okay, the codes indicate he's on the level. But he could have been caught. He could have spilled the lot. And you know too much."

"Harry, there are a hundred thousand U.S. tourists visiting Moscow these days. It's not like the old times. The KGB can't monitor them all. If the cover is perfect, it's one man among a hundred thousand. You'd have to be taken red-handed.

"They're going to torture a U.S. citizen? Nowadays? The cover will be perfect. I'm cautious. I speak Russian but pretend I don't. I'm just a harmless American goofball with a tourist guide. I don't move out of role until I know there's no surveillance. Trust me."

America possesses a vast network of foundations interested in art of every kind and description. One of them was preparing a student group to visit Moscow to study various museums, with the high point as a visit to the famous Museum of Oriental Art on Obukha Street. Monk signed on as a mature student.

All the background and papers of Dr. Philip Peters were not only perfect, they were genuine, when the student group touched down at Moscow airport in mid-June. Kruglov had been advised.

The obligatory Intourist guide met them and they stayed at the awful Rossiya Hotel, about as big as Alcatraz but without the comforts. On the third day they visited the Oriental Art Museum. Monk had studied the details back home. Between the showcases it had big open spaces where he was confident he could spot it if they were there following Kruglov.

He saw his man after twenty minutes. Dutifully he followed the guide and Kruglov trailed along behind. There was no tail; he was convinced of it by the time he headed for the cafeteria.

Like most Moscow museums the Oriental Art has a large café, and cafés have lavatories. They took their coffee separately but Monk caught Kruglov's eye. If the man had been taken by the KGB and tortured into submission, there would be something in the eyes. Fear. Desperation. Warning. Kruglov's eyes crinkled with pleasure. Either he was the greatest double the world had ever seen, or he was clean. Monk rose and went to the men's room. Kruglov followed. They waited till the single hand washer left, then embraced.

"How are you, my friend?"

"I am good. I have my own apartment now. It is so wonderful to have privacy. My children can visit and I can put them up for the night."

"No one suspected anything? I mean, the money?"

"No, I had been away too long. Everyone is on the take nowadays. All senior diplomats have many things brought back from abroad. I was too naïve."

"Then things really are changing, and we are helping them change," said Monk. "Soon the dictatorship will be over and you will live free. Not long now."

Some schoolboys came in, piddled noisily, and left. The two men washed their hands until they were gone. Monk had in any case kept the water running. It was an old trick, but unless the mike was very close or the speaker raised his voice, the sound of rushing water usually worked.

They talked for ten more minutes and Kruglov handed over the package he had brought. Real documents, hard copies, taken from Foreign Minister Eduard Shevardnadze's office.

They embraced again and left separately. Monk rejoined his group and flew back with them two days later. Before he left, he dropped the package with the CIA station inside the embassy.

Back home the documents revealed the USSR was pulling back on just about every Third World foreign aid program including Cuba. The economy was cracking up and the end was in sight. The Third World could no longer be used as a lever to blackmail the West. The State Department loved it.

It was Monk's second visit to the USSR on a black mission. When he returned home it was to learn he had secured a further promotion. Also that Nikolai Turkin, agent Lysander, was moving to East Berlin as commander of the whole Directorate K operation inside the KGB complex there. It was a prime position, the only one giving access to every single Soviet agent in West Germany.

• • •

THE hotel manager and the British Head of Station arrived at the Botkin within seconds of each other and were shown into a small ward where the draped body of the dead man awaited them with Inspector Lopatin. Introductions were made. Macdonald simply said, "From the embassy."

Lopatin's first concern was a positive identification. That was not a problem. Svenson had brought the dead man's passport and the picture in it was a perfect match. He completed the formality with a glance at the face.

"Cause of death?" asked Macdonald.

"A single bullet through the heart," said Lopatin.

Macdonald examined the jacket.

"There are two bullet holes here," he remarked mildly.

They all examined the jacket again. Two bullet holes. But only one in the shirt. Lopatin had a second look at the body. Only one in the chest.

"The other bullet must have hit his wallet, and stopped there," he said. He gave a grim smile. "At least the bastards won't be able to use all those credit cards."

"I should get back to the hotel," said Svenson. He was visibly badly shaken. If only the man had taken the proffered hotel limousine. Macdonald accompanied him to the hospital door.

"This must be terrible for you," he said sympathetically. The Swede nodded. "So let us clear things up as fast as we can. I presume there will be a wife in London. The personal effects. Perhaps you could clear his room, pack his suitcase? I'll send a car for it in the morning. Thank you so much."

Back in the private ward Macdonald had a word with Lopatin.

"We have a problem here, my friend. This is a bad business. The man was quite famous in his way. A journalist. There will be publicity. His newspaper has an office in this city. They will carry a big story. So will all the other foreign press. Why not let the embassy handle that side of things? The facts are clear, are they not? A tragic mugging that went wrong. Almost certainly the muggers called on him in Russian, but he did not understand. Thinking he was resisting, they fired. Truly tragic. But that must have been the way it was, don't you think?"

Lopatin grasped at it.

"Of course, a mugging that went wrong."

"So you will seek to find the killers, though between us, as professionals, we know you will have a hard task. Leave the matter of the repatriation of the body to our consular people. Leave the British press to us also. Agreed?"

"Yes, that seems sensible."

"I will just need the personal effects. They have no bearing on the case anymore. It's the wallet that will be the key, if ever it is found. And the credit cards, if anyone attempts to use them, which I doubt."

Lopatin looked at the kidney dish with its meager array of contents.

"You'll have to sign for them," he said.

"Of course. Prepare the release form."

The hospital produced an envelope and into it were tipped one signet ring, one gold watch with crocodile strap, one folded handkerchief, and a small plastic bag with contents. Macdonald signed for them and took them back to the embassy.

What neither man knew was that the killers had carried out their instructions but made two inadvertent mistakes. They were told to remove the wallet containing all identifying documents, including ID card, the *pazport,* and to recover the tape recorder at all costs.

They did not know that the British do not have to carry ID cards on their person inside Britain and only use the full passport for foreign travel. The old-style British passport is a stiff booklet with hard blue covers that ill fits in an inside pocket, and Jefferson had left his behind with the reception clerk at the hotel. They also missed the slim plastic room key in the top pocket. The two together had provided complete identification within two hours of the killing.

The second mistake they could not be blamed for. One of the two bullets had not hit the wallet at all. It had struck the tape recorder hanging over the chest inside the jacket. The bullet destroyed the sensitive mechanism and tore the tiny tape to pieces so that it could never be replayed.

•   •   •

INSPECTOR Novikov had secured his interview with the director of staff and personnel at the party headquarters for ten o'clock on the morning of August 10. He was somewhat nervous, expecting to be treated with blank amazement and given short shrift.

Mr. Zhilin affected a three-piece dark gray suit and a precise manner, accentuated by a toothbrush moustache and rimless glasses. He gave the appearance of a bureaucrat from an earlier age, which in fact he was.

"My time is short, Inspector. Please state your business."

"Certainly, sir. I am investigating the death of a man we think may have been a criminal. A burglar. One of our witnesses believes she saw the man lurking close to these premises. Naturally, I am concerned that he might have been attempting to make an entry by night."

Zhilin smiled thinly.

"I doubt it. These are troubled times, Inspector, and the security of this building has to be very tight."

"I'm glad to hear it. Have you ever seen this man before?"

Zhilin stared at the photograph for less than a second.

"Good God, Zaitsev."

"Who?"

"Zaitsev, the old cleaner. A burglar you say? Impossible."

"Would you tell me about Zaitsev, please."

"Nothing to tell. Engaged about a year ago. Ex-army. Seemed reliable. Came every night, Monday to Friday, to clean the offices."

"But not recently?"

"No, failed to show up. After two nights I had to engage a replacement. A war widow. Very thorough."

"When would this be, when he failed to show up?"

Zhilin went to a cabinet and extracted a file. He gave the impression there was a file for everything.

"Here we are. Work sheets. He came as usual on the night of July 15. Cleaned as usual. Left as usual sometime before dawn. Failed to appear the following night, never been seen since. That witness of yours must have seen him leaving in the small hours. Quite usual. He wasn't burgling, he was cleaning."

"That explains it all," said Novikov.

"Not quite," snapped Zhilin. "You said he was a burglar."

"Two nights after he left here he was apparently involved in a break-in at a flat on Kutuzovsky Prospekt. The householder identified him. A week later he was found dead."

"Disgraceful," said Zhilin. "This crime wave is an outrage. You people should do something about it."

Novikov shrugged.

"We try. But they are many and we are few. We want to do the job, but we get no support from on high."

"That will change, Inspector, that will change." Zhilin had a messianic light in his eye. "Six months from now Mr. Komarov will be our president. Then you will see some changes made. You have read his speeches? Crackdown on crime, that is what he is always calling for. A great man. I hope we can count on your vote."

"That goes without saying. Er, do you have a private address for this cleaner?"

Zhilin scribbled it on a scrap of paper and handed it over.

The daughter was tearful but resigned. She looked at the photo and nodded. Then she glanced at the cot along the sitting room wall. At least there would be a bit more space.

Novikov left. He would tell Volsky, but there was clearly no money here for a funeral. Better let the City of Moscow take care of it. As in the flat, the problem at the mortuary was one of space.

At least Volsky could close a file. As for Homicide, the Zaitsev murder would just pile up with the other ninety-seven percent.

Langley, September 1988

THE list of the Soviet delegation members was passed to the CIA by the State Department as a matter of routine. When the Silicon Valley conference on theoretical physics was first mooted and the notion of inviting the USSR to send a delegation was made, little chance had been given of an acceptance.

But by late 1987 the Gorbachev reforms were beginning to take effect and a distinct relaxation of official attitudes in Moscow was discernible. To the surprise of the seminar organizers, Moscow agreed to send a small participant group.

The names and details had to go to Immigration, who asked State to check them out. So secretive had the USSR been about matters scientific up to that point that the names and contributions to science of only a handful of Soviet stars were known in the West.

When the list hit Langley it went to SE Division and was given to Monk. He happened to be available. His two agents in Moscow were contributing nicely through dead drops and Colonel Turkin was in East Berlin supplying a complete breakdown of KGB activities in West Germany.

Monk ran the list of the names of the eight Soviet scientists due to attend the November conference in California through the usual checks and came up with blanks. No one on the list had even been heard of by the CIA, let alone approached or recruited.

Because he was a terrier when presented with a problem, he tried one last tack. Although relations between the CIA and its domestic counterpart, the counterintelligence wing of the FBI, had always been strained and sometimes poisonous, and since the Howard affair more the latter, he decided to approach the Bureau anyway.

It was a long shot, but he knew the Bureau had a far more comprehensive list of Soviet nationals who had sought and been granted asylum in the United States than had the CIA. The long shot was not whether the FBI would help, but whether the Soviets would ever let a scientist with a relative in America leave the USSR at all. The chances were they never would, because family in the States was considered by the KGB to be a major security flaw.

Of the eight names on the list, two appeared again on the FBI record of asylum seekers. A check revealed one name was a coincidence; the family in Baltimore had nothing whatsoever to do with the arriving Russian scientist.

The other name was odd. A Russian-Jewish refugee who had sought asylum via the U.S. Embassy in Vienna when she was in a transit camp in Austria, and been granted it, had given birth while in America, yet registered her son under a different name.

Ms. Yevgenia Rozina, now of New York, had registered her son under the name of Ivan Ivanovitch Blinov. Monk knew that meant Ivan Son-of-Ivan. Clearly the boy had been born out of wedlock. The result of a union inside the States, in the transit camp in Austria, or earlier? One of the names on the list of Soviet scientists was Professor Doctor Ivan Y. Blinov. It was an unusual name, one Monk had never seen before. He took Amtrak to New York and sought out Ms. Rozina.

·   ·   ·

INSPECTOR Novikov thought he would break the good news to his colleague Volsky over a beer after work. Again, the canteen was the place; the beer was cheap.

"Guess where I spent the morning."

"In bed with a nymphomaniac ballerina."

"Chance would be a fine thing. At the headquarters of the UPF."

"What, that dunghill they keep in Fish Alley?"

"No, that's just for show. Komarov has his real HQ in a very tasty villa up near the Boulevard Ring. By the way, the beer's on you. I solved your case for you."

"Which one?"

"The old boy found in the woods out by the Minsk Highway. He was the office cleaner at the UPF headquarters, until he turned to burglary to make a bit on the side. Here are the details."

Volsky ran his eye over the single sheet Novikov had given him.

"They're not having much luck at the UPF these days," he said.

"How so?"

"Komarov's personal secretary went and drowned himself last month too."

"Suicide?"

"No. Nothing like that. Went swimming, never came out. Well, not 'never.' They fished him out last week downstream. We have a smart pathologist. Found a wedding ring with his name on the inside."

"When does this smart pathologist say he went in the water?"

"About the middle of July."

Novikov reflected. He really should have bought the beer. After all, he was due to collect a thousand sterling pounds from the Englishman. Now he could give him a bit extra. On the house.

New York, September 1988

SHE was about forty, dark, vital, and pretty. He was waiting in the lobby of her apartment house when she arrived home after picking up her son from school. The boy was a lively lad of seven.

The laughter went out of her face when he introduced himself as an officer of the Immigration Service. For any non-American-born immigrant, even with papers in perfect order, the word *Immigration* is enough to inspire worry if not fear. She had no choice but to let him in.

When her son was absorbed in his homework at the kitchen table of her small but extremely clean apartment, they talked in the living room. She was defensive and on guard.

But Monk was unlike the abrupt, unsmiling officials she had met before during her struggle to be accepted into the United States eight years earlier. He had charm and a winning smile and she began to relax.

"You know how it is with us civil servants, Ms. Rozina. Files, files, always files. If they are complete, the boss is happy. Then what happens? Nothing. They gather dust in some archive. But when they're not, the boss gets fretful. So some small cog like me is sent out to complete the details."

"What do you want to know?" she asked. "My papers are in order. I work as an economist and translator. I pay my way, I pay my taxes. I cost nothing to the U.S.A."

"We know that, ma'am. There's no question of any irregularity in your papers. You are a citizen, naturalized. Everything in order. It's just that you registered little Ivan there under a different name. Why did you do that?"

"I gave him his father's name."

"Of course. Look, this is 1988. The son of a couple who did not marry is no problem to us. But files are files. Could you just give me his father's name? Please."

"Ivan Yevdokimovich Blinov," she said.

Bingo. The name on the list. There could hardly be two such names in all Russia.

"You loved him very much, didn't you?"

A faraway look came into her eyes, as of someone gazing at a memory of long ago.

"Yes," she whispered.

"Please tell me about Ivan."

Among his several talents Jason Monk had a peculiar ability to persuade people to talk to him. Over two hours, until the boy came out with his arithmetic homework in perfect order, she told him about her son's father.

Born in Leningrad in 1938, he was the son of a university teacher of physics, his mother a schoolteacher in mathematics. By a miracle the father survived waves of Stalinist purges before the war, but died during the German blockade in 1942. The mother, with five-year-old Vanya in her arms, was rescued, escaping the starving city in a convoy of trucks across the ice of Lake Ladoga in the winter of 1942. They were resettled in a small town in the Urals, where the boy grew up, his mother devoted to the idea that he would one day be as brilliant as his father.

At eighteen he went to Moscow to seek entry into the most prestigious technical establishment of higher education in the USSR, the Physics/Technological Institute. To his surprise he was accepted. Despite his humble circumstances, the father's fame, the mother's dedication, maybe the genes, and certainly his personal efforts had tipped the balance. Behind its modest name, the institute was the forge of the most sophisticated designers of nuclear weapons.

Six years later, still a young man, Blinov was offered a job in a scientific city so secret that it was years before the West even heard of it. Arzamas-16 became for the young prodigy at once a privileged home and a prison.

By Soviet standards, conditions were luxurious. A small apartment but all his own, better shops than anywhere in the country, a higher salary, and limitless research facilities—all were his. What he did not have was the right to leave.

Once a year there was the chance for a vacation in an approved resort, at a fraction of the usual price. Then it was back inside the barbed wire, intercepted mail, tapped phones, and monitored friendships.

Before he was thirty he met and married Valya, a young librarian and teacher of English in Arzamas-16. She taught him the language, so that he could read the harvest of technical publications pouring in from the West in the original. They were happy at first, but slowly the marriage became blighted by one flaw; they desperately wanted a child but could not have one.

In the autumn of 1977 Ivan Blinov was staying in the spa resort of Kislovodsk in the northern Caucasus when he met Zhenya Rozina. As was often the case in the gilded cage, his wife had had to take her vacation at a different time.

Zhenya was twenty-nine, ten years his junior, a divorcée from Minsk, also childless; lively, irreverent, a constant listener to the "voices"—the Voice of America and the BBC—and a reader of daring magazines like *Poland,* printed in Warsaw and much more liberal and versatile than the dreary, dogmatic Soviet publications. The shuttered scientist was entranced by her.

They agreed to correspond, but as Blinov knew his mail would be intercepted (he was a holder of secrets) he asked her to write to a friend in Arzamas-16 whose mail would not be looked at.

In 1978 they met again, by agreement, this time at the resort of Sochi on the Black Sea. Blinov's marriage was at an end in all but name. Their friendship became a torrid affair. They met again for the third and last time in 1979 at Yalta and realized they were still in love, but that it was a hopeless love.

He felt he could not divorce his wife. If there had been another man after her, that would have been different. But there was not; she was not beautiful. But she had been loyal to him for fifteen years and if love had died, that was the way of things. They were still friends and he would not shame her by divorce, not in the tiny community in which they lived.

Zhenya did not disagree, but for another reason. She told him something she had not told him before. If they married it would mar his career. She was Jewish; that was enough. She had already applied to OVIR, the Department of Visas and Permissions, to emigrate to Israel. Under Brezhnev there was a new dispensation. They kissed and made love and parted, and never saw each other again.

"The rest you know," she said.

"The transit camp in Austria, the approach to our embassy?"

"Yes."

"And Ivan Ivanovitch?"

"Six weeks after the vacation in Yalta I realized I was carrying his child. Ivan was born here, he is a U.S. citizen. At least he will grow up free."

"Did you ever correspond with him, let him know?"

"To what point?" she asked bitterly. "He is married. He lives in a gilded prison, as much a prisoner as any *zek* in the camps. What could I do? Remind him of it all? Make him yearn for what he cannot reach?"

"Have you told your son about his father?"

"Yes. That he is a great man. A kind man. But far away."

"Things are changing," said Monk gently. "He could probably get as far as Moscow nowadays. I have a friend. He travels often to

Moscow. A businessman. You could write to the man in Arzamas-16 whose mail is not intercepted. Ask the father to come to Moscow."

"Why? To tell him what?"

"He should know about his son," said Monk. "Let the boy write. I will see his father gets the letter."

Before he went to bed, the small boy wrote, in good but touchingly flawed Russian, a two-page letter that began: "Dear Papa . . ."

•   •   •

GRACIE Fields returned to the embassy just before midday on August 11. He knocked on Macdonald's door to find his Head of Station deep in gloomy thought.

"Bubble?" said the older man. Fields nodded.

When they were ensconced in Conference Room A Fields tossed a photo of the dead face of an old man on the desk.

It was one of the batch taken in the woods, similar to the picture brought to the embassy by Inspector Chernov.

"You saw your man?" asked Macdonald.

"Yep. And it's pretty traumatic stuff. He was the cleaner at UPF headquarters."

"The cleaner?"

"That's right. The office cleaner. Like Chesterton's Invisible Man. There every night but no one noticed him. Came about ten each evening from Monday to Friday, cleaned the offices from end to end, left before dawn. That's why he was a shabby old thing. Lived in a slum. Earned peanuts. There's more."

Fields recounted the story of N. I. Akopov, late personal secretary of Igor Komarov, who had elected to go for an unadvised and as it turned out terminal swim in the river about the middle of July.

Macdonald arose and paced the room.

"We're supposed, in our job, to rely on facts, facts, and only facts," he said. "But let's indulge in a little supposition. Akopov left the damn document out on his desk. The old cleaner saw it, flicked through it, didn't like something he saw, and stole it. Make sense?"

"Can't fault it, Jock. Document discovered missing the next day, Akopov fired, but as he's seen it he can't be left in the land of the living. He goes swimming with two hefty lads to hold him down."

"Probably done in a water butt. Slung in the river afterward," muttered Macdonald. "Cleaner doesn't show up and the penny drops. Then the hunt is on for him. But he's already slung it into Celia Stone's car."

"Why? Jock, why her?"

"We'll never know. He must have been aware she was with the embassy. He said something about giving it to Mr. Ambassador for the beer. What bloody beer?"

"Anyway, they find him," suggested Fields. "Work him over and he tells all. Then they finish him off and dump him. How did they find Celia's apartment?"

"Followed her car, probably. From here. She wouldn't notice. Found out where she lived, bribed the guards on the gate, checked out her car. No file lying around, so they broke into her apartment. Then she walked in."

"So Komarov knows his precious file is gone," said Fields. "He knows who took it, he knows where he threw it. But he doesn't know whether anyone took any notice of it. Celia could have chucked it away. Every crank in Russia sends petitions to the high-and-mighty. They're like autumn leaves. Perhaps he doesn't know the effect it caused."

"He does now," said Macdonald.

From his pocket he produced a small tape-player, borrowed from one of the women in the typing pool who was accustomed to playing her music tapes on it. Then he took a miniature tape and slipped it in.

"What's that?" asked Fields.

"That, my friend, is the tape of the entire interview with Igor Komarov. One hour on each side."

"But I thought the killers took the tape machine."

"They did. They also managed to put a bullet through it. I found fragments of plastic and metal at the bottom of Jefferson's right-hand inner breast pocket. It wasn't the wallet they hit, it was the tape recorder. So the tape will be unplayable."

"But . . ."

"But the fussy bugger must have stopped on the street, extracted his precious interview, and put a fresh tape in. This was found in a plastic bag in his trouser pocket. I think it shows why he died. Listen."

He switched the machine on. The voice of the dead journalist filled the room.

"Mr. President, in matters of foreign affairs, particularly those concerning relations with the other republics of the USSR, how do you intend to secure the rebirth to glory of the Russian nation?"

There was a slight pause, then Kuznetsov began translating. When he had finished, there was an even longer pause and the sound of footfalls on carpet. The machine clicked off.

"Someone rose and left the room," said Macdonald.

The machine switched back on and they heard Komarov's voice give his answer. How long Jefferson had had his machine switched off they could not know. But just before the click they could hear Kuznetsov begin to say: "I am sure the President will not be . . ."

"I don't follow," said Fields.

"It's hideously simple, Gracie. I translated that Black Manifesto myself. Through the night, back at Vauxhall Cross. It was I who translated the phrase '*Vozrozhdenie vo slavu otechestva*' as 'the rebirth to glory of the motherland.' Because that's what it means.

"Marchbanks read the translation. He must have mentioned the phrase to Jefferson's editor, who used it in turn to Jefferson. He liked the imagery so he produced it back to Komarov last night. The bastard found himself listening to his own language. And I've never heard that phrase used before."

Fields reached across and replayed the passage. When Jefferson had finished, Kuznetsov translated into Russian. For "rebirth to glory" he used the Russian words *vozrozhdenie vo slavu.*

"Jesus Christ," muttered Fields. "Komarov must have thought Jefferson had seen the whole document, read it in Russian. He must have jumped to the conclusion Jefferson was one of us, come to test him out. Do you think the Black Guards did it?"

"No, I think Grishin called up a contract hit from his underworld contacts. A very quick job. If they'd had more time they'd have snatched him from the street and questioned him at leisure. They were told to silence him and get that tape back."

"So, Jock, what are you going to do now?"

"Head back to London. The gloves are off. We know and Komarov knows we know. The Chief said he wanted proof it was no forgery. Three men have now died for that satanic document. I don't know how much more bloody proof he wants."

San Jose, November 1988

SILICON Valley really is a valley, running along a line between the Santa Cruz mountains to the west and the Hamilton range to the east. It stretches from Santa Clara to Menlo Park, which were its limits in 1988. Since then it has spread. The nickname comes from an amazing concentration of between one and two thousand industries and research foundations dedicated to the highest of high technology.

The international scientific conference of November 1988 was held in the Valley's principal city, San Jose, once a small Spanish mission town, now a sprawling conurbation of gleaming towers. The eight members of the Soviet delegation were quartered in the San Jose Fairmont. Jason Monk was in the lobby when they checked in.

The basic eight were escorted by a much larger phalanx of minders. Some were from the Soviet's U.N. mission in New York, one from the consulate in San Francisco, and four had come in from Moscow. Monk sat over a cup of iced tea, tweed-jacketed, with a copy of *New Scientist* beside him, playing spot-the-hood. There were five in all, clearly protectors from the KGB.

Before coming, Monk had had a long session with a top nuclear physicist from the Lawrence Livermore Lab. The man was ecstatic at the chance of at last meeting the Soviet physicist Professor Blinov.

"You have to realize, this guy is an enigma. He really came to prominence over the past ten years," the Livermore scientist had told him. "We began to hear rumors of him on the scientific circuit about that far back. He was a star inside the USSR before then, but he wasn't allowed to publish anything abroad.

"We do know he got the Lenin prize, along with a host of awards. He must have gotten a rack of invitations to speak abroad— hell, we sent him two—but we had to send them to the Presidium of the Academy of Sciences. They always said 'forget it.' He's made major contributions and I guess he must have wanted international recognition—we're all human—so it was probably the Academy turning down the invitations. And now he's coming. He'll be lecturing on advanced particle physics, and I'll be there."

So will I, thought Monk.

He waited until after the scientist had made his speech. It was warmly applauded. In the auditorium Monk had listened to the addresses and circulated during the coffee breaks and thought they might as well all be speaking Martian. He did not understand a word.

In the lobby of the hotel he became a familiar sight with his tweed jacket, eyeglasses hanging on a cord around his neck, and a handful of scientific journals. Even the four KGB and one GRU officers had stopped studying him.

On the last night before the Soviet delegation was due to head home, Monk waited until Professor Blinov had retired to his room before knocking on the door.

"Yes?" said a voice in English.

"Room service," said Monk.

The door opened as far as the chain would allow. Professor Blinov peered out. He saw a man in a suit holding a bowl with a display of fruit topped with a pink ribbon.

"I did not order room service."

"No, sir. I am the night manager. This is with the manager's compliments."

After five days Professor Blinov was still bewildered by this strange society of limitless material consumption. The only things he recognized were the scientific discussions and the tight security. But a free bowl of fruit was a novelty. Not wishing to be discourteous he released the chain, something the KGB had told him not to do. They of all people knew about midnight knocks on the door.

Monk entered, deposited the fruit, turned, and closed the door. Alarm sprang into the scientist's eyes.

"I know who you are. Leave now or I will ring my people."

Monk smiled and dropped into Russian.

"Sure, Professor, anytime you want. But first, I have something for you. Read this first, then ring."

Bewildered, the scientist took the boy's letter and cast his eye over the first line.

"What is this nonsense?" he protested. "You force your way in here and . . ."

"Let's just talk for five minutes. Then I'll go. Very quietly. No fuss. But first, listen please."

"There is nothing you can say that I want to hear. I have been warned about you people. . . ."

"Zhenya is in New York," said Monk. The professor stopped talking and his mouth fell open. At fifty, he was gray-haired and looked older than his years. He stooped, he needed glasses to read, and now they were perched on his nose. He peered at Monk over them and slowly sat down on the bed.

"Zhenya? Here? In America?"

"After your last holiday together in Yalta, she received her permission to leave for Israel. In a transit camp in Austria she contacted our embassy and we gave her a visa to come here instead. In the camp she realized she was carrying your child. Now, read the letter, please."

The professor read slowly, in bewilderment. When he had finished, he held the two sheets of cream paper and stared at the opposite wall. He removed his glasses and rubbed his eyes. Slowly two tears welled up and trickled down his cheeks.

"I have a son," he whispered. "Dear God, I have a son."

Monk took a photograph from his pocket and held it out. The boy wore a baseball cap high on his head and a wide grin. There were freckles and a chipped tooth.

"Ivan Ivanovitch Blinov," said Monk. "He's never seen you. Just a faded photograph from Sochi. But he loves you."

"I have a son," repeated the man who could design hydrogen bombs.

"You also have a wife," murmured Monk. Blinov shook his head.

"Valya died of cancer last year."

Monk's heart sank. He was a free man. He would want to stay in the States. That was not the game plan. Blinov preempted him.

"What do you want?"

"Two years from now, we want you to accept a lecture invitation in the West and stay here. We will fly you to the States, wherever you are. Life will be very good. A senior professorship at a major university, a large house in the woods, two cars. And Zhenya and Ivan with you. Forever. They both love you very much and I think you love them."

"Two years."

"Yes, two years more at Arzamas-16. But we need to know it all. You understand?"

Blinov nodded. Before dawn he had memorized the address in

East Berlin and accepted the can of shaving foam with, somewhere in the midst of the aerosol, the small vial of invisible ink for his one single letter. There could be no question of penetrating Arzamas-16. There would have to be one meeting and handover, and a year later the escape with everything he was able to bring.

As he walked out into the lobby, a small voice inside Jason Monk said: You are a grade-A ratfink. You should have let him stay here, now. Another voice said: You are not a Family Reunification charity. You are a fucking spy. That's what you do, it's all you do. And the real Jason Monk swore that one day Ivan Yevdokimovich Blinov would live in the States with his wife and his son, and Uncle Sam would make it all up to him, every last minute of those two years.

•   •   •

THE meeting took place two days later in Sir Henry Coombs's top-floor office at Vauxhall Cross, jocularly known as the Palace of Light and Culture. The title had originated with an old warrior, long dead, called Ronnie Bloom. An Orientalist, he had once found a building of that name in Beijing. It seemed to contain very little light and not much culture, reminding him of his own headquarters at Century House. The name stuck.

Also present were the two Controllers, East and Western Hemisphere, Marchbanks as head of Russia Section, and Macdonald. It was Macdonald who reported for close to an hour, with occasional supplementary questions from his superiors.

"Well, gentlemen?" asked the chief at last. Each gave his reactions. They were unanimous. The presumption had to be made that the Black Manifesto had indeed been stolen and was the genuine blueprint for what Komarov intended to do when he came to power: create a one-party tyranny to carry out external aggression and internal genocide.

"You'll put all you have told us in written form, Jock? By nightfall please. Then I'll have to take it higher. And I think we should share with our colleagues at Langley. Sean, you'll handle that?"

The Controller Western Hemisphere nodded. The chief rose.

"Damnable business. Has to be stopped, of course. The politicians have to give us the green light to put a stop to this man."

But that was not what happened. What did occur was that just before the end of August Sir Henry Coombs was asked to visit the senior ranking civil servant of the Foreign Office in King Charles Street.

As Permanent Under-Secretary, Sir Reginald Parfitt was not only a colleague of the chief of SIS but one of the so-called Five Wise Men who, with his opposite numbers in Treasury, Defense, Cabinet Office, and Home Office, would offer their recommendation to the Prime Minister for the chief's successor. Both men went back a long way, both had a friendly relationship, and both were acutely aware that they ruled over quite different constituencies.

"This damn document your chaps brought out of Russia last month," said Parfitt.

"The Black Manifesto."

"Yes. Good title. Your idea, Henry?"

"My station chief in Moscow. Seemed pretty apposite."

"Absolutely. Black is the word. Well, we've shared it with the Americans, but no one else. And it's been as high as it can go. Our own Lord and Master"—he meant the British Foreign Secretary—"saw it before he went off to the pleasures of Tuscany for his holidays. So has the American Secretary of State. Needless to say, the revulsion has been universal."

"Are we going to react, Reggie?"

"React. Ah, yes, well now, there's the problem. Governments react officially to governments, not foreign opposition politicians. Officially, this document"—he tapped the Foreign Office copy of the manifesto on his blotter—"almost certainly does not exist, despite the fact we both know it does.

"Officially, we are hardly in possession of it, seeing as it was undoubtedly stolen. I'm afraid the received wisdom is that officially there is nothing either government can do."

"That's officially," murmured Henry Coombs. "But our government, in its no doubt infinite wisdom, employs my Service precisely in order to be able to act, should occasion require, unofficially."

"To be sure, Henry, to be sure. And no doubt you are referring to some form of covert action."

As he spoke the last two words Sir Reginald's expression indicated that some fool must have opened a window to admit the odor from a gasworks.

"Evil maniacs have been destabilized before, Reggie. Very quietly. It's what we do, you know."

"But rarely with success, Henry. And that's the problem. All our political masters on both sides of the Atlantic seem to be seized of the notion that however covert something appears to be at the time, it always seems to leak out later. To their great discomfort.

"Our American friends have their endless succession of 'gates' to keep them awake at night. Watergate, Irangate, Iraqgate. And our own people recall all those leaks, followed by commissions of inquiry and their damning reports. Backhanders in Parliament, arms to Iraq. . . . You catch my drift, Henry?"

"You mean, they haven't the balls."

"Crude but accurate as ever. You always did have a talent for the delicate phrase. I don't think either government will dream of extending trade or aid credits to this man, should he or when he comes to power. But that's it. As for an active measure, the answer is no."

The Permanent Under-Secretary escorted Coombs to the door. His twinkling blue eyes met those of the spy chief without a hint of humor.

"And Henry, that really does mean *no*."

As his chauffeur-driven car swept him back down the quays of the drowsy River Thames toward Vauxhall Cross, Sir Henry Coombs had no choice but to accept the reality of the intergovernmental decision. Once, handshakes had been enough and discretion was both presumed and maintained. For the past decade, with official leaks one of the few growth industries, only signatures were sufficient. And they had a habit of coming back to haunt the signer. No one in London or Washington was prepared to put his signature attributably to an order to its covert services for an "active measure" to prevent the onward march of Igor Alexeivich Komarov.

Vladimir, July 1989

THE American academic Dr. Philip Peters had already entered the USSR once, ostensibly to indulge his harmless passion for the study of Oriental art and old Russian antiquities. Nothing had happened, not an eyebrow had been raised.

Twelve months later even more tourists were pouring into Moscow and the controls were even more relaxed. The question before Monk was whether to use Dr. Peters again. He decided he would.

The letter from Professor Blinov was quite clear. He had secured a rich harvest covering all the scientific questions to which the United States wanted answers. This list had been prepared after intensive discussions with the highest levels of the American research establishment even before Monk had confronted the professor in his room at the San Jose Fairmont and Ivan Blinov had taken it with him. Now he was prepared to deliver. His problem was, it would be hard for him to get to Moscow. And suspicious.

But because Gorki was another city stuffed with scientific institutions, and only ninety minutes by train from Arzamas-16, he could get there. After personal protests, the KGB had lifted his habitual tail whenever he left the nuclear research zone. After all, he reasoned, he had been to California. Why not Gorki? In this he was supported by the political commissar. Without surveillance, he could take a further train to the cathedral city of Vladimir. But that was it. He would have to be home by nightfall. He named July 19 as the day and the rendezvous as the crypt of the Cathedral of the Assumption at noon.

Monk studied the city of Vladimir for two weeks. It was a medieval city famed for two magnificent cathedrals, rich in the paintings of Rublev, the fifteenth-century iconist. The bigger was the Assumption, the smaller the San Demetrius.

Langley's research department could find no tourist group heading anywhere near Vladimir on the given date. To go as a single tourist would be risky; there was protection in groups. Finally they came up with a party of enthusiasts of Old Russian ecclesiastical architecture engaging in a visit to Moscow in mid-July with a coach trip to the fabulous monastery of Zagorsk on the nineteenth. Dr. Peters joined it.

With his hair the habitual mass of tight gray curls and his guidebook to his nose, Dr. Peters toured the superb cathedrals of the Kremlin for three days. At the end of the third their Intourist guide told them to be in the lobby of their hotel at 7:30 the following morning to board the coach for Zagorsk.

At 7:15 A.M. Dr. Peters sent a note to say he had suffered a violent stomach upset and preferred to remain in bed with his medication. At 8:00 A.M. he quietly left the Metropol and walked to the Kazan Station where he boarded a train for Vladimir. Just before 11:00 A.M. he descended at the cathedral city.

As he expected from his research, there were many parties of tourists already there, for Vladimir contained no state secrets and surveillance of tourists was almost nonexistent. He bought a city guide and wandered around the Cathedral of San Demetrius admiring its walls with its 1,300 bas-reliefs of beasts, birds, flowers, griffins, saints, and prophets. At ten minutes to twelve he wandered the three hundred meters to the Cathedral of the Assumption, and, unchallenged, went down to the two vaults beneath the choir gallery and the altar. He was admiring the Rublev icons when there was a cough at his shoulder. If he has been followed, I'm dead, he thought.

"Hello, Professor, how are you?" he said calmly, not taking his eyes off the glowing paintings.

"I am well, but nervous," said Blinov.

"Aren't we all?"

"I have something for you."

"And I have something for you. A long letter from Zhenya. Another from little Ivan, with some drawings he did at school. By the way, he must have inherited your brains. His math teacher says he is way ahead of his class."

Frightened though he was, with sweat beading his forehead, the scientist beamed with pleasure.

"Follow me slowly," said Monk, "and keep looking at the icons."

He moved away, but in a manner so as to be able to observe the entire vault. A group of French tourists left, and they were alone. He gave the professor the package of letters he had brought from America, and a second list of tasks prepared by the U.S. nuclear physicists. It went inside Blinov's jacket pocket. What he had for Monk was much bulkier—a one-inch-thick sheaf of documents he had copied in Arzamas-16.

Monk did not like it, but there was nothing for it but to stuff the lot down his shirt and work the sheaf around to the back. He shook hands and smiled.

"Courage, Ivan Yevdokimovich, not long now. One more year."

The two men parted, Blinov to return to Gorki and thence back to his gilded cage, Monk to catch the return train to Moscow. He was back in bed, his consignment deposited with the U.S. Embassy, before the coach returned from Zagorsk. Everyone was very sympathetic and told him he had missed the treat of a lifetime.

On July 20, the group flew out of Moscow for New York over the Pole. That same night another jet flew into Kennedy Airport but this one came from Rome. It bore Aldrich Ames, returning after three years in Italy to resume spying for the KGB in Langley. He was already richer by two million dollars.

Before leaving Rome he had memorized and burned a nine-page letter from Moscow. Primary among its list of assignments was to discover any more agents being run by the CIA inside the USSR, with an emphasis on any KGB, GRU, senior civil servants, or scientists. There was a postscript. Concentrate on the man we know as Jason Monk.

CHAPTER 9

AUGUST IS NOT A GOOD MONTH FOR THE GENTLEMEN'S CLUBS OF St. James's, Piccadilly, and Pall Mall. It is the month of vacations, when most of the staff wish to be away with their families and half the members are at their places in the country or abroad.

Many clubs close and those members who stay on in the capital for whatever reason find they have to make do with strange surroundings; a patchwork quilt of bilateral treaties enables members of the closed clubs to wine and dine at the few that remain open.

But by the last day of the month White's was open again, and it was there that Sir Henry Coombs invited to lunch a man fifteen years his senior and one of his predecessors in the post of Chief of the Secret Intelligence Service.

At seventy-four Sir Nigel Irvine had been out of harness for fifteen years. The first ten of those he had spent as "something in the City," meaning that like others before or since he had parlayed his experience of the world, his knowledge of the corridors of power, and his natural astuteness into a series of directorships that had enabled him to put something by for his old age.

Four years before the lunch date he had finally retired to his home near Swanage on the Isle of Purbeck in the county of Dorset, where he wrote, read, walked the wild shoreline over the English Channel, and occasionally came by train to London to see old friends. Those same friends, and some much younger ones, reckoned he was still spry and active, for his mild blue eyes hid a mind as sharp as a razor.

Those who knew him best of all were aware that the old-fashioned courtesy he demonstrated to all he met dissimulated a steely will that could on occasion turn to utter ruthlessness. Henry Coombs, despite the age gap, knew him pretty well.

They both came from the tradition of Russia specialists. After Irvine's retirement the chieftaincy of SIS had fallen to two Orientalists and an Arabist in turn before Henry Coombs marked a return to one of those who had cut his teeth in the struggle against the Soviet Union. When Nigel Irvine had been the chief, Coombs had proved himself a brilliant operator in Berlin, pitting his cunning against the KGB's East German network and the East Germans' own spymaster Marcus Wolf.

Irvine was content to let the conversation remain at the level of small talk in the crowded downstairs bar, but he would have been less than human not to wonder why his former protégé had asked him to make the train journey from Dorset to a steamy London for a single lunch. It was not until they had adjourned upstairs to a window table overlooking St. James's Street that Coombs mentioned the purpose of his invitation.

"Something happening in Russia," he said.

"Rather a lot, and all of it bad, from what the newspapers tell me," said Irvine. Coombs smiled. He knew his old chief had sources far better than the morning papers.

"I won't go into it in depth," he said. "Not here, not now. Just the outline."

"Of course," said Irvine.

Coombs gave him a sketchy outline of the events of the past six weeks, in Moscow and in London. Notably in London.

"They're not going to do anything about it and that's final," he said. "Events must take their course, lamentable though they may be. That, at any rate, is how our esteemed Foreign Secretary put it to me a couple of days ago."

"I fear you much overestimate me if you think I can do anything to put some dynamism into the mandarins of King Charles Street," said Sir Nigel. "I'm old and retired. As the poets put it, all races run, all passion spent."

"I have two documents I'd like you to have a look at," said

Coombs. "One is the full report of everything that happened, so far as we can discern it, from the moment a brave if stupid old man stole a file from the desk of Komarov's personal secretary. You can judge for yourself whether our decision that the Black Manifesto is genuine is one with which you can agree."

"And the other?"

"The manifesto itself."

"Thank you for the confidence. What am I supposed to do with them?"

"Take them home, read them both, see what you think."

As the empty bowls of rice pudding laced with jam were taken away, Sir Henry Coombs ordered coffee and two glasses of the club's vintage port, a particularly fine Fonseca.

"And even if I agree with all you say, the dreadfulness of the manifesto and the probability it is true, what then?"

"I was wondering, Nigel . . . those people I believe you are going to see in America next week . . ."

"Dear me, Henry, even you are not supposed to know about that."

Coombs shrugged dismissively, but privately he was glad his hunch had worked. The Council *would* be meeting and Irvine would be part of it.

"In the time-honored phrase, my spies are everywhere."

"Then I'm heartened things haven't changed too much since my day," said Irvine. "All right, supposing I am meeting some people in America. What about it?"

"I leave it to you. Your judgment. If you think the documents should be thrown away, please burn them both to small ashes. If you think they should cross the Atlantic, your choice."

"Dear me, how very intriguing."

Coombs produced a flat sealed package from his briefcase and handed it over. Irvine placed it in his own, along with the purchases he had just made at John Lewis, some needlepoint canvases for Lady Irvine who liked to stitch cushion covers on winter evenings.

They parted in the lobby and Sir Nigel Irvine took a taxi to the station to catch his train back to Dorset.

Langley, September 1989

WHEN Aldrich Ames moved back to Washington, his nine-year career as a spy for the KGB still had an amazing four and a half years yet to run. Rolling in money, he began his new life by buying a half-million-dollar house for cash and tooling into the parking lot in a brand-new Jaguar. All this on a $50,000-a-year salary. No one noticed anything odd.

Because he had been running the Soviet desk at the Rome mission and despite the fact that Rome came under Western Europe, Ames himself had remained part of the crucial SE Division. From the KGB's point of view it was vital that he remain where with the right access he might once again look at the 301 files. But here he had a major problem. Milton Bearden had also just returned to Langley, having supervised the covert war against the Soviets in Afghanistan. The first thing he did as new head of the SE Division was try to get rid of Ames. However, in this, like others before him, he was frustrated.

Ken Mulgrew, the quintessential bureaucrat, had risen through the nonoperational side of the hierarchy to a post that put him in charge of personnel. As such, he was highly influential in staff allocations and postings. He and Ames quickly resumed their boozy friendship, with Ames able now to afford nothing but the best. It was Mulgrew who frustrated Bearden by keeping Ames inside the SE Division.

In the interim, the CIA had computerized masses of its most covert files, confiding its innermost secrets to the most insecure tool ever invented by man. In Rome Ames had made a point of educating himself to become computer literate. All he needed were the access codes to be able to tap into the 301 files without even leaving his desk. No more plastic shopping bags full of paperwork would ever be necessary. Nor would it ever be required of him to draw and sign for the most secret files.

The first slot Mulgrew managed to fix for his pal was that of European chief of the Soviet Division's External Operations Group. But External Ops only handled Soviet assets who were outside the USSR or the Soviet Bloc. These assets did *not* include Lysander, the Spartan fighter who was in East Berlin running the KGB's Directorate K; Orion, the hunter, inside the Soviet Defense Ministry in Moscow. Delphi the oracle was in the highest reaches of Moscow's Foreign Ministry, and the fourth, the one who wanted to fly the Atlantic, code-named Pegasus, was in a sealed nuclear research facility between Moscow and the Urals. When Ames used his position rapidly to check on Jason Monk, who now outranked him as a GS-15 while Ames was still stuck at GS-14, nothing came up. But the absence of any reference to Monk in External Ops did tell him one thing: anybody run by Monk was inside the USSR. Scuttlebutt and Mulgrew told him the rest.

The word around the office was that Jason Monk was the best, the last great hope in a division ruined by Ames's earlier treachery. The word also was that he was a loner, a maverick, who worked in his own way, took his own risks, and would long ago have been elbowed except for one thing: he got results in an organization that was steadily getting fewer and fewer.

Like any paper pusher, Mulgrew resented Monk. He resented his independence, his refusal to file forms in triplicate, and most of all his seeming immunity to the complaints of people like Mulgrew. Ames played upon this resentment. Of the two of them, Ames had the better head for drink. It was he who could keep thinking despite the fumes of alcohol, while Mulgrew became boastful and loose tongued.

Thus it was that one late night in September 1989, when the subject had once again come around to the loner, Mulgrew blurted out that he had heard Monk ran an agent who was "some bigwig he recruited a couple of years ago in Argentina."

There was no name and no code name. But the KGB could work out the rest. "Bigwig" would indicate a man of Second Secretary rank or up. For "a couple of years ago" they fixed on a period from eighteen months back to three years.

Checks with Foreign Ministry postings to Buenos Aires culled a list of seventeen possibles. Ames's tip that the man had not been reposted abroad cut the list to twelve.

Unlike the CIA, the KGB's counterintelligence arm had no squeamishness. It began looking at sudden access to money, an improved lifestyle, even the purchase of a small apartment . . .

•   •   •

IT was a fine day, that first of September, with a breeze off the Channel and nothing between the cliffs and the far coast of Normandy but wind-tossed white-capped waves.

Sir Nigel strode the clifftop path between Durlston Head and St. Alban's Head and drank in the salt-tanged air. It was his favorite walk, had been for years, and a tonic after smoky boardrooms or a night of studying classified documents. He found it cleared his head, concentrated the mind, blew away the irrelevant and the deliberately deceiving, brought into focus the essential core of a problem.

He had spent the night bent over the two documents given him by Henry Coombs and he had been shocked by what he read. The detective work that had been carried out since a tramp had tossed something through the door of Celia Stone's car met with his approval. It was the way he would have done it.

He recalled Jock Macdonald vaguely, a young trainee running errands at Century House. Obviously he had come a long way. And he was convinced by the conclusion: the Black Manifesto was neither forgery nor joke.

That brought him to the manifesto itself. If the Russian demagogue really intended to carry out that program, something would happen that took him back to a hideous memory from his youth.

He was eighteen when, in 1943, he had at last been accepted into the British Army and sent to Italy. Wounded in the big push on Monte Cassino, he had been invalided back to Britain and on recovery, despite pleas to rejoin a combat unit, had been posted to Military Intelligence.

It was as a lieutenant just turned twenty that he had crossed the Rhine with the Eighth Army and come across something no one of that age, or indeed of any age, should be forced to see. He was summoned by a shocked infantry major to come and look at something the infantry had found in its path. The concentration camp of Bergen-Belsen left older men than he with nightmares they would never shake off.

He turned back inland at St. Alban's Head, following the track to the hamlet of Acton where he would turn again and follow the lane to Langton Matravers. What to do? And with what chance of having any effect at all? Burn the documents now and be done with it all? Tempting, very tempting. Or take them to America and perhaps risk ridicule from the patriarchs with whom he would spend a week? Intimidating.

He unlatched the garden gate and crossed the small patch where Penny raised fruit and vegetables in summer. There was a bonfire, some cuttings smoldering away. But at the heart the embers were hot and red. So easy to stuff the two files into the fire.

Henry Coombs, he knew, would never mention the subject again; never ask what he did, nor seek any progress report. Indeed, no one would ever know whence the documents had come, for neither man would talk. It was part of the code. His wife called from the kitchen window.

"There you are. Tea's in the sitting room. I went into the village and got muffins and jam."

"Good, love muffins."

"I should know by now."

Five years his junior, Penelope Irvine had once been a raging beauty, sought after by a dozen richer men. For reasons of her own she had chosen the impecunious young intelligence officer who read poetry to her and hid behind a shy exterior a brain like a computer.

There had been a son, just the one, their only child, long gone, fallen in the Falklands in 1982. They tried not to think about it too much, except on his birthday and the date of his death.

Through thirty years of the Secret Service she had patiently waited for him while he ran his agents deep inside the USSR or waited in the bitter chill of the shadows of the Berlin Wall for some brave but frightened man to shuffle through the checkpoint to the lights of West Berlin. When he came home, the fire was always burning and there were muffins for tea. At seventy, he still thought she was beautiful and loved her very much.

He sat and munched and stared at the fire.

"You're going away again," she said quietly.

"I think I must."

"How long?"

"Oh, a few days in London to prepare, then America for a week. After that, I don't know. Probably not again."

"Well, I'll be all right. Plenty to do in the garden. You'll ring when you can?"

"Of course."

Then he said: "It mustn't happen again, you know."

"Of course not. Now finish your tea."

Langley, March 1990

IT was the CIA's Moscow Station that sounded the first alarm. Agent Delphi had switched off. Nothing since the previous December. Jason Monk sat at his desk and pored over the cable traffic as it was decrypted and brought to him. At first he was worried, later frantic.

If Kruglov was still all right, he was breaking all the rules. Why? Twice the Moscow-based CIA had made the appropriate chalk marks in the appropriate places to indicate they had filled a drop with something for Oracle and that he should service that hiding place. Twice the alerts had been ignored. Was he out of town, suddenly posted abroad?

If so, then he should have given the standard reassuring "I'm okay" sign of life. They scoured the usual magazines, looking for the agreed small ad that would constitute an "I'm okay" message or the opposite: "I'm in trouble, help me." But there was nothing.

By March it was looking as if Oracle was either completely incapacitated by heart attack, other illness, or serious accident. Or dead. Or "taken."

For Monk, with his suspicious mind, there was an unanswered question. If Kruglov had been taken and interrogated, he would have told all. To resist was futile; it simply prolonged the pain.

Therefore he would have given away the places of the drops and the coded chalk marks that alerted the CIA to the need to pick up a package of information. Why did the KGB not then use those chalk marks to catch an American diplomat in the act? It would have been the obvious thing to do. A triumph for Moscow when they really needed one, for everything else was going America's way.

The Soviet empire in Eastern Europe was coming apart. Romania had assassinated the dictator Ceaucescu; Poland was gone, Czechoslovakia and Hungary in open revolt, the Berlin Wall torn down the previous November. To catch an American in red-handed espionage in Moscow would have done something to offset the stream of humiliations the KGB was undergoing. And yet nothing.

For Monk it meant one of two things. Either Kruglov's complete disappearance was an accident that would be explained later, or the KGB was protecting a source.

. . .

THE United States is a land rich in many things, and not least of these are nongovernmental organizations, known as NGOs. There are thousands of them. They range from trusts to endowments for research into countless subjects, some of them of mind-numbing obscurity. There are centers for policy studies, think tanks, groups for the promotion of this and that, councils for the advancement of whatever, and foundations almost too numerous to list.

Some are dedicated to research, some to charity, some to discussion; others devote themselves to single-issue propaganda, lobbying, publicity, the enhancement of public awareness of this, or the abolition of the other.

Washington alone plays host to twelve hundred NGOs, and New York has a thousand more. And they all have funds. Some are funded, in part at least, by tax dollars, others by bequests from those long dead, some by private industry and commerce, others by quixotic, philanthropic, or just plain lunatic millionaires.

They provide nesting roosts for academics, politicians, ex-ambassadors, do-gooders, busybodies, and the occasional maniac. But they all have two things in common. They admit they exist and somewhere have a headquarters. All except one.

Perhaps because of its tiny and closed membership, the quality of that membership, and its utter invisibility, the Council of Lincoln that summer of 1999 was probably the most influential of all.

In a democracy power is influence. Only in the dictatorships can raw power alone exist within the law. Nonelected power in a democracy therefore lies in the ability to influence the elected machine. This may be achieved by the mobilization of public opinion, campaigns in the media, persistent lobbying, or outright financial contributions. But in its purest form such influence may simply be quiet advice to the holders of elected office from a source of unchallenged experience, integrity, and wisdom. It is called "the quiet word."

The Council of Lincoln, denying its own existence and so small as to be invisible, was a self-sustaining group dedicated to the contemplation of issues of moment, evaluation and discussion of such issues, and a final agreement on a resolution. Based upon the quality of its membership and the ability of those members to have access to the very pinnacles of elected office, the council probably had more real influence than any other NGO or a raft of them put together.

Its character was Anglo-American and its origins in that deep sense of partnership in adversity that goes back to the First World War, although the council only came into being in the early eighties as a result of a dinner in an exclusive Washington club just after the Falklands War.

Membership was by invitation only and confined to those felt by the other members to be possessed of certain qualities. Among these were long experience, utter probity, sagacity, complete discretion, and proven patriotism.

That apart, those who had served in public office had to be retired from that office so that there could be no question of special pleading, while those in the private sector could remain at the helms of their corporations. Not all members were privately rich by any means, but at least two in the private sector were estimated to be personally worth a billion dollars.

The private sector covered experience in commerce, industry, banking, finance, and science, while the public sector included statesmanship, diplomacy, and the civil service.

In the summer of 1999 there were six British members including one woman, and thirty-four Americans including five women.

By the nature of the experience of the world that they were expected to bring to the collegial discussions, they tended to be in middle to late-middle age. Few had less than sixty years experience of life and the oldest was a very fit eighty-one.

The ethos of the council was to be found in Lincoln's words, that "government of the people, by the people, for the people shall not perish from the earth." It met once a year, by agreement reached in harmless-sounding telephone calls, and in a place of great privacy.

In each case the host was one of the wealthier members, who never declined the honor. Members paid their own way to an agreed rendezvous point, after which they became the guests of their host.

In the northwestern corner of Wyoming there is a valley known simply as Jackson Hole, named after the first trapper to have the grit to overwinter there. Bordered on the west by the towering Tetons and on the east by the Gros Ventre range, the valley is sealed in the north by Yellowstone Park. To the south the mountains converge and the Snake River rushes out between them in a canyon of white water.

North of the small ski town of Jackson, Highway 191 runs clear up to Moran Junction past the airport, and then on to Yellowstone. Just beyond the airport is the village of Moose, where a smaller road branches off to take visitors up to Jenny Lake.

West of that highway, in the very foothills of the Tetons, are two lakes: Bradley Lake, served by the torrent of Garnet Canyon, and Taggart Lake, served by Avalanche Canyon. Except for trail hikers the lakes are inaccessible. On the land between the two lakes, a tract backed by the vertical wall of the South Teton, a Washington-based financier called Saul Nathanson had built a hundred-acre vacation ranch.

Its situation granted absolute privacy to the owner and any guests. The land stretched from lake to lake on each side, with the sheer mountain behind. At the front the public trails ran below the level of the ranch, which itself was on a raised plateau.

On September 7, the first guests arrived by agreement at Denver, where they were met by Nathanson's private Grumman and transported over the mountains to the Jackson airport. Far away from the terminal, they transferred to his helicopter for the five-minute lift to the ranch. The British contingent had gone through Immigration on the East Coast, so they too could bypass the terminal and change planes far from prying eyes.

There were twenty cabins at the ranch, each with two bedrooms and a communal sitting room. The weather being warm and sunny, with a chill only after sundown, many guests chose to sit on the verandahs in front of each cabin.

Food, and it was exquisite, was served in the single large lodge that formed the focal point of the complex. After meals, the tables were cleared and rearranged to permit plenum conferences.

The staff were Nathanson's own, utterly discreet and brought in for the event. For added security, private guards posing as campers surrounded the ranch on the lower slopes to turn back any stray hikers.

The 1999 conference of the Council of Lincoln lasted five days, and when it was over no one knew that the guests had come, been, and gone.

On his first afternoon, Sir Nigel Irvine unpacked, showered, changed into slacks and a twill shirt, and went to sit on the timber deck in front of the cabin he would share with a former U.S. Secretary of State.

From his vantage point he could see some of his fellow guests stretching their legs. There were pleasant walks between the clumps of fir, birch, and lodgepole pine, and a path down to the edge of each lake.

He caught sight of the former British Foreign Secretary and ex-Secretary-General of NATO Lord Carrington, a spare, birdlike figure walking with the banker Charles Price, one of the most popular and successful of American ambassadors ever to be sent to the Court of St. James's. Irvine had been SIS chief when Peter Carrington was at the Foreign Office and therefore his boss. The six-foot-four-inch Price towered over the British peer. Further over, their host Saul Nathanson sat on a bench in the sun with American investment banker and former Attorney General Elliot Richardson.

To one side Lord Armstrong, former Cabinet Secretary and head of the Home Civil Service, was knocking on the door of the cabin where Lady Thatcher was still unpacking.

Another helicopter clattered in toward the landing pad to deposit former President George Bush, who was met by ex-Secretary of State Henry Kissinger. At one of the tables close to the central lodge an aproned waitress brought a pot of tea to another former ambassador, the British Sir Nicholas Henderson, who shared his table and his tea with London financier and banker Sir Evelyn de Rothschild.

Nigel Irvine glanced at his schedule for the five-day conference. There would be nothing that night. On the next day the membership would as usual break into its three committees, geopolitical, strategic, and economic. They would meet separately for two days. The third would be dedicated to hearing the results of their deliberations and discussing them. Day four would be for plenary sessions. He had been allocated an hour, at his own request, toward the end of that day. The last day would be consigned to further action and recommendations.

In the dense forests along the slopes of the Tetons a lone bull moose, sensing the coming rut, bellowed for a mate. On white-tipped wings an osprey drifted over the Snake, mewing in anger as a bald eagle invaded his fishing ground. It was an idyllic spot, thought the old spymaster, marred only by the black evil in the document he had brought with him from a desktop in Russia.

Vienna, June 1990

THE previous December Ames's job with External Ops of the Soviet Division had been phased out. Once again he was at a loose end and as far from the 301 files as ever. Then he landed his third job since returning from Rome. It was as branch chief for Czech Operations. But it did not authorize the computer-access codes to unlock the secret heart of the 301—the section containing the descriptions of CIA assets working inside the Soviet Bloc.

Ames protested to Mulgrew. It was unreasonable, he argued. He had once headed the entire counterintelligence desk for that very section. Moreover, he needed to cross-check for CIA assets who, although Russian, had worked in Czechoslovakia in their careers. Mulgrew promised to help if he could. Finally, in May, Mulgrew gave his friend the access code. From then on, at his desk in Czech section, Ames could surf the files until he came up with "Monk—Assets."

In June 1990 Ames flew to Vienna for another meeting with his longtime handler Vlad, a.k.a. Colonel Vladimir Mechulayev. Since his return to Washington it had been deemed unsafe for him to meet any more Soviet diplomats because of the danger of FBI surveillance. So Vienna it was.

He remained sober long enough to take possession of a huge block of cash and to make Mechulayev ecstatic. He brought with him three descriptions.

One was of a colonel of the army, probably GRU, now in the

Defense Ministry in Moscow but recruited in the Middle East in late 1985. Another was of a scientist who lived in a top-security sealed city but had been recruited in California. The third was of a colonel of the KGB, recruited outside the USSR, on the books for the past six years, now inside the Soviet Bloc but not in the USSR, who spoke Spanish.

Within three days, back at the First Chief Directorate's headquarters building at Yazenevo, the hunt was on.

•   •   •

"DO you not hear her voice upon the night wind, my brothers and sisters? Do you not hear her calling to you? Can you, her children, not hear the voice of our beloved Mother Russia?

"I can hear her, my friends. I hear her sighs through the forests, I hear her sobs across the snows. Why are you doing this to me, she asks. Have I not been betrayed enough? Have I not bled enough for you? Have I not suffered enough, that you should do this to me?

"Why do you sell me like a whore into the hands of foreigners and strangers, who pick upon my aching body as carrion crows . . . ?"

The screen erected at the end of the huge communal lodge that formed the main conference center of the ranch was the largest available. The projector stood at the back of the hall.

Forty pairs of eyes were riveted upon the image of the man addressing a mass rally at Tukhovo earlier that summer as the sonorous Russian oratory rose and fell, the voice of the interpreter, dubbed onto the sound track, a subdued counterpoint.

"Yes, my brothers, yes, my sisters, we can hear her. The men of Moscow with their fur coats and their doxies cannot hear her. The foreigners and the criminal scum who feast upon her body cannot hear her. But we can hear our mother calling to us in her pain, for we are the people of the great land."

The young filmmaker Litvinov had done a brilliant job. Into the film he had inserted cutaways of moving pathos: a young blond mother, her baby at her breast, gazing adoringly upward toward the podium; a desperately handsome soldier with tears trickling down his cheeks; a seamed laborer from the land, his scythe across his shoulder, the years of hard toil bitten into his face.

None could know that the cutaway shots had been filmed separately, using actors. Not that the crowd was faked; from a high elevation other shots revealed ten thousand supporters, rank upon rank, flanked by the uniformed cheerleaders of the Young Combatants.

Igor Komarov dropped his voice from a roar to something a little above a whisper, but the microphones caught it and brought it across the stadium.

"Will no one come? Will no one step forward to say: Enough, it shall not happen. Patience, my brothers of Russia, wait a little more, daughters of the Rodina. . . ."

The voice rose again, moving up through the scales from a murmur to a cry.

"For I am coming, dear Mother, yes, I, Igor your son, am coming. . . ."

The final word was almost lost as the rally rose in unison to the prompted chant: "KO-MA-ROV, KO-MA-ROV."

The projector was switched off and the image faded. There was a pause and then a collective exhalation of breath.

As the lights went up, Nigel Irvine moved to the head of the long rectangular refectory table of Wyoming pine.

"I think you know what you have seen," he said quietly. "That was Igor Alexeivich Komarov, leader of the Union of Patriotic Forces, the party most likely to win the elections in January and project Komarov into the presidency. As you will have seen, he is an orator of rare power and passion, and clearly enormous charisma.

"You will know also that in Russia eighty percent of the real power already lies in the hands of the president. Since the time of Yeltsin the checks and curbs on that power, such as obtain in our societies, have been abolished. A Russian president today can govern more or less as he likes and bring in, by decree, any law he likes. That could well include the restoration of a one-party state."

"Seeing the state they are in at the moment, is that such a bad idea?" asked a former ambassador to the United Nations.

"Perhaps not, ma'am," said Irvine. "But I did not ask for this presentation to discuss the possible course of events after the election of Igor Komarov, but rather to present the council with what I believe to be some hard evidence as to that course, and the nature it will take. I have brought from England two reports, and here in

Wyoming, using the office copier, have run off thirty-nine copies of each."

"I wondered why I needed to bring in so much paper," said their host, Saul Nathanson, with a grin.

"I am sorry to have worn out your machine, Saul. Anyway, I did not wish to carry forty copies of each document across the Atlantic. I will not ask you to read them now, but to take a copy of each and read them in privacy. Please read the report marked 'Verification' first, and the Black Manifesto second.

"Finally, I should tell you that three men have died already because of what you are about to read tonight. Both documents are so deeply classified that I must ask they all be returned for destruction by fire before I leave this compound."

All levity had vanished by the time the members of the Council of Lincoln took their copies and retired to their rooms. To the bewilderment of the kitchen staff, no one appeared for supper. Meals were asked for and served in the cabins.

Langley, August 1990

THE news from the CIA stations inside the Soviet Bloc was bad and getting worse. By July it was clear that something had happened to Orion, the hunter. The previous week Colonel Solomin had failed to show up for a routine brush pass, something he had never failed to do before.

A brush pass is a simple device that normally compromises nobody. At a given moment, by preagreement, one of the parties walks down a street. He may be followed, he may not. Without warning he swings off the pavement and into the door of a café or restaurant. Any crowded place will do. Just before he enters, the other man has paid his bill, risen, and is walking toward the door. Without making any eye contact they brush against each other. A hand slips a package no larger than a matchbox into the side pocket of the other man. Both continue on their way, one in, the other out. If there is a tail, by the time the followers swing through the door there is nothing to see.

In addition, Orion had failed to service two dead drops despite clear chalk-mark warnings that there was something for him in them. The only inference was that he had switched off, or been switched off by someone else. Again, the emergency sign-of-life procedure had not been utilized. Whatever had happened was instant, without warning. Heart attack, auto crash, or arrest.

Moreover, from West Berlin came the news that the regular monthly letter to the East German safe house had not been received from Pegasus. Nor had anything appeared in the Russian dog breeders' magazine.

With Professor Blinov's increasing ability to travel locally inside Russia away from Arzamas-16, Monk had suggested he send a completely harmless letter once a month to a safe East Berlin postbox address. It did not even need any secret writing on it, just the signature Yuri. He could drop the letter into a box anywhere outside the sealed complex, and it would never be traced back to him even if intercepted. With the Berlin Wall in pieces, the old trick of smuggling the letter through to the West was no longer necessary.

To add to this, Blinov had been advised to purchase a mated pair of spaniels. This had been much approved of inside Arzamas-16, for what could be more harmless for the widower academic than to breed spaniels? Each month with perfect justification he could mail a small ad to the dog breeders' weekly in Moscow notifying that there were puppies for sale, weaned, newborn, or expected. The usual monthly ad had not appeared.

Monk was by now at his wit's end. He complained to the highest levels that something was wrong, but was told he was panicking too soon. He should be patient; contact would no doubt be reestablished. But he could not be patient. He began to fire off memoranda to the effect that he believed there was a leak deep inside Langley.

Two men who would have taken him seriously, Carey Jordan and Gus Hathaway, had retired. The new regime, mostly imported since the winter of 1985, were simply annoyed. In another part of the edifice the official mole hunt, dating back to the spring of 1986, crawled on.

•   •   •

"I FIND it hard to believe," said a former U.S. Attorney General, as the plenary discussion opened after breakfast.

"My problem is, I find it hard not to believe," replied ex-

Secretary of State James Baker. "This has gone to both our governments. . . . Nigel?"

"Yes."

"And they are not going to do anything?"

The remaining thirty-nine members, grouped around the conference table, were staring at the former spymaster as if seeking some
reassurance that it was just a nightmare, a figment of the dark, that
would vanish in some way.

"The received wisdom," said Irvine, "is that officially nothing
can be done. Half of what is in the Black Manifesto could well have
the agreement of a good proportion of the Russian people. The
West is not supposed to have it at all. Komarov would denounce it
as a forgery. The effect could even be to strengthen him."

There was a gloomy silence.

"May I say something?" said Saul Nathanson. "Not as your host
but as an ordinary member. Years ago, I had a son. He died in the
Gulf War."

There was a series of somber nods. Twelve of those present had
played leading roles in the creation of the multinational coalition
that had fought the Gulf War. From the far end of the table General
Colin Powell stared intently at the financier. Because of the eminence of the father, he had personally received the news that Lieutenant Tim Nathanson, USAF, had been shot down in the closing
hours of the combat.

"If there was any comfort in that loss," said Nathanson, "it was
to know that he died fighting against something truly evil."

He paused, searching for words.

"I am old enough to believe in the concept of evil. And in the
notion that evil can sometimes be embodied in a person. I was not
old enough to fight in the Second World War. I was eight when it
ended. I know some of you here were in that war. But of course, I
learned later. I believe Adolf Hitler was evil, and what he did also."

There was utter silence. Statesmen, politicians, industrialists,
bankers, financiers, diplomats, administrators are accustomed to address the practicalities of life. They realized they were listening to a
deeply personal statement. Saul Nathanson leaned forward and
tapped the Black Manifesto.

"This document is evil. The man who wrote it is evil. I do not
see how we can walk away and let it happen again."

Nothing broke the silence of the room. By "it" everyone realized he was referring to a second Holocaust, not only against the Jews of Russia but against many other ethnic minorities.

The silence was broken by the former British premier. "I agree. This is no time to go wobbly."

Ralph Brooke, head of the giant Intercontinental Telecommunications Corporation, known in every stock exchange in the world as InTelCor, leaned forward.

"Okay, so what *could* we do?" he asked.

"Diplomatically . . . apprise every NATO government and urge them to protest," said a former diplomat.

"Then Komarov would denounce the manifesto as a crude forgery, and much of Russia would believe him. There is nothing new about the xenophobia of the Russians," said another.

James Baker leaned forward to turn sideways and address Nigel Irvine.

"You brought us this appalling document," he said. "What do you advise?"

"I advocate nothing," said Irvine. "But I offer a caveat. If the council were to sanction—not to undertake but to sanction—an initiative, it would have to be something so covert that come what may nothing would or could ever attach to any reputation in this room."

Thirty-nine members of the council knew exactly what he was talking about. Each of them had been party to, or had witnessed, supposedly covert governmental operations fail, and then unravel right up to the top.

A gravelly German-accented voice came down the table from a former U.S. Secretary of State.

"Can Nigel undertake an operation that covert?"

Two voices said "Yes" in unison. When Irvine had been Chief of British Intelligence he had served both Margaret Thatcher and her Foreign Secretary Lord Carrington.

The Council of Lincoln never passed formal, written resolutions. It reached agreements, and on the basis of these each member then used his or her influence to further the purpose of those agreements within the corridors of power in their own countries.

In the matter of the Black Manifesto, the agreement was simply to delegate to a smaller committee the members' desire that the committee consider what might be for the best. The full council agreed only not to sanction, nor condemn, nor ever be aware of anything that might ensue.

Moscow, September 1990

COLONEL Anatoli Grishin sat at his desk in his office in Lefortovo jail and surveyed the three documents he had just received. His mind was a torrent of mixed emotions.

Topmost was triumph. Through the summer the counterintelligence people of both First and Second Chief Directorates had delivered him the three traitors in quick succession.

First had come the diplomat, Kruglov, exposed by a combination of his First Secretaryship at the embassy in Buenos Aires and his purchase of an apartment for twenty thousand rubles shortly after his return.

He had confessed everything without hesitation, babbling away to the panel of officers behind the table and the turning spools of the tape machine. After six weeks he had nothing left to tell and had been consigned to one of the deep cells where the temperature, even in summer, rarely rose above one degree. There he sat and shivered, awaiting his fate. That fate was contained in one of the sheets on the colonel's desk.

July had brought the professor of nuclear physics to the cells. There were few enough scientists of his ilk who had ever lectured in California and the list quickly came down to four. A search of Blinov's apartment at Arzamas-16 had revealed a small vial of invisible ink poorly concealed in a pair of rolled-up socks in a closet.

He too had confessed all and quickly, the mere sight of Grishin and his team with the tools of their trade being enough to loosen his tongue. He had even revealed the address in East Berlin to which he had written his secret letters.

The raiding of that address had been given to a colonel of Directorate K in East Berlin, but unaccountably the tenant of the address had escaped, walking through the newly open city into the West an hour before the raid.

Last, in late July, had come the Siberian soldier, finally nailed by his rank in the GRU, his posting inside the Defense Ministry, his service in Aden, and intensive surveillance during which a raid had been made on his flat to discover that one of his children, hunting for Christmas presents, had once discovered Daddy's little camera.

Pyotr Solomin had been different, resisting amazing pain and snarling defiance through the agony. Grishin had broken him eventually; he always did. It was the threat to send the wife and children to the hardest of strict-regime camps that did it.

Each of them had described how he had been approached by the smiling American, so eager to listen to their problems, so reasonable with his proposals. That caused the other emotion in Grishin's mind, sheer rage at the elusive man he now knew to be called Jason Monk.

Not once, not twice, but three times this impudent bastard had simply walked into the USSR, talked to his spies, and walked out again. Right under the KGB's noses. The more he knew about the man, the more he hated him.

Checks had been made, of course. The passenger list of the *Armenia* for that cruise had been gone through, but no pseudonym sprang to mind. The crew vaguely remembered an American from Texas who wore Texan clothes of the type described by Solomin from their meeting at the Botanical Gardens. It was probable Monk was Norman Kelson, but not proved.

In Moscow the detectives had had more luck. Every American tourist in the capital on that day had been checked via the records of visa applications and Intourist group tours. Eventually they had homed in on the Metropol and the man who had had the so-convenient stomach upset that made him miss the Zagorsk Monastery tour the same day that Monk had met Professor Blinov in Vladimir Cathedral. Dr. Philip Peters. Grishin would remember the name.

When the three traitors had confessed to the panel of interrogators the full volume of what this one American had persuaded them to hand over, the KGB officers were pale with shock.

Grishin shuffled the three papers together and made a call on his office phone. He always appreciated the final penance.

General Vladimir Kryuchkov had been elevated from head of the First Chief Directorate to chairman of the whole KGB. It was he who had placed the three death warrants on the desk of Mikhail Gorbachev that morning in the president's office on the top floor of the Central Committee building in Novaya Ploshad for signature, and he who had sent them, duly signed, to Lefortovo jail, marked "immediate."

The colonel allowed the condemned men thirty minutes in the rear courtyard to appreciate what was going to happen. Too sudden, and there was not time for anticipation, as he had often told his pupils. When he descended the three men were on their knees in the gravel of the high-walled yard where the sun never shone.

The diplomat went first. He seemed traumatized, mumbling, "*Nyet, nyet,*" as the master-sergeant placed the 9mm Makarov to the back of his head. On a nod from Grishin the man squeezed the trigger. There was a flash, a spray of blood and bone, and Valeri Yureyvitch Kruglov slammed forward onto the gravel.

The scientist, raised a committed atheist, was praying, asking Almighty God to take his soul into safekeeping. He hardly seemed to notice what had happened two yards from him, and went facedown like the diplomat.

Colonel Pyotr Solomin was last. He stared up at the sky, perhaps seeing for the last time the forests and waters, rich in game and fish, of his homeland. When he felt the cold steel at the back of his head, he pulled his left hand across his body and held it up toward Colonel Grishin by the wall. The middle finger was raised rigid.

"Fire!" shouted Grishin, and then it was over. He ordered burial that night, in unmarked graves, in the forests outside Moscow. Even in death there must be no mercy. The families would never have a spot upon which to place their flowers.

Colonel Grishin walked over to the body of the Siberian soldier, bent over it for several seconds, then straightened up and strode away.

When he returned to his office to compile his report, the red light on his phone was flashing. The caller was a colleague he knew in the Investigation Group of the Second Chief Directorate.

"We think we are closing in on the fourth one," said the man. "It's down to two. Both colonels, both in counterintelligence, both in East Berlin. We have them under surveillance. Sooner or later we'll get our break. When we do, you want to know? You want to be in on the arrest?"

"Give me twelve hours," said Grishin, "just twelve hours and I'll be there. This one I want; this one is personal."

Both the investigator and the interrogator knew a seasoned counterintelligence officer would be the hardest to crack. After years on Line K, he would know how to spot counterintelligence when directed against himself. He would leave no invisible ink in rolled-up socks, purchase no apartments.

In the old days it had been easy. If a man was suspected he was arrested and grilled until a confession was extracted or a mistake could be proved. By 1990 the authorities insisted on proof of guilt, or at least serious evidence, before the third degree was resorted to. Lysander would leave no evidence; he would have to be caught red-handed. It would need delicacy, and time.

Moreover, Berlin was an open city. The East was still technically the Soviet sector, but the Wall was down. If spooked, the guilty party could fly the coop so easily—a fast drive through the streets to the lights of the West and safety. Then it would be too late.

CHAPTER 10

THE PROJECT COMMITTEE WAS CONFINED TO FIVE. THERE WAS THE chairman of the geopolitical group, his opposite number in the strategic committee and the chairman of the economics body. Plus Saul Nathanson at his own request and Nigel Irvine. He was very much in the chair, the others his questioners.

"Let's get one thing straight at the outset," Ralph Brooke of the economic committee began, "are you contemplating an assassination of this man Komarov?"

"No."

"Why not?"

"Because these are seldom achieved and in this case, even if achieved, it would not solve the problem."

"Why couldn't it be done, Nigel?"

"I didn't say couldn't. Just extremely difficult. The man is exceptionally well guarded. His personal bodyguard and protection squad commander is no fool."

"But even if it worked, it wouldn't work?"

"No. The man would be a martyr. Another would step into his shoes and sweep the country. Probably carry out the same program, the legacy of the lost leader."

"Then, what?"

"All practicing politicians are subject to destabilization. An American word, I believe."

There were a number of rueful grins. In its day the State Department and the CIA had sought to destabilize several left-wing foreign leaders.

"What would be required?"

"A budget."

"No problem," said Saul Nathanson. "Name it."

"Thank you. Later."

"And?"

"Some technical backup. Mostly purchasable. And a man."

"What kind of man?"

"A man to go into Russia and do certain things. A very good man."

"That's your province. If, and I say if with advisement, Komarov can be discredited, his popular support culled away from him, what then, Nigel?"

"Actually," said Irvine, "that is the principal problem. Komarov is not just a charlatan. He is skillful, passionate, and charismatic. He understands and corresponds to the instincts of the Russian people. He is an icon."

"A what?"

"An icon. Not a religious painting, but a symbol. He stands for something. All nations need something, some person or symbol, to which they can cleave; which can give a disparate mass of people a sense of identity and thus of unity. Without a unifying symbol, people drift into internecine feuds. Russia is vast, with many different ethnic groups. Communism was brutal, but it provided unity. Unity by coercion. So also in Yugoslavia; when the unity by coercion was removed we saw what happened. To achieve unity by volition, there must be that symbol. You have your Old Glory, we our Crown. At the moment Igor Komarov is their icon, and only we know how savagely flawed."

"And what is his game plan?"

"Like all demagogues, he will play on their hopes, their desires, their loves, and their hates, but mostly on their fears. That way he will win their hearts. With those he will get the votes, and with the votes the power. He can then use the power to build the machine that will carry out the aims of the Black Manifesto."

"But if he is destroyed? It's back to chaos. Even civil war."

"Probably. Unless one could introduce into the equation another and a better icon. One worthy of the loyalty of the Russian people."

"There's no such man. Never has been."

"Oh, there was," said Nigel Irvine. "Once, long ago. He was called the Czar of All the Russias."

Langley, September 1990

COLONEL Turkin, agent Lysander, sent one urgent personal message to Jason Monk. It was on a postcard that showed the open terrace of the Opera Café in East Berlin. The message was simple and innocent. "Hope to see you again, all best wishes, José-Maria." It had been posted to a CIA safe mailbox in Bonn and the frank said it had been dropped into a mailbox in West Berlin.

The CIA people in Bonn did not know who had sent it; only that it was for Jason Monk and he was in Langley. They forwarded it. That it had been posted in West Berlin meant nothing. Turkin had simply flicked it, fully stamped, through the open window of a car with West Berlin plates heading back into the west. He had simply muttered, "Bitte," to the startled driver and kept on walking. By the time his tails came around the corner, they had missed it. The kindly Berliner had posted it.

Such hit-and-miss measures are not recommended, but stranger things have happened.

It was the date scrawled above the message that was odd. It was wrong. The card was posted on September 8, and a German or Spaniard would write that as: 8/9/90 with the day first, then the month, then the year. But the date on the card seemed to have been written American-style. It said 9/23/90. To Jason Monk it meant: I need a meet at 9:00 P.M. on September 23. It was meant to be read in reverse. And the sign-off with a Spanish name meant: This is serious and urgent.

The place was obvious, the terrace of the Opera Café, East Berlin.

On October 3 the final reunification of the city of Berlin was due to take place, along with the reunification of Germany. The writ of the USSR in the east would cease. The West Berlin police would move in and take over. The KGB operation would have to withdraw to a much smaller unit inside the Soviet Embassy on Unter Den Linden. Some of the huge operation would have to be withdrawn to Moscow. Turkin might be going with them. If he wanted to run, now was the time, but he had a wife and son back in Moscow. The autumn school term had just started.

There was something he wanted to say, and he wanted to say it personally to his friend. Urgently. Unlike Turkin, Monk knew of the disappearance of Delphi, Orion, and Pegasus. As the days ticked by he became sick with worry.

•   •   •

WHEN the last guest but one had left, the copies of all the documents save Sir Nigel's personal copies were burned under supervision until there were only ashes that scattered on the wind.

Irvine left with his host, grateful for the lift in the Grumman back to Washington. From the airplane's secure phone system he made a call to the D.C. area and set up a lunch with an old friend.

Then he relaxed in the deep leather chair opposite his host.

"I know we are supposed to ask no further questions," said Saul Nathanson as he poured two glasses of a very fine Chardonnay. "But could I ask you a personal one?"

"My dear chap, of course. Can't guarantee to answer it though."

"I'll fire anyway. You came to Wyoming hoping the council would sanction some kind of action, did you not?"

"Well, I suppose so. But I thought you said it all, better than I could."

"We were all shocked. Genuinely. But there were seven Jews around that table. Why *you?*"

Nigel Irvine stared down at the passing clouds beneath. Somewhere below them were the vast wheat prairies, even now being harvested. All that food. He saw again another place, far away and long ago; British Tommies puking in the sun, the bulldozer drivers with faces masked against the stench, pushing the mounds of corpses into gaping pits, living skeleton arms coming out from the stinking bunks, human claws asking mutely for food.

"Don't know really. Been through it once. Don't want to see it all again. Old-fashioned, I suppose."

Nathanson laughed.

"Old-fashioned. Okay, I'll drink to that. Will you be going into Russia yourself?"

"Oh, I don't see how it can be avoided."

"Just you take care of yourself, my friend."

"Saul, in the Service we used to have a saying. There are old agents and there are bold agents; but there are no old, bold agents. I'll take care."

• • •

AS he was staying in Georgetown, his friend had proposed a pleasant little restaurant of French ambiance called La Chaumière, barely a hundred yards from the Four Seasons Hotel.

Irvine was there first, found a bench nearby, and sat and waited, an old man with silver hair around whom the young roller bladers wove a path.

The chief of the SIS has long been a more hands-on executive than the director of the CIA, and when he used to come to Langley it was with his fellow intelligence professionals, the Deputy Directors for Ops and Intel, with whom he felt the greater empathy. They shared a common bond not always possible with the political appointee from the White House.

The cab drew up and a white-haired American of similar age climbed out and paid. Irvine crossed the street and tapped him on the shoulder.

"Long time no see. How are you, Carey?"

Carey Jordan's face broke into a grin.

"Nigel, what the hell are you doing here? And why the lunch?"

"You complaining?"

"Absolutely not. Good to see you."

"Then I'll tell you inside."

They were a little early and the lunch crowd had not arrived. The waiter asked if they wanted a smoking or nonsmoking table. Smoking, said Jordan. Irvine raised an eyebrow. Neither of them smoked.

But Jordan knew what he was doing. They were shown to a private booth right at the back where they could talk unheard.

The waiter brought the menus and a wine list. Both men chose an appetizer, then a meat course. Irvine cast his eye down the list of

Bordeaux and spotted an excellent Beychevelle. The waiter beamed; it was not cheap and had been in-house for quite some time. In minutes he was back, offered the label, got a nod, uncorked, and decanted.

"So," said Carey Jordan when they were alone. "What brings you to this neck of the woods. Nostalgia?"

"Not exactly. A problem, I suppose."

"Anything to do with those high-and-mighty folks you've been conversing with in Wyoming?"

"Ah, Carey, dear Carey, they should never have fired you."

"I know it. What's the problem?"

"There's something serious and rather bad going on in Russia."

"What else is new?"

"This is. And it's worse than usual. The official agencies of both our countries have been warned off."

"Why?"

"Official timidity, I suppose."

Jordan snorted.

"As I said, what else is new?"

"So . . . anyway . . . the view last week was that perhaps someone ought to go and have a look."

"Someone? Despite the warning?"

"That's the general idea."

"So why come to me? I'm out of it. Have been these past twelve years."

"Do you still speak to Langley?"

"No one speaks to Langley anymore."

"Then that's why you, Carey. Fact is, I need a man. Able to go into Russia. Without drawing attention."

"On the black?"

"Afraid so."

"Against the FSB?"

When Gorbachev, just before his own ouster, broke up the KGB, the First Chief Directorate was renamed the SVR but still carried on as before from its old headquarters at Yazenevo. The Second Chief Directorate, covering internal security, was renamed the FSB.

"Probably nastier than that."

Carey Jordan chewed on his whitebait, thought, then shook his head.

"No, he wouldn't go. Never again."

"Who, pray? Who wouldn't go?"

"Guy I was thinking of. Also out of it, like me. But not as old. He was good. Cool nerve, very smart, a one-off, a natural. Fired five years ago."

"He's still alive?"

"So far as I know. Hey, this wine is good. Not often I get wine like this."

Irvine topped up his glass.

"What was his name, this fellow who wouldn't go?"

"Monk. Jason Monk. Spoke Russian like a native. Best goddam agent runner I ever had."

"Okay, even though he won't go, tell me about Jason Monk."

So the old former DDO did that.

East Berlin, September 1990

IT was a warm autumn evening and the café terrace was crowded. Colonel Turkin, in a lightweight suit of German cloth and cut, attracted no attention when he took his seat at a small table close to the sidewalk at the very moment it was vacated by a loving pair of teenagers.

When the waiter cleared away the glasses, he ordered a coffee, opened a German newspaper, and began to read.

Precisely because he had spent his career in counterintelligence, with its onus on surveillance, he was deemed to be an expert in countersurveillance. The watchers from the KGB were therefore keeping their distance. But they were there: a man and a woman across the Opera Square, seated on a bench, youthful, carefree, each with a Walkman headset over their ears.

Each could communicate with two cars parked around the corner, passing their observations and receiving instructions. In the two cars were the snatch squad, for the arrest order had finally been given.

Two last pieces of information had tipped the balance against Turkin. In his description, Ames had said Lysander was recruited outside the USSR and spoke Spanish. The language alone gave the Investigation Branch the whole of Latin America plus Spain in their hunt of the records. The alternative candidate, it recently proved, had arrived on his first South American posting, to Ecuador, five years earlier. But Ames had said the recruitment of Lysander took place six years ago.

The second and clinching piece of evidence stemmed from the bright idea of checking all the phone records out of the KGB's headquarters in East Berlin the night of the abortive raid on the CIA postbox apartment, the night the flat's occupant had made his getaway one hour before the raid.

The logs revealed a call made from the public phone in the lobby to the same number as the designated apartment. The other suspect had been in Potsdam that night, and the leader of the abortive raid had been Colonel Turkin.

The formal arrest would have taken place earlier but for the fact a very senior officer was expected from Moscow. He had insisted on being present at the arrest, and personally escorting the suspect back to the USSR. Quite suddenly the suspect had left the headquarters canteen, on foot, and the watchers had no choice but to follow.

A Spanish-Moroccan shoe cleaner shuffled along the pavement by the café, gesturing to those in the front row to ask if they wished their shoes cleaned. He received a series of shakes of the head. The East Berliners were not accustomed to see itinerant shoeshine boys at their cafés, and the West Berliners among them mostly believed there were far too many immigrants from the Third World infesting their rich city.

Eventually the shoe cleaner got a nod, whipped his small stool under his backside, and squatted in front of his customer, quickly applying a thick application of black polish to the lace-up brogues. A waiter approached to shoo him away.

"Now he has started, might as well let him finish," said the customer in accented German. The waiter shrugged and moved off.

"Been a long time, Kolya," muttered the bootblack in Spanish. "How are you?"

The Russian leaned forward to point out where he wanted more polish.

"Not so good. I think there are problems."

"Tell me."

"Two months ago I had to raid an apartment here. Denounced as a CIA postbox. I managed to make one call; the man had time to run. But how did they know? Has someone been taken—talked?"

"Possibly. Why do you think so?"

"There's more, and worse. Two weeks ago, just before my post-card, an officer came through from Moscow. I know he works in Analysis. His wife is East German, they were visiting. There was a party, he got drunk. He boasted there had been arrests in Moscow. Someone in the Defense Ministry, someone in Foreign Affairs."

To Monk the news was like a kick in the face from the brogues to which he was applying a final shine.

"Someone at the table said something like: 'You must have a good source in the enemy camp.' The man tapped the side of his nose and winked."

"You must come out, Kolya. Now, this night. Come across."

"I can't leave Ludmilla and Yuri. They are in Moscow."

"Get them back here, my friend. Any excuse in the world. This is Soviet territory for ten more days. Then it becomes West German. They will not be able to travel here after that."

"You are right. Within ten days, we come across, as a family. You will take care of us?"

"I'll handle it personally. Don't delay."

He handed the bootblack a fistful of East Marks, which could be stored for ten days, then exchanged for valuable deutsche marks. The cleaner rose, nodded his thanks, collected his gear, and shuffled away.

The two watchers across the square heard a voice in their ears.

"We are complete. Arrest is on. Go, go, go."

The two gray Czech Tatras came around the corner into Opera Square and raced to the curb beside the café. From the first car three men burst onto the sidewalk, shouldered two pedestrians out of their way, and grabbed one of the café customers in the front row. The second car ejected two more men, who held the rear door open and stood guard.

There were varied cries of alarm from the customers as the customer was picked up bodily and hurled into the rear of the second car. The door slammed and it roared away on screeching tires. The snatch squad threw themselves back into the first car and followed. The whole operation lasted seven seconds.

At the end of the block Jason Monk, a hundred yards from the assault, watched helplessly.

•   •   •

"WHAT happened after Berlin?" asked Sir Nigel Irvine.

Some of the diners were picking up their credit cards and leaving to return to work or pleasure. The Englishman lifted the bottle of Beychevelle, noted there was nothing in it, and gestured to the waiter for a replacement.

"Are you trying to get me drunk, Nigel?" asked Jordan with a wry smile.

"Tut-tut. I'm afraid we're both old enough and ugly enough to take our wine like gentlemen."

"Guess so. Anyway, I'm not often offered Château Beychevelle these days."

The waiter offered the new bottle, got a nod from Sir Nigel, uncorked, and decanted.

"So, what shall we drink to?" asked Jordan. "The Great Game? Or maybe the Great Foul-Up," he added bitterly.

"No, to the old days. And to the clarity. I think that's what I miss most, what the youngsters don't have. The absolute moral clarity."

"I'll drink to that. So, Berlin. Well, Monk came back madder than a mountain lion with his ass on fire. I wasn't there, of course, but I was still talking with guys like Milt Bearden. I mean, we went back a long way. So I got the picture.

"Monk was going around the building telling anyone who would listen that the Soviet Division had a high-placed mole right inside it. Naturally, it wasn't what they wanted to hear. Write it down, they said. So he did. It was a pretty hair-raising document. It accused just about everyone of blithering incompetence.

"Milt Bearden had finally managed to squeeze Ames out of his Soviet Division. But the guy was like a leech. In the interim the director had formed a new Counterintelligence Center. Inside it was the Analysis Group and within that the USSR Branch. The branch needed a former Directorate of Operations case officer; Mulgrew proposed Ames, and by God he got it. You can guess whom Monk had to address himself to with his complaint. Aldrich Ames himself."

"That must have been a bit of a shock to the system," murmured Irvine.

"They say the devil looks after his own, Nigel. From Ames's point of view it was the best thing that he handle Monk. He could trash the report and did. In fact he went further. He counteraccused Monk of baseless scaremongering. Where was the proof for all this, he said.

"The upshot was, there was an internal inquiry. Not on the existence of a mole, but on Monk."

"A sort of court-martial?"

Carey Jordan nodded bitterly.

"Yeah, I guess so. I would have spoken for Jason, but I wasn't in very good graces myself around that time. Anyway, Ken Mulgrew chaired it. The outcome was they decided Monk had actually made up the Berlin meeting to advance a fading career."

"Nice of them."

"Very nice of them. But by then the Ops Directorate was bureaucrats wall to wall, apart from a few old warriors serving out their time. After forty years we'd finally won the Cold War; the Soviet empire was crashing down. It should have been a time of vindication, but it was all bickering and paper pushing."

"And Monk, what happened to him?"

"They nearly fired him. Instead they busted him down. Gave him some no-no slot in Records or somewhere. Buried him. Not wanted on voyage. He should have quit, taken his pension, and gone. But he was always a tenacious bastard. He stuck it out, convinced that one day he would be proved right. He sat and rotted in that job for three long years. And eventually he was."

"Proved right?"

"Of course. But too late."

Moscow, January 1991

COLONEL Anatoli Grishin left the interrogation room and withdrew to his own office in a black rage.

The panel of officers who had carried out the questioning were satisfied they had it all. There would be no more sessions of the Monakh Committee. It was all on tape, the whole story right back to a small boy falling ill in Nairobi in 1983 up to the snatch at the Opera Café the previous September.

Somehow the men from the First Chief Directorate knew that Monk had been disgraced among his own people; busted, finished. That could only mean he had no more agents. Four had been the total, but what a four they had been. Now one was left alive, but not for long, Grishin was certain.

So the Monakh Committee was over, disbanded. It had done its job. It should have been a matter for triumph. But Grishin's rage stemmed from something that had come out of the last session. One hundred yards. One hundred miserable yards. . . .

The report of the watcher team had been adamant. On his last day of freedom Nikolai Turkin had made no contact with enemy agents. He had spent the day inside the headquarters, taken his supper in the canteen, then unexpectedly walked out and been followed to a large café where he ordered coffee and had his shoes cleaned.

It was Turkin who had let it slip. The two watchers across the square had seen the shoeshine boy do his job and shuffle away. Seconds later the KGB cars, with Grishin beside the driver of the first car, had come around the corner. At that moment he had been just one hundred yards from Jason Monk himself on Soviet-ruled territory.

In the interrogation room every eye on the panel had swiveled around to stare at him. He had been in charge of the snatch, they seemed to be saying, and he had missed the biggest prize of all.

There would be pain, of course. Not as persuasion but as punishment. This he swore. Then he was overruled. General Boyarov had told him personally that the chairman of the KGB wanted a speedy execution, fearful that in these rapidly changing times it might be refused. He was taking the warrant to the president that day and it should be carried out the following morning.

And times *were* changing, with bewildering speed. From all sides his service was under accusation from scum in the newly liberated press, scum whom he knew how to deal with.

What he did not then know was that in August his own chairman, General Kryuchkov, would lead a coup d'état against Gorbachev, and it would fail. In revenge, Gorbachev would break the KGB into several fragments; and that the Soviet Union itself would finally collapse in December.

While Grishin sat in his office that day in January and brooded, General Kryuchkov laid the execution warrant for the former KGB Colonel Turkin on the president's desk. Gorbachev lifted his pen, paused, and laid it down again.

The previous August Saddam Hussein had invaded Kuwait. Now American jets were pounding the life out of Iraq. A land invasion was imminent. Various world statesmen were seeking to intercede, proposing themselves as international brokers of peace. It was a tempting role. One of them was Mikhail Gorbachev.

"I accept what this man has done, and that he deserves to die," said the president.

"It is the law," said Kryuchkov.

"Yes, but at this moment . . . I think it would be inadvisable."

He made up his mind and handed the warrant back, unsigned.

"I have the right to exercise clemency, and I do so. Seven years at hard labor."

General Kryuchkov left in a rage. This kind of degeneracy could not go on, he vowed. Sooner or later he and others of like mind would have to strike.

For Grishin the news was the last blow of a miserable day. All he could do was ensure that the slave camp to which Turkin would be sent was of a kind and of a regimen that he could never survive.

In the early 1980s the camps for political prisoners had been moved from the too-accessible Mordovia further north to the region around Perm, Grishin's own birthplace. A dozen of them were scattered round the town of Vsesvyatskoye. The best-known were the hellholes of Perm 35, Perm 36, and Perm 37.

But there was one very special camp reserved for traitors. Nizhni Tagil was a place that caused a shudder even among the KGB.

However harsh the guards were, they lived outside the camp. Their brutalities could only be sporadic and institutional: the reduction of rations, an increase of labor. To make sure the "educated" criminals lived with the real facts of life, they were mixed inside Nizhni Tagil with a cull of the most vicious and violent of all the zeks in all the camps.

Grishin ensured that Nikolai Turkin was sent to Nizhni Tagil, and under the heading "regimen" on his sentencing form, he wrote: Special—ultra strict.

•   •   •

"ANYWAY," sighed Carey Jordan, "I guess you recall the end of that unlovely saga."

"Much of it. But remind me." He raised a hand and to the hovering waiter said, "Two espressos, if you please."

"Well, in the last year, 1993, the FBI finally took over the eight-year mole hunt. They claimed later they cracked it all themselves inside eighteen months, but a lot of elimination work had already been done, though too slowly.

"To give credit, the Feds did do what we should have done. They pissed on privacy and got covert court orders to examine the banking records of the few remaining suspects. They forced the banks to come clean. And it worked. On February 21, 1994—Jesus, Nigel, will I always remember that date?—they picked him up, just a few blocks from his house in Arlington. After that it all came out."

"Did you know in advance?"

"Nope. I guess the Bureau was smart not to tell me. If I'd known then what I know now I'd have got there before them and killed him myself. I'd have gone to the chair a happy man."

The old Deputy Director Ops stared across the restaurant, but he was actually staring at a list of names and faces, all long gone.

"Forty-five operations ruined, twenty-two men betrayed—eighteen Russians and four from the satellites. Fourteen of them executed. And all because that warped little serial killer-by-proxy wanted a big house and a Jaguar."

Nigel Irvine did not want to intrude upon private grief, but he murmured, "You should have done it yourself, in-house."

"I know, I know. We all know now."

"And Monk?" asked Irvine. Carey Jordan gave a short laugh. The waiter, now wishing to clear away the last table in the empty restaurant, shimmered by waving the bill. Irvine gestured that it be placed in front of him. The waiter hovered until a credit card was placed upon it, then went off to the cash register.

"Yes, Monk. Well, he didn't know either. That day was Presidents' Day, a federal public holiday. So he stayed at home, I guess.

There was nothing on the news until the following morning. And that was when the damn letter arrived."

Washington, February 1994

THE letter came on the 22nd, the day after President's Day, when mail deliveries resumed.

It was a crisp white envelope and from the frank Monk could see it was sent from the mail room at Langley and addressed to his home, not his office.

Inside it was another envelope bearing the crest of a U.S. Embassy. On the front was typed: Mr. Jason Monk, c/o Central Mail Room, CIA Headquarters Building, Langley, Virginia. And someone had scrawled "over." Monk turned it over. On the back the same hand had written: "Delivered by hand to our embassy, Vilnius, Lithuania. Guess you know the guy?" As it bore no stamp, the inner envelope had clearly come to the States in the diplomatic pouch.

Inside this was a third envelope, of much inferior quality, with fragments of wood pulp visible in the texture. It was addressed in quaint English: "Please"—underlined three times—"pass forward to Mr. Jason Monk at CIA. From a friend."

The actual letter was inside this. It was written on paper so frail that the leaves almost fell apart at the touch. Lavatory paper? The flyleaves of an old, cheap paperback book? Could have been.

The writing was in Russian, the hand shaky, written with an uncertain point in black ink. At the top it was headed:

Nizhni Tagil, September, 1994.

DEAR FRIEND JASON,

If you ever get this, and by the time you get it, I will be dead. It is the typhoid, you see. It comes with the fleas and the lice. They are closing this camp now, breaking it up, to wipe it off the face of the earth as if it had never been, which it should not.

A dozen among the politicals have been granted an amnesty; there is someone called Yeltsin in Moscow now. One of those is my friend, a Lithuanian, a writer and intellectual. I think I can trust him. He promises me he will hide this and send it when he reaches his home.

I will have to take another train, another cattle truck, to a new place, but I will never see it. So I send you my farewell, and some news.

The letter described what had happened after the arrest in East Berlin three and a half years earlier. Turkin told of the beatings in the cell beneath Lefortovo and how he saw no point in not telling everything he knew. He described the stinking, excrement-smeared cell with the weeping walls and the endless chill, the harsh lights, the shouted questions, the blackened eyes and broken teeth if an answer was slow in coming.

He told of Colonel Anatoli Grishin. The colonel had been convinced Turkin was going to die, so he had been happy to boast of previous triumphs. Turkin was told in detail of men he had never heard of, Kruglov, Blinov, and Solomin. He was told what Grishin had done to the Siberian soldier to make him talk.

When it was over, I prayed for death as I have many times since. There have been many suicides in this camp, but somehow I always hoped that if I could hold on, I might one day be free. Not that you would recognize me, nor would Ludmilla or my boy Yuri. No hair left, no teeth, not much body and that torn by wounds and fever. I do not regret what I did, for it was a foul regime. Perhaps now there will be freedom for my people. Somewhere there is my wife, I hope she is happy. And my son Yuri who owes his life to you. Thank you for that. Good-bye, my friend.

Nikolai Ilyich

Jason Monk folded the letter, placed it on a side table, put his head in his hands, and cried like a child. He did not go in to work that day. He did not ring and explain why. He did not answer the phone. At 6:00 P.M. when it was already dark, he checked the phone book, got into his car, and drove across to Arlington.

He knocked quite politely on the door of the house he sought, and when it opened he nodded at the woman, said "Good evening, Mrs. Mulgrew," and walked on past, leaving her speechless in the doorway.

Ken Mulgrew was in the living room, his jacket off and a large glass of whiskey in one hand. He turned, saw the intruder, and said: "Hey, what the hell? You burst—"

It was the last thing he said without whistling uncomfortably for several weeks. Monk hit him. He hit him on the jaw and he hit him very hard.

Mulgrew was the bigger man, but he was out of condition and still feeling the effects of a very liquid lunch. He had been to the office that day, but no one was doing anything except discuss in traumatized whispers the news that was raging through the building like a forest fire.

Monk hit him four times in all, one for each of his lost agents. Apart from breaking his jaw, he blacked both his eyes and broke his nose. Then he walked out.

•   •   •

"SOUNDS like a bit of an active measure," suggested Nigel Irvine.

"About as active as you can get," agreed Jordan.

"What happened?"

"Well, thankfully Mrs. Mulgrew didn't call the cops, she called the agency. They sent a few guys around, just in time to find Mulgrew being shoveled into the ambulance, en route to the nearest emergency room. They calmed down the wife and she identified Monk. So the guys drove around to his place.

"He was there, and they asked him what the fuck he thought he had done and he gestured at the letter on the table. Of course, they couldn't read it, but they took it with them."

"He was busted? Monk?" asked the Englishman.

"Right. This time they busted him for good. There was a lot of sympathy, of course, when the letter was read out in translation at the hearing. They even let me speak for him, whatever good that did. But the outcome was foregone. Even in the aftermath of the Ames arrest, you couldn't have spooks with a grudge going around turning senior officers into hamburger. They fired him outright."

The waiter was back again, looking plaintive. Both men rose and headed toward the door. The relieved waiter nodded and smiled.

"What about Mulgrew?"

"Ironically, he was dismissed in disgrace a year later, when the full measure of what Ames had done was more widely known."

"And Monk?"

"He left town. He was living with a girl at the time, but she was away on a seminar and when she came back they parted. I heard Monk took his pension as a lump sum, but anyway he left Washington."

"Any idea where for?"

"Last I heard he was in your neck of the woods."

"London? Britain?"

"Not quite. One of Her Majesty's colonies."

"Dependent territories—they're not called colonies anymore. Which one?"

"Turks and Caicos Islands. You know I said he loved deep-sea fishing? Last I heard he had a boat down there, working as a charter skipper."

It was a brilliant autumn day and Georgetown was looking lovely as they stood on the sidewalk in front of La Chaumière waiting for a cab for Carey Jordan.

"You really want him to go back to Russia, Nigel?"

"That's the general idea."

"He won't go. He swore he'd never go back. I loved the lunch and the wine, but it was a waste of time. Thanks all the same, but he won't go. Not for money, not for threats, not for anything."

A cab came. They shook, Jordan climbed in and the cab drove off. Sir Nigel Irvine crossed the street to the Four Seasons. He had some phone calls to make.

CHAPTER 11

THE *FOXY LADY* WAS TIED UP AND CLOSED DOWN FOR THE NIGHT.
Jason Monk had bidden farewell to his three Italian clients who,
although they had not caught much, seemed to have enjoyed the
outing almost as much as the wine they had brought with them.

Julius was standing at the filleting table beside the dock, slicing
off the heads and removing the offal from two modest-sized dorado.
His own back pocket contained his wages for the day plus his share
of the gratuity the Italians had left behind.

Monk strolled past the Tiki Hut toward the Banana Boat, whose
open-sided plank-floored drinking and dining area was thronged
with early imbibers. He walked up to the bar and nodded to
Rocky.

"The usual?" The barman grinned.

"Why not, I'm a creature of habit."

He had been a regular for years and there was an understanding
that the Banana Boat would take calls for him while he was at sea.
Indeed its telephone number was on the cards he had placed with
all the hotels on the island of Providenciales to attract clients for a
fishing charter.

Rocky's wife, Mabel, called over:

"Grace Bay Club called."

"Uh-huh. Any message?"

"No, just call 'em back."

She pushed the telephone she kept behind her cash desk toward him. He dialed and got the operator at the reception desk. She recognized his voice.

"Hi, Jason, had a good day?"

"Not bad, Lucy. Seen worse. You called?"

"Yeah. What you doin' tomorrow?"

"You bad girl, what had you in mind?"

There was a scream of laughter from the big, jolly woman at the reception desk of the hotel three miles down the beach.

The permanent residents of the island of Provo did not constitute an enormous group, and within the community serving the tourists who made up the island's sole source of dollar income, just about everyone knew everyone, islander or settler, and the lighthearted badinage helped the time go by. The Turks and Caicos were still the Caribbean as it used to be: friendly, easygoing, and not in too much of a hurry.

"Don't you start, Jason Monk. You free for a client tomorrow?"

He thought it over. He had intended to spend the day working on the boat, a task that never ends for boat owners, but a charter was a charter and the finance company in Miami that still owned half the *Foxy Lady* never tired of repayment checks.

"Guess I am. Full day or half day?"

"Half day. Morning. Say about nine o'clock?"

"Okay. Tell the party where to find me. I'll be ready."

"It's not a group, Jason. Just one man, a Mr. Irvine. I'll tell him. Bye now."

Jason put the phone down. Single clients were unusual; normally they were two or more. Probably a husband whose wife did not want to come; that was pretty normal too. He finished his daiquiri and went back to the boat to tell Julius they would have to meet at seven to fuel up and get some fresh bait onboard.

The client who appeared at a quarter to nine the next morning was older than the usual fisherman, elderly in fact, in tan slacks, cotton shirt, and white Panama hat. He stood on the dock and called up:

"Captain Monk?"

Jason clambered down from his flying bridge and went to greet him. He was evidently English, by his accent. Julius helped him aboard.

"You tried this before, Mr. Irvine?" Jason asked.

"Actually, no. My first time. Bit of a new boy."

"Don't worry about it, sir. We'll take care of you. The sea's pretty calm, but if you find it's too much, just say."

It never ceased to surprise him how many tourists went out to sea with the presumption that the ocean would be as calm as the water inside the reef. Tourist brochures never show a whitecap wave on the Caribbean, but it can produce some seriously bumpy seas.

He eased the *Foxy Lady* out of Turtle Cove and turned half-right toward Sellar's Cut. Out beyond Northwest Point there would be wild water, probably too much for the old man, but he knew a spot off Pine Key in the other direction where the seas were easier and reports had it there were dorado running.

He ran at full cruise for forty minutes, then saw a large mat of floating weed, the sort of place where dorado, locally called dolphin, were wont to lie in the shade just below the surface.

Julius streamed four rigs and lines as the power eased off and they started to cruise around the bed of reed. It was on the third circuit that they got a strike.

One of the rods dipped violently, then the line began to scream out of the Penn Senator. The Englishman got up from beneath the awning and sedately took his place in the fighting chair. Julius handed him the rod, slotted the butt into the cup between the client's thighs, and began to haul in the other three lines.

Monk turned the nose of the *Foxy Lady* away from the reed bed, set her power just above idle, and came down to the afterdeck. The fish had stopped taking line, but the rod was well bent.

"Just haul back," said Monk gently. "Haul back until the rod is upright, then ease forward and wind in as you go."

The Englishman tried it. After ten minutes he said:

"I think this is a bit too much for me, you know. Strong things, fish."

"Okay, I'll take it if you like."

"I'd be most grateful if you would."

Monk slipped into the fighting chair as the client climbed out and returned to the shade of the awning. It was half past ten and the heat was fierce. The sun was astern and the glare came off the water like a blade.

It took ten minutes of hard pumping to bring the fish close to the transom. Then it saw the hull and made another run for freedom, taking a further thirty yards of line.

"What is it?" asked the client.

"Big bull dolphin," said Monk.

"Oh, dear, I rather like dolphins."

"Not the bottle-nosed mammal. Same name but different. Also called dorado. It's a game fish, and very good to eat."

Julius had the gaff ready and as the dorado came alongside he swung expertly and brought the forty-pounder over the edge.

"Good fish, mister," he said.

"Ah, but I think Mr. Monk's fish, not mine."

Monk climbed out of the chair, disengaged the hook from the dorado's mouth, and unclipped the steel trace from the line. Julius, about to put the catch into the stern locker, looked surprised. With the dorado on board, the routine would be to stream the four lines again, not put them away.

"Go topside and take the helm," Monk told him quietly. "Head for home, trolling speed."

Julius nodded without understanding and his lean ebony form went up the ladder to the upper control panel. Monk bent to the chilled locker, extracted two cans of beer, and popped both, offering one to his client. Then he sat on the locker and looked at the elderly Englishman in the shade.

"You don't really want to come fishing, do you, Mr. Irvine." It was not a question but a statement.

"Not my passion, actually."

"No. And it's not Mr. Irvine, is it? Something bothering me all this trip. A VIP visit at Langley, way back, by the big honcho from the British Intelligence Service."

"Quite a memory, Mr. Monk."

"The name Sir Nigel seems to ring a bell. Okay, Sir Nigel Irvine, can we please stop fooling around? What is all this about?"

"Sorry for the deception. Just wanted to have a look. And a talk. In privacy. Few places more private than the open sea."

"So . . . we're talking. What about?"

"Russia, I'm afraid."

"Uh-huh. Big country. Not my favorite. Who sent you here?"

"Oh, nobody sent me. Carey Jordan told me about you. We

lunched in Georgetown a couple of days ago. He sends his best wishes."

"Nice of him. Thank him if you see him again. But you must have noticed that he is out of it these days. Know what I mean by 'it'? Out of the game. Well, so am I. Whatever you came for, sir, it was a wasted journey."

"Ah, yes, that's what Carey said. Don't bother, he said. But I did anyway. It's a long journey. Mind if I make my pitch? Isn't that what you chaps say? Make my pitch, put my proposal?"

"That's the expression. Well, it's a hot and sunny day in paradise. You have two hours left of a four-hour charter. Talk if you wish, but the answer's still *no*."

"Have you ever heard of a man called Igor Komarov?"

"We get the papers here, a couple of days late, but we get 'em. And we listen to the radio. Personally I don't have a satellite dish, so I don't get TV. Yes, I've heard of him. The coming man, isn't he?"

"So they say. What have you heard of him?"

"He heads the right wing. Nationalist, appeals to patriotism a lot. That sort of thing. Makes a mass appeal."

"How far right-wing would you think he is?"

Monk shrugged.

"I don't know. Pretty much, I guess. About as far as some of those Deep South ultraconservative senators back home."

"A bit more than that, I'm afraid. He's so far right he's off the map."

"Well, Sir Nigel, that's terribly tragic. But right now my major concern is whether I have a charter for tomorrow and whether the wahoo are running fifteen miles off Northwest Point. The politics of the unlovely Mr. Komarov do not concern me."

"Well, they will, I fear. One day. I . . . we . . . some friends and colleagues, feel he really should be stopped. We need a man to go into Russia. Carey said you were good . . . once. Said you were the best . . . once."

"Yes, well, that was once." Monk stared at Sir Nigel for several seconds in silence. "You're saying this isn't even official. This is not government policy, yours or mine."

"Well done. Our two governments take the view there is nothing they can do. Officially."

"And you think I am going to pull anchor, cross the world, and go into Russia to tangle with this yo-yo at the behest of some group of Don Quixotes who don't even have government backing?"

He stood up, crushed the empty beer can in one fist and tossed it in the trash bucket.

"I'm sorry, Sir Nigel. You really did waste your airfare. Let's get back to the harbor. The trip's on the house."

He went back to the flying bridge, took the helm, and headed for the Cut. Ten minutes after they entered the lagoon the *Foxy Lady* was back at her slot on the quayside.

"You're wrong about the trip," said the Englishman. "I engaged you in bad faith, but you took the charter in good faith. How much is a half-day charter?"

"Three-fifty."

"With a gratuity for your young friend." Irvine peeled four hundred-dollar bills from a wad. "By the by, do you have an afternoon charter?"

"No, I don't."

"So you'll be going home?"

"Yep."

"Me too. I'm afraid at my age a short nap after lunch is called for in this heat. But while you're sitting in the shade, waiting for the heat of the day to pass, would you do something?"

"No more fishing," warned Monk.

"Oh, Lord no." The elderly man burrowed into the shoulder bag he had brought and produced a brown envelope.

"There is a file in here. It is not a joke. Just read it. No one else sees it, you do not let it out of your sight. It is more highly classified than anything Lysander or Orion or Delphi or Pegasus ever brought you."

He might as well have punched Jason Monk in the solar plexus. As the former chief ambled up the dock to find his rented buggy, Monk stood with his mouth open. Finally he shook his head, stuffed the envelope beneath his shirt, and went to the Tiki Hut for a burger.

On the northern side of the chain of six islands that make up the Caicos—West, Provo, Middle, North, East, and South—the reef is close to the shore, giving speedy access to the open sea. On the south the reef is miles away, enclosing a huge thousand-square-mile shallow called the Caicos Bank.

When he came to the islands, his money was short and prices on the north shore where the tourists went and the hotels were built were high. Monk had costed out his budget and with harbor dues, fuel, maintenance costs, a business license, and a fishing permit, there was not much left. For a small rental he was able to take a timber-frame bungalow on the less fashionable Sapodilla Bay, south of the airport and facing the glittering sheet of the bank where only boats of shallow draft could venture. That and a beat-up Chevy pickup comprised his worldly assets.

He was sitting on his deck watching the sun go down to his right when a vehicle engine coughed to a halt on the sandy track behind his house. Presently the lean figure of the elderly Englishman came around the corner. This time his white Panama was complemented by a creased alpaca tropical jacket.

"They said I'd find you here," he said cheerfully.

"Who said?"

"That nice young gal at the Banana Boat."

Mabel was well into her forties. Irvine stumped up the steps and gestured to the spare rocking chair.

"Mind if I do?"

Monk grinned.

"Be my guest. Beer?"

"Not just now, thanks."

"Make a mean daiquiri. No fruit except fresh lime."

"Ah, much more like it."

Monk prepared two straight-up lime daiquiris and brought them out. They sipped appreciatively.

"Manage to read it?"

"Yep."

"And?"

"It's sick. It's also probably a forgery."

Irvine nodded understandingly. The sun tipped the low hump of West Caicos across the bank. The shallow water glowed red.

"We thought that. Obvious deduction. But worth checking out. That's what our people in Moscow reckoned. Just a quick check."

Sir Nigel did not produce the verification report. He narrated it, stage by stage. Monk, despite himself, was interested.

"Three of them, all dead?" he said at length.

" 'Fraid so. It really does seem Mr. Komarov wants that file of his back. Not because it's a forgery. He'd never have known about it if another hand had written it. It's true. It's what he intends to do."

"And you think he can be terminated? With extreme prejudice? Taken out?"

"No, I said 'stopped.' Not the same. Terminating, to borrow your quaint CIA phraseology, would not work."

He explained why.

"But you think he can be stopped, discredited, finished as a force?"

"Yes, actually I do."

Irvine eyed him keenly, sideways.

"It never quite leaves you, does it? The lure of the hunt. You think it will, but it's always there, hiding."

Monk had been in a reverie, his mind going back many years and many miles. He jerked out of his thoughts, rose, and refilled their glasses from the pitcher.

"Nice try, Sir Nigel. Maybe you're right. Maybe he can be stopped. But not by me. You'll have to find yourself another boy."

"My patrons are not ungenerous people. There'd be a fee of course. Laborer's worthy of his hire and all that. Half a million dollars. U.S., of course. Quite a tidy sum, even in these times."

Monk contemplated a sum like that. Wipe out the debt on the *Foxy Lady,* buy the bungalow, a decent truck. And half left over shrewdly invested to produce ten percent per annum. He shook his head.

"I came out of that damn country, and I came out by the skin of my teeth. And I swore I'd never go back. It's tempting, but no."

"Ah, hum, sorry about this, but needs must. These were waiting in my keyhole back at the hotel today."

He reached into his jacket pocket and handed over two slim white envelopes. Monk eased a single sheet of formal letterhead paper out of each.

One was from the Florida finance company. It stated that due to changes in policy, extended loan facilities in certain territories were no longer deemed acceptable risks. The loan on the *Foxy Lady* should therefore be repaid in one month, failing which foreclosure and repossession would be the company's only choice. The language involved the usual weasel words, but the meaning was plain enough.

The other sheet bore the emblem of Her Majesty's Governor of the Turks and Caicos Islands. It regretted that His Excellency, who was not required to give reasons, intended to terminate the residence permit and business license of one Jason Monk, U.S. citizen, with effect from one month from the date of the letter. The writer signed himself as Mr. Monk's obedient servant.

Monk folded both letters and placed them on the table between the two rocking chairs.

"That's dirty pool," he said quietly.

"I'm afraid it is," said Nigel Irvine, staring over the water. "But that's the choice."

"Can't you find somebody else?" asked Monk.

"I don't want anybody else. I want you."

"Okay, bust me. It's been done before. I survived. I'll survive again. But I ain't going back to Russia."

Irvine sighed. He picked up the Black Manifesto.

"That's what Carey said. He told me, he won't go for money and he won't go for threats. That's what he said."

"Well, at least Carey hasn't turned into a fool in his old age." Monk rose. "I can't say it's been a pleasure, after all. But I don't think we have anything else to say to each other."

Sir Nigel Irvine rose too. He looked sad.

"Suppose not. Pity, great pity. Oh, one last thing. When Komarov comes to power, he will not be alone. By his side stands his personal bodyguard and commander of the Black Guard. When the genocide starts, he will be in charge of it all, the nation's executioner."

He held out a single photograph. Monk stared at the cold face of a man about five years older than he. The Englishman was walking up the sand track to where he had left his buggy behind the house.

"Who the hell's he?" Monk called after him. The old spymaster's voice came back through the deepening dusk.

"Oh, him. That is Colonel Anatoli Grishin."

•   •   •

PROVIDENCIALES Airport is not the world's greatest aviation terminal but it is a pleasant place to arrive and depart, being small enough to process passengers without much delay. The following day Sir Nigel Irvine had checked his single suitcase, was nodded through passport control, and sauntered into the departure area. The American Airlines plane for Miami was waiting in the sun.

Because of the heat, most of the buildings are open sided and only a chain-link fence separates them from the open tarmac beyond. Someone had wandered around the building and was standing beside the chain-link looking in. Irvine walked over. At that moment boarding was called and the passengers began to stream toward the airplane.

"All right," said Jason Monk through the wire. "When and where?"

Irvine drew an airline ticket from his breast pocket and pushed it through the wire.

"Providenciales-Miami-London. First class of course. Five days from now. Time to clear things up here. Be away about three months. If the January elections take place, we're too late. If you're on the plane at Heathrow, you'll be met."

"By you?"

"Doubt it. By someone."

"How will they know me?"

"They'll know you."

A ground crew attendant, a young woman, tugged at his jacket. "Passenger Irvine, please, boarding now."

He turned to head for the plane.

"By the way, the dollar offer still stands."

Monk produced two formal letters and held them up.

"What about these?"

"Oh, burn them, dear boy. The file wasn't forged but they were. Didn't want a chap who folds, don't you see."

He was halfway to the aircraft with the attendant trotting beside him when they heard a shout from behind.

"You, sir, are a cunning old bastard."

The woman looked up at him, startled. He smiled down.

"One does hope so," he said.

●   ●   ●

ON his return to London Sir Nigel Irvine threw himself into a week of extremely high-pressure activity.

With Jason Monk, he had liked what he had seen, and the narration of his former boss Carey Jordan had been impressive. But ten years is a long time to be out of the game.

Things were very different now. Russia had changed out of all recognition from the old USSR that Monk had briefly known and duped. Technology had changed, almost every place name had reverted from its Communist designation to its old pre-Revolutionary name. Dumped into modern Moscow without the most intensive briefing, Monk could become bewildered by the transformation. There could be no question of his contacting either the British or American embassies to seek help. These were out of bounds. Yet he would need some place to hide, some friend in need.

Other things in Russia remained much the same. The country still had its huge internal security service, the FSB, inheritor of the mantle of the KGB's old Second Chief Directorate. Anatoli Grishin might have left the service, but he would assuredly have maintained contacts within it.

Even that was not the principal hazard. Worst was the pandemic level of corruption. With virtually limitless funds, which Komarov and therefore Grishin seemed to have from the Dolgoruki mafia that underpinned their drive for power, there was no level of cooperation from the organs of state that they could not simply buy by bribery.

The plain fact was, hyperinflation had driven every employee of the central government into moonlighting for the highest bidder. Enough money could buy complete cooperation from any state security organization, or a private army of Special Forces soldiers.

Add to that Grishin's own Black Guard and the thousands of fanatical Young Combatants, plus the invisible street army of the underworld itself, and Komarov's henchman would have an army out to track down the man who had come to challenge him.

Of one thing the old spymaster was certain: Anatoli Grishin would not long be ignorant of the return of Jason Monk to his private turf, and he would not be pleased.

The first thing Irvine did was to assemble a small but trustworthy and thoroughly professional team of former soldiers from Britain's own Special Forces.

After decades fighting IRA terrorism within the United Kingdom, declared wars in the Falklands and the Gulf, a score of undeclared wars from Borneo to Oman, from Africa to Colombia, and deep-penetration missions into a dozen other "denied territories," Britain had produced a labor pool of some of the most experienced undercover men in the world.

Many of these had left the army, or whatever other service they had been with, and parlayed their strange talents into a livelihood. The natural areas in which one could find them were bodyguard work, asset protection, industrial counterespionage, and security consultancy.

Saul Nathanson, true to his word, had caused an untraceable deposit to be established in a British-owned offshore bank where banking secrecy was trustworthy. On demand, by an innocent-sounding code word in a harmless telephone call, Irvine could transfer what he needed to the London branch for immediate use. Within forty-eight hours he had six younger men at his beck and call, two of them fluent in Russian.

There was something Jordan had said that intrigued Irvine, and in pursuit of this lead one of the Russian speakers flew to Moscow with a bundle of hard currency. He would not return for two weeks, but when he did his news was encouraging.

The other five were sent on errands. One of them went to America with a letter of introduction to Ralph Brooke, chairman and president of InTelCor. The remainder went looking for the various experts in a variety of arcane areas that Irvine felt would be needed. When he had them all busy on his behalf, he addressed the problem he wished to handle personally.

During World War II, fifty-five years earlier, returning to Europe after convalescence, he had been attached to the intelligence staff of General Horrocks, commanding XXX Corps as it pushed up the Nijmegen road in Holland desperately trying to relieve the British paratroopers holding the Arnhem bridgehead.

One of the regiments in XXX Corps was the Grenadier Guards. Among its youthful officers was a certain Major Peter Carrington; another, with whom Irvine had much to do, was Major Nigel Forbes.

Upon the death of his father, Major Forbes had acceded to the hereditary title of Lord Forbes, premier lord of Scotland. After a number of calls to Scotland, Irvine finally tracked him down at the Army and Navy Club in London's Piccadilly.

"I know it's a long shot," he said when he had reintroduced himself, "but I need to conduct a little seminar. Rather private, really. Very private."

"Oh, that kind of seminar."

"Exactly. One is looking for somewhere out of the way, a bit off the beaten track, capable of hosting about a dozen people. You know the Highlands. Anywhere you can think of?"

"When would you want it?" asked the Scottish peer.

"Tomorrow."

"Ah, like that. My own place is no good, it's rather small. I long ago made over the castle to my lad. But I think he's away. Let me check."

He called back in an hour. His "lad," son and heir Malcolm, bearing the courtesy handle Master of Forbes, was in fact fifty-three that year and had confirmed he was leaving the following day for a month in the Greek islands.

"I suppose you'd better borrow his place," said Lord Forbes. "No rough stuff, mind."

"Certainly not," said Irvine. "Just lectures, slide shows, that sort of thing. Every expense will be fully covered, and more."

"All right then. I'll call Mrs. McGillivray and tell her you're coming. She'll look after you."

With that Lord Forbes put down the phone and went back to his interrupted lunch.

It was dawn on the sixth day when the British Airways overnight from Miami touched down at Heathrow's Terminal Four and decanted Jason Monk among four hundred other passengers into the world's busiest airport. Even at that hour there were thousands of passengers arriving from various points on the globe and heading for passport control. Monk had been in first class and was among the earliest to reach the barrier.

"Business or pleasure, sir?" asked the passport officer.

"Tourism," said Monk.

"Enjoy your stay."

Monk pocketed his passport and headed for the luggage carousel. There was a ten-minute wait until the bags rolled off. His own was within the first twenty. He walked through the Green Channel and was not stopped. As he emerged he glanced at the waiting crowd, many of them chauffeurs holding up cards with the names of individual passengers or companies. Nothing said "Monk."

With people coming up behind him he had to move on. Still nothing. He moved along the twin lines of barriers that formed a passageway to the main concourse and as he emerged a voice in his ear said: "Mr. Monk?"

The speaker was about thirty, in jeans and tan leather jacket. He was short-haired and looked extremely fit.

"That's me."

"Your passport, sir, if you please."

Monk produced it and the man checked his identity. He had ex-soldier written all over him, and looking at the hammer-knuckled hands holding his passport, Monk would have taken any bet the man's military career had not been spent in the paymaster's office. The passport was handed back.

"My name's Ciaran. Please follow me."

Instead of heading for a parked car, the guide took Monk's suit-case and headed for the courtesy shuttle bus. They sat in silence as the coach took them to Terminal One.

"We're not going to London?" asked Monk.

"No, sir. We're going to Scotland."

Ciaran had their tickets. An hour later the London-Aberdeen businessmen's flight took off for the Highlands. Ciaran buried himself in his own copy of the *Army Quarterly and Defence Review*. Whatever else he could do, small talk was not his forte. Monk accepted his second airline breakfast of the morning and caught up on some sleep lost across the Atlantic.

At the Aberdeen airport there was transportation, a long-base Land Rover Discovery with another taciturn ex-soldier at the wheel. He and Ciaran exchanged eight syllables, which seemed to rank as a pretty long conversation.

Monk had never seen the mountains of the Scottish Highlands, which they entered after leaving the airport on the outskirts of the east-coast city of Aberdeen. The unnamed driver took the A96 Inverness road and seven miles later pulled off to the left. The sign-post said simply: KEMNAY. They went through the village of Monymusk to hit the Aberdeen-Alford road. Three miles later the

Land Rover turned right, ran through Whitehouse, and headed for Keig.

There was a river on the right. Monk wondered if there were salmon or trout in it. Just before Keig the vehicle suddenly pulled off the road, crossed the river and went up a drive. Around two bends the stone bulk of an ancient castle sat on a slight eminence looking out over the hills. The driver turned and spoke.

"Welcome to Castle Forbes, Mr. Monk."

The spare figure of Sir Nigel Irvine, a flat cloth cap on his head, white wings of hair blowing on either side, came out of the stone porch.

"Good trip?" he asked.

"Fine."

"Tiring all the same. Ciaran will show you to your room. Have a bath and a nap. Lunch in two hours. We've a lot of work to do."

"You knew I was coming," said Monk.

"Yes."

"Ciaran made no phone call."

"Ah, yes, see what you mean. Mitch there"—he pointed at the driver unloading the suitcase—"was also at Heathrow. And on the Aberdeen plane. Right at the back. Got through Aberdeen airport before you, didn't have to wait for luggage. Reached the Land Rover with five minutes to spare."

Monk sighed. He had not spotted Mitch at Heathrow, nor on the plane. The bad news was, Irvine was right; there *was* a lot of work to do. The good news was, he was with a rather professional outfit.

"Are these guys coming where I'm going?"

"No, 'fraid not. When you get there, you'll be on your own. What we're going to do for the next three weeks is try to help you survive."

Lunch was a kind of minced lamb covered in a potato crust. His hosts called it shepherd's pie and soaked it all in a spicy black sauce. There were five at the table: Sir Nigel Irvine, the genial host, Monk himself, Ciaran and Mitch, who always referred to both Monk and Irvine as "Boss," and a short alert man with thin white hair who spoke good English but with an accent Monk recognized as Russian.

"There will have to be some English spoken, of course," said Irvine, "because not many of us speak Russian. But for four hours a day, minimum, you will be speaking Russian with Oleg here. You have to get back to the point where you can actually pass for one."

Monk nodded. It had been years since he had spoken the language and he was going to discover how rusty he had become. But a natural linguist never forgets and enough practice will always bring it back.

"So," his host continued, "Oleg, Ciaran, and Mitch here will be permanent residents. Others will come and go. That includes myself. In a few days, when you're settled, I'll have to fly south and get on with . . . other things."

If Monk had thought some consideration might be given to jet lag, he was mistaken. After lunch he had four hours with Oleg.

The Russian invented a range of scenarios. One minute he was a militiaman on the street, stopping Monk to challenge his papers, demand where he had come from, where he was going and why. Then he would become a waiter, seeking details of a complicated meal order, an out-of-town Russian asking directions of a Muscovite. Even after four hours Monk could feel the sense of the language coming back.

Hauling on fishing lines in the Caribbean, Monk had reckoned he was pretty fit, despite a thickening of the waistline. He was wrong. Before dawn the next morning he had his first cross-country run with Ciaran and Mitch.

"We'll start with an easy one, Boss," said Mitch, so they only did five miles through thigh-deep heather. At first Monk thought he was going to die. Then he wished he would.

There were only two staff on duty. The housekeeper, the formidable Mrs. McGillivray, widow of an estate worker, cooked and cleaned, accepting with a disapproving sniff the series of experts coming and going with their English accents. Hector looked after the grounds and the vegetable garden, motoring into Whitehouse for groceries. No tradesman ever called. Mrs. McGee, as the men called her, and Hector lived in two small cottages in the grounds.

A photographer came and took a range of pictures of Monk for the various identification papers being prepared for him somewhere else. A hair stylist cum makeup man appeared, skillfully changing Monk's appearance and showing him how to do so again with minimum materials and nothing that could not be easily bought or carried in luggage without anyone suspecting the true use of the item.

When his appearance had been changed, the photographer took more pictures for yet another *pazport*. From somewhere Irvine had obtained the real things and the services of an engraving artist and calligrapher to alter them to the new identity.

Monk spent hours with a huge map of Moscow, memorizing the city and its hundreds of new names—new to him, anyway. Maurice Thorez Quay, named after the dead French Communist leader, had reverted to its old name of Sofia Quay. All references to Marx, Engels, Lenin, Dzerzhinski, and the other Communist notables of their day had vanished.

He memorized the hundred most prominent buildings and their locations, how to use the new telephone system, and how to hail an instant taxi by waving down any driver anytime anywhere and offering him a dollar.

There was a screening room, where he sat for hours with a man from London, another Russian speaker but an Englishman, looking at faces, faces, and more faces.

There were books to read, Komarov's speeches, Russian newspapers and magazines. Worst of all, there were private telephone numbers to memorize, figure perfect, until he had fifty of them stored away in his head. Figures had never been his forte.

Sir Nigel Irvine returned in the second week. He appeared tired but satisfied. He did not say where he had been. He brought something one of his team had purchased after scouring the antiques shops of London. Monk turned it over in his hands.

"How the hell did you know about this?" he asked.

"Never mind. My ears are long. Is it the same?"

"Identical. So far as I recall."

"Well, it should work then."

He also brought a suitcase, created by a skilled craftsman. It would take an ace customs inspector to discern the inner compartment where Monk would conceal two files: the Black Manifesto in its original Russian, and the verification report that authenticated the manifesto, now translated into Russian.

By the second week Jason Monk was feeling fitter than he had in ten years. His muscles were hard and his stamina was improved, though he knew he would never match Ciaran and Mitch, who could march on hour after hour, through the barriers of pain and exhaustion into that limbo near death where only the will keeps the body moving.

Halfway through that week, George Sims arrived. He was about the same age as Monk and a former Warrant Officer (One) of the SAS Regiment. The following morning he took Monk out onto the lawn. Both men were dressed in track suits. He turned and addressed Monk from four yards.

"Now, sir," he said in a lilting Scottish accent, "I would be most grateful if you would try and kill me."

Monk raised an eyebrow.

"But dinna fash yoursel, for you'll not succeed."

He was right. Monk approached, feinted, and then lunged. The Highlands turned upside down and he found himself on his back.

"A wee bit slow to block me there," said Sims.

Hector was in the kitchen depositing some fresh-dug carrots for lunch when Monk, upside down again, went past the window.

"What on earth are they doing?" he asked.

"Away with you," said Mrs. McGee. "It's just the young laird's gentlemen friends enjoying themselves."

Out in the woods, Sims introduced Monk to the Swiss-made Sig Sauer 9mm automatic.

"Thought you guys used the Browning thirteen-shot," said Monk, hoping to demonstrate his inside knowledge.

"Used to, but that was years ago. Changed to this over ten years back. Now, you know the two-handed hold and the crouch, sir?"

Monk had had small arms training back at the Farm, Fort Peary in Virginia, when he was a trainee with the CIA. He had been at the top of his class, the inheritance of hunting with his dad in the Blue Ridge Mountains as a boy. But that too was a long time back.

The Scot set up a target of a crouching man, walked fifteen paces, turned, and blew five holes in the heart. Monk took off the crouching figure's left ear and creased his thigh. They used a hundred rounds twice a day for three days until finally Monk could put three out of five rounds into the face.

"That usually slows them up," admitted Sims, in the tone of one who knew he would not get anything better.

"With luck I'll never have to use one of these damn things," said Monk.

"Aye, sir, that's what they all say. Then the luck runs out. Best to know how, if you have to."

At the start of the third week Monk was introduced to his communicator. A surprisingly young man called Danny came up from London.

"It's a perfectly ordinary laptop computer," he explained. And it was. No larger than a normal book, the top when raised revealed a screen on its underside, and the keypad, whose two halves could be lifted up, spread apart, and relocked to become a full-sized typewriter-style keyboard. It was the sort of thing eight executives out of ten now carried in their attaché cases.

"The floppy disk"—Danny held up what looked like a credit card and waved it under Monk's nose before inserting it into the side of the laptop—"carries the normal range of information needed by a businessman of the kind that you will be. If anyone interferes with it, all they will get is commercial information of zero interest to anyone but the owner."

"So?" asked Monk. He realized this disarmingly young man was one of those born long after his time who had been weaned on computers and found their inner workings much easier than Egyptian hieroglyphics. Monk would have picked the Egyptians any day.

"Now this," said Danny, holding up another card, "is what?"

"It's a Visa card," said Monk.

"Look again."

Monk examined the thin sheet of plastic with its "smart" magnetic strip along the back.

"Okay, it looks like a Visa card."

"It will even act as a Visa card," said Danny, "but don't use it as such. Just in case some piece of duff technology wipes it by mistake. Keep it safe, wherever you live, preferably hidden from prying eyes, and use it only when necessary."

"What does it do?" asked Monk.

"A lot. It encodes anything you want to type. It has memorized a hundred one-time pads, whatever they may be. That's not my field, but I gather they are unbreakable."

"They are," said Monk, glad to hear at least one phrase he recognized. It made him feel better.

Danny ejected the original floppy disk and inserted the Visa card in its place.

"Now, the laptop is powered by a lithium-ion battery with enough power to reach the satellite. Even if you have a regular circuit available, use the battery in case of a drop or surge in the domestic current. Use the circuit to recharge the battery. Now, switch it on."

He pointed to the power/off switch and Monk did so.

"Type your message to Sir Nigel onto the screen, in clear language."

Monk typed a twenty-word message to confirm safe arrival and first contact made.

"Now touch this key here. It says something different, but it gives the order to encode."

Monk touched the key. Nothing happened. His words stayed on the screen.

"Now touch power/off."

The words vanished.

"They have vanished forever," said Danny. "They have been completely erased from the computer's memory. In the code of a one-time pad, they are inside Virgil the Visa, waiting to be transmitted. Now switch the laptop back on again."

Monk did so. The screen illuminated but remained blank.

"Touch this one. It says something else, but when Virgil is inserted it means 'transmit/receive.' Now you just leave it on. Twice a day a satellite will swing over the horizon. As it approaches the place you are in, it is programmed to beam a message downward. The down call is on the same frequency as Virgil, but it takes a nanosecond and it's in code. What it is saying is, Are you there, baby? Virgil hears this call, identifies Mother, acknowledges, and transmits your message. We call it handshaking."

"That's it?"

"Not quite. If Mother has a message for Virgil, *she* will transmit. Virgil will receive it, all in the one-time pad code. Then Mother passes over the horizon and vanishes. She will already have passed on your message to the receiving base, wherever that may be. I don't know and I don't need to know."

"Do I have to stay with the machine while it does all this?" asked Monk.

"Certainly not. You can be out and about. When you come back, you find the screen still glowing. Just touch this button. It doesn't say 'decrypt' but that's what it does if Virgil is inside there. What Virgil will do is decode your message from home. Learn it, hit power/off, and you erase it. Forever.

"Now, one last thing. If you really want to blow Virgil's little brain to pieces, you hit these four numbers in sequence." He showed Monk the four, written on a slip of card. "So never punch in those four numbers unless you want to return Virgil to just a Visa card with no other function."

They spent two days going through the procedures over and over again, until Monk was touch perfect. Then Danny left, for whatever world of silicon chips he dwelt in.

By the end of the third week at Castle Forbes, all the instructors pronounced themselves satisfied. Monk saw them leave.

"Is there a phone I could use?" Monk asked that evening as he, Ciaran, and Mitch sat in the drawing room after supper.

Mitch looked up from the chessboard where he was being trounced by Ciaran and nodded toward the telephone in the corner.

"A private one," said Monk.

Ciaran also raised his head, and both former soldiers looked at him.

"Sure," said Ciaran, "use the one in the study."

Monk sat among the books and hunting prints in Lord Forbes's private den and dialed an overseas number. It rang in a small frame house in Crozet, south-central Virginia, where the sun was low over the Blue Ridge Mountains, five hours behind Scotland. Someone answered at the tenth ring and a woman's voice said, "Hello?"

He could imagine the small but cozy living room where a log fire would burn through the winter and the light always gleamed from the surfaces of her cherished, highly polished wedding furniture.

"Hi, Mom, it's Jason."

The frail voice rose with pleasure.

"Jason. Where are you, son?"

"I've been traveling, Mom. How's Dad?"

Since the stroke his father had spent much of his time in his rocking chair out on the stoop, staring at the small town and the forested mountains beyond where, forty years earlier and able to trek all day, he had taken his firstborn son hunting and fishing.

"He's fine. He's dozing on the porch right now. It's hot. It's been a long, hot summer. I'll tell him you called. He'll be pleased. Will you be coming to visit soon? It's been so long."

There were two brothers and a sister, long gone from the small home, one brother an insurance adjuster, the other a real estate broker along the Chesapeake, his sister married to a country doctor and raising a family. All in Virginia. They visited frequently. He was the absent one.

"Soon as I can make it, Mom. That's a promise."

"You're going away again, aren't you son?"

He knew what she meant by "away." She had known about Vietnam before he got word he was shipping out and used to call him in Washington before the foreign journeys as if she sensed something she could not possibly know. Something about mothers . . . three thousand miles and she could sense the danger.

"I'll be back. Then I'll come visit."

"Take care of yourself, Jason."

He held the phone and stared through the windows at the stars over Scotland. He should have gone home more often. They were both old now. He should have made the time. If he came back from Russia he would make the time.

"I'll be fine, Mom, I'll be fine."

There was a pause, as if neither knew what to say.

"I love you, Mom. Tell Dad I love you both."

He put the phone down. Two hours later Sir Nigel Irvine read the transcript at his home in Dorset. On the following morning Ciaran and Mitch drove Monk back to the Aberdeen airport and escorted him on the southbound flight.

He spent five days in London, staying with Sir Nigel Irvine at the Montcalm, a quiet and discreet hotel tucked away in a Nash terrace behind Marble Arch. During those days the old spymaster explained in detail what Monk should do. Finally, there was nothing more but to say good-bye. Irvine slipped him a piece of paper.

"If ever that wonderful hi-tech communications system goes down, there's a chap here who might get a message out. Last resort of course. Well, good-bye, Jason. I'll not come to Heathrow. Hate airports. I think you can do it, you know. Yes, dammit, I really think you might."

Ciaran and Mitch drove him to Heathrow and took him as far as the security checkpoint. Then each held out his hand.

"Good luck, Boss," they said.

It was an uneventful flight. No one knew that he looked nothing like the Jason Monk who had flown into Terminal Four nearly a month earlier. No one knew he was not the man on his passport. He was nodded through.

Five hours later, with his watch adjusted three more hours forward, he approached passport control at Sheremetyevo Airport, Moscow. His visa was in order, apparently applied for and granted at the Russian Embassy in Washington. He was passed through.

At Customs he filled out the lengthy currency-declaration form and humped his single suitcase onto the examination table. The Customs man looked at it, then gestured to the attaché case.

"Open," he said in English.

Nodding and smiling, the eager American businessman, Monk did so. The officer poked through his papers, then held up the laptop. He looked at it approvingly, said, "Nice," and put it back. There was a quick chalk mark on each case, and he turned to his next customer.

Monk took his bags, passed through the glass doors, and emerged into the land to which he had sworn he would never return.

PART TWO

CHAPTER 12

THE METROPOL HOTEL WAS STILL WHERE HE REMEMBERED IT, A BIG cube of gray stone facing the Bolshoi Theatre across the square.

In the reception area Monk approached the desk, introduced himself, and offered his American passport. The clerk checked a computer screen, tapping in the numbers and letters until the confirmation flashed up on the screen. He glanced at the passport, then at Monk, nodded, and gave a professional smile.

Monk's room was the one he had asked for, acting on the advice of the Russian-speaking soldier Sir Nigel had sent to Moscow four weeks earlier on a reconnaissance trip. It was a corner room on the eighth floor, with a view toward the Kremlin and, more important, a balcony that ran along the length of the building.

Owing to the time difference with London, it was early evening by the time he was settled in and the October dusk was already cold enough for those on the street who could afford an overcoat to wear one. That night Monk dined inside the hotel and went to sleep early.

The following morning there was a new reception clerk on duty.

"I have a problem," Monk told him. "I have to go to the U.S. Embassy for them to check my passport. It's a minor matter, you know, bureaucracy. . . ."

"Unfortunately, sir, we have to retain visitors' passports during their stay," said the clerk.

Monk leaned across the desk and the hundred-dollar bill crinkled in his fingers.

"I understand," he said soberly, "but you see, that's the problem. After Moscow I have to travel widely across Europe, and with the passport close to its expiration date, my embassy needs to prepare a replacement. I'd only be gone a couple of hours. . . ."

The clerk was young, recently married and a baby on the way. He thought how many rubles at the black market rate a hundred-dollar bill would buy him. He glanced left and right.

"Excuse me," he said, and disappeared behind the glass partition dividing the reception desk from the complex of offices behind it. Five minutes later he was back. He carried the passport.

"Normally, these are only returned upon checkout," he said. "I must have it back unless you are leaving."

"Look, as I said, as soon as the Visa Section has finished with it, I'll bring it right back. When do you go off duty?"

"Two this afternoon."

"Well, if I can't make it by then, your colleagues will have it by tea time."

As the passport came one way, the hundred-dollar bill went the other. Now both were co-conspirators. They nodded, smiled, and parted.

Back in his room, Monk hung the Do Not Disturb notice and locked the door. In the bathroom the dye-solvent described on the label as eyewash liquid came out of his toilet case and he ran a bowl of warm water.

The cluster of tight gray curls belonging to Dr. Philip Peters disappeared, to be replaced by the blond hair of Jason Monk. The moustache gave way before the razor blade and the smoked glasses that masked the weak eyes of the academic went into a trash can down the hall.

The passport he withdrew from his attaché case was in his own name with his own photograph, and bore the entry stamp of the airport's immigration officer, copied from the one brought back by Irvine's soldier from his earlier mission but with the appropriate date. Inside the flyleaf was a duplicate currency-declaration form, also bearing the forged stamp of the currency desk.

At midmorning Monk descended to the ground floor, crossed the vaulted atrium, and left by the door facing away from the reception desk. There was a rank of licensed taxis outside the Metropol and Monk took one, by now speaking fluent Russian.

"Olympic Penta," he said. The driver knew the hotel, nodded, and set off.

The entire Olympic complex, built for the 1980 games, lies due north of the center of the city, just outside the Sadovaya Spasskaya or Garden Ring Road. The stadium still towered over the surrounding buildings, and in its shadow was the German-built Penta Hotel. Monk had himself deposited under the marquee, paid off the cab, and entered the lobby. When the cab was gone he left the hotel and walked the rest of the way. It was only a quarter of a mile.

The whole area south of the stadium had degenerated into that atmosphere of drabness that prevails when upkeep and maintenance become too much trouble. The Communist-era buildings housing a dozen embassies, offices, and some restaurants carried a patina of summer dust that would turn to crust in the coming cold. Bits of paper and Styrofoam fluttered along the streets.

Just off Durova Street was a railed enclave whose gardens and buildings showed a different spirit, one of care and attention. There were three principal buildings within the railings: a hostel for wayfarers visiting from the provinces, a very fine school built in the mid-1990s, and the place of worship itself.

Moscow's principal mosque had been built in 1905, a dozen years before Lenin struck, and it bore the stamp of pre-Revolutionary elegance. For seventy years under Communism it had languished, like the Christian churches persecuted on the orders of the atheist state. After the fall of Communism a generous gift from Saudi Arabia had enabled a five-year program of enlargement and restoration. The hostel and school dated from the mid-1990s program.

The mosque had not changed in size, a quite small edifice in pale blue and white, with tiny windows, entered through a pair of antique carved oak doors. Monk slipped off his shoes, put them in one of the pigeonholes to the left of the lobby, and went in.

As with all mosques, the interior was completely open and devoid of chairs or benches. Rich carpets also donated by Saudi Arabia covered the floor; pillars held up a gallery that ran around the building above the central space.

According to the faith, there were no graven images or paintings. Panels on the walls contained various quotations from the Koran.

The mosque served the spiritual needs of Moscow's resident Moslem community, excluding the diplomats who mainly worshiped at the Saudi Embassy. But Russia contains tens of millions of Moslems, and its capital two public mosques. As it was not a Friday, there were only a few dozen worshipers.

Monk found a place against the wall near the entrance, sat cross-legged, and watched. Mainly the men were old: Azeris, Tatars, Ingush, Ossetians. They all wore suits, frayed but clean.

After half an hour an old man in front of Monk rose from his knees and turned toward the door. He noticed Monk and an expression of curiosity crossed his face. The suntanned face, the blond hair, the lack of a string of prayer beads. He hesitated, then sat down with his back to the wall.

He must have been well over seventy and three medals won in the Second World War dangled from his lapel.

"Peace be unto you," he murmured.

"And to you be peace," Monk replied.

"Are you of the faith?" asked the old man.

"Alas, no, I come seeking a friend."

"Ah. A particular friend?"

"Yes, one of long ago. We lost contact. I hoped I might find him here. Or someone who might know him."

The old man nodded.

"Ours is a small community. Many small communities. Which one would he belong to?"

"He is a Chechen," said Monk. The old man nodded again, then climbed stiffly to his feet.

"Wait," he said.

He came back ten minutes later, having found someone outside. He nodded in the direction of Monk, smiled, and left. The newcomer was younger, but not much.

"I am told you seek one of my brothers," said the Chechen. "Can I help?"

"Possibly," said Monk. "I would be grateful. We met years ago. Now that I am visiting your city I would be happy to see him again."

"And his name, my friend?"

"Umar Gunayev."

Something flickered in the older man's eyes.

"I know of no such man," he said.

"Ah, then I shall be disappointed," said Monk, "for I had brought him a gift."

"How long will you be among us?"

"I would like to sit here awhile longer and admire your beautiful mosque," replied Monk.

The Chechen rose.

"I will ask if anyone has heard of this man," he said.

"Thank you," said Monk. "I am a man of great patience."

"Patience is a virtue."

It was two hours before they came, and there were three of them, all young. They moved quietly, stockinged feet making no sound on the deep pile of the Persian carpets. One stayed by the door, dropping to his knees and leaning back on his heels, hands on the tops of his thighs. He might seem to be at prayer, but Monk knew no one would get past him.

The other two walked over and sat on either side of Monk. Whatever they carried under their jackets was hidden. Monk stared ahead. The questions when they came were murmurs that would not disturb the worshipers in front of them.

"You speak Russian?"

"Yes."

"And you ask about one of our brothers?"

"Yes."

"You are a Russian spy."

"I am American. There is a passport in my jacket."

"Forefinger and thumb," said the man. Monk eased out his U.S. passport and let it fall to the carpet. It was the other man who leaned forward, retrieved it, and scanned the pages. Then he nodded and handed it back. He spoke in Chechen across Monk. The American suspected the burden of what he said was to the effect that anyone can have a forged American passport. The man to Monk's right nodded and resumed.

"Why do you seek our brother?"

"We met, long ago. In a faraway land. He left something behind. I promised myself that if ever I came to Moscow I would return it to him."

"You have it with you?"

"In that attaché case."

"Open."

Monk flicked the catches on the case and lifted the lid. Inside was a flat cardboard box.

"You expect us to bring this to him?"

"I would be grateful."

The one on the left said something else in Chechen.

"No, it is not a bomb," said Monk in Russian. "For if it were, and it were opened now, I too would die. So open it."

The two men glanced at each other, then one leaned forward and lifted the lid of the cardboard box. They stared at what lay inside.

"That is it?"

"That is it. He left it behind."

The one on his left closed the box and lifted it out of the attaché case. Then he arose.

"Wait," he said.

The man by the door watched him leave but made no sign. Monk and his two watchers sat for another two hours. The hour of lunch had come and gone. Monk felt the yearning for a big hamburger. Beyond the small windows the light was fading by the time the messenger returned. He said nothing, just nodded to his two companions and jerked his head toward the door.

"Come," said the Chechen who squatted to Monk's right. All three arose. In the lobby they retrieved their shoes and put them on. The two flankers took up position on either side; the watcher by the door brought up the rear. Monk was marched out of the compound to Durova Street where a big BMW waited at the curb. Before he was allowed to enter it he was expertly frisked from behind.

Monk went into the center of the backseat with a flanker on either side. The third man slipped into the front beside the driver. The BMW moved off and headed for the ring road.

Monk had calculated the men would never defile the mosque by offering violence within it, but their own car was a different matter, and he knew enough of men like those around him to be aware they were all supremely dangerous.

After a mile the one in the front reached into the glove compartment and withdrew a pair of wraparound dark glasses. He gestured to Monk to put them on. They were better than a blindfold, for the lenses had been painted black. Monk completed the journey in darkness.

In the heart of Moscow, down a side street that it is wiser not to penetrate, is a small café called the Kashdan. It means "chestnut" in Russian and has been there for years.

Any tourist wandering idly toward the doors will be met by a fit-looking young man who will indicate to the stranger that he would be advised to take his morning coffee elsewhere. The Russian militia do not even bother to go near it.

Monk was helped out of the car and his black glasses were removed as he was led through the door. As he entered, the buzz of conversation in the Chechen language died. Twoscore eyes watched in silence as he was led to a private room at the back beyond the bar. If he failed to come out of that room, no one would have seen a thing.

There was a table, four chairs, and a mirror on the wall. From a nearby kitchen came a smell of garlic, spices, and coffee. For the first time the senior of the three watchers, the one who had sat by the entrance of the mosque while his subordinates did the questioning, spoke.

"Sit," he said. "Coffee?"

"Thank you. Black. Sugar."

It came and it was good. Monk sipped the steaming liquid and kept his eyes away from the mirror, convinced it was a one-way device and that he was being studied from behind it. As he put down his empty cup a door opened and Umar Gunayev entered.

He had changed. The shirt collar was no longer worn outside the jacket, and the suit was not cheaply cut. It was of an Italian designer label and the tie of heavy silk probably from Jermyn Street or Fifth Avenue.

The Chechen had matured over twelve years, but at forty was darkly handsome, urbane, and polished. He nodded several times at Monk, with a quiet smile, then sat down and put the flat cardboard box on the table.

"I received your gift," he said. He flicked the lid open, and picked out the contents, holding the Yemeni gambiah to the light and running a fingertip down the cutting edge.

"This is it?"

"One of them left it on the cobblestones," said Monk. "I thought you might use it for a letter-opener."

This time Gunayev smiled with genuine amusement.

"How did you know my name?"

Monk told him about the mug shots the British in Oman had collected of the incoming Russians.

"And since then, what have you heard?"

"Many things."

"Good or bad?"

"Interesting."

"Tell me."

"I heard that Captain Gunayev, after ten years with the First Chief Directorate, finally became tired of the racial jokes and having no chance of promotion. I heard he left the KGB to take up another line of work. Also covert, but different."

Gunayev laughed. At this the three watchers seemed to relax. The master had set the mood for them.

"Covert, but different. Yes, that is true. And then?"

"Then I heard that Umar Gunayev had risen in his new life to become the undisputed overlord of all the Chechen underworld west of the Urals."

"Possibly. Anything else?"

"I heard that this Gunayev is a traditional man, though not old. That he still clings to the ancient standards of the Chechen people."

"You have heard much, my American friend. And what are these standards of the Chechen people?"

"I have been told that in a world of degeneracy the Chechens still abide by their code of honor; that they pay their debts, the good and the bad."

There was tension from the three men behind Monk. Was the American making fun of them? They watched their leader. Gunayev nodded at last.

"You have heard correctly. What do you want of me?"

"Shelter. A place to live."

"There are hotels in Moscow."

"Not very safe."

"Someone is trying to kill you?"

"Not yet, but soon."

"Who?"

"Colonel Anatoli Grishin."

Gunayev shrugged dismissively.

"You know him?" asked Monk.

"I know of him."

"And what you know, you like?"

Gunayev shrugged again.

"He does what he does. I do what I do."

"In America," said Monk, "if you wished to disappear, I could make you disappear. But this is not my city, not my country. Can you make me disappear in Moscow?"

"Temporarily or permanently?"

Monk laughed.

"I should prefer temporarily."

"Then of course I can. That is what you want?"

"If I am to stay alive, yes. And I would prefer to stay alive."

Gunayev rose and addressed his three gangsters.

"This man saved my life. Now he is my guest. No one will touch him. While he is here he will become one of us."

The three hoods were all around Monk, offering their hands, grinning, giving their names. Aslan, Magomed, Sharif.

"Has the hunt for you begun already?" asked Gunayev.

"No, I don't think so."

"Then you must be hungry. The food here is foul. We will go to my office."

Like all mafia chieftains, the leader of the Chechen clan had two personae. The more public one was that of a highly successful "*biznizman*" controlling a score of prosperous companies. In the case of Gunayev his chosen specialty was that of property.

In the early years he had simply bought prime development sites all over Moscow by the simple expedient of purchasing or shooting the bureaucrats who, as Communism collapsed and state property became available for public purchase, had the sales of these prime sites at their disposal.

Having taken title to the development sites, Gunayev was able to take advantage of the wave of collaborative planning ventures set up between the Russian tycoons and their Western partners. Gunayev provided the building sites and guaranteed strike-free labor, while the Americans and West Europeans erected their office buildings and skyscrapers. Ownership then became a shared venture, as did the profits and rents from the offices.

With similar procedures, the Chechen took over control of six of the top hotels in the city, branching out into steel, concrete, timber, bricks, and glazing. If one wanted to restore, convert, or build, one dealt with a subsidiary owned and controlled by Umar Gunayev.

That was the overt face of the Chechen mafia. The less visible side of the operation, as with all Moscow gangsterdom, remained in the provinces of black marketeering and embezzlement.

Russian state assets such as gold, diamonds, gas, and oil were simply purchased locally in rubles, at the official rate and even then at knockdown prices. The "sellers," being bureaucrats, could all be bought anyway. Exported abroad, the assets were sold for dollars, pounds, or deutsche marks at world market prices.

A fraction of the sale price could then be reimported, converted into a blizzard of rubles at the unofficial rate, and used to purchase the next consignment and pay the necessary bribes. The balance, in the region of eighty percent of the foreign sale, was the profit.

In the early days, before some of the state officials and bankers got the hang of things, a number refused to cooperate. The first warning was verbal, the second involved orthopedic surgery, and the third was permanent. The successor official to the one who had shuffled off the mortal coil usually grasped the game rules.

By the late 1990s violence against members of officialdom or the legitimate professions was hardly ever necessary, but by then the growth of private armies meant that every underworld chieftain had to match all his rivals if need be. Among all the men of violence none matched the speed and unconcern of the Chechens if they felt they were being crossed.

From the late winter of 1994 a new factor had entered the equation. Just before Christmas that year Boris Yeltsin launched his incredibly foolish war against the homeland of Chechnya, ostensibly to oust the breakaway president Dudayev who was claiming independence for it. If the war had been a quick surgical operation, it might have worked. In fact, the supposedly mighty Russian Army took a pasting from lightly armed Chechen guerrillas, who simply headed for the mountains of the Caucasus and fought on.

In Moscow any semblance of hesitation the Chechen mafia

might have felt toward the Russian state vanished. Ordinary life became almost impossible for a law-abiding Chechen. With every man's hand turned against them, the Chechens became a tightly knit and fiercely loyal clan within the Russian capital, far more impenetrable than the Georgian, Armenian, or native Russian underworlds. Within that community the head of the underworld became both a hero and a resistance leader. In the late autumn of 1999 this was the former captain of the KGB, Umar Gunayev.

And yet as businessman Gunayev he could still circulate freely and live like the multimillionaire he was. His office was in fact the entire top floor of one of his hotels, a collaborative enterprise with an American chain, situated near the Helsinki Station.

The journey to the hotel was accomplished in Umar Gunayev's Mercedes limousine, proofed against bullet and bomb. He had his own driver and bodyguard, and the three from the café came behind in the Volvo. Both cars drove into the underground garage of the hotel, and after the basement area had been searched by the three from the BMW, Gunayev and Monk walked to a high-speed elevator that took them to the tenth and penthouse floor. The electric power to the elevator was then disconnected.

There were more guards in the lobby on the tenth floor, but they finally found privacy in the Chechen leader's apartment. A white-jacketed steward brought food and drink at a command from Gunayev.

"There is something I have to show you," said Monk. "I hope you will find it interesting, even educational."

He opened his attaché case and activated the two control buttons to release the false base. Gunayev watched with interest. The case and its potential clearly excited his admiration.

Monk handed over the Russian translation of the verification report first. It comprised thirty-three pages between stiff gray paper covers. Gunayev raised an eyebrow.

"Must I?"

"It will reward your patience. Please."

Gunayev sighed and began to read. As he became more involved in the narrative he left his coffee untouched and concentrated on the text. It took twenty minutes. Finally he put the report back on the table between them.

"So. This manifesto is no joke. The real thing. So what?"

"This is your next president talking," said Monk. "This is what he intends to do when he has the power to do it. Quite soon now."

He slipped the black-covered manifesto across the table.

"Another thirty pages?"

"Forty, actually. But even more interesting. Please. Humor me."

Gunayev ran his eye quickly over the first ten pages, taking in the plans for the single-party state, the recommissioning of the nuclear arsenal, the reconquest of the lost republics, and the new Gulag archipelago of slave camps. Then his eyes narrowed and he slowed his pace.

Monk knew the point he had reached. He could envisage the messianic sentences as he had first read them in front of the sparkling water of Sapodilla Bay in the Turks and Caicos Islands.

"The final and complete extermination of every last Chechen on the face of Russia . . . the destruction of the rat-people so that they will never rise again . . . the reduction of the tribal homeland to a wild-goat pasture . . . not a brick on brick nor a stone on stone . . . forever . . . the surrounding Ossetians, Dagomans, and Ingush will watch the process and learn due and proper respect and fear of their new Russian masters. . . ."

Gunayev read to the end and put the manifesto down.

"It's been tried before," he said. "The Czars tried, Stalin tried, Yeltsin tried."

"With swords, tommy guns, rockets. What about gamma rays, anthrax, nerve gases? The art of extermination has modernized."

Gunayev rose, stripped off his jacket, draped it over his chair, and walked to the picture window with its view over the roofs of Moscow.

"You want him eliminated? Taken down?" he asked.

"No."

"Why not? It can be done."

"It won't work."

"It usually does."

Monk explained. A nation already in chaos plunged into the abyss, probably civil war. Or another Komarov, perhaps his own right-hand man Grishin, storming to power on a wave of outrage.

"They are two sides of the same coin," he said. "The man of

thought and words, and the man of action. Kill one and the other takes over. The destruction of your people continues."

Gunayev turned from the window and walked back. He leaned over Monk, his face taut.

"What do you want of me, American? You come here as a stranger who once saved my life. So for that I owe you. Then you show me this filth. What has it to do with me?"

"Nothing, unless you decide so. You have many things, Umar Gunayev. You have great wealth, enormous power, even the power of life and death over any man. You have the power to walk away, to let what will happen happen."

"And why should I not?"

"Because there was a boy, once. A small and ragged boy who grew up in a poor village in the northern Caucasus among family, friends, and neighbors who clubbed together to send him to university and thence to Moscow to become a great man. The question is, Did that boy die somewhere along the road, to become an automaton, triggered only by wealth? Or does the boy still remember his own people?"

"You tell me."

"No. The choice is yours."

"And your choice, American?"

"Much easier. I can walk out of here, take a cab to Sheremetyevo, fly home. It's warm there; comfortable, safe. I can tell them not to bother; that it doesn't matter, that no one over here cares anymore, they're all bought and paid for. Let night descend."

The Chechen seated himself and stared into some distance long past. Finally he said, "You think you can stop him?"

"There is a chance."

"And then what?"

Monk explained what Sir Nigel Irvine and his patrons had in mind.

"You're crazy," said Gunayev flatly.

"Maybe. What else faces you? Komarov and the genocide carried out by his beastmaster, chaos and civil war, or the other."

"And if I help you, what do you need?"

"To hide. But in plain sight. To move but not be recognized. To see the people I have come to see."

"You think Komarov will know you are here?"

"Quite soon. There are a million informants in this city. You know that. You use many yourself. All can be bought. The man is no fool."

"He can buy all the organs of the state. Even I never take on the entire state."

"As you will have read, Komarov has promised his partners and financial backers, the Dolgoruki mafia, the world and all therein. Soon now, they will *be* the state. What happens to you?"

"All right. I can hide you. Though for how long even I do not know. Inside our community no one will find you until I say so. But you cannot live here. It is too obvious. I have many safe houses. You will have to pass from one to the other."

"Safe houses are fine," said Monk. "To sleep in. To move about, I will need papers. Perfectly forged ones."

Gunayev shook his head.

"We don't forge papers here. We buy the real thing."

"I forgot. Everything is for money."

"What else do you need?"

"To start with, these."

Monk wrote several lines on a sheet of paper and handed it over. Gunayev ran his eye down the list. Nothing was a problem. He reached the last item.

"What the hell do you need that for?"

Monk explained.

"You know that I own half the Metropol Hotel," Gunayev sighed.

"I'll try and just use the other half."

The Chechen failed to see the joke.

"How long until Grishin knows you are in town?"

"It depends. About two days, maybe three. When I start to move about, there are bound to be some traces left. People talk."

"All right. I will give you four men. They will watch your back, move you from place to place. The leader is one you have met. In the front seat of the BMW, Magomed. He's good. Give a list of what you need to him from time to time. It will be provided. And I still think you are crazy."

By midnight Monk was back in his room at the Metropol. At the end of the corridor was an open area by the elevators. There were four leather club chairs. Two of them were occupied by silent men who read newspapers and would do so all night. In the small hours of the morning two suitcases were delivered to Monk's room.

•   •   •

MOST Muscovites and certainly all foreigners presume that the Patriarch of the Russian Orthodox Church lives in a sumptuous suite of apartments deep in the heart of the medieval Danilovsky Monastery, with its white crenellated walls and its complex of abbeys and cathedrals.

This is certainly the impression, and it is a carefully cultivated one. In one of the great office buildings within the monastery guarded by fiercely loyal Cossack soldiers, the Patriarch does indeed keep his offices, and these are the heart and center of the Patriarchate of Moscow and All the Russias. But he does not actually live there.

He lives in a quite modest town house at Number Five Chisti Pereulok, meaning "Clean Passage," a narrow side street just outside the central district of the city.

Here he is attended by a priestly staff of personal private secretary, valet/butler, two manservants, and three nuns who cook and clean. There is also a driver on call and two Cossack guards. The contrast with the magnificence of the Vatican or the splendor of the palace of the Patriarch of the Greek Orthodox Church could not be greater.

In the winter of 1999 the holder of that office was still His Holiness Alexei II, elected ten years earlier, just before the fall of Communism. Still only in his early fifties then, he became the inheritor of a church demoralized and traduced from within and persecuted and corrupted from without.

From the very earliest days, Lenin, who loathed the priesthood, realized that Communism had only one rival for the hearts and minds of the teeming mass of the Russian peasantry, and he determined to destroy it. Through systematic brutality and corruption he and his successors nearly succeeded.

Even Lenin and Stalin balked at the complete extermination of the priesthood and the church, fearful they might inspire a backlash not even the NKVD could control. So after the first pogroms in which churches were burned, their treasures stolen, and the priests hanged, the Politburo sought to destroy the church by discrediting it.

The measures were numerous. Aspirants of high intelligence were banned from the seminaries, which were controlled by the NKVD and later the KGB. Only plodders from the periphery of the USSR, Moldavia in the west and Siberia in the east, were accepted. The level of education was kept low and the quality of the priesthood degraded.

Most churches were simply closed and allowed to rot. A few remained open, patronized mainly by the elderly and very old, i.e., the harmless. The officiating priests were required to report regularly to the KGB and did so, acting as informers against their own parishioners.

A young person seeking baptism would be reported by the priest he approached. After that he would lose his high school place and a chance at university, and his parents would probably be ousted from their apartment. Virtually nothing went unreported to the KGB. Almost the entire priesthood, even if not involved, became tainted by popular suspicion.

The Communists used the stick-and-carrot technique, a crippling stick and a poisoned carrot.

Defenders of the church point out that the alternative was complete extirpation, and thus that keeping the church, any church, alive was a factor that outweighed the humiliation.

What the mild, shy, and retiring Alexei II inherited, therefore, was a college of bishops steeped in collaboration with the atheist state and a pastoral priesthood discredited among the people.

There were exceptions, wandering priests without parishes who preached and dodged arrest, or failed to do so and were sent to the labor camps. There were ascetics who withdrew to the monasteries to keep the faith alive by self-denial and prayer, but these hardly ever met the masses of the people.

In the aftermath of the collapse of Communism the opportunity occurred for a great renaissance, a rebirth that would put the church and the word of the Gospel back at the center of the lives of the traditionally deeply religious Russian people.

Instead the turning back to religion was experienced by the newer churches, vigorous, vibrant, dedicated, and prepared to go and preach to the people where they lived and worked. The Pentecostalists multiplied, the American missionaries poured in with their Baptism, Mormonism, and Seventh-Day Adventism. The reaction of the Russian Orthodox leadership was to beg Moscow for a ban on foreign preachers.

Its defenders argued that root-and-branch reform of the Orthodox hierarchy was impossible because the lower levels were also dross. The seminary-trained priests were of poor caliber, spoke in the archaic language of the scriptures, were possessed of pedantic or didactic speech, and had no training in nonacademic public delivery. Their sermons were delivered to captive audiences, few in number and elderly in years.

The opportunity missed was vast, for as dialectical materialism was proved a false god and as democracy and capitalism failed to provide for the body, let alone the soul, the appetite for comfort was pan-national and profound. It went largely unanswered. Instead of sending out its best younger priests on missionary work, to proselytize for the faith and spread the word, the Orthodox Church sat in bishoprics, monasteries, and seminaries waiting for the people. Few came.

If a passionate and inspirational leadership was desperately needed after the fall of Communism, the mild scholar Alexei II was not the man to provide it. His election was a compromise between the various factions among the bishops, a man who, the inadequate hierarchs hoped, would not make waves.

Yet despite the burden he inherited and his own personal lack of charisma, Alexei II was not without some reforming instinct, which took courage. He did three important things.

His first reform was to divide the land of Russia into one hundred bishoprics, each far smaller than in the past. This enabled him to create new and younger bishops from among the best and most motivated priests, the least tarred by the brush of collaboration with the defunct KGB. Then he visited every see, making himself more visible to the people than any patriarch in history.

Second, he silenced the violent anti-Semitic outpourings of Metropolitan Ioann of St. Petersburg and made plain that any bishop preferring to offer hatred of man above love of God as his message to the faithful would depart his office. Ioann died in 1995, still privately railing against the Jews and Alexei II.

Finally he gave his personal sanction, over considerable opposition, to Father Gregor Rusakov, a charismatic young priest who steadfastly refused to accept either a parish of his own or the discipline of the bishops through whose territory he moved on his itinerant pastoral mission. Many a Patriarch would have condemned the maverick monk and forbidden him the pulpit, but Alexei II had refused to take this path, preferring to accept the risk of giving the nomad priest his head. With his moving and passionate oratory Father Gregor reached out to the young and the agnostic, something that the bishops were failing to do.

One night in early November 1999 the gentle-mannered Patriarch was disturbed at his prayers just before midnight with the news that an emissary from London was waiting at the street door and asking for an audience.

The Patriarch was dressed in a plain gray cassock. He rose from his knees and crossed the floor of his small private chapel to take the letter from the hand of his secretary.

The missive was on the letterhead of the London bishopric, based in Kensington, and he recognized the signature of his friend Metropolitan Anthony. Nevertheless he frowned in perplexity that his colleague should contact him in such an unusual way.

The letter was in Russian, which Bishop Anthony both spoke and wrote. It asked his brother in Christ to receive as a matter of some urgency a man who bore news that concerned the church, news of great confidentiality and very disturbing.

The Patriarch folded the letter and glanced at his secretary.

"Where is he?"

"On the pavement, Holiness. He came by taxi."

"He is a priest?"

"Yes, Holiness."

The Patriarch sighed.

"Let him be admitted. You may return to your sleep. I will see him in my study. In ten minutes."

The Cossack guard on night duty received a whispered command from the secretary and reopened the street door. He glanced at the gray taxi from Central City Cabs and the black-clad priest beside it.

"His Holiness will see you, Father," he said. The priest paid off the cab.

Inside the house he was shown to a small waiting room. After ten minutes a plump priest entered and murmured: "Please come with me."

The visitor was shown into a room that was clearly the study of a scholar. Apart from one exquisite Rublev icon on a white plaster wall, the room was adorned only with shelving on which row upon row of ancient books gleamed in the light from a table lamp on a desk. Behind the desk sat Patriarch Alexei. He gestured his guest to a chair.

"Father Maxim, would you bring us refreshments. Coffee? Yes, coffee for two, and some biscuits. You will take Communion in the morning, Father? Yes? Then there is just time for a biscuit before midnight."

The plump valet/butler withdrew.

"So, my son, and how is my friend Anthony of London?"

There was nothing false about the visitor's black cassock, nor even the black stovepipe that he had now removed to reveal blond hair. The only odd thing was that he wore no beard. Most Orthodox priests do, but not all the English ones.

"I'm afraid I could not say, Your Holiness, for I have not met him."

Alexei stared at Monk without comprehension. He gestured at the letter in front of him.

"And this? I do not understand."

Monk took a deep breath.

"First, Holiness, I have to confess that I am not a priest of the Orthodox Church. Neither is the letter from Bishop Anthony, though the paper is genuine and the signature skillfully forged. The purpose of this disrespectful charade is that I had to see you. You personally, in privacy and in conditions of great secrecy."

The Patriarch's eyes flickered in alarm. Was the man a lunatic? An assassin? There was an armed Cossack guard down below, but could he be summoned in time? He kept his face impassive. His butler would return in a few moments. Perhaps that would be the time to escape.

"Please explain," he said.

"First, sir, I am by birth an American, not a Russian. Second, I come from a group of people in the West, discreet and powerful, who wish to help Russia and the church, not harm either of them. Third, I come only with news that my patrons feel you may believe to be important and troubling. Finally, I come to seek your help, not your blood. You have a phone at your elbow. You may use it to summon help. I will not stop you. But before you denounce me, I beg you to read what I have brought."

Alexei frowned. Certainly the man did not appear to be a maniac, and he had already had time to kill him. Where was that fool Maxim with his coffee?

"Very well. What is it you have for me?"

Monk reached beneath his cassock and produced two slim folders, which he placed on the desk. The Patriarch glanced at the covers, one gray, the other black.

"What do these concern?"

"The gray one should be read first. It is a report that proves beyond any reasonable doubt that the black file is no forgery, no joke, no hoax, no trick."

"And the black file?"

"It is the private and personal manifesto of one Igor Alexeivich Komarov, who it appears will soon be president of Russia."

There was a knock on the door. Father Maxim entered with a tray of coffee, cups, and biscuits. The mantel clock struck twelve.

"Too late," sighed the Patriarch. "Maxim, you have deprived me of my biscuit."

"I am terribly sorry, Holiness. The coffee . . . I had to grind fresh . . . I . . ."

"I am only jesting, Maxim." He glanced at Monk. The man appeared hard and fit. If he was going to commit murder, he could probably kill them both. "Away to your bed, Maxim. May God give you good rest."

The butler shuffled toward the door.

"Now," said the Patriarch, "what does Mr. Komarov's manifesto tell us?"

Father Maxim closed the door behind him, hoping no one had noticed the start he gave at the mention of Komarov's name. In the corridor he glanced up and down. The secretary was already back in bed, the religious sisters would not appear for hours, the Cossack was downstairs. He knelt by the door and applied his ear to the keyhole.

Alexei II read the verification report first, as he was asked. Monk sipped his coffee. Finally the Patriarch had finished.

"An impressive story. Why did he do it?"

"The old man?"

"Yes."

"We shall never know. As you see, he is dead. Murdered beyond any doubt. Professor Kuzmin's report is adamant on that."

"Poor fellow. I shall pray for him."

"What we may surmise is that he saw something in these pages that so disturbed him that he risked and finally gave his life to reveal the inner intentions of Igor Komarov. Would Your Holiness now read the Black Manifesto?"

An hour later the Patriarch of Moscow and All the Russias leaned back and stared at a point above Monk's head.

"He cannot mean this," he said finally. "He cannot intend to do these things. They are satanic. This is Russia on the threshold of the third millennium of Our Lord. We are beyond these things."

"As a man of God, you must believe in the forces of evil, Holiness?"

"Of course."

"And that sometimes those forces can take human form? Hitler, Stalin . . ."

"You are a Christian, Mr. . . . ?"

"Monk. I suppose so. A bad one."

"Aren't we all? So inadequate. But then you know the Christian view of evil. You do not need to ask."

"Holiness, the passages concerning the Jews, the Chechens, and the other ethnic minorities apart, these plans would send your Holy Church spinning back into the Dark Ages, either a willing tool and accomplice, or a fellow victim of the Fascist state, as godless in its way as the Communist one."

"If this is true."

"It is true. Men do not hunt down and kill for a forgery. Colonel Grishin's reaction was too fast for the document not to have come from Secretary Akopov's desk. They would have been unaware of a forgery. They were aware within hours that something of priceless value had gone missing."

"What have you come to seek of me, Mr. Monk?"

"An answer. Will the Orthodox Church of All the Russias oppose this man?"

"I shall pray. I shall seek guidance. . . ."

"And if the answer is that, not as a Patriarch but as a Christian, and a man, and a Russian, you have no choice. What then?"

"Then I shall have no choice. But how to oppose him? The presidential elections of January are seen as a foregone conclusion."

Monk arose, gathered the two files, and pushed them inside his cassock. He reached for his hat.

"Holiness, shortly a man will come, also from the West. This is his name. Please receive him. He will propose what can be done."

He handed over a small pasteboard card.

"Will you need a car?" asked Alexei.

"Thank you, no. I shall walk."

"May God walk with you."

Monk left him standing erect beside his Rublev, a deeply troubled man. As he crossed the floor he thought he heard the rustle of foot on carpet outside, but when he opened the door the passage was empty. Downstairs he met the Cossack, who showed him out. The wind on the street was bitter. He pushed his priestly hat firmly onto his head, leaned into the wind, and walked back to the Metropol.

Before the dawn a plump figure slipped out of the home of the Patriarch and scurried through the streets and into the lobby of the Rossiya. Although he had a portable telephone beneath his dark coat, he knew that the lines from public booths were far safer.

The man he spoke to at the dacha off Kiselny Boulevard was one of the night guards but he agreed to take a message.

"Tell the colonel my name is Father Maxim Klimovsky. Got that? Yes, Klimovsky. Tell him I work in the private residence of the Patriarch. I must speak to him. It is urgent. I will phone back on this number at ten this morning."

He got his connection at that hour. The voice at the other end was quiet but authoritative.

"Yes, Father, this is Colonel Grishin."

In the booth the priest held the receiver in a damp hand, a bead of sweat across his forehead.

"Look, Colonel, you do not know me. But I am a passionate

admirer of Mr. Komarov. Last night a man came to visit the Patriarch. He brought documents. He referred to one as a Black Manifesto. . . . Hello? Hello? Are you there?"

"My dear Father Klimovsky, I think we should meet," said the voice.

CHAPTER 13

AT THE FAR SOUTHEASTERN END OF STARAYA PLOSHAD IS SLAVYAN-sky Square, where stands one of the smallest, oldest, and most beautiful churches in Moscow. All Saints of Kulishki was originally built in the thirteenth century of wood, when the Russ capital comprised only the Kremlin and a few surrounding acres. After burning down, it was rebuilt in stone in the late sixteenth and early seventeenth centuries and remained in constant use until 1918.

Moscow was then still known as the city of Twenty-Times-Twenty Churches, for there were over four hundred of them. The Communists closed down ninety percent and destroyed three-quarters. Among those that remained abandoned but otherwise intact was All Saints of Kulishki.

After the fall of Communism in 1991, the little church underwent four years of meticulous restoration at the hands of teams of craftsmen until it reopened as a place of worship. It was here that Father Maxim Klimovsky came on the day following his phone call. He attracted no attention because he was dressed in the standard full-length black cassock and stovepipe hat of an Orthodox priest, and there were several of them in and around the church. He took a votive candle, lit it, and walked to the wall on the right of the entrance, where he stood contemplating the restored icons as if in prayer and contemplation.

In the center of the church, ablaze with gold and paintings, a resident priest stood behind the altar chanting the litany to a small group in street clothes who answered with the responses. But the right-hand wall, behind a series of arches, was unoccupied apart from the single priest.

Father Maxim glanced nervously at his watch. Five minutes after the appointed hour. He did not know he had been seen from the parked car across the little square, nor had he noticed the three men alight after he entered the building. He did not know they had checked to see if he was being followed; he knew none of these things, or how they were done.

He heard the slight scrape of a shoe on the flagstone behind him and felt the man move into position beside him.

"Father Klimovsky?"

"Yes."

"I am Colonel Grishin. I believe you have something to tell me."

He glanced sideways. The man was taller than him, slim, in a dark winter coat. He turned and looked down at Father Maxim. The priest met his eyes and was frightened. He hoped he was doing the right thing and would not regret it. He nodded and swallowed.

"First tell me why, Father. Why the phone call?"

"You must understand, Colonel, that I have long been a keen admirer of Mr. Komarov. His policies, his plans for Russia—all admirable."

"How gratifying. And what happened the night before last?"

"A man came to see the Patriarch. I am his valet and butler. The man was dressed as a priest of the church, but he was blond and wore no beard. His Russian was perfect, but he might have been a foreigner."

"Was he expected, this foreigner?"

"No. That was what was so strange. He came unannounced, in the middle of the night. I was in bed. I was told to get up and prepare coffee."

"So, the stranger was received after all?"

"Yes, that was odd, too. The Western appearance of the man, the hour of his arrival . . . The secretary should have told him to make a formal appointment. No one just walks in on the Patriarch in the middle of the night. But he seemed to have a letter of introduction."

"So, you served them coffee."

"Yes, and as I was leaving I heard His Holiness say: What does Mr. Komarov's manifesto tell us?"

"And you were intrigued?"

"Yes. So after closing the door I listened at the keyhole."

"Very astute. And what did they say?"

"Not a lot. There were long periods of silence. I looked through the keyhole and could see His Holiness was reading something. It took almost an hour."

"And then?"

"The Patriarch seemed very disturbed. I heard him say something and then use the word 'satanic.' Then he said, 'We are beyond these things.' The stranger was talking in a low voice, I could hardly hear him. But I caught the words 'the Black Manifesto.' They came from the stranger. That was just before His Holiness spent an hour reading. . . ."

"Anything else?"

The man, thought Grishin, was a babbler; nervous, sweating in the warmth of the church but not from it. But what he had to say was cogent enough, even though he, the priest, did not understand the significance of it.

"A little more. I heard the word 'forgery' and then your name."

"Mine?"

"Yes, the stranger said something about your reaction being too fast. Then they talked about an old man and the Patriarch said he would pray for him. They mentioned 'evil' several times, then the stranger rose to leave. I had to get down the corridor fast, so I did not see him go. I heard the street door slam, that was all."

"You saw no car?"

"No. I peered from an upper window, but he left on foot. The next day I have never seen His Holiness so disturbed. He was pale, spent hours in his chapel. That was how I could get away to call you. I hope I did the right thing."

"My friend, you did exactly the right thing. There are antipatriotic forces at work seeking to spread lies about a great statesman who will soon be the president of Russia. You are a patriotic Russian, Father Klimovsky?"

"I long for the day when we can purify Russia from this trash and garbage that Mr. Komarov denounces. This foreign filth. That is why I support Mr. Komarov with all my heart."

"Excellent, Father. Believe me, you are one of those whom Mother Russia must look to. I think a great future awaits you. Just one thing. This stranger . . . have you no idea where he came from?"

The candle had burned low. Two other worshipers now stood a few yards to their left, gazing at the sacred images and praying.

"No. But though he left on foot, the Cossack guard told me later he came by cab. Central City Cabs, the gray ones."

A priest, at midnight. Going to Chisti Pereulok. The log would record it. And the pickup point. Colonel Grishin gripped the upper arm of the cassock beside him, felt his fingers dig into the soft flesh, and sensed the man start. He turned Father Klimovsky to face him.

"Now listen, Father. You have done well and in due course will be rewarded. But there is more, you understand?"

Father Klimovsky nodded.

"I want you to keep a record of everything that happens in that house. Who comes, who goes. Especially high-ranking bishops or strangers. When you have something, you call me. Just say 'Maxim is calling,' and leave a time. That is all. The meetings will be here, at that time. If I need you, I will have a letter delivered by hand. Just a card with a time. If by any chance you cannot make that time, without arousing suspicion just ring and give an alternate. Do you understand?"

"Yes, Colonel. I will do what I can for you."

"Of course you will. I can see that one day we shall have a new bishop in this land. You had better go now. I shall follow later."

Colonel Grishin continued to stare at the images he despised and reflect on what he had been told. That the Black Manifesto had returned to Russia he had no doubt. The cassocked fool would not know what he was talking about, but the words were too accurate.

So someone was back, after months of silence, and circulating quietly: showing the document but not leaving a copy behind. To create enemies, of course. To try to influence events.

Whoever it was, he had miscalculated with the primate. The church had no power. Grishin recalled with appreciation Stalin's sneer: How many divisions has the Pope? But whoever it was could cause trouble.

On the other hand, the man had retained his copy of the manifesto. Indicating he might have only one or two copies in his possession. The problem was clearly to find him and eliminate him, and in a manner such that not a shred of the stranger or his document would be left.

As it turned out, the problem was much easier than Grishin could have hoped.

On the matter of his new informant, he had no problems. Years in counterintelligence had taught him to recognize and evaluate informants. The priest, he knew, was a coward who would sell his grandmother for preferment. Grishin had noted the sudden spark of lust when he mentioned elevation to a bishopric.

And something else, he mused as he left the icons and passed between the two men he had stationed just inside the doors. He really must search among the Young Combatants to find a seriously handsome friend for the traitor-priest.

The raid by the four men in black balaclava masks was quick and efficient. When it was over the director of Central City Cabs reckoned it was hardly worth reporting to the militia. In the general lawlessness of Moscow there was nothing the best detective could do to find the raiders, nor would any seriously try. To report that nothing was stolen and no one harmed would invite a torrent of form-filling and several wasted days making statements that would gather dust in a file.

The men simply barged into the ground-floor office, closed it down, drew the blinds, and demanded to see the manager. As they all had handguns, no one argued, presuming it was a holdup for money. But no, all they wanted when they stuck a pistol in the manager's face were the worksheets of three nights previously.

The leader among them studied the sheets until he came to an entry that seemed to interest him. Though the manager could not see the pages, because he happened to be on his knees facing the corner at the time, the entry referred to a pickup and a destination logged about midnight.

"Who is driver Fifty-two?" snapped the leader.

"I don't know," squealed the manager. He was rewarded with a crack on the side of the head from a pistol barrel. "It'll be in the staff file," he screamed.

They made him get out the staff list. Driver Fifty-two was Vassili. There was an address in the suburbs.

After telling him that if he even let the thought cross his mind of calling Vassili to warn him, he would quickly move from his present accommodation to a long wooden box, the leader tore off a chunk of the worksheet and left.

The manager nursed his head, took an aspirin, and gave a thought to Vassili. If the fool was daft enough to cheat men like that, he deserved a visit. Clearly the driver had shortchanged someone with an even shorter temper, or been rude to his girlfriend. This was Moscow, 1999, he thought; you survived or you made trouble for men with guns. The manager intended to survive. He reopened his office and went back to work.

Vassili was taking a late lunch of sausage and black bread when the doorbell rang. Seconds later his wife came back into the room white-faced, with two men behind her. Both had black ski masks and guns. Vassili opened his mouth and a piece of sausage fell out.

"Look, I'm a poor man, I don't have . . ." he began.

"Shut up," said one of the men while the other pushed the trembling wife into a chair. Vassili found a torn sheet of paper pushed under his nose.

"You're driver Fifty-two, Central City Cabs?" asked the man.

"Yes, but honestly, guys . . ."

A black-gloved finger pointed out a line on the work sheet.

"Two nights ago, a fare to Chisti Pereulok. Just before midnight. Who was it?"

"How should I know?"

"Don't get smart, pal or I'll blow your balls off. Think."

Vassili thought. Nothing came.

"A priest," said the gunman.

That was it. The light went on.

"Right, I remember now. Chisti Pereulok, a small side street. I had to check the street map. Had to wait there ten minutes before he was let in. Then he settled up and I left."

"Describe."

"Medium height, medium build. Late forties. A priest, come on, they all look the same. No, wait a minute, he had no beard."

"A foreigner?"

"Don't think so. His Russian was perfect."

"Seen him before?"

"Never."

"Or since?"

"Nope. I offered to come back for him, but he said he didn't know how long he'd be. Look, if anything happened to him, it was nothing to do with me. I just drove him for ten minutes. . . ."

"One last thing. Where from?"

"The Metropol, of course. That's what I do. Night shift at the rank outside the Metropol."

"He came up the pavement or out the doors?"

"Out the doors."

"How do you know?"

"I was head of the line. Standing by the cab. You have to be careful or you wait an hour, then some asshole down the line takes your fare. So I was watching the doors for the next tourist. Out he comes. Black cassock, tall hat. I remember thinking: What's a priest doing in a place like that? He looks up and down the line, then comes straight for me."

"Alone? Any companion?"

"No. Alone."

"He gave a name?"

"No, just the address he wanted to go. Paid cash in rubles."

"Any conversation?"

"Not a word. Just where he wanted to go, then silence. When we got there he said, 'Wait here.' When he came back from the door, he said, 'How much?' That was it. Look, guys, I swear I didn't lay a finger . . ."

"Enjoy your lunch," the interrogator said, and pushed his face in the sausage. Then they left.

Colonel Grishin listened to the report impassively. It could mean nothing. The man came out of the doors of the Metropol at half-past eleven. He could be staying there, he could have been visiting, he could have walked right through the lobby from the other entrance. But worth a check.

Grishin maintained a number of informers inside the headquarters building of the Moscow militia. The senior was a major general on the ruling Presidium. The most consistently useful was the senior clerk in Records. For this job the one was too high and the other confined to his rows of shelves. The third was a detective inspector in Homicide, Dimitri Borodin.

The detective entered the hotel just before sundown and asked to see the front office manager, an Austrian who had worked in Moscow for eight years. He flashed his militia pass.

"Homicide?" asked the manager in concern. "I hope nothing has happened to any of our guests."

"So far as I know, no. Just routine," said Borodin. "I need to see the complete guest list for three nights ago."

The manager sat in his office and punched up the information on his computer.

"You want it printed out?" he asked.

"Yes, I like paper lists."

Borodin began to work his way down the columns. To judge by the names, there were only a dozen Russians among the six hundred guests. The rest were from countries all over Western Europe, plus the United States and Canada. The Metropol was expensive, for visiting tourists and businessmen. Borodin had been told to look for the title Father preceding a guest's name. He could see none.

"Do you have any priests of the Orthodox Church staying here?" he asked. The manager was startled.

"No, not so far as I am aware. . . . I mean, no one has checked in as such."

Borodin scanned all the names without success.

"I'll have to keep the list," he said at length. The manager was happy to see him go.

It was not until the following morning that Colonel Grishin was able to study the list himself. Just after ten o'clock one of the two stewards at the dacha entered his office with his coffee to find the Head of Security for the UPF pale and shaking.

He asked timorously if the colonel was feeling himself, but was waved away irritably. When he had gone, Grishin looked at his hands on the blotter and tried to stop the shaking. He was no stranger to rage, and when it seized him he came very close to losing control.

The name was on the third page of the printout, halfway down. Dr. Philip Peters, American academic.

He knew that name. For ten years he had guarded that name. Twice, ten years earlier, he had scoured the files of the Immigration Division of the old Second Chief Directorate, to which the Foreign Ministry passed copies of every application for a visa to visit the

USSR. Twice he had found that name. Twice he had procured and stared at the photo accompanying the application; the tight gray curls, the smoked glasses hiding the weak eyes that were not weak at all.

In the cellars beneath Lefortovo he had shaken those pictures beneath the noses of Kruglov and Professor Blinov, and they had confirmed this was the man who met them covertly in the lavatory of the Museum of Oriental Art and the crypt beneath the Cathedral of the Assumption in Vladimir.

Many more times than twice he had sworn that if the man who bore that face and pseudonym ever came back to Russia he would settle accounts.

And now he was back. Ten years later he must have thought he could get away with the crass impudence, the insulting arrogance of coming back to the territory ruled by Anatoli Grishin.

He arose, went to a cabinet, and burrowed for an old file. When he had it he extracted another picture, a blowup of a smaller one provided long ago by Aldrich Ames. After the end of the Monakh Committee, a contact in the First Chief Directorate had given it to him as a souvenir. A mocking souvenir. But he had kept it like a treasure.

The face was younger than it would be now, but the gaze was still direct. The hair was blond and rumpled, there was no gray moustache and no smoked glasses. But it was the same face, the face of the young Jason Monk.

Grishin made two phone calls and left his listeners in no doubt that he would not tolerate delay. From the contact in the Immigration Department at the airport he wanted to know when this man arrived, from where, and whether he had left the country.

To Borodin he ordered that the detective return to the Metropol and discover when Dr. Peters checked in, if he had left, and if not what his room was.

He had both answers by midafternoon. Dr. Peters had arrived on the scheduled British Airways flight from London seven days earlier, and if he had left the country it was not via Sheremetyevo. From Borodin he learned that Dr. Peters had checked into the hotel with a prearranged reservation from a reputable London travel agent the same day he arrived at the airport, had not left, and was in Room 841.

There was only one odd thing, said Borodin. Dr. Peters's passport was nowhere to be found. It ought to have remained with reception, but it had been removed. All staff denied any knowledge of how this came to be.

It was no surprise to Grishin. He knew how far a hundred-dollar bill would stretch in Moscow. The passport for getting in would have been destroyed. Monk would now be under a new identity, but among the six hundred foreigners at the Metropol no one would notice. When he wished to leave he would just go without paying; vaporize, disappear. The hotel would shrug and write off the loss.

"Two last things," he told Borodin, who was still at the hotel. "Obtain a passkey and tell the manager that if a word of this is breathed to Dr. Peters, the manager will not be expelled, he will be spending ten years cutting salt. Spin him any story you like."

Grishin decided this was not a job for his Black Guards. They were too recognizable and this affair might end up with a protesting American Embassy. Ordinary criminals could do it and take the blame. Within the Dolgoruki mafia there was a team who specialized in high-quality break-ins.

During the evening, after repeated calls to Room 841 to ensure no one was at home, the room was entered by two men with a passkey. A third waited among the leather chairs at the end of the hall in case the room's occupant returned.

A thorough search was made. Nothing of interest was found. No passport, no files, no attaché case, no personal papers of any kind. Wherever he was, Monk must have his alternative identity papers with him. The room was left exactly as the burglars found it.

From across the corridor the Chechen who had taken the facing room eased his door open a fraction, watched the men enter and leave, then reported back on his mobile phone.

At 10:00 P.M. Jason Monk entered the hotel lobby as one who has dined and wishes to retire to bed. He made no approach to the reception desk, having his plastic key on him. Both entrances were covered by observers, two at each, and as he entered one of the elevators, two of the watchers sauntered to the other. Two took the stairs.

Monk walked down the corridor to his room, tapped on the opposite door, was passed a suitcase from inside, and went into 841.

The first two gangsters, having taken the second elevator, appeared at the end of the corridor in time to see the door close. Shortly after, the other pair arrived by the stairs. There was a brief conversation. Two settled themselves in the club chairs from where they could survey the corridor while their companions went back down to report.

At half-past ten they saw a man leave the room opposite the target, pass them in the lobby area, and head for the elevators. They took no notice. Wrong room.

At 10:45 Monk's phone rang. It was Housekeeping, asking if he wished for any more towels. He said he did not, thanked them, and hung up.

With the contents of the suitcase Monk made his last dispositions and prepared to leave. At eleven he went onto the narrow balcony and pulled the glass doors closed behind him. As he could not lock them from outside he secured them with a strip of strong adhesive tape.

With a length of stout cord from around his waist he lowered himself one floor to the balcony of Room 741 just below his own. From there he hopped over four intervening barriers to the windows of 733.

At 11:10 a Swedish businessman was lying naked on his bed with his organ in his hand, watching a porno movie, when he was electrified by a tap on the window.

In a panic-stricken choice between a terrycloth robe and the freeze-frame button, he chose the robe first, then the remote control. Decently covered, he arose and went to the window. A man was outside gesturing that he be allowed to enter. Completely mystified, the Swede unlocked the catch to the balcony door. The man stepped into the room and addressed him in the molasses drawl of the American Deep South.

"Mighty neighborly, friend, yes sir. I guess you'll be wondering what I was doing on your balcony . . ."

He was right, there. The Swede had not the faintest idea.

"Well, I'll tell you. It was the darnedest thing. I'm right next door to you here, and I just stepped out to smoke a seegar, not wanting to smoke in the room and all, and would you believe it the goddam door swung shut in the wind? So I figured I had no choice but to hop over the divider and see if you'd be kind enough to let me through."

It was cold outside, the cigar-smoker was fully dressed with an attaché case in his hand, there was no wind, and the balcony doors were not self-locking, but the businessman was beyond caring.

His unwelcome guest was still babbling his gratitude and apologies when he let himself out into the corridor and wished the Swede a mighty fine evening.

The businessman, who very fittingly marketed toilet fixtures, resecured the balcony door, drew the curtains, disrobed, hit the "play" button, and returned to his econobudget pastime.

Monk walked unobserved down the corridor of the seventh floor, descended by the stairs, and was met on the curb by Magomed in the BMW.

At midnight three men entered Room 741 with a small suitcase, again using the passkey. They worked for twenty minutes before leaving.

At 4:00 A.M. a device later shown to have contained three pounds of plastic explosive in a shaped charge detonated just below the ceiling of Room 741. Forensic experts would deduce that it had been placed on top of a pyramid of furniture on the bed, and had gone off precisely beneath the center of the bed in the replica room upstairs.

Room 841 was completely gutted. The mattress and duvet on the bed had been turned into a layer of fabric and down, most of it charred, which had settled on everything else. Beneath this were fragments of timber from the bed frame, wardrobe, and cupboards, shards of glass from the mirrors and lamps, and numerous slivers of human bone.

Four emergency services arrived. The ambulances came and soon went, for there was nothing for them save the hysterical occupants of three other rooms along the corridor. However, the screaming occupants spoke no Russian and the ambulance men spoke nothing else. Seeing there were no physical injuries, they left the screamers to the night manager.

The fire service appeared, but though everything in both the affected rooms was charred by the white heat of the explosion, nothing was actually blazing. The forensic team had plenty to do, bagging every last crumb of the debris, part of it human, for later analysis.

Homicide was represented, on the orders of a major general, by Detective Borodin. He could see at a glance there was nothing in the room bigger than the palm of a hand, and a dangerous four-foot-diameter hole in the floor, but there was something in the bathroom.

The door had evidently been closed, for it had fragmented and the bits hurled into the sink. The wall in which it was set had also come down, being forced into the bathroom by the blast from the other side.

But under the rubble was an attaché case, scored, charred, and deeply scratched. Its contents, however, had survived. Apparently at the moment of explosion the case must have been standing in the most sheltered place in either room, up against the inside bathroom wall between the toilet and the bidet. The water from the shattered appliances had soaked the case, but its contents had survived. Borodin checked to see that he was unobserved, then slipped both documents under his jacket.

Colonel Grishin had them in time for his coffee. Twenty-four hours can make a difference to a mood. He gazed at them both with deep satisfaction. One was a file, in Russian, which he recognized as the Black Manifesto. The other was an American passport. It was in the name of Jason Monk.

"One to get in," he thought, "and one to get out. But this time, my friend, you are not getting out."

•   •   •

TWO other things happened that day and neither attracted a whit of attention. A British visitor whose passport gave his name as Brian Marks flew into Sheremetyevo Airport on the scheduled afternoon flight from London, and two other Englishmen drove a Volvo sedan across the border from Finland.

So far as the officials at the airport were concerned the new arrival was one of hundreds and appeared to speak no Russian. But like the others he made his way through the various controls and finally emerged to hail a taxi and ask to be driven to central Moscow.

Dismissing his taxi on a street corner, he made sure he was not being followed, then continued by foot to the small second-class hotel where he had a reservation for a single room.

His currency declaration form showed he had admitted to a modest amount of British sterling pounds, which he would need to redeclare on departure, or produce official exchange receipts in lieu of them, and some traveler's checks to which the same stipulation would apply. His currency form made no mention of the bricks of hundred-dollar bills taped to the back of each thigh.

His surname was not really Marks but the similarity with Marx as in Karl Marx had amused the engraver who had prepared his passport. Given the choice, he had elected to retain his real first name of Brian. He was in fact the same Russian-speaking ex-soldier with a career in Special Forces whom Sir Nigel Irvine had sent on the reconnaissance mission in September.

Having settled in, he set about his various tasks and purchases. He rented a small car from a Western agency and explored one of the outer suburbs of the city, the district of Vorontsovo in the far south of the capital.

For two days, at varying intervals so as not to attract attention to himself, he staked out and observed one particular building, a large windowless warehouse constantly visited during daylight hours by heavy trucks.

By night he observed the building on foot, walking past it a number of times, always clutching a half-empty bottle of vodka. On the few occasions another pedestrian came the opposite way, he would simply weave from side to side like any drunk, and be ignored.

What he saw he liked. The chain-link fence would prove no obstacle. The truck bay for deliveries and pickups was locked at night, but there was a small door with a padlock at the rear of the warehouse, and a single guard on foot made occasional tours of the outside during the hours of darkness. In other words, the building was a soft target.

At the old South Port secondhand car market, where everything from a decrepit wreck to a nearly new limousine just stolen in the West could be bought for cash, he acquired a set of Moscow license plates and an assortment of tools, including a pair of heavy-duty bolt cutters.

In the center of the city he purchased a dozen cheap but reliable

Swatch watches and a variety of batteries, rolls of electrical wire, and tape. When he was finally satisfied that he could find the warehouse with complete accuracy at any time of the day or night and get back to the city center by a score of different routes, he returned to his hotel to wait for the Volvo pushing south from St. Petersburg.

The rendezvous with Ciaran and Mitch was at the McDonald's hamburger bar on Tverskaya Street. The other two Special Forces soldiers had had a slow but uneventful journey south.

In a garage in south London the Volvo had been endowed with its unusual cargo. Both front wheels had been removed and replaced with old-fashioned tires containing inner tubes. Before this, each inner tube had been slit. Into the tubes were dropped hundreds of thumb-sized pellets of Semtex plastic explosive. The tubes were then patched, slipped back inside the tires, and inflated.

With the spinning of the wheels, the puttylike explosive, extraordinarily stable unless subjected to the attentions of a mercury-fulminate detonator, had melded into a skin lining the inside of each inner tube. In this manner, after being shipped to Stockholm, the Volvo had rolled sedately for a thousand kilometers via Helsinki to Moscow. The detonators came in the lower layer of a box of Havana cigars, apparently bought on the ferry but in fact prepared in London.

Ciaran and Mitch stayed at a different hotel. Brian accompanied them in the Volvo to a patch of waste ground near South Port where the car was jacked up and the two spare wheels the tourists had thoughtfully brought with them replaced the two front wheels. No one took any notice; the car thieves of Moscow were always cannibalizing cars around the South Port area. It took only a few more minutes to deflate and remove the inner tubes, stuff them in a carryall, return to the hotel, and strip away the melded Semtex that lined them.

While Ciaran and Mitch assembled their goodies in the hotel room, Brian took the shredded rubber tubes out into the streets to lose them in a variety of public garbage bins.

The three pounds of plastic explosive were divided into twelve small pieces, each about the size of a crushproof cigarette pack. To these were added one detonator, one battery, and one watch, with the wires connecting the components at the appropriate places. The bombs were finally held together with stout plastic tape.

"Thank God," said Mitch as they worked, "we don't have to use that kipper rubbish."

Semtex-H, the most popular of all the RDX plastic explosive derivatives, has always been a Czech product, and under Communism was made completely odor-free, which made it the terrorists' favorite device. After the fall of Communism, however, the new Czech president Vaclav Havel quickly acceded to a Western request to change the formula and add a particularly foul odor to make the stuff detectable in transit. The odor was similar to rotten fish, hence Mitch's reference to kippers.

By the mid-nineties detection devices had become so sophisticated that they could even identify the nonsmell variety. But warm rubber has its own very similar odor, hence the use of the tires as a transporting device. In fact the Volvo had not been subjected to that sort of test, but Sir Nigel believed in extreme caution, a quality of which Ciaran and Mitch totally approved.

The raid on the factory took place six days after Colonel Grishin received the Black Manifesto and the passport of Jason Monk.

The trusty Volvo, with its new front wheels and equally new and false Moscow license plates, was driven by Brian. If anyone stopped them, he was the Russian speaker.

They parked three streets away from their target and walked the rest of the way. The chain-link fence at the rear of the premises proved no match for the bolt cutters. The three men ran at a crouch across the intervening fifty feet of concrete and disappeared into the shadows cast by a pile of ink drums.

Fifteen minutes later the solitary night guard made his round. He heard a loud burp from a patch of shadow, spun around, and fixed his flashlight on the source. He saw a drunk, collapsed against the warehouse wall, clutching a bottle of vodka.

He had no time to work out how the man had got into the sealed compound, for having turned his back on the pile of drums he never saw the figure in black overalls who emerged from between them and hit him hard on the back of the head with a piece of lead pipe. So far as the guard was concerned there was a brief flash of fireworks and then darkness.

Brian cinched the man's ankles, wrists, and mouth with heavy tape while Ciaran and Mitch took the padlock off the door. When it was open they dragged the senseless guard inside, laid him by the wall, and closed the door.

Inside the cavernous factory a string of night-lights burned among the girders of the roof, casting a dim glow over the interior. Much of the floor space was taken up by great reels of newsprint and stacked drums of ink. But the center of the factory contained what they had come for: three huge web-offset printing presses.

Somewhere near the front doors of the building they knew the second guard would be ensconced in his warm glass booth, watching the television or reading his newspaper. Brian slipped quietly between the machines to take care of him. Having done so he returned, went out the back, and stood guard over the exit route.

Ciaran and Mitch were no strangers to the three machines in front of them. They were Baker-Perkins presses, made in the United States and not replaceable in Russia. Resupply would require a long sea journey from Baltimore to St. Petersburg. Provided the mainframes were distorted, not even a Boeing 747 could bring the needed components by air.

Posing as Finnish newspaper executives contemplating the re-equipping of their plant with Baker-Perkins presses, both men had kindly been given a tour of the factory by a company in Norwich, England, which used the same machines. After that a retired engineer, handsomely rewarded, had completed their education.

Their targets were four in type. Each press was fed by giant reels of paper, and the feeders for these rolls of newsprint, the reel stands, were of sophisticated technology, capable of ensuring that as one reel ran out it was seamlessly replaced by another. The reel stands were the first target and there was one for each machine. Ciaran began to place his small bombs precisely where they would guarantee that the reel stands would never work again.

Mitch took care of the ink-supply mechanism. These were four-color presses, and the supply of the exact amounts of four different inks at the right moment in the press run depended on a mixer unit fed by four great drums containing different colors. With both these pieces of technology taken care of, the two saboteurs addressed the actual presses.

The parts they chose for their remaining bombs were the mainframes and the bearings of the impression cylinders, one per machine.

They spent twenty minutes inside the press shop. Then Mitch tapped his watch and nodded at Ciaran. It was one in the morning and the timers were set for one-thirty. Five minutes later they were back outside, dragging the guard, now awake but still helpless, behind them. He would be colder out there, but shielded from flying fragments. The guard at the front, lying on the floor of his office, was too far away to be hurt.

At ten past one they were in the Volvo and moving. At half past, they were too far away to hear the almost simultaneous series of booms and cracks as the presses, reel stands, and ink feeders crashed to the concrete floor.

So discreet were the explosions that the sleeping denizens of the Vorontsovo suburb were hardly roused. It was not until the guard lying outside had hopped laboriously around the building to the front gate and hit the alarm button with his elbow that the police were called.

The liberated guards found the phones were still working and called the factory foreman, whose home number was pinned up in the office. He arrived at half-past three and examined the devastation with horror. Then he called Boris Kuznetsov.

The Union of Patriotic Forces' propaganda chief was there by five and listened to the factory manager's tale of woe. At seven he phoned Colonel Grishin.

Before that hour the rented car and the Volvo had been abandoned just off Manege Square, where the rental would soon be found and returned to the agency. The Volvo, which was unlocked with its keys in the ignition, would certainly be stolen before then, and was.

The three former soldiers took their breakfast in the insalubrious café at the airport and boarded their flight to Helsinki, the first of the morning, an hour later.

As they flew out of Russia, Colonel Grishin was surveying the wrecked printing plant with black anger. There would be an inquiry; he would institute one, and woe betide anyone who had collaborated. But his professional eye told him the perpetrators were experts and he doubted he would find them.

Kuznetsov was distraught. Every week for the past two years the Saturday tabloid *Probudis!*, Russian for *"Awake!,"* had carried the words and policies of Igor Komarov to five million homes across

Russia. The idea of establishing a major newspaper owned and run entirely by the UPF had been his, as had been the monthly magazine *Rodina, "Motherland."*

These two vehicles, a mixture of easy contests with big prizes, sex confessions, and race propaganda, had carried the words of the leader into every corner of the land and contributed enormously to his electoral popularity.

"When can you be back in production?" he asked the head printer. The man shrugged.

"When we have new presses," he said. "These cannot be mended. Two months, perhaps."

Kuznetsov was pale with shock. He had not yet told the leader himself. It was Grishin's fault, he assured himself, the place should have been better guarded. But one thing was certain: There would be no *Probudis!* this Saturday and no special edition of *Rodina* in a fortnight. Nor even for eight weeks at a minimum. And the presidential elections were in six.

It was not a very good morning for Detective Inspector Borodin either, though he had entered the office in the Homicide Division of the militia HQ on Petrovka in good humor. His geniality during the previous week had been noted by his colleagues, but had remained unexplained. In fact the explanation was simple: his delivery of two valuable documents to Colonel Anatoli Grishin after the still unexplained bomb explosion at the Metropol had brought him a very handsome bonus to his monthly retainer.

Privately he knew there was not the slightest point in continuing inquiries into the outrage at the hotel. Restoration work had already begun, the insurers were almost certainly foreigners who would pick up the tab, the American guest was dead, and the mystery was total. If he suspected that his own inquiries concerning the American, ordered by Grishin himself, had something to do with his almost immediate death, he, Borodin, was not going to make an issue of it.

Igor Komarov was certainly going to be the new president of the Russian Federation in less than two months, the second most powerful man in the country would be Colonel Grishin, and there would be rewards to almost dizzying heights for those who had served him well during the years of opposition.

The office was abuzz with news of the destruction during the night of the printing presses of the UPF Party. Borodin put it down to Zyuganov's Communists or some paid hoodlums from one of the mafia gangs, motive obscure. He was just airing his theories when his phone rang.

"Borodin?" said a voice.

"Detective Borodin speaking, yes."

"Kuzmin here."

He rattled his memory but it stayed blank.

"Who?"

"Professor Kuzmin, forensic pathology lab, Second Medical Institute. Did you send me the specimens recovered from the Metropol bombing? The file has your name on it."

"Ah, yes, I am the officer in charge of the case."

"Well, you're a bloody fool."

"I don't understand."

"I have just finished my examination of the remains of the body recovered from that hotel room. Along with a lot of bits of wood and glass that have nothing to do with me," said the irascible pathologist.

"So what's the problem, Professor? He's dead, isn't he?"

The voice on the phone was becoming shrill with rage.

"Of course he's dead, poltroon. He wouldn't be in bits in my lab if he was running around."

"Then I can't see the problem. I've been years in Homicide, and I've never seen anyone more dead."

The voice from the Second Medical Institute took a grip on itself and dropped to the coaxing tone of one speaking to a small and rather dim child.

"The question, my dear Borodin, is, *Who* is dead?"

"Well, the American tourist of course. You have his bones there."

"Yes, I have bones, Detective Borodin." The voice stressed the word *detective* to imply the policeman would have trouble finding his way to the washroom without a guide dog. "I would also expect to have fragments of tissue, muscle, cartilage, sinew, skin, hair, nails, entrails—even a couple of grams of marrow. But what do I have? Bones, just bones, nothing but bones."

"I don't follow you. What's wrong with the bones?"

The professor finally exploded. Borodin had to hold the phone away from his ear.

"There's nothing wrong with the bloody bones. They're lovely bones. They've been lovely bones for about twenty years, which is the period I estimate their former owner has been dead. What I am trying to get into your pin-size brain is that someone took the trouble to blow to bits an anatomical skeleton, the sort every medical student keeps in the corner of his room."

Borodin's mouth opened and shut like a fish's.

"The American wasn't in that room?" he asked.

"Not when the bomb went off," said Dr. Kuzmin. "Who was he anyway? Or, as he is presumably still alive, who is he?"

"I don't know. Just a Yankee academic."

"Ah, you see, another intellectual. Like myself. Well, you can tell him I like his sense of humor. Where do you want me to send my report?"

The last thing Borodin wanted was for it to land on his own desk. He named a certain major general in the militia Presidium.

The major general received it the same afternoon. He rang Colonel Grishin to give him the news. He did not get a bonus.

By nightfall Anatoli Grishin had mobilized his private army of informants, and it was a formidable force. Thousands of replicas of the photo of Jason Monk, the one taken from his passport, were circulated to the Black Guard and the Young Combatants, who were spewed onto the streets of the capital in the hundreds to search for the wanted man. The effort and the numbers were greater than during the hunt for Leonid Zaitsev, the missing office cleaner.

Other copies went to the clan chiefs of the Dolgoruki underworld mafia with orders to locate and hold. Informants in the police and immigration services were alerted. A reward of one hundred billion rubles was offered for the fugitive, a sum to take the breath away.

Against such a locust plague of eyes and ears there would be nowhere for the American to hide, Grishin advised Igor Komarov. This network of informants could penetrate every nook and cranny of Moscow, every hideaway and bolthole, every corner and crevice. If he did not lock himself inside his own embassy, where he could do no further harm, he would be found.

Grishin was almost right. There was one place his Russians could not penetrate: the tightly sealed world of the Chechens.

Jason Monk was inside that world, in a safe apartment above a spice shop, protected by Magomed, Aslan, and Sharif, and beyond them a screen of invisible street people who could see a Russian coming a mile away and communicate in a language no one else could understand.

In any case, Monk had already made his second contact.

CHAPTER 14

OF ALL THE SOLDIERS OF RUSSIA, SERVING OR RETIRED, THE ONE who in terms of prestige was worth any dozen others was General of the Army Nikolai Nikolayev.

At seventy-three and just a few days short of his seventy-fourth birthday, he was still an impressive figure. Six-feet one-inch tall, he carried himself bolt upright; a mane of white hair, a ruddy face weathered by a thousand bitter winds, and his trademark moustache jutting in two defiant points on either side of his upper lip marked him out in any gathering.

He had been a tank man all his life, a commander of mechanized infantry, had served in every theater and on every front over a fifty-year career, and to those who had served under him, numbering several millions in all by 1999, he had become a legend.

It was common knowledge that he would and should have retired with the rank of marshal, but for his habit of speaking his mind to the politicians and time servers.

Like Leonid Zaitsev, the Rabbit, whom he would never remember but whom he had once clapped on the back at a camp outside Potsdam, the general had been born near Smolensk, west of Moscow. But twelve years earlier, in the winter of 1925, the son of an engineer.

He could still recall the day he and his father had been passing a church and the older man had forgotten himself and made the sign of the cross. The son had asked what he was doing. Startled and fearful, his father had told him never to tell a soul.

Those were the days when another Soviet youth had been officially declared a hero for betraying his parents to the NKVD for anti-Party remarks. Both parents had died in the camps, but the son had been made a role model for Soviet youth.

But young Kolya loved his father and never said a word. Later he learned the meaning of the gesture, but accepted the word of his teachers that it was all complete rubbish.

He was fifteen when the Blitzkrieg erupted out of the west, on June 22, 1941. Within a month Smolensk fell to the German tanks and with thousands of others the boy was on the run. His parents did not make it and he never saw them again.

A strapping youth, he helped his ten-year-old sister along for a hundred miles until one night they jumped a train heading east. They did not know it, but it was a special train. Along with others it carried a disassembled tank factory out of the danger zone and east toward the safety of the Urals.

Cold and hungry, the children clung to the roof until the train came to rest at Chelyabinsk in the foothills of the mountains. There the engineers reerected the factory called Tankograd.

There was no time for schooling. Galina went to an orphanage, Kolya was put to work in the factory. He stayed there for almost two years.

By the winter of 1942 the Soviets were taking horrendous losses in men and tanks around Kharkov and Stalingrad. The tactics were traditional and lethal. There was neither time nor talent for subtlety; the men and tanks were thrown into the muzzles of the German guns without thought or care for losses. In Russian military history that was how it had always been.

At Tankograd the demand was for more and more production; they worked sixteen-hour shifts and slept beneath the lathes. What they were building was the KV1, named after Marshal Klimenti Voroshilov, a useless article as a soldier but one of Stalin's favorite toadies. The KV1 was a heavy tank, the Soviets' main battle tank at the time.

By the spring of 1943 the Soviets were reinforcing the bulge around the city of Kursk, an enclave 150 miles from north to south that jutted 100 miles into the German lines. In June, the seventeen-year-old was detailed to accompany a trainload of KV1s west to the salient, unload them at the railhead, deliver them, and return to Chelyabinsk. He did all but the last.

The new tanks were lined up by the track when the regimental commander for whom they were destined strode up. He was amazingly young, not twenty-five, a colonel, bearded, haggard, and exhausted.

"I've got no fucking drivers," he screamed at the tank factory official in charge of the delivery. Then he turned to the big flaxen-haired youth. "Can you drive these bloody things?"

"Yes, Comrade, but I have to go back to Tankograd."

"No chance. You can drive, you're drafted."

The train steamed east. Private Nikolai Nikolayev found himself in a rough cotton smock, deep inside the hull of a KV1, heading toward the town of Prokhorovka. The Battle of Kursk began two weeks later.

Though referred to as the "Battle" of Kursk, it was in fact a series of raging and bloody clashes that spanned the whole enclave and lasted two months. By the time it was over, Kursk had become the biggest tank battle the world has ever seen, before or since. It involved 6,000 tanks on both sides, 2 million men, and 4,000 aircraft. It was the battle that finally proved the German Panzer was not invincible after all. But it was a close-run thing.

The German army was just deploying its own wonder weapon, the Tiger, packing a fearsome 88mm cannon in its turret, which, with armor-piercing shells, could take out anything in its path. The KV1 carried a much smaller 76mm gun, even though the new model Nikolai had delivered mounted the improved ZIS-5 longer-range version.

On July 12, 1943, the Russians began to counterattack, and the key was the Prokhorovka sector. The regiment Nikolai had joined was down to six KV1s when the commander saw what he thought were five Panzer Mark IVs and decided to attack. The Russians rolled in line abreast over the crest of a ridge and down into a shallow valley; the Germans were on the opposite crest.

The young colonel was wrong about the Panzer IVs; they were Tigers. One by one they picked off the six KV1s with armor-piercing sabot.

Nikolai's tank was hit twice. The first shell tore off all the tracks on one side and peeled open the hull. Down in the driver's seat he felt the tank shudder and halt. The second shell took the turret a glancing blow and careened off into the hillside. But the impact was enough to kill the crew.

There were five men in the KV1 and four of them were dead. Nikolai, battered, bruised, and shaken, crawled out of his living tomb to the smell of running diesel fuel on hot metal. Bodies got in his way; he pushed them to one side.

The gun commander and gunner were sprawled over the breech, blood and mucus running from mouth, nose, and ears. Through the gap in the hull Nikolai could see the Tigers racing past, through the smoke of the other blazing KV1s.

To his surprise, he found the gun turret still worked. He hauled a shell up from the rack, pushed it into the breech, and closed the mechanism. He had never done it before, but he had seen it done. Usually it took two men. Feeling sick from the blow to his head down below and the stench of fuel up above, he turned the turret around, put his eye to the periscopic sight, found a Tiger barely three hundred yards away, and fired.

It turned out the one he had picked was the last of the five. The four Tigers up ahead did not notice. He reloaded, found another target, and fired again. The second Tiger took his shell in the gap between turret and hull, and exploded. Somewhere beneath Nikolai's feet there was a low whump and flames began to trickle across the grass, spreading as they found more pools of fuel. After his second shell the remaining three Tigers noticed they were under attack from behind and turned. He took his third one side-on as it pulled around. The other two completed their turn and came back at him. That was when he knew he was dead.

He threw himself down and fell out of the rent in the KV's side just before the Tigers' answering shell took away the turret in which he had been standing. The ammunition began to explode; he could feel his blouse smoldering. So he rolled in the long grass, over and over, away from the wreck.

Then something happened that he did not expect and did not see. Ten SU-152s came over the ridge and the Tigers decided they had had enough. There were two left of five. They raced for the opposite slope and the crest above it. One got there and disappeared.

Nikolai felt someone hauling him to his feet. The man was a full colonel. The shallow valley was studded with wrecked tanks, six Russian and four German. His own tank was surrounded by three of the dead Tigers.

"Did you do this?" asked the colonel.

Nikolai could hardly hear him. His ears were ringing; he felt sick. He nodded.

"Come with me," said the colonel. There was a small GAZ truck behind the ridge. The colonel drove for eight miles. They came to a bivouac. In front of the main tent was a long table covered in maps, being studied by a dozen high-ranking officers. The colonel halted the truck, strode forward, and threw up a salute. The senior general looked up.

Nikolai sat in the front passenger seat of the truck. He could see the colonel talking and the officers looking at him. Then the senior among them raised his hand and beckoned. Fearful that he had let two Tigers escape, Nikolai came down from the truck and marched over. His cotton blouse was scorched, his face blackened, and he stank of petrol and cordite.

"Three Tigers?" said General Pavel Rotmistrov, Commanding Officer, First Guards Tank Army. "From the rear? From a wrecked KV1?"

Nikolai stood there like an idiot and said nothing.

The general smiled and turned to a short, chunky man with piggy eyes and the insignia of a political commissar.

"I think that's worth a bit of metal?"

The chunky commissar nodded. Comrade Stalin would approve. A box was brought from the tent. Rotmistrov pinned the order of Hero of the Soviet Union on the seventeen-year-old. The commissar, who happened to be Nikita Khrushchev, watched and nodded again.

Nikolai Nikolayev was told to report to a field hospital, where his scorched hands and face were treated with a smelly salve, and then return to the general's headquarters. There he was given a field commission, a lieutenancy, and a platoon of three KV1s. Then it was back into combat.

That winter, with the Kursk salient miles behind him and the Panzers on the retreat, he received a captaincy and a company of brand-new heavy tanks fresh from the factory. They were the IS-2s, named after Josef Stalin. With a 122mm gun and thicker armor, they became known as the Tiger Killers.

At Operation Bagration he got his second Hero of the Soviet Union medal for outstanding personal bravery and on the outskirts of Berlin, fighting under Marshal Chuikov, the third.

This was the man, almost fifty-five years later, that Jason Monk had come to see.

If the old general had been a bit more tactful with the Politburo he would have got his marshal's baton and with it a big retirement dacha out along the Moskva River at Peredelkino with the rest of the fat cats, all free as a gift of the state. But he always told them what he really thought, and they did not always like it.

So he built his own more modest bungalow for his declining years, off the Minsk road on the way to Tukhovo, an area studded with army camps where he could at least be close to what remained of his beloved army.

He had never married—"no life for a young girl" he would say of his numerous postings to the bleakest outposts of the Soviet empire—and at seventy-three he lived with a faithful valet, a former master sergeant with one foot, and an Irish wolfhound with four feet.

Monk had tracked down his rather humble abode simply by asking the villagers in the nearby communities where Uncle Kolya lived. Years earlier, when he had entered middle age, the old general had been given the nickname by his younger officers, and it stuck. His hair and moustache had turned prematurely white so that he looked old enough to be the uncle of all of them. General of the Army Nikolayev was good enough for the newspapers, but every ex-soldier in the country knew him as Dyadya Kolya.

As Monk was driving a Defense Ministry staff car that evening and was dressed as a full colonel of the General Staff, the villagers saw no reason not to point out that Uncle Kolya lived at such-and-such a place.

It was pitch-black and freezing cold when Monk knocked at the door a little after nine in the evening. The limping valet answered, and seeing the uniform let him in.

General Nikolayev was expecting no visitors, but the staff colonel's uniform and the attaché case caused him no more than mild surprise. He was in his favorite armchair by a roaring log fire reading a military memoir by a younger general and occasionally snorting in derision. He knew them all, he knew what they had done and, more embarrassing, he knew what they had never done, no matter what they claimed now that they could make money by writing fictitious history.

He looked up when Valodya announced he had a visitor from Moscow and left.

"Who are you?" he growled.

"Someone who needs to talk to you, General."

"From Moscow?"

"Just now, yes."

"Well, since you've come, better get on with it." The general nodded at the briefcase. "Papers from the Ministry?"

"Not quite. Papers, yes. From somewhere else."

"Cold outside. Better sit down. Well, spit it out. What's your business?"

"Let me be perfectly frank. This uniform was to persuade you to receive me. I am not in the Russian Army, I am not a colonel, and I am certainly not on anyone's general staff. In fact I am an American."

Across the fireplace the Russian stared at him for several seconds as if he could not believe his ears. Then the points of his bristling moustache twitched in outrage.

"You're an impostor," he snapped. "You're a damned spy. I'm not having impostors and spies in my house. Get out."

Monk remained where he was.

"All right, I will. But as six thousand miles is a long way to come for thirty seconds, will you answer me one single question?"

General Nikolayev glowered at him.

"One question. What?"

"Five years ago when Boris Yeltsin asked you to come out of retirement and command the attack on Chechnya and the destruction of the capital Grozny, rumor has it you looked at the plans and told the then Defense Minister Pavel Grachev: 'I command soldiers, not butchers. This is a job for slaughterers.' Is that true?"

"What of it?"

"Was it true? You allowed me a question."

"All right, yes. And I was right."

"Why did you say it?"

"That's two questions."

"I've still got six thousand more miles to get home."

"All right. Because I don't believe genocide is a job for soldiers. Now get out."

"You know that's a rotten book you're reading?"

"How do you know?"

"I've read it. It's bunk."

"True. So what?"

Monk slipped a hand into his briefcase and extracted the Black Manifesto. He opened it at a page he had tagged. Then he held it out across the fire.

"Since you have the time to read rubbish, why not glance at something really unpleasant?"

The general's anger vied with his curiosity.

"Yankee propaganda?"

"No. Russian future. Have a look. That page and the next."

General Nikolayev grunted and took the proffered file. He read quickly the two marked pages. His face mottled.

"Bloody rubbish," he shouted. "Who wrote this crap?"

"Have you heard of Igor Komarov?"

"Don't be a fool. Of course. Going to be president in January."

"Good or bad?"

"How should I know? They're all as bent as corkscrews."

"So he's no better or worse than the rest of them?"

"That's about it."

Monk described the events of the previous July 15, covering the ground as fast as he could, fearful of losing the old man's attention or, worse, his patience.

"Don't believe it," the general snapped. "You come here with some fancy story . . ."

"If it's a fancy story, then three men did not die in attempts to recover it. But they did. Are you going anywhere this evening?"

"Eh, no. Why?"

"Then why not put down Pavel Grachev's memoirs and read Igor Komarov's intentions? Some parts you will like. The reempowerment of the army. But it's not to defend the Motherland. There's no external threat to the Motherland. It is to create an army that will carry out genocide. You may not like Jews, Chechens, Georgians, Ukrainians, Armenians, but they were in those tanks too, remember. They were at Kursk and Bagration, Berlin and Kabul. They fought beside you. Why not spare a few minutes to see what Mr. Komarov has in store for them?"

General Nikolayev stared at the American a quarter of a century his junior, then grunted.

"Do Americans drink vodka?"

"They do on freezing nights in the middle of Russia."

"There's a bottle over there. Help yourself."

While the old man read, Monk treated himself to a slug of Moskovskaya and thought of the briefing he had had in Castle Forbes.

"He's probably the last of the Russian generals with an old-fashioned sense of honor. He's no fool and he's got no fear. There are ten million veterans who will still listen to Uncle Kolya," the Russian tutor Oleg had told him.

After the fall of Berlin and a year in occupation, the young Major Nikolayev was sent back to Moscow, to Armored Officer School. In the summer of 1950 he was appointed to command one of the seven regiments of heavy tanks on the Yalu River in the Far East.

The Korean War was at its height, with the Americans rolling back the North Koreans. Stalin was seriously thinking of saving the Koreans' bacon by throwing in his own new tanks against the Americans. Two things prevailed to prevent him: wiser counsels and his own paranoia. The IS-4s were so ultrasecret that details of them were never revealed, and Stalin feared to lose one intact. In 1951 Nikolayev returned to a lieutenant-colonelcy and a posting to Potsdam. He was still only twenty-five.

At thirty he commanded a Special Ops tank regiment in the Hungarian uprising. That was where he first upset Soviet Ambassador Yuri Andropov, who went on to become chairman of the KGB for fifteen years and General Secretary of the USSR. Colonel Nikolayev refused to use his tanks' machine guns to rake the crowds of protesting Hungarian civilians on the streets of Budapest.

"They're seventy percent women and children," he told the ambassador and architect of the crushing of the revolt. "They're throwing rocks. Stones don't hurt tanks."

"They must be taught a lesson!" shouted Andropov. "Use your machine guns."

Nikolayev had seen what heavy machine guns can do to massed

civilians in a confined space. At Smolensk in 1941. His parents had
been among them.

"You want it, you do it," he told Andropov. A senior general
calmed things down but Nikolayev's career hung by a thread. Andropov was not a forgiving man.

In the early and mid-sixties he got the outposts, years along the
banks of the Amur and Ussuri rivers facing China across the flowing
water while Khrushchev debated whether to try to teach Mao Tse-
tung a lesson in tank warfare.

Khrushchev fell, Brezhnev succeeded him, the crisis calmed
down, and Nikolayev gladly forsook the frozen barren wastes of the
Manchurian border to return to Moscow.

In 1968, as a forty-two-year-old major general, he commanded a
division in the Prague uprising, far and away the best-performing
division in the operation. He won the undying gratitude of the
airborne, the VDVs, when he saved one of their units from the
frying pan. A too-small company had been dropped into central
Prague, was surrounded by Czechs and in trouble, when Nikolayev
personally led a tank company into the city to get them out.

He spent four years lecturing on tank warfare at the Frunze
Academy, turning out an entire new generation of tank corps officers who adored him, and in 1973 was adviser on armored warfare
to the Syrians. It was the year of the Yom Kippur War.

Though he was supposed to remain in the background, he knew
the Soviet-supplied tanks so well that he planned and mounted an
attack against the Israeli Seventh Armored Brigade out of the Golan
Heights. The Syrians were no match for it, but the planning and
tactics were brilliant. The Israeli Seventh Armored survived, but for
a while the Syrians had them severely worried; it ranked as one of
the few occasions when Arab armor gave them any problems at all.

On the basis of Syria he was invited onto the general staff, planning offensive operations against NATO. Then in 1979 up came
Afghanistan. He was fifty-three, and was offered the command of
the 40th Army that would do the job. The post meant promotion
from lieutenant general to colonel general.

General Nikolayev looked at the plans, looked at the terrain,
looked at the indigenous people, and wrote a report that said the
operation and occupation would prove a mankiller, had no point,

and would constitute a Soviet Vietnam. It was the second time he upset Andropov.

They assigned him the wilderness again—recruit training. The generals who went to Afghanistan got their medals and their glory—for a while. They also got their body bags, tens of thousands of body bags.

"This is garbage. I won't believe this rubbish."

The old general tossed the black file across the hearth to land in Monk's lap. "You have a nerve, Yankee. You come barging into my country, into my house . . . try to fill my head with these pernicious lies. . . ."

"Tell me, General, what do you think of us?"

"Us?"

"Yes, us. The Americans, the people from the West. I have been sent here. I am no freelance. Why have I been sent? If Komarov is a fine man and a great leader-to-be, why should we give a fuck?"

The old man stared at him, not so much shocked by the language, which he had heard many times before, but by the intensity of the younger man.

"I know I've spent my whole life fighting you."

"No, General, you've spent your whole life opposing us. And you did so in the service of regimes you know have done terrible things. . . ."

"This is my country, American. Insult it at your peril."

Monk leaned forward and tapped the Black Manifesto.

"But nothing like this. Not Khrushchev, not Brezhnev, not Andropov, nothing like this. . . ."

"If it's true, if it's true," shouted the old soldier. "Anybody could write that."

"So try this. This is the story of how it came into our possession. An old soldier gave his life to get this out."

He handed the general the verification report and poured him a generous slug of his own vodka. The general threw it back Russian-style, in one gulp.

It was not until the summer of 1987 that someone reached to a high shelf, brought down the 1979 Nikolayev report on Afghanistan, dusted it off, and gave it to the Foreign Ministry. In January 1988, Foreign Minister Eduard Shevardnadze told the world, "We're pulling out."

Nikolayev was made colonel general at last, and brought from the general staff to supervise the withdrawal. The last commander of the 40th Army was General Gromov, but he was told the overall plan would be Nikolayev's. Amazingly the whole 40th Army came out with hardly any more casualties, though the mujahedin were snapping at their heels.

The last Soviet column drove over the Amu Darya bridge on February 15, 1989. Nikolai Nikolayev brought up the rear. He could have flown in a staff jet, but he drove out with the men.

He sat alone in the back of an open GAZ jeep with a driver in front. No one else. He had never retreated before. He sat bolt upright in his battle dress uniform of combat smock, with no shoulder boards to give his rank. But the men recognized the mane of white hair and the points of the bristling moustache.

They were sick and tired of Afghanistan, glad to be going home despite the defeat. Just north of the bridge the cheering began. They pulled over when they saw the white hair, poured out of the trucks, and cheered him. There were VDV airborne men among them who had heard of the Prague affair and they cheered too. The BMD troop transporters were mostly driven by ex-tank men, and they waved and shouted.

He was sixty-three then, driving north into retirement, to a life of lectures, memoirs, and reunions. But he was still their Uncle Kolya, and he was bringing them home.

In his forty-five years as a tank man he had done three things that made him a legend. He had banned "hazing"—the systematic bullying of new recruits by three-year men, which led to hundreds of suicides—in every unit under his command, causing the other generals to copy him. He had fought the political establishment tooth and claw for better conditions and food for his men, and he had insisted on unit pride and intensive training, over and over again, until every unit he commanded from platoon to division was the best in the line when it counted.

Gorbachev gave him his General of the Army rank and then fell from power. If he had agreed to butcher Chechnya for Yeltsin he would have got his marshal's baton and his free dacha.

"What do you expect, American?"

General Nikolayev threw down the verification report and stared at the fire.

"If it's all true, then the man's a shit after all. And what am I supposed to do about it? I'm old, retired these eleven years, past it, over the hill. . . ."

"They are still out there," said Monk as he stood up and put the files back in his case. "Millions of them. Veterans. Some served under you, others remember you, most have heard of you. They will still listen if you speak."

"Look, Mr. American, this land of mine has suffered more than you can ever understand. This Motherland of mine is soaked in the blood of her sons and daughters. Now you tell me there is more to come. I grieve, if it is true, but I can do nothing."

"And the army, which will be made to do these things? What of the army, your army?"

"It is not my army anymore."

"It's as much your army as anyone else's."

"It's a defeated army."

"No, not defeated. The Communist regime was defeated. Not the soldiers, not your soldiers. They were withdrawn. Now here is a man who wants to rebuild them. But for a new purpose. Aggression, invasion, enslavement, slaughter."

"Why should I?"

"Do you have a car, General?"

The old man looked up from the fire, startled.

"Of course. A small one. It gets me about."

"Drive into Moscow. To the Alexandrovsky Gardens. To the big polished red granite stone. By the flame. Ask them what they would want of you. Not me. Them."

Monk left. By dawn he was back in yet another safe house with his Chechen bodyguards. It was the night the printing presses blew up.

•   •   •

AMONG the many arcane and historic institutions that still exist in Britain, few are more so than the College of Arms, whose existence goes back to the reign of Richard III. The senior officers of the college are the Kings of Arms and Heralds.

In medieval times, as their name implies, the heralds were first used to convey messages between warlords across the battlefield under a flag of truce. Between wars they were given a different job.

In peacetime it was customary for knights and nobles to gather for mock warfare in tournaments and jousts. As the knights were covered in body armor, often with the visor pulled down, the herald whose job it was to announce the next tourney might have a problem identifying the man inside the armor. To solve this problem, nobles carried an emblem or device upon their shields. Thus a herald seeing a shield with the sign of the bear and ragged staff would know that the Earl of Warwick was inside there somewhere.

From this function the heralds became the experts and arbiters of who was who, and more important, who had the right to call himself who. They traced and recorded the bloodlines of aristocracy down the generations.

This was not simply a matter of snobbery. Along with the titles went huge estates, castles, farms, and manors. In modern terms it could be the equivalent of proving legal ownership of the majority stock in General Motors. Great wealth and power were involved.

Nobles tended on their deathbeds to leave behind a gaggle of offspring, some legitimate and many not, so disputes concerning who was the legitimate heir flared up. Wars broke out over rival claims. The heralds, as keepers of the archive, were the final arbiters of true bloodline and of who had the right "to bear arms," meaning not weapons but a coat of arms describing the ancestry in pictorial terms.

Even today, the college will adjudicate on rival claims, devise a coat of arms for a newly ennobled banker or industrialist, or for a fee trace the genealogical tree of anyone as far back as records go.

Not surprisingly, the heralds are scholars, steeped in their strange science with its arcane Norman-French language and emblems, mastery of which requires many years of study. Some specialize in the ancestry of the noble houses of Europe, linked to the British aristocracy by constant intermarriage. By discreet but sedulous inquiry, Sir Nigel Irvine discovered that one in particular was the world's leading expert on the Romanov dynasty of Russia. It was said of Dr. Lancelot Probyn that he had forgotten more about the Romanovs than the Romanovs ever knew. After introducing himself over the phone as a retired diplomat preparing a paper for the Foreign Office on possible monarchic trends in Russia, Sir Nigel asked him for tea at the Ritz.

Dr. Probyn turned out to be a small cuddly man who treated his subject with great good humor and no pomposity. He reminded the old spymaster of the illustrations of Dickens's Mr. Pickwick.

"I wonder," said Sir Nigel as the crustless cucumber sandwiches arrived with the Earl Grey, "if we might contemplate the matter of the Romanov succession?"

The post of Clarenceux King of Arms, to give Dr. Probyn his glorious title, is not vastly paid and the rotund little scholar was unaccustomed to tea at the Ritz. He tucked into the sandwiches with eager industry.

"The Romanov line is only my hobby, you know. Not my real job."

"Nevertheless, I believe you are the author of the definitive work on the subject."

"Kind of you to say so. How can I help?"

"What about the Romanov succession? Is it clear?"

Dr. Probyn demolished the last sandwich and eyed the cakes.

"Far from it. They're a mess, a complete mess. The surviving bits of the old family are at sixes and sevens. Claimants all over the place. Why do you ask?"

"Let us suppose," said Sir Nigel carefully, "that for some reason the Russian people decided as a people that they wished to restore constitutional monarchy in the form of a czar."

"Well, they couldn't, because they never had one. The last Emperor—incidentally, that is the correct title and has been since 1721, but everyone still uses the word *czar*—was Nicholas the Second, an absolute monarch. They never had a constitutional one."

"Indulge me."

Dr. Probyn slipped the last fragment of an éclair into his mouth and took a sip of tea.

"Good cakes," he said.

"I'm glad."

"Well, in the extremely unlikely event of that ever happening, they would have a problem. As you know, Nicholas, along with the Czaritza Alexandra and all five of their children, were butchered at Yekaterinburg in 1917. That wiped out the direct line. All the claimants today are of indirect line, some going back to Nicholas's grandfather."

"So no strong, unassailable claim?"

"No. I could give you a more cogent briefing back at my office. Got all the charts. Couldn't spread them out here. They're quite large, lots of names, branches all over the place."

"But in theory, could the Russians reinstitute the monarchy?"

"Are you serious, Sir Nigel?"

"We are just talking theoretically."

"Well, theoretically anything is possible. Any monarchy can choose to become a republic by expelling its king. Or queen. Greece did. And any republic can choose to institute a constitutional monarchy. Spain did. Both in the last thirty years. So, yes, it could be done."

"Then the problem would be the candidate?"

"Absolutely. General Franco chose to create the legislation to restore the Spanish monarchy after his death. He chose the grandson of Alfonso XIII, Prince Juan Carlos, who reigns to this day. But there no counterclaim emerged. The bloodline was clear. Counterclaims can be messy."

"There are counterclaims in the Romanov line?"

"All over the place. Extremely messy."

"Anyone stand out?"

"No one springs to mind. I'd have to look hard. It's been a long time since anyone seriously asked."

"Would you have another look?" asked Sir Nigel. "I have to travel. Say, when I return? I'll call you at your office."

•   •   •

BACK in the days when the KGB was simply one vast organization for espionage, suppression, and control, with a single chairman, its tasks were so varied that it had to be subdivided into Chief Directorates, Directorates, and Departments.

Among these were the Eighth Chief Directorate and the Sixteenth Directorate, both charged with electronic surveillance, radio interception, phone tapping, and spy satellites. As such they were the Soviet equivalent of the American National Security Agency and National Reconnaissance Organization, or the British Government Communications Headquarters, GCHQ.

For the old-timers of the KGB like Chairman Andropov, electronic intelligence gathering, or ELINT, was hi-tech and scarcely understood, but at least its importance was recognized. In a society where technology was years behind the West save in military- or espionage-related matters, the very latest and best hi-tech facilities were nevertheless procured for the Eighth CD.

After Gorbachev's breakup of the KGB monolith in 1991, the Eighth and Sixteenth Chief Directorates were amalgamated and re-named the Federal Agency for Government Communication and Information, or FAPSI.

FAPSI was already endowed with the most advanced computers, the country's best mathematicians and codebreakers, and anything in interception technology that money could buy. But after the fall of Communism, this exceptionally expensive-to-run department ran into a major problem: funding.

With the introduction of privatization FAPSI literally went to the open market for funds. It offered emerging Russian business the ability to intercept, meaning steal, the commercial traffic of its rivals, domestic and foreign. For at least four years prior to 1999 it had been perfectly possible for a commercial operation in Russia to hire this government department to monitor the movements of a foreign subject in Russia whenever that foreigner made a phone call, sent a fax, cable, or telex, or made a radio transmission.

Colonel Anatoli Grishin estimated that wherever Jason Monk might be, the chances were he would have some means of communication with whoever had sent him. This could not be via his embassy, which was under surveillance, unless he called in by phone, which would be overheard and traced.

Therefore, reasoned Grishin, he had brought in or collected in Moscow some form of transmitter.

"If I were he," said the senior ranking scientist of FAPSI whom Grishin consulted for a substantial fee, "I would use a computer. Businessmen do it all the time."

"A computer that transmits and receives?" asked Grishin.

"Of course. Computers talk to satellites, and via satellites computers talk to computers. That's what the information superhighway, the Internet, is all about."

"The traffic must be vast."

"It is. But so are our computers. It's a question of filtering out. Ninety percent of computer-generated traffic is chitchat, idiots talking to each other. Nine percent is commercial, companies discussing products, prices, progress, contracts, delivery dates. One percent is governmental. That one percent used to be half the traffic flying around up there."

"How much is coded?"

"All governmental and about half the commercial. But most of the commercial codes we can break."

"Where in all that would my American friend be transmitting?"

The FAPSI official, who had spent his working life in the covert world, knew better than to ask for details.

"Probably among the commercial traffic," he said. "The governmental stuff, we know the source. We may not be able to crack it, but we know it comes from this or that embassy, legation, consulate. Is your man in one of those?"

"No."

"Then he's probably using the commercial satellites. The American government's equipment is mainly used for watching us and listening to us. It also carries diplomatic traffic. But now there are scores of commercial satellites up there; companies rent time and communicate with their branch offices all around the world."

"I think my man is transmitting from Moscow. Probably receiving, too."

"Receiving doesn't help us. A message pumped out by a satellite over us could be received anywhere from Archangel down to the Crimea. It's when he transmits we might spot him."

"So, if a Russian commercial company were to engage you to find the sender, you could do it?"

"Maybe. The fee would be substantial, depending on the number of men and the amount of computer time assigned, and the number of hours per day the watch has to be kept."

"Twenty-four hours a day," said Grishin, "all the men you have got."

The FAPSI scientist stared at him. The man was talking millions of U.S. dollars.

"That's quite an order."

"I'm serious."

"You want the messages?"

"No, the location of the sender."

"That's harder. The message, if intercepted, we can study at leisure, take time to break it. The sender will only be on-line for a nanosecond."

The day after Monk had his interview with General Nikolayev, FAPSI caught a blip. Grishin's contact rang him at the dacha off Kiselny Boulevard.

"He's been on-line," he said.

"You have the message?"

"Yes, and it's not commercial. He's using a one-time pad. It's unbreakable."

"That's not good enough," said Grishin. "Where did he transmit from?"

"Greater Moscow."

"Marvelous. Such a tiny place. I need the building."

"Be patient. We think we know the satellite he is using. It's probably one of the two InTelCor machines that overfly us daily. There was one over the horizon at the time. We can concentrate on them in the future."

"You do that," said Grishin.

For six days Monk had evaded the army of watchers Grishin had put on the streets. The Head of Security of the UPF was puzzled. The man had to eat. Either he was holed up in some small place, afraid to move, in which case he could do little harm; or he was out and about pretending to be a Russian, in heavy disguise, which would soon be penetrated; or he had slipped out after his one useless contact with the Patriarch. Or he was being protected: fed, given a place to sleep, moved around, disguised, protected, guarded. But by whom? That was the enigma whose answer still eluded Anatoli Grishin.

•   •   •

SIR Nigel Irvine flew into Moscow two days after his talk at the Ritz with Dr. Probyn. He was accompanied by a personal interpreter, for although he had once had a working knowledge of Russian, it was far too rusty to be reliable for delicate discussions.

The man he brought back was the ex-soldier and Russian speaker, Brian Marks, except that Marks was now on his real passport in the name of Brian Vincent. At Immigration the passport control officer punched both names into his computer but neither came up as a recent or frequent visitor.

"You are together?" he asked. One man was clearly the senior, slim, white-haired, and according to his passport in his mid-seventies; the other was late thirties, dark-suited, and looked fit.

"I am the gentleman's interpreter," said Vincent.

"My Russky not good," said Sir Nigel helpfully, in bad Russian.

The Immigration officer was less than interested. Foreign businessmen often needed interpreters. Some could be hired from agencies in Moscow; some tycoons brought their own. It was normal. He waved them through.

They checked into the National, where the unfortunate Jefferson had stayed. Waiting for Sir Nigel, deposited twenty-four hours earlier by an olive-skinned man no one recalled but who happened to be a Chechen, was a single envelope. It was handed to him with his room key.

It contained a slip of blank paper. Had it been intercepted or lost no particular harm would have come. The writing was not on the paper, but on the inside of the envelope in lemon juice.

With the envelope sliced open and laid flat, Brian Vincent gently warmed it with a match from the complimentary box on the bedside table. In pale brown, seven figures became discernible, a private phone number. When he had memorized it, Sir Nigel ordered Vincent to burn the paper totally and flush the ashes down the toilet. Then the two men had a quiet dinner in the hotel and waited until ten o'clock.

When the phone rang, it was answered personally by Patriarch Alexei II, for it was his private phone situated on the desk in his office. He knew that very few people possessed that number, and he ought to know them all.

"Yes?" he said carefully.

The voice that responded was one he did not know, speaking good Russian but not a Russian.

"Patriarch Alexei?"

"Who speaks?"

"Your Holiness, we have not met. I am merely the interpreter for the gentleman who accompanies me. Some days ago you were kind enough to receive a father from London."

"I recall it."

"He said another man would come, more senior, for a private discussion of great importance with you. He is here beside me. He asks if you will receive him."

"Now, tonight?"

"Speed is of the essence, Your Holiness."

"Why?"

"There are forces in Moscow who will soon recognize this gentleman. He could be put under surveillance. Utter discretion is the key."

That was an argument that certainly rang a bell with the edgy prelate.

"Very well. Where are you now?"

"Within a few minutes' drive. Ready to move."

"In half an hour then."

This time, with forewarning, the Cossack guard opened the street door without question and a nervous but intensely curious Father Maxim conducted the two visitors to the Patriarch's private study. Sir Nigel had taken advantage of the National's own limousine and asked it to wait at the curb.

Patriarch Alexei was again in a pale gray cassock with a simple pectoral cross on a chain round his neck. He greeted his visitors and bade them be seated.

"Permit me first to apologize that my poor grasp of Russian is so unsatisfactory that I have to converse through an interpreter," said Sir Nigel.

Vincent translated rapidly. The Patriarch nodded and smiled.

"And, alas, I speak no English," he replied. "Ah, Father Maxim, please place the coffee on a table. We will serve ourselves. You may go."

Sir Nigel began by introducing himself, though avoiding specifying that he had once been a very senior intelligence officer combating Russia and all her works. He confined himself to saying that he was a veteran of Britain's Foreign Service (almost right), now in retirement but recalled for the present task of negotiation.

Without mentioning the Council of Lincoln, he related that the Black Manifesto had been privately shown to men and women of enormous influence, all of whom had been deeply shocked by it.

"As shocked no doubt as yourself, Holiness."

Alexei nodded somberly as the Russian translation ended.

"I have come, therefore, to suggest to you that the present situation involves us all, people of goodwill inside and outside Russia. We had a poet in England who said: No man is an island. We are all part of the whole. For Russia, one of the greatest countries in the world, to fall under the hand of a cruel dictator again would be a tragedy for us in the West, for the people of Russia, and most of all for the holy church."

"I do not doubt you," said the Patriarch, "but the church cannot involve itself in politics."

"Overtly, no. Yet the church must struggle against evil. The church is always involved in morality, is it not?"

"Of course."

"And the church has the right to seek to protect itself from destruction, and from those who would seek to destroy her and her mission on earth?"

"Beyond doubt."

"Then the church may speak to urge the faithful against a course of action that would help evil and hurt the church?"

"If the church speaks out against Igor Komarov, and still he wins the presidency, the church will have accomplished her own destruction," said Alexei II. "That is how the hundred bishops will see it, and they will vote overwhelmingly to stay silent. I will be overruled."

"But there is possibly another way," said Sir Nigel. For several minutes he outlined a constitutional reform that caused the Patriarch's jaw to drop.

"You cannot be in earnest, Sir Nigel," he said at length. "Restore the monarchy, bring back the czar? The people would never encompass it."

"Let us look at the picture before you," suggested Irvine. "We know that the choice before Russia is more bleak than can be imagined. On the one hand lies continuing chaos, possible disintegration, even civil war in the Yugoslav style. There can be no prosperity without stability. Russia is rocking like a ship in a gale with no anchor and no rudder. Soon she must founder, her timbers split apart, and her people perish.

"Or there is dictatorship, a terrible tyranny to match anything your long-suffering country has ever seen. Which would you choose for your people?"

"I cannot," said the Patriarch. "Both are too terrible."

"Then remember that a constitutional monarch is always a bulwark against single-tyrant despotism. The two cannot coexist, one has to go. All nations need a symbol, human or not, to which they can cleave when times are bad, that can unite them across barriers of language and clan. Komarov is building himself into that national symbol, that icon. No one will vote against him and in favor of vacuum. There must be an alternative icon."

"But to preach for restoration . . ." protested the Patriarch.

"Would not be preaching against Komarov, which is what you fear to do," argued the Englishman. "It would be preaching for a new stability, an icon above politics. Komarov could not accuse you of meddling in politics, of being against him, even though he might privately suspect what is afoot. And there are the other factors. . . ."

Skillfully Nigel Irvine trailed the temptations before the Patriarch. The union of church and throne, the full restoration of the Orthodox Church in all its panoply, the return of the Patriarch of Moscow and All the Russias to his palace within the Kremlin walls, the resumption of credits from the West as stability returned.

"What you say has much logic, and it appeals to my heart," said Alexei II when he had thought it over. "But I have seen the Black Manifesto. I know the worst. My brothers in Christ, the convocation of bishops, have not seen it and would not believe it. Publish it, and half of Russia might even agree with it. . . . No, Sir Nigel, I do not overestimate my flock."

"But if another voice were to speak? Not yours, Holiness, not officially, but a strong and persuasive voice, with your silent backing?"

He meant the maverick Father Gregor Rusakov, to whom the Patriarch had, with considerable moral courage, given his personal authority to preach.

Father Rusakov had been turned down in his youth by seminary after seminary. He was far too intelligent for the KGB's taste and far too passionate. So he had withdrawn to a small monastery in Siberia and taken holy orders before becoming a wandering priest, with no parish, preaching where he could before moving on ahead of the secret police.

They caught him of course, and he got five years in a labor camp for anti–State utterances. In court he had refused the state's paid–off defense counsel, defending himself with such brilliance that he forced the judges to admit they were raping the Soviet constitution.

Liberation under Gorbachev's amnesty for priests showed he had lost none of his fire. He resumed preaching, but also castigated the bishops for their timidity and corruption, so offending most of them that they ran to Alexei to beg him to have the younger man locked up again.

In the robes of a parish priest Alexei II went to one of his rallies to listen. If only, he thought as he stood unrecognized in the crowd, I could turn all that fire, all that passion, all that oratory into the service of the Church.

The point was, Father Gregor packed them in. He talked the language of the people, in the syntax of the workers. He could pepper his sermon with barracks-room language learned in the labor camp; he could talk the language of the young, knew their pop idols by name and group, knew how hard it was for a housewife to make ends meet, knew how vodka could blunt the hardship.

At thirty-five he was celibate and ascetic but knew more of the sins of the flesh than any seminary could teach. Two popular teen magazines had even proposed him to their readers as a sex symbol.

So Alexei II did not run to the militia asking for an arrest. He invited the wild one to dinner. In the Danilovsky Monastery where they ate a frugal supper at a wooden table. Alexei served. They talked through the night. Alexei explained the task before him, the slow reform of a church too long the servant of dictatorship, trying to find its way back to a pastoral role among the one hundred forty million Christians of Russia.

By dawn he had his compact. Father Gregor agreed to urge his listeners to seek God in their homes and their work, but also to return to the church, flawed though it might be. The silent hand of the Patriarch enabled many things. A major TV station carried weekly coverage of Father Gregor's hugely attended rallies, and his sermons were thus watched by millions whom he could never have addressed in the flesh. By the winter of 1999 this single priest was widely considered to be the most powerful orator in Russia, even including Igor Komarov.

The Patriarch was silent for a while. Finally he said, "I will speak with Father Gregor on the matter of the return of a czar."

CHAPTER 15

As always in late November, the wind bore the first snows of winter whipping across Slavyansky Square, harbinger of the bitter chill to come.

The tubby priest bowed his head toward the wind and scurried through the outer gates, across the small yard, and into the warmth of All Saints of Kulishki, redolent of damp clothing and incense.

Once again he was watched from a parked car, and when the watchers were certain no one was tailing him, Colonel Grishin followed him inside.

"You called," he said as they stood side by side away from the few worshipers, apparently contemplating the icons on the wall.

"Last night. There was a visitor. From England."

"Not America? You are sure, not America?"

"No, Colonel. Just after ten His Holiness told me to receive a gentleman from England and let him in. He came with his interpreter, a much younger man. I let them in and escorted them to the study. Then I brought a tray of coffee."

"What did they say?"

"When I was in the room, the elderly Englishman was apologizing that he spoke poor Russian. The younger man translated everything. Then the Patriarch told me to put the coffee down and dismissed me."

"You listened at the door?"

"I tried to. But the younger *Anglichanin* seemed to have hung his scarf over the knob. It blocked my vision and most of what I could hear. Then someone came, the Cossack on his rounds, and I had to get away."

"He mentioned his name, this elderly Englishman?"

"No, not while I was there. Perhaps when I was away making the coffee. Because of the scarf I could see nothing and hear very little. What I did hear did not make sense."

"Try me, Father Maxim."

"The Patriarch only raised his voice once. I heard him say 'Bring back the czar?' He seemed amazed. Then they dropped their voices."

Colonel Grishin stood staring at the paintings of the Madonna holding her Child as if he had been slapped in the face. What he had heard might make no sense to the stupid priest, but it made sense to him.

With a constitutional monarch as head of state, there would be no post of president. The head of government would be the prime minister, leader of the government party but still subject to parliament, the Duma. That was a thousand miles from Igor Komarov's scenario for a one-party dictatorship.

"His appearance?" he asked quietly.

"Medium height, spare, silver hair, early to mid-seventies."

"No idea where he came from?"

"Ah, he was different from the young American. He came by car and it waited for him. I showed them out. The car was still there. Not a taxi, but a limousine. I took its number as it drove away."

He passed a slip of paper to the colonel.

"You have done well, Father Maxim. This will not be forgotten."

Anatoli Grishin's detectives did not take long. A call to the Bureau of Automobiles had the number within an hour—the limousine belonged to the National Hotel.

Kuznetsov the propaganda chief was the errand boy. His near-perfect American English could persuade any Russian clerk that he was indeed American. He turned up at the National just after lunch and approached the concierge.

"Hi, sorry to ask, but do you speak English?"

"Yes, sir, I do."

"Great. Look, I was dining in a restaurant not far from here last night and there was this English gentleman at the next table. We got talking. When he left, he forgot this on the table."

He held up a lighter. It was gold and expensive, a Cartier. The concierge was puzzled.

"Yes, sir?"

"Anyway, I ran after him, but I was too late. He was driving away . . . in a long black Mercedes. But the commissionaire thought it might be one of yours. I managed to grab the number."

He passed over a slip of paper.

"Ah, yes, sir. One of ours. Excuse me."

The concierge checked his log for the previous evening.

"That must have been Mr. Trubshaw. Shall I take the lighter?"

"No problem. I'll just hand it in to reception and they can put it in his cubbyhole."

With a cheery wave, Kuznetsov strolled over to the reception desk. He pocketed the lighter.

"Hi there. Could you give me Mr. Trubshaw's room number?"

The Russian girl was dark and pretty and occasionally moonlighted with Americans. She flashed a smile.

"One moment, sir."

She punched the name into her desktop computer and shook her head.

"I'm sorry. Mr. Trubshaw and his companion left this morning."

"Oh, damn. I hoped to catch him. Do you know if he has left Moscow?"

She punched in more figures.

"Yes, sir, we confirmed his flight this morning. He returned to London on the midday plane."

Kuznetsov was not really aware of the reason why Colonel Grishin wanted to trace the mysterious Mr. Trubshaw but he reported what he had found. When he had gone, Grishin used his contact in the visa applications section of the Immigration division of the Interior Ministry. The details were faxed to him, and the photo that had accompanied the application through the Russian Embassy in Kensington Palace Gardens, London, came by messenger.

"Blow that photo up to a eight-by-ten," he told his staff. The face of the elderly Englishman meant nothing to him, but he thought he might know a man to whom it would.

Three miles down Tverskaya Street, at a point where the highway to Minsk has already changed its name twice, is the great Victory Arch, and just to one side lies Maroseyka Street. Here two big apartment houses are dedicated entirely to senior retirees of the old KGB, pensioners of the state, living out their retirement in reasonable comfort.

Among them in the winter of 1999 was one of the most formidable of Russia's old spymasters, General Yuri Drozdov. In the high days of the Cold War he had run all KGB operations on the eastern seaboard of America, before being recalled to Moscow to head the ultrasecret Illegals Directorate.

"Illegals" are those who go into enemy territory without any diplomatic cover, burrowing into the alien society as businessmen, academics, whatever, to run the indigenous assets they have recruited. If caught, they face not expulsion but arrest and trial. Drozdov had trained and sent out the KGB's illegals for years.

Grishin had come across him briefly when Drozdov in his last days as an active officer had headed the small and discreet group at Yazenevo assigned to analyze the tidal wave of product being sent across by Aldrich Ames. Grishin had been the chief interrogator of the spies thus betrayed.

Neither man had taken to the other. Drozdov preferred skill and subtlety to brute force, while Grishin, who had never left the USSR apart from one brief and inglorious expedition to East Berlin, despised those in the First Chief Directorate who had spent years in the West and become infected by foreign mannerisms. Nevertheless, Drozdov agreed to see him at his apartment on Maroseyka Street. Grishin placed the enlarged photograph in front of him.

"Have you ever seen him before?" he asked.

To his horror the old spymaster threw back his head and roared with laughter.

"Seen him? Not personally, no. But that face is stamped on the mind of everyone my age who ever worked at Yazenevo. Don't you know who he is?"

"No. Or I wouldn't be here."

"Well, we called him The Fox. Nigel Irvine. Ran operations against us for years through the sixties and seventies, then became chief of the British Secret Intelligence Service for six years."

"A spy."

"A master of spies, a runner of spies," Drozdov corrected him. "Not the same thing. And he was one of the best ever. Why are you interested?"

"He came to Moscow yesterday."

"Good God. Do you know why?"

"No," lied Grishin. Drozdov stared at him intently. He did not believe the answer.

"What's it got to do with you, anyway? You're out of it now. You run those black-uniformed thugs for Komarov, don't you?"

"I am the Head of Security for the Union of Patriotic Forces," said Grishin stiffly.

"Same difference," muttered the old general. He escorted Grishin to the door.

"If he comes back, tell him to stop by for a drink," he called after the departing Grishin. Then he muttered "Asshole," and closed the door.

Grishin warned his informants in the Immigration Division that he needed to know if ever Sir Nigel Irvine, or Mr. Trubshaw, sought to reenter Moscow.

The following day General of the Army Nikolai Nikolayev gave an interview to *Izvestia*, the country's biggest national newspaper. The paper regarded the event as something of a scoop, for the old warrior never gave interviews.

Ostensibly the interview was to mark the general's up-and-coming seventy-fourth birthday, and it began with general inquiries about his health.

He sat bolt upright in a leather-backed chair in a private room at the Officers' Club of the Frunze Academy and told the reporter his health was fine.

"My teeth are my own," he barked. "I don't need eyeglasses and I can still outmarch any whippersnapper your age."

The reporter, who was in his early forties, believed him. The photographer, a woman in her mid-twenties, gazed at him with awe. She had heard her grandfather tell of following the young tank commander into Berlin fifty-four years before.

The conversation drifted to the state of the country.

"Deplorable," snapped Uncle Kolya. "A bloody mess."

"I suppose," suggested the reporter, "you will be voting for the UPF and Igor Komarov in the January election?"

"Him, never," snapped the general. "A bunch of Fascists, that's all they are. Wouldn't touch them with a sterilized barge-pole."

"I don't understand," quavered the journalist, "I would have thought . . ."

"Young man, don't think for one minute that I have fallen for that phoney patriotism crap Komarov keeps churning out. I've seen patriotism, boy. Seen men bleed for it, seen good men die for it. Got to recognize the real thing, don't you see? This man Komarov is no patriot, it's all bullshit and catcrap."

"I see," said the reporter, who did not see at all and was completely bewildered. "But surely there are many people who feel his plans for Russia . . ."

"His plans for Russia are bloodshed," snarled Uncle Kolya. "Think we haven't had enough bloodshed in this land already? I've had to wade through the damn stuff, and I don't want to see anymore. The man's a Fascist. Look, boy, I've fought Fascists all my life. Fought 'em at Kursk, fought 'em at Bagration, across the Vistula, right to the bloody bunker. German or Russian, a Fascist's a Fascist, and they're all . . ."

He could have used any of forty words that in Russian refer to private parts, but as there was a woman present he settled for *merzavtsi*—villains.

"But surely," protested the journalist, who was completely out of his depth, "Russia needs to be cleaned up of all the filth?"

"Oh, there's filth all right. But a lot of it is not ethnic minority filth, it's home-grown Russian crap. What about the crooked politicians, the corrupt bureaucrats hand in hand with the gangsters?"

"But Mr. Komarov is going to clean out the gangsters."

"Mr. bloody Komarov is financed by the gangsters, can't you see that? Where do you think the tidal wave of his money is coming from? The tooth fairy? With him in charge this country is bought and paid for by the gangsters. I tell you, boy, no man who ever wore the uniform of his country and wore it with pride should ever put those black-uniformed thugs of his guard in charge of the Motherland."

"Then what should we do?"

The old general reached for a copy of the day's paper and gestured at the back page.

"Did you see that priest fella on the box last night?"

"Father Gregor, the preacher? No, why?"

"I think he may have got it right. And we may have got it wrong all these years. Bring back God and the czar."

The interview caused a sensation, but not for what it said. It was the source that caused the furor. Russia's most famous old soldier had delivered a denunciation that would be read by every officer and trooper in the land and a large number of the twenty million veterans.

The interview was syndicated in its entirety in the weekly *Our Army,* successor to the *Red Star,* which went into every barracks in Russia. Extracts were included in the TV national news and repeated on the radio. After that the general declined to give any more interviews.

In the dacha off Kiselny Boulevard, Kuznetsov was almost in tears as he confronted a stony-faced Igor Komarov.

"I don't understand, Mr. President, I just don't understand. If there was one figure in the entire country whom I would have assumed to be a staunch supporter of the UPF and of yourself, it would have been General Nikolayev."

Igor Komarov, and Anatoli Grishin who was standing staring out of the window onto the snowy forecourt, heard him out in bleak silence. Then the young propaganda chief returned to his office to continue calling the media to try to limit the damage.

It was not an easy task. He could hardly denounce Uncle Kolya as a geriatric who had lost his wits, for this was clearly not true. His only plea was that the general had got it all wrong. But the questions about where the UPF's funding was coming from were getting harder and harder to handle.

A fuller restoration of the UPF position would have been made easier by devoting the whole next issue of *Awake* to the topic, along with the monthly edition of *Motherland.* Unfortunately they had been silenced and the new presses were only now leaving Baltimore.

Back in the president's office the silence was finally broken by Komarov.

"He saw my manifesto, didn't he?"

"I believe so," said Grishin.

"First the presses, then the secret meetings with the Patriarch, now this. What the hell is going on?"

"We're being sabotaged, Mr. President."

Igor Komarov's voice remained deceptively quiet, too quiet. But his face was deathly pale and bright spots burned red on each cheek. Like the late secretary Akopov, Anatoli Grishin too had seen the rages of which his leader was capable and even he feared them. When Komarov spoke again, his voice had dropped to a whisper.

"You are retained, Anatoli, at my side, the closest man to me, the man destined to have more power in Russia than any save me, to prevent me from being sabotaged. Who is doing this?"

"An Englishman called Irvine, and an American called Monk."

"Two of them? Is that all?"

"They obviously have backing, Mr. President, and they have the manifesto. They are showing it around."

Komarov arose from his desk, took up a heavy cylindrical ebony ruler, and began to tap it into the palm of his left hand. As he spoke his voice began to rise.

"Then find them, and suppress them, Anatoli. Find out what the next stage is, and prevent it. Now listen to me carefully. On January sixteenth, in just a few short weeks, one hundred and ten million Russian voters will have the right to cast their ballot for the next president of Russia. I intend that they shall vote for me.

"On a seventy percent poll, that means seventy-seven million votes cast. I want forty million of those votes. I want a first-round win, not a runoff. A week ago I could have counted on sixty million. That fool of a general has just cost me at least ten."

The word *ten* came out close to a scream. The ruler was rising and falling, but Komarov was now hammering the desktop with it. Without warning he began to shriek his rage at his persecutors, using the ruler to hit his own telephone until the plastic cracked and shattered. Grishin stood rigid; down the corridor there was utter silence as the office staff froze where they were.

"Now some demented priest has started a new hare running, calling for the return of the czar. There will be no czar in this land other than me, and when I rule they will learn the meaning of discipline such that Ivan the Terrible will seem like a choirboy."

As he shouted, he brought the ebony ruler down again and again on the wreckage of the telephone, staring at the fragments as if the once-useful tool was itself the disobedient Russian people, learning the meaning of discipline under the knout.

The last scream of *choirboy* died away and Komarov dropped the ruler back on his desk. He took several deep inhalations and resumed his grip on himself. His voice returned to normal levels but his hands were shaking, so he placed all ten fingertips on the desk to steady them.

"Tonight I will address a rally at Vladimir, the greatest of the whole campaign. It will be broadcast, nationwide, tomorrow. After that I shall address the nation every night until the election. The funds have been arranged. That is my business. The publicity belongs to Kuznetsov."

From behind his desk he reached out an arm and pointed his forefinger straight at Grishin's face.

"Your business, Anatoli Grishin, is one and one only. *Stop the sabotage.*"

The last sentence was also a shout. Komarov slumped into his chair and waved his hand in dismissal. Grishin, without a word, crossed the carpet to the door and let himself out.

•   •   •

IN the days of Communism there was only one bank, the Narodny, or People's Bank. After the fall, and with the onset of capitalism, banks sprang up like mushrooms until there were over eight thousand of them.

Many were blink-and-you-miss-it affairs that quickly folded, taking their depositors' money with them. Others vaporized in the night, with the same effect. The survivors learned their banking almost as they went along, for such experience in the Communist state was sparse.

Nor was banking a safe occupation. In ten years over four hundred bankers had been assassinated, usually for failing to see eye to eye with gangsters on the matter of unsecured loans or other forms of illegal cooperation.

By the late nineties the business had settled down to a basic four hundred reasonably reputable banks. With the top fifty of these the West was prepared to do business.

Banking was centered in St. Petersburg and Moscow, mainly in the latter. In an ironic mirror of organized crime, banking too had amalgamated, with the so-called Top Ten doing eighty percent of the business. In some cases, the level of investment was so high that the enterprise could only be undertaken by consortia of two or three banks acting together.

Chief among the major banks in the winter of 1999 were the Most Bank, the Smolensky, and biggest of all, the Moskovsky Federal.

It was to the head office of the Moskovsky that Jason Monk addressed himself in the first week of December. The security was like Fort Knox.

Because of the dangers to life and limb the chairmen of the major banks had private protection squads that would make the personal security of an American president look puny. At least three had long since removed their families to London, Paris, and Vienna respectively, and commuted to their Moscow offices in private jets. When inside Russia their personal protectors ran into the hundreds. It took thousands more to protect the bank's branches.

To achieve a personal interview with the chairman of the Moskovsky Federal without an appointment made days ahead was at the very least unheard of. But Monk managed it. He brought with him something equally unheard of.

After a body search and an inspection of his leather briefcase on the ground floor of the tower building, he was allowed to go up under escort to the executive reception, three floors below the chairman's personal suite.

There the letter he offered was examined by a smooth young Russian who spoke perfect English. He asked Monk to wait and disappeared through a stout wooden door that opened only to a code in a keypad. Two armed guards watched Monk as the minutes dragged by. To the surprise of the receptionist behind the desk, the personal aide returned and asked Monk to follow him. Beyond the door he was frisked again and an electronic scanner was run over him as the smooth Russian apologized.

"I understand," said Monk. "Times are hard."

Two floors further up he was shown into another anteroom, and then ushered into the private office of Leonid Grigoreivitch Bernstein.

The letter he had brought lay on the blotter of the desk. The banker was a short, broad man with crinkly gray hair, sharp, questioning eyes, and a beautifully cut charcoal-gray suit from Savile Row. He arose and held out his hand. Then he waved Monk to a chair. Monk noticed that the smooth one sat at the back of the room, complete with the bulge under his left armpit. He might have attended Oxford University but Bernstein had ensured he also completed his studies on the range at Quantico.

The banker gestured to the letter.

"So, how are things in London? You have just arrived, Mr. Monk?"

"Some days ago," said Monk.

The letter was on very expensive paper of cream linen weave, topped by the five splayed arrows that recall the five original sons of Mayer Amschel Rothschild of Frankfurt. The stationery itself was perfectly genuine. Only the signature of Sir Evelyn de Rothschild at the bottom of the text was a forgery. But it is a rare banker who will not receive a personal emissary from the chairman of N. M. Rothschild of St. Swithin's Lane, City of London.

"Sir Evelyn is well?" asked Bernstein. Monk dropped into Russian.

"So far as I know," said Monk, "but he did not sign that letter." He heard a soft rustle behind him. "And I really would be most grateful if your young friend didn't put one of those bullets in my back. I'm not wearing body armor and I would prefer to stay alive. Besides, I am not carrying anything dangerous, and I did not come here for the purpose of trying to hurt you."

"Then why did you come?"

Monk explained the events since July 15.

"Rubbish," said Bernstein at last. "Never heard such rubbish in my life. I know about Komarov. I make it my business to know. He's too far right for my taste, but if you think insulting Jews is anything new you know nothing about Russia. They all do it, but they all need banks."

"Insults are one thing, Mr. Bernstein. What I am carrying in this case promises more than insults."

Bernstein stared at him long and hard.

"This manifesto, you brought it with you?"

"Yes."

"If Komarov and his thugs knew you were here, what would he do?"

"Have me killed. His men are all over the city looking for me now."

"You've got a nerve."

"I agreed to do a job. After reading the manifesto, it seemed worth doing."

Bernstein held out his hand.

"Show me."

Monk gave him the verification report first. The banker was accustomed to reading complex documents at great speed. He finished it in ten minutes.

"Three men, eh?"

"The old cleaner, the secretary Akopov who foolishly left it out on his desk to be stolen, and Jefferson, the journalist who Komarov wrongly thought had read it."

Bernstein punched a button on his intercom.

"Ludmilla, get into the agency clipping files for late July and early August. See if the local papers carried anything on Akopov, a Russian, and an English reporter called Jefferson. On the first name, try the obituaries as well."

He stared at his desktop screen as the microfiches were flashed up. Then he grunted.

"They're dead all right. And now you, Mr. Monk, if they catch you."

"I'm hoping they won't."

"Well, since you've taken the risk, I'll look at Mr. Komarov's private intentions for us all."

He held out his hand again. Monk gave him the slim black file. Bernstein began to read. One page he read several times, flicking back and forward as he reread the text. Without looking up, he said:

"Ilya, leave us. It's all right, lad, go."

Monk heard the door close behind the aide. The banker looked up at last and stared at Monk.

"He can't mean this."

"Complete extermination? It's been tried before."

"There are a million Jews in Russia, Mr. Monk."

"I know. Ten percent can afford to get out."

Bernstein arose and walked to the windows that looked across the whitescape of the roofs of Moscow. The glass had a slight greenish tint; it was five inches thick and would stop an antitank shell.

"He can't be serious."

"We believe he is."

"We?"

"The people who sent me, powerful, influential people. But frightened of this man."

"Are you Jewish, Mr. Monk?"

"No, sir."

"Lucky you. He's going to win, isn't he? The polls say he's unstoppable."

"Things may be changing. He was denounced by General Nikolayev the other day. That might have an effect. I hope the Orthodox Church may play a role. Perhaps he could be stopped."

"Huh, the church. No friend of the Jews, Mr. Monk."

"No, but he has plans for the church too."

"So it's an alliance you're after?"

"Something like that. Church, army, banks, ethnic minorities. Every little bit helps. Have you seen the reports of the wandering priest? Calling for a return of the czar?"

"Yes. Foolishness, my personal view. But better a czar than a Nazi. What do you want of me, Mr. Monk?"

"I? Nothing. The choice is yours. You are the chairman of the four-bank consortium that controls the two independent TV channels. You have your Grumman at the airport?"

"Yes."

"It is only two hours by air to Kiev."

"Why Kiev?"

"You could visit Babi Yar."

Leonid Bernstein spun round from the windows.

"You may leave now, Mr. Monk."

Monk retrieved his two files from the desk and slipped them into the slim leather case in which he had brought them.

He knew he had gone too far. Babi Yar is a ravine outside Kiev. Between 1941 and 1943 one hundred thousand civilians were machine-gunned on the edge of the ravine so that their corpses fell inside. Some were commissars and Communist officials, but ninety-five percent were the Jews of Ukraine. Monk had reached the door when Leonid Bernstein spoke again.

"Have you been there, Mr. Monk?"

"No, sir."

"And what have you heard of it?"

"I have heard that it is a bleak place."

"I have been to Babi Yar. It is a terrible place. Good-day to you, Mr. Monk."

•   •   •

DR. Lancelot Probyn's office in the headquarters of the College in Queen Victoria Street was small and cluttered. Every horizontal space was occupied by bundles of paper that seemed to be in no particular order, yet presumably made some sense to the genealogist.

When Sir Nigel Irvine was shown in, Dr. Probyn leaped to his feet, swept the entire House of Grimaldi onto the floor, and bade his visitor take the chair thus liberated.

"So, how goes the succession?" asked Irvine.

"To the throne of Romanov? Not well. As I thought. There's one who might have a claim but doesn't want it, one who lusts after it but is excluded on two counts, and an American who hasn't been approached and hasn't a chance anyway."

"Bad as that, eh?" said Irvine. Dr. Probyn bounced and twinkled. He was in his element, his own world of bloodlines, intermarriages, and strange rules.

"Let's start with the fraudsters," he said. "You remember Anna Andersen? She was the one who all her life claimed she was Grand Duchess Anastasia, who had survived the massacre at Yekaterinburg. All lies. She's dead now, but DNA tests have finally proved she was an impostor.

"A few years ago another died in Madrid, self-styled Grand Duke Alexei. He turned out to be a con man from Luxembourg. That leaves three who are occasionally mentioned in the press, usually inaccurately. Ever heard of Prince Georgi?"

"Forgive me, no, Dr. Probyn."

"Well, no matter. He's a young man who has been hawked around Europe and Russia for years by his avidly ambitious mother,

Grand Duchess Maria, the daughter of the late Grand Duke Vladimir.

"Vladimir himself might have had a claim as the great grandson of a reigning emperor, though it would have been a thin one because his mother was not a member of the Orthodox Church at the time of his birth, which is one of the conditions.

"Anyway, his daughter Maria was not eligible to be his successor, even though he kept claiming she was. The Pauline Law, you see."

"And that is . . . ?"

"Czar Paul the First laid it down. Succession, save in exceptional circumstances, is by the male line only. No daughters count. Very sexist, but that's the way it was and is. So Grand Duchess Maria is really Princess Maria, and her son Georgi is not in line. The Pauline Law also specified that not even the sons of daughters count."

"So they are just hoping for the best?"

"Exactly. Very ambitious, but no true claim."

"You mentioned an American, Dr. Probyn?"

"Now there's an odd story. Before the Revolution Czar Nicholas had an uncle called Grand Duke Paul, youngest brother of his father.

"When the Bolsheviks came, they murdered the czar, his brother, and his uncle Paul. But Paul had a son, cousin of the czar. By chance this wild young man, Grand Duke Dmitri, had been involved in the murder of Rasputin. Because of that he was in exile in Siberia when the Bolsheviks struck. It saved his life. He fled via Shanghai and ended up in America."

"Never heard of that," said Irvine. "Go on."

"Well, Dmitri lived, married, and had a son, Paul, who fought as a major in the U.S. Army in Korea. He also married, and had two sons."

"That looks like a pretty straight male line to me. Are you saying the true czar might be an American?" asked Irvine.

"Some do, but they delude themselves," said Probyn. "You see, Dmitri married an American commoner, and so did his son Paul. Under Rule 188 of the Imperial House, you can't marry someone not of equal rank and expect your offspring to succeed. This rule was later relaxed a bit, but not for grand dukes. So Dmitri's marriage was morganatic. His son who fought in Korea cannot succeed and neither can either of the two grandchildren by yet a second marriage to a commoner."

"So they're out."

" 'Fraid so. Not that they have ever shown much interest, actually. Live in Florida, I think."

"Who does that leave?"

"The last, with the strongest claim by blood. This is Prince Semyon Romanov."

"He is related to the murdered czar? No daughters, no commoners?" asked Irvine.

"True, but it's a long way back. You have to imagine four czars. Nicholas the Second came after his father Alexander the Third. *He* came after his father Alexander the Second and his father was Nicholas the First. Now, Nicholas the First had a junior son, Grand Duke Nicholas, who of course never became czar. His son was Peter, his son was Kyrill, and *his* son is Semyon."

"So from the murdered Czar you have to go back three generations to Great-Granddad, then sideways to a junior son, then down four generations to reach Semyon."

"Exactly."

"Seems pretty well-stretched elastic to me, Dr. Probyn."

"It is a long way, but that's family trees for you. Technically, Semyon is the nearest we can get to direct bloodline. However, that's academic. There are practical difficulties."

"Such as?"

"For one thing he's over seventy. So even if he were restored, he wouldn't last long. Second, he has no children, so the line would die with him and Russia would be back to square one. Third, he has repeatedly said he has no interest and would refuse the office even if it were offered."

"Not very helpful," admitted Sir Nigel.

"There's worse. He's always been a bit of a rake, interested in fast cars, the Riviera, and taking his pleasures with young girls, usually servants. That habit has led to three broken marriages. And worst of all, I have heard it whispered, he cheats at backgammon."

"Good God."

Sir Nigel Irvine was genuinely shocked. Humping the staff one might overlook, but cheating at backgammon . . .

"Where does he live?"

"On an apple farm in Normandy. Grows apples to make Calvados."

Sir Nigel Irvine was pensive for a while. Dr. Probyn gazed at him sympathetically.

"If Semyon has stated publicly that he renounces any part in a restoration, would that count as a legal disclaimer?"

Dr. Probyn puffed out his cheeks.

"I should think so. Unless a restoration actually came about. Then he might change his mind. Think of all those fast cars and serving wenches."

"But without Semyon, what's the picture? What, as our American friends say, is the bottom line?"

"My dear chap, the bottom line is that if the Russian people want, they can choose any damn person they like to become their monarch. It's as simple as that."

"It's precedented, choosing a foreigner?"

"Oh, massively. It's been done time and again. Look, we English have done it three times. When Elizabeth the First died single, if not a virgin, we invited James the Sixth of Scotland down to become James the First of England. Four kings later, we threw out James the Second and invited the Dutchman William of Orange to take the throne. When Queen Anne died without surviving issue, we asked George of Hannover to come across as George the First. And he hardly spoke a word of English."

"The Europeans have done the same?"

"Of course. The Greeks twice. In 1833 after winning their freedom from the Turks, they invited Otto of Bavaria to become King of Greece. He wasn't up to much, so they deposed him in 1862 and asked Prince William of Denmark to take over. He became King George the First. Then they proclaimed a republic in 1924, restored the monarchy in 1935, and abolished it again in 1973. Can't make up their minds.

"The Swedes a couple of hundred years ago were at a loss, so they looked round and invited the Napoleonic General Bernadotte to become their king. Worked pretty well; his descendants are still there.

"And, finally, in 1905 Prince Charles of Denmark was asked to become Haakon the Seventh of Norway, and his descendants are still there too. If you've got an empty throne, and you want a monarch, it's not always a bad thing to pick a good outsider rather than a useless local boy."

Sir Nigel was silent again, lost in thought. By now Dr. Probyn had suspected his inquiries were not entirely academic.

"May I ask something?" said the herald.

"Certainly."

"If the question of restoration ever did occur in Russia, what would be the American reaction? I mean, they control the purse strings, the only superpower left."

"The Americans are traditionally antimonarchist," admitted Irvine, "but they're no fools either. In 1918, America was instrumental in exiling the German Kaiser. That led to the chaotic vacuum of the Weimar Republic, and into that vacuum stepped Adolf Hitler with results we all know. In 1945, Uncle Sam specifically did not terminate the Japanese imperial house. The result? For fifty years Japan has been the most stable democracy in Asia, anti-communist and a friend of America. I think Washington would take the view if the Russians choose to go that road, it's their choice."

"But it would have to be the entire Russian people, by plebiscite?"

Sir Nigel nodded.

"Yes, I think it would. The Duma alone wouldn't suffice. Too many allegations of corruption. It would have to be the nation's decision."

"Then whom have you in mind?"

"That's the problem, Dr. Probyn. No one. From what you've told me, a playboy or an itinerant pretender won't work. Look, let's think what qualities a restored czar would need to have. Do you mind?"

The herald's eyes sparkled.

"Much more fun than my usual job. What about age?"

"Forty to sixty, wouldn't you say? No job for a teenager, nor a geriatric. Mature but not elderly. What next?"

"Have to be born a prince of a reigning house, look and behave the part," said Probyn.

"A European house?"

"Oh, surely yes. I don't suppose the Russians want an African, Arab, or Asian."

"No. Caucasian then, Doctor."

"He'd need a living legitimate son and they'd both have to convert to the Orthodox Church."

"That's not insuperable."

"But there is a real stinker," said Probyn. "His mother would have to have been a member of the Orthodox Church at the time of his birth."

"Ow. Anything else?"

"Royal blood on both sides of his parentage, preferably Russian on one side at least."

"And a senior or former army officer. The support of the Russian officer corps would be vital. I don't know what they'd think of an accountant."

"You've forgotten one thing," said Probyn. "He'd have to speak fluent Russian. George the First arrived speaking only German, and Bernadotte spoke only French. But those days are gone. Nowadays a monarch must address his people. The Russians wouldn't take kindly to a stream of, say, Italian."

Sir Nigel Irvine arose and took a slip of paper from his breast pocket. It was a check, and a generous one.

"I say, that's awfully decent," said the herald.

"I'm sure the college has its overhead, my dear doctor. Look, would you do me a favor?"

"If I can."

"Cast your eye about. Run through the reigning houses of Europe. See if there is any man who fits all those categories."

• • •

FIVE miles to the north of the Kremlin in the suburb of Kashenkin Lug lies the complex of the television centers from which are transmitted all the TV programs beamed across Russia.

On either side of the Boulevard Akademika Koroleva are the TV Center (Domestic) and the International TV Center. Three hundred yards away the needle spire of the Ostankino TV tower juts into the sky, the highest point in the capital. State TV, very much under the control of the incumbent government, is broadcast from here, as are the two independent or commercial TV stations that carry advertising to pay their way. The buildings are shared, but on different levels.

Boris Kuznetsov was deposited at the domestic center by one of the UPF's chauffeur-driven Mercedeses. He carried with him the videocassette of the hugely impressive rally at Vladimir that Igor Komarov had conducted the previous day.

Cut and edited by the young genius of a director Litvinov, it had emerged as a triumph. To a wildly cheering crowd, Komarov had trashed the itinerant preacher who was calling for a return to God and the czar, and treated with thinly veiled sarcasm posing as regret the maunderings of the old general.

"Yesterday's men with yesterday's hopes," he roared at his supporters, "but we, my friends, you and I, must think of tomorrow, for tomorrow belongs to us."

Five thousand people had been at the rally, which Litvinov's skillful camera work had made to look three times that number. But broadcast across the nation, despite the awesome cost of buying an entire hour at commercial rates, the rally would reach not five thousand but fifty million Russians, or a third of the nation.

Kuznetsov was shown directly into the office of the head of programs for the larger commercial station, a man he regarded as a personal friend and whom he knew to be a supporter of Igor Komarov and the UPF. He dropped the cassette onto the desk of Anton Gurov.

"It was wonderful," he said enthusiastically, "I was there. You'll love it."

Gurov fiddled with his pen.

"And I've got better news for you. A major contract, cash on the barrelhead. President Komarov wishes to address the nation every night from now until election day. Think of it, Anton, the biggest single commercial contract this station has ever had. Some credit to you, eh?"

"Boris, I'm glad you came personally. I'm afraid something has cropped up."

"Oh, not a technical hitch. Can't you ever sort them out?"

"No, not exactly technical. Look, you know I support President Komarov to the hilt, right?"

As a senior program planner, Gurov knew exactly how the coverage by TV, the most persuasive single medium in any modern society, was playing in the countdown to the election.

Only Britain, with its BBC, continued to attempt unbiased political coverage using state television channels. In all other countries across Western and Eastern Europe, the incumbent governments used their national television to support the regime of the moment, and had done so for years.

In Russia the state TV network carried copious coverage of the campaign of acting president Ivan Markov, while giving only occasional mentions, always within a dry news context, to the other two candidates.

Those other two candidates, the smaller fry having dropped out along the way, were Gennadi Zyuganov for the neo-Communist Socialist Union and Igor Komarov of the Union of Patriotic Forces.

The former was clearly having problems raising money for his campaign; the latter appeared to enjoy a cornucopia of it. With these funds, Komarov had been able to buy publicity in the American manner by paying for hours of TV time on the two commercial channels. By buying this time, he could ensure that he was not cut, edited, or censored. Gurov had long been happy to oblige with prime-time slots for the full-length screenings of Komarov's speeches and rallies. He was no fool. He realized that if Komarov won there would be some heavy firings among the state TV staff. A lot of the bigwigs would go; Komarov would see to that. For those with their hearts in the right place, there would be transfers and promotions.

But something was wrong now. Kuznetsov stared at Gurov in puzzlement.

"The fact is, Boris, there's been a sort of policy shift. At board level. Nothing to do with me, you understand. I'm just the errand boy. This is way up above my head, in the stratosphere."

"What policy shift, Anton? What are you talking about?"

Gurov shifted uncomfortably and again cursed the managing director who had saddled him with the task.

"You probably know, Boris, like all big enterprises, we are heavily indebted to the banks. When push comes to shove, they have a lot of clout. They rule. Normally, they leave us alone. The returns are good. But . . . they're pulling the plug."

Kuznetsov was aghast.

"Hell, Anton, I'm sorry. It must be awful for you."

"Not quite for me, Boris."

"But surely, if the station is going belly-up, down the tubes . . ."

"Yes, well now, it seems that wasn't quite what they said. The station can survive, but there's a price."

"What price?"

"Now look, friend, this is nothing to do with me. If it was down to me, I'd screen Igor Komarov twenty-four hours a day, but . . ."

"But what? Spit it out."

"Okay. The station won't be screening any more of Mr. Komarov's speeches or rallies. That's the order."

Kuznetsov was on his feet, face scarlet with rage.

"You're out of your fucking mind! We buy this time, remember. We pay for it. This is a commercial station. You can't refuse our money."

"Apparently we can."

"But this one has been prepaid!"

"It seems that the money is being returned."

"I'll go next door. You're not the only commercial TV channel in this town. I always favored you, Anton. Well, no more."

"Boris, they're owned by the same banks."

Kuznetsov sat down again. His knees were shaking.

"What the hell's going on?"

"All I can say, Boris, is, someone's been got at. I don't understand this any more than you. But the board handed it down yesterday. Either we decline to screen Mr. Komarov for the next thirty days or the banks pull."

Kuznetsov stared at him.

"That's a lot of screen time you're passing up. What are you going to air instead? Cossack dancing?"

"No, that's the odd thing. The station is going to program coverage of the rallies of that priest fellow."

"What priest fellow?"

"You know, the revivalist preacher. Always urging people to turn to God."

"God and the czar," muttered Kuznetsov.

"That's him."

"Father Gregor."

"The same. I can't understand it myself but . . ."

"You're crazy. He hasn't two rubles to rub together."

"That's just the point. The money seems to be in place. So we're carrying him on the news and the special events slot. He's got a hell of a schedule. Want to see it?"

"No, I do not want to see his bloody schedule."

With that, Kuznetsov stormed out. How he was going to face his idol with the news, he had no idea. But a suspicion that had been in his head for three weeks had concretized into total belief. There had been looks between Komarov and Grishin when he broke the news of the printing presses and then General Nikolayev. They knew something that he did not. But one thing he did know; something was going catastrophically wrong.

*   *   *

THAT night, on the other side of Europe, Sir Nigel Irvine was interrupted at his dinner. The club servant held out the phone to him.

"A Dr. Probyn, Sir Nigel."

The herald's chirpy voice came down the line from his office where he was clearly working late.

"I think I've got your man."

"Your office, tomorrow, ten o'clock? Splendid."

Sir Nigel handed the phone back to the hovering steward.

"I think this calls for a port, Trubshaw. Club vintage, if you please."

CHAPTER 16

IN RUSSIA, WHAT WESTERN COUNTRIES WOULD CALL THE POLICE IS named the militia and comes under the direction of the Ministry of the Interior, the MVD.

Like most police forces, it has two main strands: the federal police on the one hand, and the local, state, or regional police on the other.

The regions are called Oblasts. The largest of them is the Moscow Oblast, a chunk of territory encompassing the entire capital of the federal republic and the surrounding countryside. It is like the District of Columbia with a third of Virginia and Maryland thrown in.

Moscow therefore plays host, though in different buildings, to both the federal militia and the Moscow militia. Unlike Western police establishments, the Russian Interior Ministry also has at its disposal a private army—one hundred thirty thousand heavily armed MVD troops, almost a match for the real army under the Defense Ministry.

Shortly after the fall of Communism the mushroomlike rise of organized crime became so open, so pervasive, and so scandalous that Boris Yeltsin was forced to order the formation of entire divisions within the federal and Moscow Oblast police to fight the spread of the mafia.

The job of the feds was to fight crime across the entire country, but so concentrated in Moscow was organized crime, much of it economic, that the Moscow Organized Crime Combat Department, or GUVD, became almost as big as its federal counterpart.

The GUVD had only moderate success until the mid-nineties, when it was taken over by General-of-Police Valentin Petrovsky. Petrovsky became the senior ranking general of the Collegium controlling it. He was an out-of-town appointment, brought in from the industrial city of Nizhny Novgorod, where he had established the reputation of a no-bribe "hard man." Like Elliott Ness, he inherited a situation resembling Chicago under Al Capone. Unlike the leader of the Untouchables, he had a lot more firepower and a lot fewer civil rights to bother about.

He started his reign by firing a dozen top officers whom he designated as being "too close" to the subject at hand, organized crime. "Too close!" yelled the FBI Liaison Officer at the U.S. Embassy. "They were on the goddam payroll."

Petrovsky then ran a series of covert will-they-take-a-bribe tests on some of the senior investigators. Those who told the bribe offerers to get lost received promotions and big pay hikes. When he had a reliable and honest task force to hand, he declared war on organized crime. His Anti-Gang Squad became more feared among the underworld than any such previously, and he was nicknamed "Molotov." This was not a tribute to the long-dead foreign minister and cohort of Stalin; the word means "hammer."

Like any honest cop he did not win them all. The cancer ran too deep. Organized crime had friends in high places. Too many gangsters went into court and came back out again with their smiles still in place.

Petrovsky's response was not to be overly careful about taking prisoners. To back up their detectives, both the federal and city anti-gang divisions had armed troops. Those of the federal police were called the OMON, and Petrovsky's own rapid reaction force, the SOBR.

In his early days Petrovsky led raids personally and without forewarning to prevent leaks. If the raided gangsters came quietly they got a trial; if one of them reached under his armpit or sought to destroy evidence or escape, Petrovsky waited until it was all over, said "Tut-tut," and called for the body bags.

By 1998 he realized that the largest mafia group by far, and seemingly the most impregnable, was the Dolgoruki gang, based in Moscow, controlling much of Russia west of the Urals, immensely rich and with its wealth able to buy awesome influence. For two years prior to the winter of 1999 he had waged personal war against the Dolgoruki and they hated him for it.

·   ·   ·

UMAR Gunayev had told Jason Monk at their first meeting that there was no need for him to forge identity papers in Russia; money could simply buy the real article. In early December Monk put that boast to the test.

What he had in mind would be the fourth time he had secured a private talk with a Russian notable while flying under false colors. But the forged letter from Metropolitan Anthony of the Russian Orthodox Church in London had been created in that city. So had the letter purporting to come from the House of Rothschild. General Nikolayev had asked for no identity papers; the uniform of a General Staff officer had been enough. General Valentin Petrovsky, living under daily threat of assassination, was guarded night and day.

Where the Chechen leader got them from, Monk never asked. But they looked good. They bore the photograph of Monk with his short-cropped blond hair and identified him as a police colonel on the personal staff of the First Deputy Head, Organized Crime Control Directorate, Federal Interior Ministry. As such he would not be personally known to Petrovsky, but would be a colleague from the federal police.

One of the things that did not change after the fall of Communism was the Russian habit of setting aside entire apartment blocks for senior officers in the same profession. While in the West politicians, civil servants, and senior officers usually live in their own private homes scattered through the suburbs, the tendency in Moscow is to live rent-free in groups in state-owned apartment houses.

This is mainly because the post-Communist state simply took over these apartments from the old Central Committee and created rent-free residences. Many of these buildings were, and remain, strung along the north side of Kutuzovsky Prospekt where Brezhnev and most of the Politburo once lived. Petrovsky lived on the eighth floor, just below the top floor of a building on Kutuzovsky Prospekt. A dozen other senior police officers had apartments there too. There was at least one advantage to lumping all these men from the same profession into one building. Private citizens would have become exasperated by the security; police generals completely understood the need for it.

The car that Monk drove that evening, miraculously acquired or "borrowed" by Gunayev, was a genuine MVD militia black Chaika, which came to a stop at the barrier leading to the inner courtyard of the apartment building. One OMON guard gestured for the rear window to come down, while a second covered the car with his submachine gun.

Monk offered his ID and his destination, and held his breath. The guard studied the pass, nodded, and retired to his booth to make a phone call. Then he returned.

"General Petrovsky asks what your business concerns."

"Tell the general I have papers from General Chebotaryov, a matter of urgency," said Monk. He had named the man who would have been his real superior. A second phone conversation took place. Then the OMON guard nodded to his colleague and the barrier came up. Monk parked in a vacant slot and walked inside.

There was a guard on the ground floor reception desk who nodded him through, and two more outside the elevator on the eighth. They frisked him, checked his attaché case, and studied his ID papers. Then one spoke through an intercom. The door opened ten seconds later. Monk knew he had been studied through a peephole in the door.

There was a manservant in a white jacket, whose build and demeanor indicated he could serve a lot more than canapés if the occasion required, and then the family atmosphere became clear. A small girl ran out of the living room, stared at him, and said, "This is my dolly." She held up a flaxen-haired doll in a nightdress. Monk grinned.

"She's lovely. And what's your name?"

"Tatiana."

A woman in her late thirties appeared, smiled apologetically, and ushered the child away. From behind her a man emerged in his shirtsleeves, wiping his mouth, as any citizen interrupted at dinner.

"Colonel Sorokin?"

"Sir."

"Odd hour to call."

"I'm sorry. Things just came up in a rush. I can wait while you finish dinner."

"No need. Just finished. Anyway, it's cartoon time on the telly now, so I'm well out of it. Come in here."

He led the way into a study off the hall. In the better light Monk could see that the crime buster was no older than he was and just as fit.

Three times, with the Patriarch, the general, and the banker, he had begun by revealing that his identity-of-access was false and had just got away with it. This time he calculated he could well end up dead, with apologies later. He flipped open his attaché case. The guards outside had searched it, but seen only two files in Russian and had not read a word. Monk offered the gray file, the verification report.

"It's this, General. We take the view it is pretty disturbing."

"Can I read it later?"

"It really could be an action-this-night affair."

"Oh, screw it. Do you drink?"

"Not on duty, sir."

"Then they're improving down at the MVD. Coffee?"

"Love some, it's been a long day."

General Petrovsky smiled.

"When isn't it?"

He summoned the manservant and ordered coffee for two. Then he began to read. The valet came, delivered coffee, and left. Monk served himself. Finally General Petrovsky looked up.

"Where the hell did this come from?"

"British Intelligence."

"What?"

"But it's not a *provokatsia*. It's been checked out. You could double-check in the morning. N. I. Akopov, the secretary who left the manifesto lying around, is dead. Ditto the old cleaner, Zaitsev. Ditto the British journalist, who actually knew nothing."

"I remember him," said Petrovsky pensively. "It looked like a gang killing, but no motive. Not for a foreign reporter. You think it was Komarov's Black Guards?"

"Or Dolgoruki killers hired for the job."

"So where is this mysterious Black Manifesto?"

"Here, General."

Monk tapped his briefcase.

"You've got a copy? You brought it with you?"

"Yes."

"But according to this it went to the British Embassy. Then to London. How did you get hold of it?"

"I was given it."

General Petrovsky was staring at him with open suspicion.

"And how the hell does the MVD get hold of a copy? . . . You're not from the MVD. Who the hell are you from? SVR? FSB?"

The two organizations he named were the Russian Foreign Intelligence Service and the Federal Security Service, successors to the First and Second Chief Directorates of the old KGB.

"Neither, sir. I'm from America."

General Petrovsky showed no fear. He just stared at his visitor hard, looking for a trace of threat, for his family was next door and the man could be a paid assassin. But he could work out that the impostor carried no bomb or gun.

Monk began to talk, explaining how the black-covered file in his case had come to the embassy, then London, then Washington. How it had been read by less than a hundred people in two governments. He made no mention of the Council of Lincoln; if General Petrovsky wished to believe Monk represented the U.S. government, it would do no harm.

"What's your real name?"

"Jason Monk."

"You're really American?"

"Yes, sir."

"Well, your Russian's damn good. So, what's in this Black Manifesto?"

"Among other things, Igor Komarov's death sentence on you and most of your men."

In the silence Monk heard the words in Russian "That's my boy" coming through the wall. Tom and Jerry on the television. Tatiana squealed with laughter. Petrovsky held out his hand.

"Show," he said.

He spent thirty minutes reading the forty pages, divided into twenty subject headings. Then he tossed it back.

"Bullshit."

"Why?"

"He couldn't get away with it."

"He has so far. A private army of Black Guards, all superbly equipped and paid for. A bigger but less well trained corps of Young Combatants. And enough money to drown in. The Dolgoruki godfathers struck their deal with him two years ago. A war chest of a quarter of a billion U.S. dollars to buy supreme power in this land."

"You have no proof."

"That manifesto is proof. The reference to rewarding the fund providers. The Dolgoruki will want their pound of flesh. All the turf of all their rivals. After the extermination of the Chechen and the banishment of the Armenians, Georgians, and Ukrainians, that won't be a problem. But they'll want more. Revenge against those who have persecuted them. Starting with the Collegium of the anti-gang units.

"They'll need fodder for their new slave camps, to mine the gold, salt, and lead. Who better than the young men you command, the SOBR and the OMON? Of course, you won't live to see that."

"He may not win."

"True, General, he may not. His star is falling. General Nikolayev denounced him a few days ago."

"I saw that. Damn surprising, I thought. Anything to do with you?"

"Maybe."

"Smart."

"Now the commercial TV stations have stopped broadcasting him. His magazines have ceased production. The latest opinion polls put him at sixty percent, against seventy last month."

"So, his ratings are falling, Mr. Monk. He may not win."

"But if he does?"

"I can't go against the entire presidential election. I may be a general, but I'm still just a policeman. You should go to the acting president."

"Palsied by fear."

"I still can't help."

"If he thinks he can't win, he could strike at the state."

"If anyone strikes at the state, Mr. Monk, the state will defend itself."

"Have you ever heard of *Sippenschaft,* General?"

"I don't speak English."

"It's German. May I have your private number here?"

Petrovsky nodded at the nearby phone. Monk memorized it. He collected his files and put them in his case.

"That German word. What does it mean?"

"When parts of the German officer corps struck at Hitler, they were hanged by piano wire. Under the law of *Sippenschaft* their wives and children went to the camps."

"Not even the Communists did that," snapped Petrovsky. "Families lost their apartments, their school places. But not the camps."

"He's mad, you know. Behind the urbane facade, he's not sane. But Grishin will do his bidding in all things. May I go now?"

"You'd better get out of here before I arrest you."

Monk was at the door.

"If I were you, I would make some precautionary dispositions. If he wins, or looks like losing, you may have to fight for that wife and child of yours."

Then he was gone.

•   •   •

DR. Probyn was like a small and excited schoolboy. Proudly he led Sir Nigel Irvine to a chart, three feet by three, pinned to one wall. He had obviously created it himself.

"What do you think?" he said.

Sir Nigel stared at it without comprehension. Names, scores of names, linked by vertical and horizontal lines.

"The Mongolian Underground without the translation," he suggested. Probyn chuckled.

"Not bad. You're looking at the interwoven parts of four European royal houses. Danish, Greek, British, and Russian. Two still in existence, one out of office, and one extinct."

"Explain," begged Irvine. Dr. Probyn took large red, blue, and black markers.

"Let's start at the top. The Danes. They're the key to it all."

"The Danes? Why the Danes?"

"Let me tell you a true story, Sir Nigel. A hundred and sixty years ago there was a king of Denmark who had several children. Here they are."

He pointed to the top of the chart, where the King of Denmark was named, and, beneath his name in a horizontal line, those of his offspring.

"Now, the oldest boy became crown prince and succeeded his father. No more interest to us. But the youngest one . . ."

"Prince William was invited to become King George the First of Greece. You mentioned that the last time I was here."

"Splendid," said Probyn. "What a memory. So here he is again; he's shot off to Athens and becomes King of Greece. What does he do? He marries Grand Duchess Olga of Russia, and they produce Prince Nicholas, prince of Greece but ethnically half-Danish and half-Russian, that is, Romanov. Now, let's leave Prince Nicholas on the back burner, still a bachelor."

He marked Nicholas in blue, for Greece, and pointed back to the Danes at the top.

"The old king also had daughters, and two did pretty well for themselves. Dagmar went off to Moscow to become Empress of Russia, changed her name to Maria, converted to the Orthodox Church, and gave birth to Nicholas the Second of All the Russias."

"Murdered with his entire family at Yekaterinburg."

"Precisely. But look at the other one. Alexandra of Denmark came over here and married our prince, who became Edward the Seventh. They produced the eventual George the Fifth. See?"

"So Czar Nicholas and King George were cousins."

"Exactly. Their mothers were sisters. So in the First World War the Czar of Russia and the King of England were cousins. When King George referred to the Czar as 'cousin Nicky' he was being completely accurate."

"Except that ended in 1917."

"It did indeed. But now look at the British line."

Dr. Probyn reached up and circled in red both King Edward and Queen Alexandra. His red pen ran down a generation to circle King George V.

"Now, he had five sons. John died as a boy, the others grew up. Here they are: David, Albert, Henry, and George. It's the last we're interested in, Prince George."

The red pen ran down from George V to envelop his fourth son, Prince George of Windsor.

"Now, he died in a plane crash in the Second World War, but he had two sons, both alive today. Here they are, but it's the younger one we must concentrate on."

The red pen ran down to the bottom line to circle the second English prince.

"Now follow the line back," said Dr. Probyn. "His father was Prince George, his grandfather King George, but his great-grandma was the sister of the czar's mum. Two Danish princesses, Dagmar and Alexandra. This man is linked to the House of Romanov by marriage."

"Mmmm. A long time back," said Sir Nigel.

"Ah, there's more. Look at these."

He tossed on the desk two photographs. Two bearded, somber faces staring directly at the camera.

"What do you think?"

"They could be brothers."

"Well, they're not. There's eighty years between them. This one is the dead Czar Nicholas the Second; the other is the living English prince. Look at the faces, Sir Nigel. They're not typically British faces—anyway the czar was half-Russian, half-Danish. They're not typical Russian faces. They're Danish faces; it's the Danish blood coming through, from those two Danish sisters."

"That it? Linkage by marriage?"

"Far from it. The best is yet to come. Remember Prince Nicholas?"

"The one on the back burner? Prince of Greece, but actually half-Danish, half-Russian?"

"That's the one. Now, the Czar Nicholas had a cousin, Grand Duchess Elena. What did she do? Shot off to Athens and married Nicholas. So he's half Romanov and she's a hundred percent. Their offspring therefore is three-quarters Russian and Romanov. And *she* was Princess Marina."

"Who came over here . . ."

"And married Prince George of Windsor. So these two living men, his sons, are three-eighths Romanov, and nowadays that's about as near as you'll get. That doesn't mean there's a linear claim—too many women in the way, which is banned by the Pauline Law. But the linkage by marriage is through the father line and by blood through the mother line."

"That applies to both brothers?"

"Yes, and something else. Their mother, Marina, was a member of the Orthodox Church at the time of both births. That's a crucial condition for acceptance by the Orthodox hierarchy, and there aren't many others like that."

"That applies to both brothers?"

"Yes, of course. And both served in the British Army, rising to the rank of major."

"Then what about the elder brother?"

"Ah, you mentioned age, Sir Nigel. The elder is sixty-four, outside your guideline. The younger was fifty-seven this year. That's almost all you asked for. Born a prince of a reigning house, cousin of the queen, one marriage, a son of twenty, married to an Austrian countess, quite accustomed to all those ceremonies, still vigorous, a former army man. But the killer is, he was in the Intelligence Corps, did the full Russian course, and is damn near bilingual."

Dr. Probyn stood back from his multicolored chart beaming. Sir Nigel stared at the face in the photograph.

"Where does he live?"

"During the week, here in London. On weekends, at his place in the country. It's listed in Debrett."

"Perhaps I should have a word," mused Sir Nigel. "One last thing, Dr. Probyn. Is there any other man who fulfills all the qualifications so completely?"

"Not on this planet," said the herald.

That weekend Sir Nigel Irvine, having obtained his appointment, drove to western England to see the younger of the two princes at his country house. He was courteously received and gravely listened to. Finally the prince escorted him to his car.

"If half what you say is true, Sir Nigel, I find it perfectly extraordinary. Of course, I have followed events in Russia from the media. But this . . . I shall have to consider carefully, consult my family extensively, and of course ask for a private meeting with Her Majesty."

"It may never happen, sir. There may never be a plebiscite. Or the people's reply might be the reverse."

"Then, we shall have to wait until that day. Safe journey, Sir Nigel."

•   •   •

ON the third floor of the Metropol Hotel is situated one of the
finest traditional Russian restaurants of Moscow. The Boyarsky Zal,
or Boyars' Hall, is named after the body of aristocrats who once
flanked the czar and, if he was weak, ruled in his place. It is vaulted,
paneled, and decorated with superb ornamentation recalling a long-
bygone age. Excellent wines vie with iced vodka, the trout, salmon,
and sturgeon are from the rivers, the hare, deer, and boar from the
steppes of Russia.

It was here on the evening of December 12 that General Nikolai
Nikolayev was taken by his sole living relative to celebrate his
seventy-fourth birthday.

Galina, the little sister he had once carried on his back through
the burning streets of Smolensk, had grown up to be a teacher, and
in 1956, aged twenty-five, she had married a fellow teacher called
Andreev. Their son, Misha, was born late that same year.

In 1963 she and her husband had been killed in a car crash, one
of those stupid affairs in which a vodka-drunk idiot had driven right
into them.

Colonel Nikolayev had flown home from the Far Eastern Command to attend the funeral. But there was more, a letter from his
sister written two years earlier.

"If anything should ever happen to me and Ivan," she wrote, "I
beg you to look after little Misha." Nikolayev stood at the grave
beside a solemn little boy just turned seven who refused to weep.

Because both the parents had been employees of the state—under
Communism everyone was an employee of the state—their apartment was repossessed. The tank colonel, who was then thirty-seven,
had no Moscow apartment. When home on furlough he lived in
bachelor quarters at the Frunze Officers' Club. The commandant
agreed the boy could stay with him on a strictly temporary basis.

After the funeral, he took the boy to the mess hall for a meal, but
neither had much appetite.

"What the hell am I going to do with you, Misha?" he asked, but
the question was more to himself.

Later he tucked the boy into his single bed and threw a handful
of blankets onto the sofa for himself. Through the wall he could
hear the boy starting to cry at last. To take his mind off things, he

turned on the radio, to learn that Kennedy had just been shot in Dallas.

One thing about wearing the medals of a triple-Hero was that it gave the wearer a certain clout. Normally boys go to the prestigious Nakhimov Military Academy at the age of ten, but in this case the authorities agreed to make an exception. Very small and very frightened, the seven-year-old was fitted out in a cadet uniform and inducted into the Nakhimov. Then his uncle went back to the Far East to complete his tour.

Over the years General Nikolayev had done his best, visiting whenever he was home on leave and, when seconded to the general staff, acquiring his own apartment in Moscow where the growing youth could stay during vacations.

At eighteen Misha Andreev had graduated as a lieutenant and not unnaturally had opted for tanks. Twenty-five years later he was forty-three, and a major general commanding an elite division of tanks outside Moscow.

The two men entered the restaurant just after eight, their table booked and awaiting them. Viktor, the headwaiter, was a former tank man; he rushed forward with his hand out.

"Good to see you, General. You won't remember me. I was a gunner with the One thirty-first Maikop in Prague in 1968. Your table's over here facing the gallery."

Heads turned to see what all the fuss was about. The American, Swiss, and Japanese businessmen stared in curiosity. Among the few Russian diners there was a muttered "That's Kolya Nikolayev."

Viktor had prepared two brimming tumblers of freezing Moskovskaya, on the house. Misha Andreev raised his glass to his uncle and the only father he could really remember.

"*Za vashe zdrovye*. Another seventy-four to come."

"Bullshit. *Za vashe zdrovye*."

Both men threw back the liquid in one, paused, grunted as it hit the spot.

Above the bar at the Boyarsky Zal is a gallery from which the diners are serenaded with traditional Russian songs. That night the singers were a statuesque blonde in the robes of a Romanov princess, and a man in tuxedo possessed of a rich baritone voice.

When they finished the ballad they were performing as a duet, the male singer stepped forward alone. The live band at the end of the gallery paused and the deep, rich voice launched into the soldier's love song to the girl he left back home, "Kalinka."

The Russians stopped chattering and sat in silence; the foreigners followed suit. The baritone voice filled the hall . . . "Kalinka, Kalinka, Kalinka maya . . ."

When the last chords died away the Russians rose to toast the white-moustached man seated with his back to the tapestries. The singer bowed and took his applause. Viktor was next to a group of six Japanese diners.

"Who is old man?" asked one of them in English.

"War hero, Great Patriotic War," replied Viktor.

The English speaker translated for the rest.

"Ah, so," they said, and raised their glasses. *"Kampei."*

Uncle Kolya nodded and beamed, raised his glass to the singer and the room, and drank.

It was a good meal, trout and duck, with Armenian red wine and coffee to follow. At the Boyarski's prices, it was costing the major general a month's salary. He reckoned his uncle was worth it.

It was probably not until he was thirty, and had seen some thoroughly bad officers, not a few in high office, that he understood why his uncle had become a legend among tank men. He possessed something bad officers never had, a passionate concern for the men serving under him. By the time he got his first division and his first red tab, Major General Andreev, looking about him at the shambles in Chechnya, recognized that Russia would be lucky to see another like Uncle Kolya.

The nephew had never forgotten something that happened when he was ten. Between 1945 and 1965 neither Stalin nor Khrushchev had thought fit to erect a cenotaph to the war dead in Moscow. Their own cults of personality had been more important, despite the fact neither of them would have been on top of Lenin's Mausoleum to take the salute on May Day had it not been for the millions who died between 1941 and 1945.

Then in 1966, with Khrushchev gone, the Politburo had finally ordered the construction of a cenotaph and an eternal flame to the memory of the Unknown Soldier.

Still, no open space was employed. The memorial was tucked away under the trees of the Alexandrovsky Gardens, close by the

Kremlin wall, in a position that would never catch the eye of those in the endless queue to see Lenin's embalmed remains.

After the May Day parade that year, when the wide-eyed ten-year-old cadet had watched the rolling tanks, guns, and rockets, the goose-stepping troops and the dancing gymnasts pouring across Red Square, his uncle had taken him by the hand and led him down Kremlev Alley between the gardens and the Manege.

Under the trees was a flat-topped slab of red polished granite. Beside it burned a flame in a bronze bowl.

On the slab was written the words: *Your grave is unknown, your achievement immortal.*

"I want you to make me a promise, boy," said the colonel.

"Yes, Uncle."

"There are a million of them out there, between here and Berlin. We don't know where they lie, in many cases who they were. But they fought with me, and they were good men. Understand?"

"Yes, Uncle."

"Whatever they promise you, whatever money, or promotion, or honors they offer you, I don't want you ever to betray these men."

"I promise, Uncle."

The colonel slowly raised his hand to the peak of his cap. The cadet followed suit. A passing crowd in from the provinces, sucking ice cream bars, watched curiously. Their guide, whose job was to tell them what a great man Lenin had been, was clearly embarrassed and shooed them round the corner toward the mausoleum.

"Saw your piece in *Izvestia* the other day," said Misha Andreev. "Caused quite a stir on the base."

General Nikolayev stared at him keenly.

"Didn't like it?"

"Surprised, that's all."

"Meant it, you know."

"Yes, I suppose you did. You usually do."

"He's an arsewipe, boy."

"If you say so, Uncle. Looks like he's going to win, though. Perhaps you should have kept your mouth shut."

"Too old for that. Speak as I find."

The old man seemed lost in thought for a while, staring up at the "Romanov princess" singing in the gallery above. Foreign diners thought they recognized "Those Were the Days, My Friend," which is not a Western song at all but an old Russian ballad. Then the general reached across and gripped his nephew's forearm.

"Look, lad, if anything ever happens to me . . ."

"Don't be daft, you'll outlive the lot of us."

"Listen, if anything happens, I want you to plant me in Novodevichi. All right? I don't want a miserable civil affair, I want a bishop and all the trimmings, the whole deal. Understand?"

"You, a *bishop*? I didn't think you believed in all that."

"Don't be a fool. No man who's had a German eighty-eight land six feet away and not explode doesn't believe there must be Somebody up there. Of course I had to pretend, we all did. Party membership, indoctrination lectures, it all went with the job, and it was all crap. So that's what I want. Now let's toss back the coffee and go. Got a staff car?"

"Yes."

"Good, because we're both plastered. You can run me home."

•   •   •

THE overnight sleeper train from Kiev, capital of the independent republic of the Ukraine, rumbled through the freezing darkness toward Moscow.

In the sixth carriage, compartment 2B, the two Englishmen sat and played gin rummy. Brian Vincent checked his watch.

"Half an hour to the border, Sir Nigel. Better get ready for bed."

"I suppose so," said Nigel Irvine. Still fully dressed he clambered to the top bunk and drew the blankets to his chin.

"Look the part?" he asked. The ex-soldier nodded.

"Leave the rest to me, sir."

There was a brief halt at the border. The Ukrainian officials on the train had already checked the two passports. The Russians boarded at the halt.

Ten minutes later there was a tap on the door of the sleeper compartment. Vincent opened up.

"*Da?*"

"*Pazport, pozhaluysta.*"

There was only a dim blue light inside the compartment and though the light in the corridor was yellow and brighter, the Russian inspector had to peer.

"No visa," he said.

"Of course not. These are diplomatic passports. Require no visa."

The Ukrainian pointed to the word in English on the cover of each passport.

"Diplomat," he said.

The Russian nodded, slightly embarrassed. He had an instruction from the FSB in Moscow, an all-crossing-point alert, to watch for a name and a face or both.

"The old man," he said, gesturing at the second passport.

"He's up there," said the young diplomat. "Actually, as you see he's very old. He's not feeling well. Do you have to disturb him?"

"Who is he?"

"Well, actually he's the father of our ambassador in Moscow. That's why I'm escorting him there. To see his son."

The Ukrainian pointed up to the recumbent figure in the bunk.

"Father of ambassador," he said.

"Thank you, I can understand Russian," said the Russian. He was perplexed. The round-faced, bald man in the passport bore no relationship to the description he had been given. Nor did the name. No Trubshaw, no Irvine. Just Lord Asquith.

"It must be cold in the corridor," said Vincent. "Cold to the bones. Please. For friendship. From our Kiev embassy's special stock."

The liter of vodka was of exceptional quality, the sort no money could buy. The Ukrainian nodded, smiled and nudged his Russian counterpart. The Russian grunted, stamped both passports and passed on.

"Couldn't hear much under all those blankets, but it sounded good," said Sir Nigel when the door was closed. He swung down from the upper bunk.

"Let's just say, the fewer of those the better," Vincent said, and set about destroying the two phony passports in the sink. The fragments would go down the lavatory hole and be scattered in the snows of southern Russia. One to get in, and one to get out. The exit passports, with their beautifully created entry stamps, were locked away.

Vincent looked at Sir Nigel with curiosity. At thirty-three he was aware the older man could not only be his father, but biologically his grandfather. As a former special forces soldier he had been in some tough places, not excluding lying in the desert of Western Iraq waiting to cream a passing Scud missile. But always there had been mates, a gun, grenades, a way of fighting back.

The world into which Sir Nigel Irvine had inducted him, albeit for a very large fee, a world of deception and disinformation, of endless smoke and mirrors, left him feeling in need of a double vodka. Fortunately there was a second bottle of the special stuff in his bag. He helped himself.

"Would you like one, Sir Nigel?"

"Not for me," said Irvine. "Upsets the tummy, burns the throat. But I will join you with something else."

He unscrewed a silver hip flask from his attaché case, and tipped a measure into the silver cup attached. He raised it toward Vincent and took an appreciative sip. It was Mr. Trubshaw's vintage port from St. James's.

"I actually think you're enjoying all this," said ex-Sergeant Vincent.

"My dear boy, I haven't had such fun in years."

The train deposited them at the Moscow terminus just after dawn. The temperature was fifteen below zero. However bleak a railway station in winter may appear to those hurrying home to a blazing hearth, they are still a lot warmer than the streets. When Sir Nigel and Vincent stepped down from the Kiev overnight express, the concourse of the Kursk Station was awash with the cold and hungry poor of the city.

They huddled as close as they could to the warm engines, sought to catch the occasional wave of heat emerging from a café, or simply lay on the concrete trying to survive another night.

"Stay very close to me, sir," muttered Vincent as they moved toward the ticket barrier, beyond which was the open concourse. As they were heading to the taxi stand, a swarm of the derelicts approached, hands out, heads muffled in scarves, faces unshaven, eyes sunken.

"Dear God, this is awful," muttered Sir Nigel.

"Don't reach for your money, you'll start a riot," snapped his bodyguard. Despite his age, Sir Nigel was carrying his own grip and attaché case, leaving Vincent with one free hand. The former special forces soldier had it lodged under his left armpit, indicating that he had a gun and would use it if he had to.

In this manner he shepherded the older man ahead of him through the crowd, toward the outside pavement where a few taxis waited hopefully. As he brushed aside a supplicant hand Sir Nigel heard the voice of its owner shouting at his back:

"Foreigner! Damned foreigner!"

"It's because they think we're rich," said Vincent in his ear. "We're foreign so we're rich."

The cries followed them to the pavement. "Fucking foreigner. Wait for Komarov."

When they were safely seated in the clattering taxi, Irvine leaned back.

"I hadn't realized it had got so bad," he muttered. "Last time, I just went from the airport to the National and back out again."

"It's full winter now, Sir Nigel. Always worse in winter."

As they drove out of the forecourt a militia truck swung in front of them. Two stone-faced policemen in heavy greatcoats and fur shapkas sat in the warmth of the cab. The truck swerved past and they could see into the back.

Rows of feet, the rag-bound soles of human feet, were visible for a second as the canvas flaps swung open with the movement of the truck. Bodies. Bodies frozen rock solid and stacked one on top of the other like corded timber.

"The stiff wagon," said Vincent shortly. "The dawn pickup shift. Five hundred of them are dying every night in the doorways, along the quays."

They were booked into the National, but did not wish to check in until late afternoon. So the taxi dropped them at the Palace Hotel and they spent the day in deep leather armchairs in the residents' lounge.

•   •   •

TWO days earlier Jason Monk had made a brief transmission, in code, from his specially adapted laptop computer. It was brief and to the point. He had seen General Petrovsky and all seemed to be well. He was still being moved around the city by the Chechens, often in the guise of a priest, an army or police officer, or a tramp. The Patriarch was ready to receive his English guest for a second time.

It was the message which, beamed across the world to the headquarters of InTelCor, had been retransmitted to Sir Nigel in London, still in code. Sir Nigel alone had the replica one-time pad to unlock the cipher.

It was the message that had brought him from London-Heathrow to Kiev and thence by train to Moscow.

But the message had also been caught by FAPSI, now working almost full-time for Colonel Grishin. The senior director of FAPSI conferred with Grishin while the Kiev–Moscow train steamed through the night.

"We damn near had him," said the director. "He was in the Arbat district, while last time he was out near Sokolniki. So he's moving around."

"The Arbat?" queried Grishin angrily. The Arbat district is barely half a mile from the Kremlin walls.

"There is another danger I should warn you about, Colonel. If he's using the sort of computer we think he is, he need not necessarily be present when transmissions take place or are received. He can preset it and leave."

"Just find the set," ordered Grishin. "He'll have to return to it, and when he does, I'll be waiting."

"If he makes two more, or a single one lasting half a second, we'll have the source. To within a city block, maybe the building."

What neither man knew was that according to Sir Nigel Irvine's plan, Monk would need to make at least three more transmissions to the West.

•   •   •

"HE'S back, Colonel Grishin."

The voice of Father Maxim down the phone was squeaky with tension. It was six in the evening, pitch-dark outside, and freezing cold. Grishin was still at his desk in the dacha off Kiselny Boulevard. He had just been about to leave when the call came. As per instructions, the switchboard operator heard the word *Maxim* and passed the call straight to the head of security.

"Calm yourself, Father Maxim. Who's back?"

"The Englishman. The old Englishman. He's been with His Holiness for an hour."

"He can't be."

Grishin had spread a large sum of money throughout the Immigration Division of the Interior Ministry and the FSB Counterintelligence apparat to receive forewarning, and it had not come.

"Do you know where he is staying?"

"No, but he used the same limousine."

The National, thought Grishin. The old fool has gone to the same hotel. He was still bitterly conscious that he had lost the old spymaster the last time because Mr. Trubshaw had moved too fast for him. This time there would be no mistake.

"Where are you now?"

"In the street, using my portable."

"It's not secure. Go to the usual place and wait for me there."

"I should get back, Colonel. I will be missed."

"Listen, fool, ring the residence and tell them you are feeling unwell. Say you have gone to the pharmacy for medication. But get to the meeting place and wait."

He slammed down the phone, picked it up again, and ordered his deputy, an ex-major of Border Guards Directorate, KGB, to report to his office immediately.

"Bring ten men, the best, in civilian clothes, and three cars."

Fifteen minutes later he spread a photograph of Sir Nigel Irvine in front of his deputy.

"That's him. Probably accompanied by a younger man, dark-haired, fit looking. They're at the National. I want two in the lobby, covering the elevators, the reception desk, and the doors. Two in the downstairs café. Two on the street on foot, four in two cars. If he arrives, watch him go in, then let me know. If he's there, I don't want him to come out without my knowing."

"If he leaves by car?"

"Follow, unless it's clear he's heading for the airport. Then arrange a car crash. He does not reach the airport."

"Yes, Colonel."

When the deputy had gone to brief his team, Grishin phoned another expert he had on the payroll, a former thief specializing in hotels who reckoned he could unlock any hotel door in Moscow.

"Get your kit together, get to the Intourist Hotel, sit in the lobby, and keep your mobile phone switched on. I want you to take a hotel room for me, tonight, hour unknown. I'll call you when I need you."

The Intourist Hotel is two hundred yards from the National, around the corner in Tverskaya Street.

Colonel Grishin was at the church of All Saints of Kulishki thirty minutes later. The worried priest, beaded with sweat, was waiting for him.

"When did he arrive?"

"Unannounced, about four o'clock. But His Holiness must have been expecting him. I was asked to show him straight up. With his interpreter."

"How long were they together?"

"About an hour. I served a samovar of tea, but they ceased talking while I was in the room."

"You listened at the door?"

"I tried, Colonel. It was not easy. The cleaning staff were about, those two nuns. Also the archdeacon, his private secretary."

"How much did you hear?"

"A bit. There was much talk of some prince. The Englishman was proposing a foreign prince to the Patriarch, in some capacity. I heard the phrase 'The Romanov blood' and 'extremely suitable.' The old man speaks softly, not that it matters; I can't understand English. Fortunately the interpreter speaks louder.

"The Englishman did most of the talking, His Holiness most of the listening. Once I could see him studying a plan of some sort. Then I had to move.

"I knocked and went back in to ask if they wanted the samovar replenished. There was silence because His Holiness was writing a letter. He said no, and waved me away."

Grishin was pensive. The word *prince* made perfect sense to him, if not to the valet.

"Anything else?"

"Yes, there was one last thing. As they were leaving, the door opened a fraction. I was waiting outside with their coats. I heard the Patriarch say, 'I will intercede with our acting president at the first suitable moment.' That was quite clear, the only whole sentence I heard."

Grishin turned to Father Maxim and smiled.

"I'm afraid the Patriarch is conspiring with foreign interests against our future president. It is very sad, very unfortunate, because it will not work. I'm sure His Holiness means well, but he is being most foolish. After the election, all this nonsense can be forgotten. But you, my friend, will not be forgotten. During my time with the KGB I learned to recognize the difference between a traitor and a patriot. Traitors may in certain circumstances be forgiven. His Holiness, for example. But a true patriot will always be rewarded."

"Thank you, Colonel."

"Do you ever have time off?"

"One evening a week."

"After the election, you must come and dine at one of our Young Combatants camps. They're rough-hewn lads but good-hearted. And of course extremely fit. All fifteen to nineteen. The best of them we take into the Black Guards."

"That would be very . . . agreeable."

"And of course after the election I shall suggest to President Komarov that the Guards and the Combatants will need an honorary chaplain. Certainly the rank of bishop will be necessary."

"You're very kind, Colonel."

"You will find I can be, Father Maxim. Now back to the residence. Keep me informed. You had better take this. You will know what to do with it."

When the informer had left, Colonel Grishin ordered his driver to take him to the National Hotel. It was time, he thought, that this interfering Westerner and his American troublemaker learned some of the facts of modern Moscow.

CHAPTER 17

COLONEL GRISHIN ORDERED HIS DRIVER TO PARK A HUNDRED yards down Okhotny Ryad, Hunter's Row, which makes up the northwestern side of Manege Square where the National is situated.

From inside his car he could see the two vehicles of his watcher team parked near the shopping mall facing the facade of the hotel.

"Wait here," he told his driver, and got out. Even at seven in the evening it was almost twenty below zero. A few huddled figures shuffled past.

He crossed the street and tapped on the driver's side window. It creaked in the cold as the electric motor brought it down.

"Yes, Colonel."

"Where is he?"

"He must be inside, if he was in there before we arrived. No one has left that even looks like him."

"Call Mr. Kuznetsov. Tell him I need him here."

The propaganda chief arrived twenty minutes later.

"I need you to play your American tourist again," said Grishin. He pulled a photograph from his pocket and showed it to Kuznetsov.

"That's the man I'm looking for," he said. "Try the names of Trubshaw or Irvine."

Kuznetsov was back ten minutes later.

"He's in there, under the name of Irvine. He's in his room."

"Number?"

"Two-five-two. Is that all?"

"That's all I need."

Grishin returned to his own car and used his mobile phone to call the professional thief he had stationed around the corner in the lobby of the Intourist.

"Are you ready?"

"Yes, Colonel."

"Stay on listening watch. When I give the command, the room I want searched is two-five-two. I want nothing taken, everything searched. One of my own men is in the lobby. He will come with you."

"Understood."

At eight o'clock one of the two men Grishin had posted in the lobby came out. He nodded across the road to his colleagues in the nearest car, then drifted off.

Minutes later two figures in heavy winter coats and fur hats emerged. Grishin could see wisps of white hair escaping from under one of the hats. The men turned left, up the street toward the Bolshoi Theatre.

Grishin called up his thief.

"He's left the hotel. The room is vacant."

One of Grishin's cars began to crawl slowly after the walking men. Two more of the watchers, who had been in the National's ground-floor café, came out and turned after the Englishmen. There were four walkers on the street, four more watchers in two cars. Grishin's driver spoke.

"Shall we pick them up, Colonel?"

"No, I want to see where they go."

There was a chance Irvine would make contact with the American, Monk. If he did, Grishin would have them all.

The two Englishmen paused at the lights where Tverskaya Street leaves the square, waited for the green, and crossed. Seconds later the thief came around the corner from Tverskaya.

He was a thoroughly experienced man and always looked the part of a foreign executive, almost the only breed who could still afford the top Moscow hotels. His coat and suit were from London, both stolen, and his air of self-confident ease would fool almost all hotel employees.

Grishin watched him push at the revolving doors of the hotel and disappear inside. Nigel Irvine, the colonel had been happy to notice, carried no attaché case. If he had one, it would be in his room.

"Move," he told his driver. The Mercedes eased away from the curb and closed to within a hundred yards of the walking men.

"You know we are being followed," said Vincent conversationally.

"Two walkers up ahead, two behind, a crawling car on the opposite side of the street," said Sir Nigel.

"I'm impressed, sir."

"My dear boy, I may be old and gray, but I hope I can still spot a tail when it's that big and clumsy."

Because of its supreme power, the old Second Chief Directorate had seldom bothered to dissimulate on the streets of Moscow. Unlike the FBI in Washington or MI5 in London, the cult of the unspottable tail was never really its specialty.

After passing in front of the illuminated splendor of the Bolshoi Theatre and then the smaller Maly Theatre, the two walkers approached a narrow side street, Theatre Alley.

There was a doorway just before the turning, and a bundle of rags trying to sleep there despite the biting cold. Sir Nigel stopped.

Ahead and behind him the Black Guards tried to pretend they were studying empty shop windows.

In the doorway, dimly lit by the streetlamps, the bundle stirred and looked up. He was not drunk, but old, the tired face beneath the woolen comforter pinched and lined with years, hard work, and deprivation. On the lapel of the threadbare greatcoat hung an array of faded medal ribbons. Two deep-set, exhausted eyes looked up at the foreigner.

Nigel Irvine, when based in Moscow, had taken the time to study Russian medals. There was one in the stained row of ribbons he recognized.

"Stalingrad?" he asked softly in Russian. "You were at Stalingrad?"

The bundle of wool around the old head nodded slowly.

"Stalingrad," croaked the old man.

He would have been less than twenty then, in that freezing winter of 1942, fighting Von Paulus's Sixth Army for every brick and cellar of the city on the Volga.

Sir Nigel dug into the pocket of his trousers and came up with a banknote. Fifty million rubles, about thirty U.S. dollars.

"Food," he said. "Hot soup. A slug of vodka. For Stalingrad."

He straightened up and walked on, stiff and angry. Vincent caught up. The followers moved away from their shop windows and resumed the patrol.

"Sweet heaven, what have they come to?" Irvine said to no one in particular, and turned into the side street.

Grishin's car radio crackled as one of the walkers used his walkie-talkie.

"They've turned off. They're going into a restaurant."

The Silver Age is another completely traditional old-Russian restaurant, situated in a recessed alley around the back of the theaters. It was formerly the Central Russian Bathhouse, its walls covered in tiles and mosaics depicting rustic scenes of long ago. Coming from the bitter cold of the street, the two visitors felt the rush of warm air wash over them.

The restaurant was crowded, almost every table taken. The headwaiter scurried forward.

"I'm afraid we are fully booked, gentlemen," he said in Russian. "A large private party. I am so sorry."

"I see there is one table left," replied Vincent in the same language. "Look, over there."

There was indeed a single table for four standing empty against the back wall. The waiter looked worried. He realized the two tourists were foreigners, and that would mean payment in dollars.

"I shall have to ask the host of the dinner," he said, and bustled away. He addressed a handsome olive-skinned man who sat surrounded by companions at the largest table in the room. The man gazed thoughtfully at the two foreigners near the door, and nodded.

The headwaiter came back.

"It is permitted. Please follow me."

Sir Nigel Irvine and Vincent took their seats side by side on the banquette along the wall. Irvine looked across and nodded his thanks to the patron of the private party. The man nodded back.

They ordered duck with cloudberry sauce and allowed the waiter to propose a Crimean red wine that turned out to be reminiscent of bull's blood.

Outside, Grishin's four foot soldiers had sealed the alley at both ends. The colonel's Mercedes drew up at the entrance to the narrow street. He got out and had a quick conference with his men. Then he returned to his car and used his phone.

"How is it going?" he asked.

From the corridor on the second floor of the National he heard a voice say, "Still working on the lock."

Of the four men who had been posted inside the hotel, two had remained. One was now at the end of the corridor, close to the elevators. His job was to see if anyone got out at the second floor and turned toward Room 252. If someone did, he would overtake the person, whistling a tune, to warn the thief to leave the door and move on.

His colleague was with the thief, who was bent over the lock of 252 doing what he did best.

"Tell me when you're in," said Grishin.

Ten minutes later the lock gave a low click and yielded. Grishin was informed.

"Every paper, every document, photograph and replace," he said.

Inside Sir Nigel Irvine's room the search was fast and thorough. The thief spent ten minutes in the bathroom, then emerged and shook his head. The drawers of the chest revealed only the to-be-expected array of ties, shirts, undershorts, handkerchiefs. The drawers of the bedside table were empty. The same applied to the small suitcase stacked on top of the wardrobe, and the pockets of the two suits within it.

The thief went onto his knees and gave a low, satisfied "Aaaaah."

The attaché case was under the bed, pushed right to the center where it was well out of sight. The thief retrieved it with a coat hanger. The numbered locks needed his attention for three minutes.

When the lid came up, he was disappointed. There was a plastic envelope of traveler's checks, which normally he would have taken but for his orders. A wallet with several credit cards and a bar bill from White's Club in London. A silver hip flask whose liquid gave an odor with which he was not familiar.

The pockets inside the lid yielded the return half of an airline ticket from Moscow back to London and a street map of Moscow. He scoured the latter to see if any sites were marked, but could find none.

With a small camera he photographed them all. The Black Guard with him reported their finds to Colonel Grishin.

"There should be a letter," came the metallic voice from the street five hundred yards away.

The thief, thus forewarned, reexamined the attaché case and found the false bottom. It contained a long cream envelope, and inside it a single sheet of matching paper with the embossed heading of the Patriarchate of Moscow and All the Russias. This was photographed three times, just to make sure.

"Pack up and leave," said Grishin.

The two men restored the case to exactly the way it had been before, with the letter back in its envelope and the envelope in the hidden compartment beneath the base of the case. The case itself, relocked with the numbers on the rollers in exactly the same sequence as found, was pushed back beneath the bed. When the room looked as if no one had entered it since Sir Nigel Irvine left, the two men departed.

•   •   •

THE door of the Silver Age opened and closed with a soft hiss. Grishin and four men crossed the small lobby and pushed aside the heavy drapes that led to the dining area. The headwaiter trotted over.

"I am so sorry, gentlemen . . ."

"Get out of my way," said Grishin without even looking at him.

The waiter was jolted, looked at the four men behind the tall man in the black coat, and backed away. He knew enough to recognize serious trouble when he saw it. The four bodyguards might be in civilian clothes, but they were all heavily built, with faces that had been in a few brawls. Even without their uniforms, the elderly waiter recognized them for Black Guards. He had seen them in their uniforms, on television, strutting battalions flashing their arms up to the leader on the podium, and was wise enough to know that waiters did not tangle with the Black Guards.

The man in charge of them swept the room until his gaze fell on the two foreigners dining in the banquette against the rear wall. He nodded to one of his men to accompany him and the other three to give support from the door. Not, he knew, that he needed any. The younger of the two Englishmen might try to give trouble, but he would last a few seconds.

"Friends of yours?" asked Vincent quietly. He felt nakedly unarmed, and wondered how far the serrated steak knife by his plate might get him. Not very far, was his mental answer.

"I think they are the gentlemen whose printing presses you dented a few weeks ago," said Irvine. He wiped his mouth. The duck had been delicious. The man in the black coat walked over, stopped, and looked down at them. The Black Guard stood behind him.

"Sir Irvine?" Grishin spoke only Russian. Vincent translated.

"It's Sir Nigel, actually. And to whom do I have the pleasure?"

"Do not play games. How did you get into the country?"

"Through the airport."

"Lies."

"I assure you, Colonel—it *is* Colonel Grishin, is it not?—my papers are in perfect order. Of course, they are with the hotel reception, or I could show you."

Grishin experienced a flicker of indecision. When he gave orders to most of the organs of state, with the necessary bribes to back them up, those orders were obeyed. But there *could* have been a failure. Someone would pay.

"You are interfering in the internal affairs of Russia, *Anglichanin*. And I do not like it. Your American puppy, Monk, will soon be caught and I shall personally settle accounts with him."

"Have you finished, Colonel? Because if you have, and since we are in the mood to be frank, let me be equally candid with you."

Vincent translated rapidly. Grishin stared in disbelief. No one talked to him like that, least of all a helpless old man. Nigel Irvine raised his eyes from staring at his glass of wine and looked straight at Grishin.

"You are a deeply loathsome individual, and the man you serve is, if possible, even more repugnant."

Vincent opened his mouth, shut it again, then muttered in English: "Boss, is this wise?"

"Just translate, there's a good chap."

Vincent did so. There was a vein tapping rhythmically in Grishin's forehead. The thug behind him looked as if his collar would soon cease to contain his throat.

"The Russian people," resumed Irvine in a conversational tone of voice, "may have made many mistakes, but they do not deserve, nor indeed does any nation deserve, scum like you."

Vincent paused at the word *scum*, swallowed, and used the Russian word *pizdyuk*. The tapping vein increased tempo.

"In summary, Colonel Grishin, the chances are even that you and your whoremaster will never rule this great land. Slowly the people are beginning to see through the facade and in thirty days' time you may find that they will change their minds. So, what are you going to do about it?"

"I think," said Grishin carefully, "that I shall begin by killing you. Certainly you will not leave Russia alive."

Vincent translated and then added in English: "I think he will, too."

The room had fallen silent and the diners at tables on either side had heard via Vincent the Russian interchange between Grishin and Irvine. Grishin was not worried. Muscovites out for an evening dinner were neither going to interfere nor recall what they had seen. The Homicide Division was still aimlessly looking for the killers of the London journalist.

"Not the wisest choice you could make," said Irvine.

Grishin sneered.

"And who do you think will help you? These pigs?"

Pigs was the wrong word. There was a thump at a table to Grishin's left. He half-turned. A gleaming switchblade had been jammed into the tabletop and was still quivering. It might have been the diner's steak knife, but he already had one of those. To the left another diner removed his white napkin from in front of him. Lying underneath it was a Steyr 9mm.

Grishin muttered over his shoulder to the Black Guard behind him.

"Who are these?"

"They're Chechens," hissed the guard.

"All of them?"

"I'm afraid so," said Irvine gently as Vincent translated. "And they really don't like being called pigs. Moslems, you see. With long memories. They can even remember Grozny."

At the mention of the name of their destroyed capital, there was a rattle of metallic clicks as safety catches came off among the fifty diners. Seven handguns were pointing at the three Black Guards by the curtains at the door. The headwaiter was crouched behind his cash desk praying that he would see his grandchildren again.

Grishin looked down at Sir Nigel.

"I underestimated you, *Anglichanin*. But never again. Get out of Russia and stay out. Cease interfering in her internal affairs. Resign yourself to never seeing your American friend again."

He turned on his heel and stalked toward the door. His guards followed him out.

Vincent let out a long exhalation.

"You knew about the people around us, didn't you?"

"Well, I hoped my message had got through. Shall we go?"

He raised his glass with the last of the strong red wine to the room.

"Gentlemen, your very good health, and my thanks."

Vincent translated and they left. They all left. The Chechens staked out the hotel through what remained of the night and escorted the visitors to Sheremetyevo the next morning where they boarded their flight for London.

"I don't care what the offer, Sir Nigel," said Vincent as the British Airways jet banked over the Moskva and turned west. "But I am not, repeat *not*, going back to Moscow."

"Well, that's fine, because neither am I."

"And who's the American?"

"Ah, I'm afraid he's still down there somewhere. Living at the edge, right at the edge. And he's rather special."

•   •   •

UMAR Gunayev let himself in without knocking. Monk was at a table, studying a large-scale map of Moscow. He looked up.

"We have to talk," said the Chechen leader.

"You are not happy," said Monk. "I'm sorry."

"Your friends have left. Alive. But what happened at the Silver Age last night was crazy. I agreed because I owe you a debt, from long ago. But we are running out of debt. And the debt is from me alone. My men do not need to be put in danger because your friends want to play crazy games."

"I'm sorry. The old man had to come to Moscow. He had a meeting, very important. No one could handle it except him. So he came. Grishin discovered he was here."

"Then he should have stayed in the hotel to eat. He would have been reasonably safe in there."

"Apparently he needed to see Grishin, to talk to him."

"To talk to him like that? I was sitting three tables away. He practically asked to be killed."

"I don't understand why either, Umar. Those were his instructions."

"Jason, there are twenty five hundred private security companies in this country and eight hundred of them in Moscow. He could have hired fifty men from any one of them."

With the rise of gangsterdom, another mushroom industry had been that of private guards. Gunayev's figures were quite accurate. The security companies tended to draw their men from the same ex-military units; there were ex-army, marines, special forces, paratroops, police, KGB, all available for hire.

By 1999 the number of private guards across the Russian nation was 800,000, a third of them in Moscow. In theory the militia was the licensing authority for all such companies, and had a duty under the law to check out all recruits to the payroll, their criminal records if any, their suitability, sense of responsibility, weapons carried, how many, what type, and what for.

That was the theory. In practice the well-stuffed envelope could procure all the licenses needed. So useful was the cover of "security company" that the gangs simply formed and registered their own, so that every hoodlum in town could produce identification to show he was a security guard permitted to carry what he wore under his left armpit.

"The trouble is, Umar, they're buyable. They see Grishin, they know they can double their fee; they would change sides and do the job themselves."

"So you use my men, because they will not betray you?"

"I had no choice."

"You know Grishin will now be completely aware who has been

shielding you? If he was ever puzzled before, he will not be now. Life is going to get very hard from now on. Already I hear word from the street that the Dolgoruki have been told to tool up for a major gang war. The last thing I need is a gang war."

"If Komarov comes to power, the Dolgoruki will be the least of your problems."

"What the hell have you started here, you and your damned black file?"

"Whatever it is, we can't stop now, Umar."

"We? What is all this about 'we'? You came to me for help. You needed shelter. I offered you my hospitality. It is the way of my people. Now I'm threatened with open war."

"I could try and head it off."

"How?"

"Speak to Major General Petrovsky."

"Him? That Chekist? You know how much damage he and his GUVD have done to my operations? You know how many raids he has conducted against my clubs, warehouses, casinos?"

"He hates the Dolgoruki more than he hates you. I also need to see the Patriarch. One last time."

"Why?"

"I need to talk to him. There are things to tell him. But this time I will need to be helped to get away."

"No one suspects him. Dress as a priest and go see him."

"It's more complicated than that. I think the Englishman used a hotel limousine. If Grishin checks the records, and he probably will, the log will reveal the Englishman visited the Patriarch. The house in Chisti Pereulok could be under surveillance."

Umar shook his head in disbelief.

"You know, my friend, that Englishman of yours is an old fool."

•　　•　　•

COLONEL Grishin sat at his desk in the dacha and surveyed the blown-up eight-by-ten photograph with unalloyed satisfaction. Finally he pressed a button on his intercom.

"Mr. President, I need to speak to you."

"Come."

Igor Komarov studied the photograph of the letter found in Sir Nigel Irvine's attaché case. It was clearly on the official paper of the

Patriarchate and began with the words: "Your Royal Highness." The signature and seal were those of His Holiness Alexei II.

"What is this?"

"Mr. President, the foreign conspiracy being mounted against you is perfectly clear. It is in two parts. Internally, here in Russia, it is one of destabilization of your election campaign, the spreading of alarm and despondency, based on the selective showing of your private manifesto to certain persons.

"That has resulted in the sabotage of the printing presses, the pressure by the banks to terminate the nationwide broadcasts, and the denunciation from that old fool of a general. It has caused damage but it cannot stop your victory.

"The second part of the conspiracy is in its way even more dangerous. It proposes the replacement of yourself by a restoration of the Throne of All the Russias. For his own self-interest, the Patriarch has fallen for this. What you have before you is his personal letter to a certain prince, living in the West, supporting the concept of restoration and agreeing that if this is accepted the church will propose the invitation go to this man."

"And your proposal, Colonel?"

"Quite simple, Mr. President. Without a candidate, the conspiracy collapses."

"You know of a man who can . . . discourage this noble gentleman?"

"Permanently. He is very good. Accustomed to working in the West. Speaks several languages. He works for the Dolgoruki, but can be hired. His last contract concerned two renegades from the mafia who were charged with depositing twenty million dollars in London but decided to divert it to themselves. They were found two weeks ago in a flat in Wimbledon, a suburb of London."

"Then I think we need the services of this man, Colonel."

"Leave it to me, Mr. President. Within ten days there will be no candidate."

Then, Grishin thought as he returned to his office, with Sir Nigel's precious prince on a marble slab and Jason Monk traced by FAPSI and hanging in a cellar, we shall send Sir Nigel Irvine a packet of photographs that will really make his Christmas.

●　　　●　　　●

THE Head of the GUVD had finished his dinner and was sitting with his small daughter on his knee watching her favorite cartoon show when the phone rang. His wife answered.

"It's for you."

"Who is it?"

"He just says, 'The American.'"

The militia general eased Tatiana onto the floor and rose.

"I'll take it in the study."

When he had closed the door and lifted the receiver he heard the click of his wife replacing the extension.

"Yes."

"General Petrovsky?"

"Yes."

"We spoke the other day."

"We did."

"I have some information you might find useful. Do you have pen and paper?"

"Where are you speaking from?"

"A phone booth. I don't have long. Please hurry."

"Go ahead."

"Komarov and Grishin have persuaded their friends the Dolgoruki gang to launch a war. They are going to take on the Chechen mafia."

"So it's dog-eat-dog. I should worry."

"Except that the World Bank delegation is in Moscow negotiating the next round of economic credits. Maybe. If the streets are a hail of bullets, acting president Markov, trying to look good both in the eyes of the world and for his election prospects, will not be happy. He might wonder why it had to be now."

"Go on."

"Six addresses. Please take them down."

Monk reeled them off while Major General Petrovsky noted them.

"What are they?"

"The first two are arsenals, packed with Dolgoruki weaponry. The third is a casino; in the basement are most of their financial records. The last three are warehouses. They contain twenty million dollars worth of contraband goods."

"How do you know this?"

"I have friends in low places. Do you know these two officers?"
Monk gave him two names.

"Of course. One senior deputy of mine and one squad commander of the SOBR troops. Why?"

"They are both on the Dolgoruki payroll."

"You'd better be certain, American."

"I am. If you want to mount any raids, I'd keep the notice very short and those two out of the picture."

"I know how to do my job."

The line disconnected. General Petrovsky replaced the receiver thoughtfully. If this bizarre foreign agent was right, the information was priceless. He had a choice. Let the gang war rip, or mount a series of body blows on the major mafia syndicate at a moment likely to receive ringing congratulations from the presidency.

He had three thousand rapid reaction force troops at his disposal, the SOBR, mainly young and eager. If the American was only half-right about Igor Komarov and his plans after taking power, there would be no place in the New Russia for him, his gangbusters, or his troops. He returned to the sitting room.

The cartoons were over. Now he would never know if Wiley Coyote had got the Roadrunner for supper or not.

"I'm going back to the office," he told his wife. "I'll be there all night and most of tomorrow."

•   •   •

IN winter the city authorities are accustomed to flood the paths and walkways of the Gorki Park with water, which soon freezes rock solid, creating the country's biggest ice rink. It extends for miles and is popular with Muscovites of all classes and ages, who bring their skates and a good supply of vodka to forget for a while their cares and troubles in the freedom of the ice.

Some drives remain ice-free and terminate in small parking areas. It was in one of these that two men, muffled and fur-hatted against the cold, met ten days before Christmas. Each got out of his car and walked alone to the edge of the trees, facing the sheet of ice where the skaters glided and swooped around one another.

One was Colonel Anatoli Grishin, the other a solitary man known in the underworld as Mekhanik, or the Mechanic.

While killers for hire were two-a-penny in Russia, several mafia gangs but most usually the Dolgoruki regarded the Mechanic as special.

He was in fact a Ukrainian, a former army major, who years earlier had been assigned to the Spetsnaz special forces and thence to the military intelligence arm, the GRU. After language school he had enjoyed two postings to Western Europe. Leaving the army, he had realized he could parlay his fluency in English and French, his ability to move easily in societies most Russians regarded as alien and strange, and his lack of inhibitions in the matter of killing other human beings into a lucrative profession.

"I understand you wanted to see me," he said.

He knew who Colonel Grishin was, and that inside Russia the head of security for the Union of Patriotic Forces Party would have no need of him. Within the Black Guards, not to mention the party's allies in the Dolgoruki mafia, there were triggermen enough who had but to be given the order. But working abroad was special.

Grishin passed him a photograph. The Mechanic glanced at it and turned it over. A name and the address of a manor house in the countryside, far to the west, were typed on the back.

"A prince," he murmured. "I *am* going up in the world."

"Keep your sense of humor to yourself," said Grishin. "It's a soft target. No personal security worth the name. By Christmas Day."

The Mechanic considered. Too quick. He needed to prepare. He was alive and free because he took meticulous precautions, and they took time.

"New Year's Day," he said.

"Very well. You have a price."

The Mechanic named it.

"Agreed."

Plumes of white frosted breath rose from both men. The Mechanic recalled seeing on the television a religious revivalist rally at which a charismatic young priest had been calling for a return to God and the czar. So that was Grishin's game. He regretted not doubling his price.

"That's it?" he asked.

"Unless you have more you need to know."

The executioner slipped the photograph inside his coat.

"No," he said, "I think I know all I need to. Nice to do business with you, Colonel."

Grishin turned and gripped the man's arm. The Mechanic looked down at the gloved hand until the grip was released. He did not like to be touched.

"There must be no mistakes, on target or timing."

"I do not make mistakes, Colonel. Or you would not have asked for me. I will mail you the number of my Liechtenstein account. Good-day to you."

•   •   •

IN the small hours of the morning following the meeting by the skating rink in Gorki Park, General Petrovsky's six simultaneous raids went in.

The two informers had been invited to a private dinner in the officers club at the SOBR barracks and plied with enough vodka to render them gloriously drunk. Rooms had been provided for them to sleep off the effects. To make sure, there was a guard on each door.

A tactical "exercise," arranged during the day, had been converted into the real thing just before midnight. By then the troops in their trucks had been confined to a series of closed garages. At two in the morning the drivers and detail commanders had been given their missions and the addresses they needed. For the first time in months surprise had been total.

The three warehouses had proved little problem. Four guards protecting the treasure stores had tried to resist and been gunned down. Eight more had surrendered just in time. The warehouses had yielded ten thousand cases of imported vodka, all without duty paid, that had rolled in from Finland and Poland over the previous two months. It was the wheat famine that had forced the biggest vodka-drinking nation in the world to import its own tipple, with prices rising to three times those in the countries of manufacture.

Other consignments in the warehouses turned out to be dishwashers, washing machines, televisions, video recorders, and computers, all from the West and all hijacked.

The two arsenals had yielded enough weaponry to fit out a fullstrength infantry regiment, with types running from normal assault rifles up to shoulder-borne antitank rockets and flamethrowers.

Petrovsky personally had led the raid on the casino, which was still full of gamblers who fled screaming into the night. The manager continued to protest that his was a perfectly legitimate and city-licensed business until the desk in his office was removed, the carpet lifted, and the trapdoor to the cellar revealed. Then he fainted.

At midmorning the SOBR troops were still removing box after box of financial records, which were put in vans and taken back to the GUVD headquarters at 6 Shabolovka Street for analysis.

By midday two generals of the Presidium of the MVD, the Interior Ministry, five hundred yards away at Zhitny Square, had been on the phone to offer their congratulations.

The midmorning radio news carried the first bulletins of the affair, and at noon there was a fairly full report on the TV news. The number of fatalities among the gangsters, the newscaster intoned, had risen to sixteen, while among the rapid reaction force the casualties were limited to one seriously injured with a bullet in the stomach and one slight flesh wound. Twenty-seven mafiosi had been detained alive, of whom seven were in the hospital, and two were delivering lengthy statements to the GUVD.

This last allegation was not actually true, but had been released to the media by Petrovsky to cause even further panic among the leaders of the Dolgoruki clan.

The latter were indeed in a state of trauma as they met in a sumptuous, heavily guarded dacha well out of town, a mile and a half from the Archangelskoye Bridge over the Moskva. The only emotion transcending their panic was that of rage. Most were convinced that the sidelining of their two informers, the element of complete surprise the SOBR had achieved, and the accuracy of their knowledge pointed the finger in the direction of a major leak.

Even as they deliberated word came in from their street people that the buzz was about to the effect the leak had come from a loose-talking senior officer of the Black Guard. Considering the millions of dollars the Dolgoruki had put behind Igor Komarov's election campaign, they were not amused.

They would never learn that the street rumor had in fact been started by the Chechens on the advice of Jason Monk. The clan chiefs resolved that before any further money was released to the UPF, there would have to be a serious explanation.

Just after three, Umar Gunayev, backed by heavy personal protection, came to visit Monk. This time he was living with a Chechen family in a small apartment just north of the Sokolniki Park Exhibition Center.

"I don't know how you managed it, my friend, but a very large bomb went off last night."

"It's a question of self-interest," said Monk. "Petrovsky had a considerable interest in pleasing his superiors right up to the office of the acting president during the week of the visit of the World Bank team. That's all."

"All right. Well, the Dolgoruki are in no position to launch a war against me. They will spend weeks trying to repair the damage."

"And to trace the leak inside the Black Guards," Monk reminded him.

Umar Gunayev tossed a copy of *Sevodnya* onto his lap.

"Have a look at page three," he suggested.

There was a report from Russia's leading opinion poll organizers to suggest electoral support for the UPF was at fifty-five percent and falling.

"These polls are mainly taken in the cities," said Monk, "for ease and convenience. Komarov is stronger in the cities. The key will lie with the overlooked teeming masses in the countryside."

"You really think Komarov can actually be defeated at the polls?" asked Gunayev. "Six weeks ago there would not have been a chance."

"I don't know," said Monk.

This was not the moment to tell the Chechen leader that defeat at the polls was not what Sir Nigel Irvine had in mind. He recalled the old spymaster, still revered in the world of the Great Game as the ultimate practitioner of deception by disinformation, sitting in the library at Castle Forbes with the family Bible open in front of him.

"The key is Gideon, dear boy," he was saying. "Think like Gideon."

"You're miles away," said Gunayev. Monk snapped out of his reverie.

"Sorry, you were right. Tonight I have to visit the Patriarch again. For the last time. I will need your help."

"To get in?"

"I think to get out. There is a good chance Grishin has the place under surveillance, as I told you. One man would do, but that man will call up others while I am inside."

"We'd better start planning," said the Chechen.

*   *   *

COLONEL Anatoli Grishin was in his apartment preparing for bed when his mobile phone rang. He recognized the voice without introduction.

"He's here. He's here again."

"Who?"

"The American. He's back. He's with His Holiness now."

"He suspects nothing?"

"I don't think so. He came alone."

"As a priest?"

"No. All in black, but civilian dress. The Patriarch seemed to be expecting him."

"Where are you?"

"In the pantry, making coffee. I must go."

The phone disconnected. Grishin tried to control his elation. The hated American agent was almost in his grasp. This time there would be no East Berlin. He called the leader of the inner-core group of the Black Guards' enforcers.

"I need ten men, three cars, mini-Uzis, now. Seal both ends of a street called Chisti Pereulok. I'll meet you there in thirty minutes."

It was half-past midnight.

At ten minutes after one o'clock Monk arose and bade the Patriarch good night.

"I don't suppose we shall meet again, Your Holiness. I know you will do the best you can for this land and people you love so much."

Alexei II arose also and accompanied him to the door.

"With God's good grace, I shall try. Good-bye, my son. May angels guard you."

For the moment, thought Monk, as he descended the stairs, a few warriors from the North Caucasus will do nicely.

The fat valet was there as usual, holding out his coat.

"No coat, thank you, Father," he said. The last thing he needed was something to slow him up. He took out his mobile phone and tapped in a number. It was answered at the first ring.

"Monakh," he said.

"Fifteen seconds," replied a voice. Monk recognized Magomed, the senior of the protectors Gunayev had assigned to him. Monk pulled the street door open a few inches and peered out.

Down the narrow street a single Mercedes waited near a dim streetlight. It contained four men, one at the wheel and three with mini-Uzi machine pistols. The white plume rising from the rear in the bitter night indicated the engine was running.

In the other direction Chisti Pereulok debouched into a small square. Waiting in the shadows of the square were two other black cars. On foot or four wheels, anyone wishing to leave the alley would have to pass the ambush.

At the end where the single car waited, another vehicle approached, its "Taxi" light burning yellow above the windshield. The watchers let it come abreast. Clearly it had come to pick up their target. Bad luck for the taxi driver; he would die too.

The taxi came abreast of the Mercedes and there was a double clink as two grapefruit-sized pieces of metal hit the icy road and skittered under the sedan. Hardly had the taxi cleared it than Monk, behind the street door, which was by then an inch open, heard the double *whump* of the grenades going off.

Simultaneously a large delivery truck rolled into the square at the other end, rumbled across the entrance to the alley, and stopped. The driver leaped from the cab into the road and began to sprint down the alley.

Monk nodded once at the trembling priest, opened the door wide, and stepped into the street. The taxi was almost opposite him, rear door swinging open. He threw himself inside. From the front seat a strong arm reached back and dragged him the rest of the way in. The running truck driver followed.

In reverse gear the taxi roared back the way it had come. From behind the immobile truck came a spray of bullets as someone flat on the ground used a submachine gun. Then the two charges under the chassis of the truck went off and the firing ceased.

One of the men had managed to get out of the Mercedes and was standing groggily by the rear door, trying to raise his gun. The rear fender of the taxi caught him in the shins and sent him flying.

Out of the alley, the taxi slewed sideways, skidded on the ice, recovered, moved into forward gear, and sped off. The gas tank in the Mercedes exploded and finished the job.

Magomed turned from the front seat and Monk caught the flash of his teeth beneath the black Zapata moustache.

"You make life interesting, Amerikanets."

In the small square at the far end of the alley Colonel Grishin stood contemplating the ruined truck that blocked the access. Beneath it, two of his men were lying dead, killed by the two small charges lashed beneath the chassis and triggered from inside the cab. Peering around the edge of the vehicle he could see his other car burning at the far end of the narrow street.

He took his mobile phone and punched in seven numbers. He heard the mobile phone he had dialed trill twice. Then a panicky whisper said, *"Da."*

"He got away. You have what I want?"

"Da."

"Usual place. At ten this morning."

•   •   •

THE small church of All Saints of Kulishki was almost empty at that hour. A verger tended the altar and two babushkas, cleaning women, were dusting. A young priest entered, genuflected at the altar, crossed himself, and disappeared through a panel in the wall toward the vestry behind the altar.

Father Maxim was standing by the right-hand wall, holding a guttering candle bought from the store by the main door, when Colonel Grishin appeared beside him.

"The American got away," he said quietly.

"I am sorry. I tried."

"How did he guess?"

"He seemed to suspect the residence might be under some kind of surveillance." As usual the priest was sweating. "He produced a mobile phone from his waistband and called somebody."

"Start at the beginning."

"He arrived about ten past twelve. I was about to go to bed. His Holiness was still up, working in his study. He always is, at that hour. The street doorbell rang, but I did not hear it. I was in my room. The Cossack night guard answered it. Then I heard voices. I came out of my room and there he was, standing in the hall.

"I heard His Holiness call from upstairs. 'Show the gentleman up,' he said. Then he leaned over the banister, saw me, and asked for some coffee. I went back to my pantry and phoned you."

"How long until you entered the room?"

"Not long. A few minutes. I hurried as fast as I could in order to miss as little as possible. I was there within five minutes."

"And the tape recorder I gave you?"

"I switched it on before I went in with the coffee. They stopped talking when I knocked. While putting down the coffee I spilled some sugar lumps onto the floor, and went down on my knees to pick them up. His Holiness said not to bother, but I insisted and while down there slipped the recorder under the desk. Then I left."

"And at the end?"

"He came downstairs alone. I was waiting with his coat, but he did not want it. The Cossack was in his small room beside the door. The American seemed nervous. He produced a mobile phone and dialed. Someone answered, and he just said, 'Monakh.' "

"Nothing else?"

"No, Colonel, just Monakh. Then he listened. I didn't hear the answer because he kept the phone close to his ear. Then he waited. He pulled the street door open a little way and looked out. I was still holding his coat."

Grishin considered. The old Englishman could have told Monk he had himself been traced via the hotel limousine. It would be enough to warn the American the Patriarchal residence could be under surveillance.

"Go on, Father."

"I heard the roar of a car engine, then two explosions. The American tore the door open and ran. Then I heard gunfire and jumped back from the open door."

Grishin nodded. The American was smart, but he had arrived at the right answer for the wrong reasons. He, Grishin, had indeed had the Patriarchal residence under surveillance, but from the inside, from the renegade priest.

"And the tape?"

"When the explosions took place outside, the Cossack rushed out with his gun. The American had left the door open. The Cossack looked out, shouted 'Gangsters,' and slammed the door closed. I ran upstairs just as His Holiness came out of his library to lean over the banister and ask what was going on. While he was there I recovered the coffee cups and the tape recorder."

Without a word Grishin held out his hand. Father Maxim delved into a side pocket of his cassock and produced a small tape, the sort used by miniature recorders of the type the priest had been given at their last meeting.

"I hope I did the right thing," said Father Maxim tremulously. Grishin sometimes felt he would dearly like to strangle the toad with his bare hands. Perhaps one day he would.

"You have done exactly the right thing, Father," he said. "You have done exceptionally well."

In his car on the way back to his office Colonel Grishin looked at the tape again. He had lost six good men during the small hours, and lost his quarry. But he held in his hand the record of exactly what the interfering American had said to the Patriarch, and vice versa. One day, he vowed, both would pay for their crimes. For the moment, so far as he was concerned, the day would certainly end much better than it started.

CHAPTER 18

COLONEL ANATOLI GRISHIN SAT ALL THE REST OF THAT MORNING, through the lunch hour, and into the afternoon locked in his office listening to the tape of the conference between Patriarch Alexei II and Jason Monk.

At times there were mumbles or the tinkle of cups being stirred, but most of the passages were clear enough.

The tape began with the sound of a door opening—Father Maxim entering the room with a tray of coffee. The sounds were muffled because at that point the recorder had been in the side pocket of his cassock.

Grishin heard the tray being placed on the desk, then a muffled voice saying, "Don't bother."

There was an equally muffled response as Father Maxim knelt on the carpet, presumably picking up the dropped sugar lumps.

The sound quality improved as the recorder was slipped under the desk. The voice of the Patriarch was clear enough saying to Father Maxim: "Thank you, Father, that will be all."

There was silence until the sound of a door closing, the withdrawal of the informer. Then the Patriarch said:

"Now, perhaps you will explain what you have come to tell me."

Monk began to speak. Grishin could distinguish the slight nasal twang of the American speaking fluent Russian. He began to take notes.

He listened to the forty-minute conversation three times before he began to write a verbatim transcript. This was not a job for a secretary, however trusted.

Page after page was covered in his neat Cyrillic script. Sometimes he paused, played back, craned to hear the words, and then resumed writing. When he was certain he had every word, he stopped.

There was the sound of a chair moving back, then Monk's voice saying, "I don't suppose we shall meet again, Your Holiness. I know you will do the best you can for this land and people you love so much."

Two sets of footsteps moved across the carpet. More faintly, as they reached the door, Grishin heard Alexei's reply: "With God's good grace, I shall try."

The door evidently closed behind Monk. Grishin heard the sound of the Patriarch resuming his seat. Ten seconds later the tape ran out.

Grishin sat back and mulled over what he had heard. The news was as bad as it could conceivably be. How one man, he reflected, could cause such systematic damage was hard to understand. The key of course was that damnable act of stupidity by the late N. I. Akopov in leaving the manifesto lying around to be stolen. The damage caused by that single leak was already incalculable.

Monk clearly had done most of the talking. The earlier interventions by Alexei II had been to indicate that he understood and approved. His own contribution came toward the end.

The American had not been idle. He revealed that immediately after the New Year a concerted campaign would begin to destroy the electoral chances of Igor Komarov across the country by a process of discreditation and massive publicity.

General Nikolai Nikolayev, it seemed, would resume a series of newspaper, radio, and television interviews in which he would denounce the UPF, calling on every soldier and ex-soldier to repudiate the party and vote elsewhere. There were 20 million veterans among the 110 million enfranchised voters. The damage that one man would do could scarcely be contemplated.

The shutdown of all publicity for Igor Komarov being exercised by both commercial TV channels was the work of the bankers, three out of four of them Jewish, and the leader and inspirator of them all Leonid Bernstein of the Moskovsky Federal. That constituted two scores that would have to be settled.

Monk's third contribution concerned the Dolgoruki mafia. Grishin had long regarded all of them as scum concentration camp fodder for the future. But for the moment their financial backing was crucial.

No politician in Russia could hope to aspire to the presidency without a nationwide campaign costing trillions of rubles. The secret deal with the most powerful and richest mafia west of the Urals had provided that treasure chest, which vastly exceeded anything available to other candidates. Several had already folded their tents, unable to keep up with the expenditure of the UPF.

The six raids of the previous day in the small hours had been disastrous for the Dolgoruki, but none more so than the discovery of the financial records. There were few sources from which the GUVD could have learned such details. A rival mafia was the obvious choice, but in the closed world of the gangsters no one, despite the internecine rivalry, would inform to the hated GUVD. Yet here was Monk informing the Patriarch of the source of the leak—a disgusted and turncoat senior officer of Grishin's own Black Guards.

If the Dolgoruki ever proved such a thing—and Grishin knew rumors were flying around the streets, rumors he had passionately denied—the alliance would be over.

To make matters worse, the tape revealed that a team of skilled accountants had already begun work on the papers found beneath the casino and were confident that by the New Year they would be able to prove the funding link between the mafia and the UPF. Those findings would be delivered directly to Acting President Markov. During the same period, Major General Petrovsky of the GUVD, who could be neither bribed nor intimidated, would keep up the pressure on the Dolgoruki gang with raid after raid.

If he did so, Grishin calculated, there was no way the Dolgoruki gang would continue to accept his assurances that a Black Guard source was not behind the GUVD.

The Patriarch's intervention, coming as it did toward the end of the tape, was perhaps the most potentially damaging of all.

The acting president would be spending the New Year celebrations with his family away from Moscow. He would return on January 3. On that day he would receive the Patriarch, who intended to make a personal intercession, urging Markov to invalidate the candidature of Igor Komarov as an "unfit person," based upon existing evidence.

With the proof of gangster linkage provided by Petrovsky and the personal intervention of the Patriarch of Moscow and All the Russias, Markov would be extremely likely to do just that. Apart from anything else, he was himself a candidate and did not want to face Komarov at the polls.

Four traitors, Grishin brooded. Four traitors to the New Russia that was destined to come into existence after January 16, with himself at the head of an elite corps of 200,000 Black Guards ready to carry out the orders of the leader. Well, he had spent his life rooting out and punishing traitors. He knew how to deal with them.

He personally typed out a copy of his handwritten transcript and asked for an uninterrupted two hours of President Komarov's time that evening.

•   •   •

JASON Monk had moved from the flat by Sokolniki Park and was installed in another from whose windows he could see the crescent atop the mosque where he had first met Magomed, the man now sworn to protect him but who on that day would just as easily have killed him.

He had a message to send to Sir Nigel Irvine in London, according to his schedule the second-from-last, if all went according to the old man's plan.

He typed it carefully into his laptop computer, as he had done all the others. When he was finished, he pressed the 'encode' button and the message vanished from the screen, safely encrypted into the jumbled blocks of numbers of the one-time pad and logged inside the floppy disk to await the next pass of the InTelCor satellite.

He did not need to attend the machine. Its batteries were fully charged and it was switched on, waiting for the handshake from the comsat rolling in space.

He never heard of Ricky Taylor of Columbus, Ohio, never met

him and never would. But the pimply teenager probably saved his life.

Ricky was seventeen and a computer freak. He was one of those dysfunctional young men bred by the computer age, most of whose life was spent gazing into a dully fluorescent screen.

Having been given his first PC at the age of seven, he had progressed through the various stages of expertise until the legitimate challenges ran out and only the illegal ones created the necessary buzz, the required periodic "high" of the true addict. Not for Ricky the gentle rhythm of the passing seasons outside, nor the camaraderie of his fellows or even the lust for girls. Ricky's fix was to hack into the most jealously guarded databanks.

By 1999 InTelCor was not only a major player in global communications for strategic, diplomatic, and commercial use; it was also preeminent as deviser and marketer of the most complex of computer games. Ricky had surfed the Internet until he was bored, and had mastered every known and freely available game sequence. He yearned to pit himself against InTelCor's Ultra programs. The problem was, to log in to them legitimately cost a fee. Ricky's allowance did not run to that fee. So he had tried for weeks to enter the InTelCor mainframe by the back door. After so much effort he figured he was almost there.

Eight time zones west of Moscow his screen read, for the thousandth time: ACCESS CODE PLEASE. He tapped in what he thought might do it. Again the screen told him: ACCESS DENIED.

Somewhere south of the mountains of Anatolia the InTelCor comsat was drifting through space on its heading north for Moscow.

When the technicians of the multinational had devised Monk's coded sender/receiver they had, on instructions, included a total wipeout code of four digits. These were the numbers Danny had him memorize at Castle Forbes, and were intended to protect Monk in the event of capture, provided he could punch in the code before he was taken.

But if his machine was captured intact, so reasoned the chief encoder, a former CIA cryptographer from Warrenton brought out of retirement for the job, the bad guys could use the machine to send false messages.

So to prove his authenticity, Monk had to include certain harmless words, all in sequence. If a transmission took place without those words, the ex-CIA man would know that whoever was out there was off the payroll. At that point he could use the Compuserve mainframe to log in to Monk's PC via the satellite and use the same four digits to obliterate its memory, leaving the bad guys with a useless tin can.

Ricky Taylor was already into InTelCor's mainframe when he hit those four digits. The satellite rolled over Moscow and sent down its "Are you there, baby?" call. The laptop replied "Yes, I am," and the satellite, obedient to its instructions, wasted it.

The first Monk knew about it was when he went to check his machine and found his message, in clear, back on the screen. That meant it had been rejected. He negated the message manually, aware that, for reasons beyond his comprehension, something had gone wrong and he was out of contact.

There was an address Sir Nigel Irvine had given him just before he left London. He did not know where it was or who lived there. But it was all he had. With economy he could compress his last two messages into one, something the spymaster would have to know. That might work for getting a message out. Receiving any more was out of the question. For the first time, he was completely on his own. No more progress reports, no more confirmations of action taken, no more instructions.

With the billion-dollar technology down, he would rely on the oldest allies in the Great Game: instinct, nerve, and luck. He prayed they would not let him down.

•   •   •

IGOR Komarov finished the last page of the transcript and leaned back. He was never a man of high color, but now, Grishin noted, his face was like a sheet of paper.

"This is bad," said Komarov.

"Very bad, Mr. President."

"You should have captured him before now."

"He is being sheltered by the Chechen mafia. This we now know. They live like rats in their own subterranean world."

"Rats can be exterminated."

"Yes, Mr. President. And they will be. When you are undisputed leader of this country."

"They must be made to pay."

"They will. Every last one of them."

Komarov was still staring at him with those hazel eyes, but they were unfocused, as if their owner were looking to another time and another place, a time in the future, a place of settlement of accounts with his enemies. The two red spots were bright upon the cheekbones.

"Retribution. I want retribution. They have attacked me, they have attacked Russia, attacked the Motherland. There can be no mercy for scum like this. . . ."

His voice was rising, the hands starting to tremble as the rage cracked his habitual self-control. Grishin knew that if he could argue his point with enough skill he would win his argument. He leaned forward over the desk, forcing Komarov to look him in the eyes. Slowly the rage subsided and Grishin knew he had his attention.

"Listen to me, Mr. President. Please listen. What we now know enables me to turn the tables completely. You will have your revenge. Just give me the word."

"What do you mean, Anatoli Grishin?"

"The key to counterintelligence, Mr. President, is knowledge of the enemy's intentions. This we now have. From that stems prevention. It is already taking place. In a few days, there will be no selected candidate for the throne of All the Russias. Now we have a second revelation of their intentions. Once again I must propose both prevention and retribution, all in one."

"All four men?"

"There can be no choice."

"Nothing must be traced back. Not yet. It is too early for that."

"Nothing will be traced back. The banker? How many bankers have been killed in the past ten years? Fifty? At least. Armed and masked men, a settlement of accounts. It happens all the time.

"The policeman? The Dolgoruki gang will be happy to take the contract. How many cops have been wasted? Again, it happens all the time.

"As for the fool of a general, a burglary that went wrong. Nothing could be more common. And for the priest, a house servant caught ransacking his study during the night. Shot down by the Cossack guard, who in turn is killed by the thief as he dies."

"Will anyone believe that?"

"I have a source inside the residence who will swear to it."

Komarov looked at the papers he had finished reading and the tape beside them. He smiled thinly.

"Of course you do. I need to know no more about all this. I insist I know nothing more of all this."

"But you do wish the four men bent upon your destruction to cease to function?"

"Certainly."

"Thank you, Mr. President. That is all I need to know."

• • •

THE room at the Spartak Hotel had been booked in the name of Mr. Kuzichkin, and a man of that name had indeed checked in. Having done so he then walked out again, slipping his room key to Jason Monk as he did so. The Chechen guards filtered through the lobby, the stairwell, and the access to the elevators as he went upstairs. It was as safe a way as any of having twenty minutes on a telephone which, if traced, would reveal only a room in a non-Chechen-owned hotel far from the center of town.

"General Petrovsky?"

"You again."

"You seem to have stirred up a hornet's nest."

"I don't know where you get your information from, American, but it seems to be good."

"Thank you. But Komarov and Grishin will not take this lying down."

"What about the Dolgoruki?"

"Bit players. The key danger is Grishin and his Black Guards."

"Was it you who put out the rumor that the source was a senior officer in the Black Guard?"

"Friends of mine."

"Smart. But dangerous."

"The weak point for Grishin lies in those papers you captured. I think they prove the mafia has been funding Komarov all along."

"They are being worked on."

"So are you, General."

"What do you mean?"

"Are your wife and Tatiana still there?"

"Yes."

"I wish you would get them out of town. Now, tonight. Somewhere far away and safe. Yourself too. Move out. Go and live in the SOBR barracks. Please."

There was silence for a while.

"Do you know something, American?"

"Please, General. Get out of there. While there is time."

He put the phone down, waited awhile, and dialed another number. The phone rang on Leonid Bernstein's desk at the Moskovsky Federal Bank headquarters. It was late at night and only a tape machine answered. Without the banker's private home phone number, Monk could only pray that Bernstein would access his messages within the next few hours.

"Mr. Bernstein, this is the man who reminded you of Babi Yar. Please don't go to the office, however pressing the business. I am certain Komarov and Grishin now know who is behind the shutdown of their TV exposure. You keep your family out of the country; go and join them until it is safe to return."

He put the phone down again. Though he did not know it, a light flashed on a console in a heavily guarded house miles away and Leonid Bernstein listened to the message in silence.

The third call was to the residence.

"Yes."

"Your Holiness?"

"Yes."

"You know my voice?"

"Of course."

"You should go to the monastery at Zagorsk. Get inside and stay inside."

"Why?"

"I fear for you. Last night proved that matters are becoming dangerous."

"I have High Mass tomorrow at the Danilovsky."

"The Metropolitan can take your place."

"I will consider what you say."

The phone went down. The fourth call was answered at the tenth ring and a gruff voice said, "Yes."

"General Nikolayev?"

"Who is . . . wait a minute, I know you. You're that damned Yankee."

"That's me."

"Well, no more interviews. Did what you wanted, said my piece. No more. That's it. Hear me?"

"Let's keep it short. You should get out and go to live with your nephew on the base."

"Why?"

"Certain thugs did not appreciate what you said. I think they might pay you a visit."

"Ruffians, eh? Well, bollocks. Stuff 'em all. Never retreated in my life, boy. Too late to start now."

The phone went dead. Monk sighed and replaced his own. He checked his watch. Twenty-five minutes. Time to go. Back to the warren of rat runs in the Chechen underworld.

•   •   •

THERE were four killer groups and they struck two nights later, on December 21.

The biggest and best-armed took the private dacha of Leonid Bernstein. There were a dozen guards on duty and four of them died in the firefight. Two Black Guards were also cut down. The main door was blown out with a shaped charge and the men in combat black, their faces hidden by ski masks of the same color, raced through the house.

The surviving guards and staff were rounded up and herded into the kitchen. The guard commander was badly beaten but kept repeating that his employer had flown to Paris two days earlier. The rest of the staff, above the screaming of the women, confirmed this. Finally the men in black retreated to their trucks, taking their two dead with them.

The second assault was on the apartment house in Kutuzovsky Prospekt. A single black Mercedes pulled under the arch and drew up at the barrier. One of the two OMON guards came out of his warm hut to examine papers. Two men crouching behind the car ran forward with silenced automatics and shot him through the base of the neck, just above the body-armor. The second guard was killed before he could emerge.

In the ground floor lobby the man at the reception desk suffered the same fate. Four Black Guards, running in from the street, secured the lobby while six went up in the elevator. This time there were no men in the corridor at all, though the attackers did not know why.

The door to the apartment, although steel-lined, was taken apart by half a pound of plastic explosive and the six rushed in. The white-jacketed steward winged one in the shoulder before he was cut down. A thorough search of the flat revealed there was no one else there and the squad retreated frustrated.

Back on the ground floor they exchanged fire with two more OMON guards who had appeared from the rest area at the back of the building, killed one, and lost one of their own. Empty-handed, they retreated under fire into the avenue and took off in three waiting GAZ jeeps.

At the Patriarchal Residence the approach was more subtle. A single man knocked at the street door while six more crouched on either side of him out of the line of sight of the peephole.

The Cossack inside peered through the hole and used the street intercom to ask who was there. The man at the door held up a valid militia identification and said: "Police."

Duped by the ID, the Cossack opened the door. He was shot immediately and his body carried upstairs.

The plan had been to shoot the private secretary with the Cossack's gun, and kill the primate with the same piece that had been used on the Cossack. This gun would then be placed in the hand of the dead secretary, to be found behind the desk.

Father Maxim would then be forced to swear both Cossack and primate had disturbed the secretary rifling the drawers and in the ensuing interchange of fire all three had died. Apart from a huge ecclesiastical scandal, the militia would close the case.

Instead the killers found a fat priest in a soiled dressing gown at the top of the stairs screaming, "What are you doing?"

"Where's Alexei?" snarled one of the men in black.

"He left," babbled the priest. "He's gone to Zagorsk."

A search of the private apartments revealed that the Patriarch and the two nuns were not there. Leaving the body of the Cossack, the killer team withdrew.

There were only four men sent to the lonely cottage out along the Minsk Highway. They came out of their car and while one approached the door the other three waited in the darkness of the trees.

It was old Valodya who answered. He was shot in the chest and the four men poured into the house. The wolfhound came at them across the floor of the sitting room and went for the throat of the leading Black Guard. He threw up an arm and the hound's teeth went deeply into it. A companion blew its head off.

By the embers of the log fire an old man with bristling white whiskers pointed a Makarov at the group in the doorway and fired twice. One bullet lodged in the doorjamb and the other hit the man who had just killed his dog.

Then three bullets in quick succession struck the old general in the chest.

•   •   •

UMAR Gunayev called shortly after ten in the morning.

"I just drove to my office. There's all hell going on."

"In what way?"

"Kutuzovsky Prospekt is blocked off. Militia all over the place."

"Why?"

"Some kind of attack last night on a building inhabited by senior militia officers."

"That was quick. I'm going to need a safe phone."

"What about the one where you are?"

"Traceable."

"Give me half an hour. I'll send some men for you."

By eleven Monk was installed in a small office in a warehouse full of contraband liquor. A telephone engineer was just finishing.

"It's linked to two cutouts," he said to Monk, gesturing at the phone. "If anyone tries to trace a call on it, they'll end up in a café two miles away. It's one of our joints. If they get past that, they'll be led to a phone booth down the street. By then we'll know."

Monk started with the private number of General Nikolayev. A male voice answered.

"Give me General Nikolayev," said Monk.

"Who is that?" asked the voice.

"I could ask the same thing."

"The general is not available. Who are you?"

"General Malenkov, Defense Ministry. What's going on?"

"I'm sorry, General. This is Inspector Novikov, Homicide Division, Moscow militia. I'm afraid General Nikolayev is dead."

"What? What are you talking about?"

"There was an attack. Last night. Burglars, it seems. Killed the general and his valet. Plus the dog. The cleaning woman found them just after eight."

"I don't know what to say. He was a friend of mine."

"I'm sorry, General Malenkov. The times we live in . . ."

"Get on with your job, Inspector. I'll tell the Minister."

Monk put the phone down. So, Grishin had finally lost his head. It was what Monk had been working toward, but he cursed the obstinacy of the old general. Then he rang the headquarters of the GUVD in Shabolovka Street.

"Put me through to Major General Petrovsky."

"He is busy. Who is that?" said the telephone operator.

"Interrupt him. Tell him it is about Tatiana."

Petrovsky came on the phone ten seconds later. There was an edge of fear in his voice.

"Petrovsky."

"It's me, the late-night visitor."

"Damn you, I thought something had happened to my child."

"Are they both out of town, she and your wife?"

"Yes, miles away."

"I believe there was an attack."

"Ten of them, all masked and armed to the teeth. They killed four OMON guards and my own steward."

"They were looking for you."

"Of course. I took your advice. I'm living inside the barracks. Who the hell were they? Bloody gangsters."

"They weren't gangsters. They were Black Guard."

"Grishin's thugs. Why?"

"I think because of those papers you confiscated. They are probably afraid you'll prove there's a link between the Dolgoruki mafia and the UPF."

"Well, they don't. They're trash, mostly casino receipts."

"Grishin doesn't know that, General. He fears the worst. Have you heard about Uncle Kolya?"

"The tank general. What about him?"

"They got him. A similar killer squad. Last night."

"Shit. Why?"

"He denounced Komarov. Remember?"

"Of course. But I never thought they'd go that far. Bastards. Thank God politicals aren't my territory. I do gangsters."

"I know. You have contacts in the Militia Collegium?"

"Of course."

"Why not tell them? You got it from an underworld contact."

Monk replaced the receiver and rang the Moskovsky Federal.

"Ilya. Mr. Bernstein's personal assistant. Is he there?"

"One moment, caller."

Ilya came on the line.

"Who's that?"

"Let's say you nearly put a bullet in my back the other day," said Monk in English.

There was a low laugh.

"Yes, I did."

"Is the boss safe?"

"Miles away."

"Advise him to stay there."

"No problem. His private house was attacked last night."

"Casualties?"

"Four of our people dead, two of theirs, we think. They ransacked the place."

"You know who they were?"

"We think so."

"Grishin's Black Guard. And the reason was clearly retribution. The shutdown of Komarov's propaganda broadcasts."

"They may pay for that. The boss has a lot of clout."

"The key lies in the commercial TV companies. Their reporters should have a word with a couple of senior generals of the militia. Ask if they have any intention of interviewing Colonel Grishin concerning widespread rumors, etc., etc."

"They'd better have some proof."

"That's what newshounds are for. They sniff, they dig. Can you get in touch with the boss?"

"If I have to."

"Why not put it to him?"

His next call was to the national newspaper *Izvestia*.

"Newsroom."

Monk affected a gruff accent.

"Get me senior reporter Repin."

"Who is this?"

"Tell him General of the Army Nikolai Nikolayev needs to speak to him urgently. He will remember."

Repin was the one who had done the interview in the Frunze Officers' Club. He came on the line.

"Yes, General. Repin here."

"This is not General Nikolayev," said Monk. "The general is dead. He was murdered last night."

"What? Who are you?"

"Just a former tank man."

"How do you know?"

"Never mind. Do you know where he lived?"

"No."

"He had a house just off the Minsk Highway. Near the village of Kobyakovo. Why not take a photographer and get the hell out there? Ask for Inspector Novikov."

He put the phone down. The other major newspaper was *Pravda,* the former organ of the Communist Party, which politically supported the renascent neo-Communist Socialist Union Party. But to prove its new non-Communist credentials the party had been trying to woo the Orthodox Church. Monk had studied the paper enough to have memorized the name of the chief crime reporter.

"Put me through to Mr. Pamfilov, please."

"He's out of the office right now."

Reasonable. He was almost certainly up at Kutuzovsky Prospekt with the rest of the press pack clamoring for details of the attack on Petrovsky's flat.

"He has a mobile?"

"Of course. But I can't give you the number. Can he call you back?"

"No. Contact him and say one of his sources in the militia needs to speak to him urgently. A major tipoff. I need his mobile number. I'll call you back in five."

On the second call he obtained the number of Pamfilov's mobile phone and reached him in his car outside the senior police officers' apartment building.

"Mr. Pamfilov?"

"Yes. Who is this?"

"I had to lie to get your phone number. We don't know each other. But I may have something for you. There was another attack last night. On the residence of the Patriarch. An attempt to assassinate him."

"You're crazy. An attempt on the Patriarch? Rubbish. There'd be no motive."

"Not for the mafia, no. Why not get over there?"

"The Danilovski Monastery?"

"He doesn't live there. He lives at Number Five Chisti Pereulok."

Pamfilov sat in his car listening to the whine of the disconnected phone. He was stunned. Nothing like this had ever happened in his career. If it was half true, it was the biggest story he would ever handle.

When he arrived at the side street he found it blocked off. Normally he could flash his press pass and walk past the cordon. Not this time. Fortunately he spotted a militia detective inspector whom he knew personally and called out to him. The man walked over to the cordon.

"What's going on?" asked the reporter.

"Burglars."

"You're Homicide."

"They killed the night watchman."

"The Patriarch. Alexei, is he safe?"

"How the fuck do you know he lives here?"

"Never mind. Is he safe?"

"Yes, he's away at Zagorsk. Look, it was just a burglary that went wrong."

"I have a tip they were after the Patriarch."

"Bullshit. Just robbers."

"What's to rob?"

The detective looked worried.

"Where did you get that from?"

"Never mind. Could it be true? Did they steal anything?"

"No. Just shot the guard, searched the house, and ran."

"So they *were* looking for someone. And he wasn't there. Boy, what a story."

"You be bloody careful," warned the detective. "There's no evidence."

But the detective was becoming worried. He became even more so when a militiaman beckoned him over to his car. On the phone was a full general of the Presidium. Within a few sentences he began to hint at the same thing as the reporter.

•   •   •

ON December 23, the media were in uproar. In the early editions each newspaper concentrated on the particular story to which Monk had directed it. As the journalists read one another's stories, there were copious rewrites that knitted the four attacks together.

The morning television news carried composite accounts of four separate assassination attempts, one of them successful. In the other three cases, they reported, only extreme luck had saved the intended victims.

No credence was being given to the notion of burglaries that went wrong. Analysts were at pains to point out that there would be no point in a burglary at the home of a pensioned-off general, nor the apartment of a single senior police officer while ignoring all the other flats in the building, nor on the home of the Patriarch.

Burglary might be the justification for raiding the home of the hugely wealthy banker Leonid Bernstein, but his surviving guards testified that the onslaught had all the hallmarks of a military attack. Moreover, they reported, the attackers had been looking specifically for their employer. Kidnaping was also a possibility, or murder. But in two cases there was no point in a kidnap and in the case of the general it had not been attempted.

Most pundits speculated that the perpetrators must have been the all-pervading gangster underworld, long since the cause of hundreds of murders and kidnapings. Two commentators went further, however, pointing out that while organized crime might well have reason to hate Major General Petrovsky of the gang-busting GUVD, and some might have a score to settle with the banker Bernstein, who could hate an old general who was a triple-Hero to boot, or the Patriarch of Moscow and All the Russias?

The editorial writers deplored for the thousandth time the astronomical crime levels in the country and two called on Acting President Markov to do precisely that—act—to forestall a total breakdown of law and order in the countdown to the crucial elections in twenty-four days' time.

Monk began his second day of anonymous telephoning in the late morning, when the hacks, exhausted from their labors of the previous day, began to trickle into their offices.

A rolled-up tissue in each cheek disguised his voice sufficiently for it not to be recognized as the caller of the day before. To each of the possessors of the major bylines in the seven morning and evening newspapers who had carried the four-assassinations story, he conveyed the same message, starting with Pamfilov of *Pravda* and Repin of *Izvestia*.

"You don't know me, and I cannot give you my name. It is more than my life is worth. But as one Russian to another I ask you to trust me.

"I am a very senior officer in the Black Guard. But I am also a practicing Christian. For many months now I have been more and more distressed by the increasing anti-Christ, anti-Church sentiments being expressed in the inner heart of the UPF, mainly by Komarov and Grishin. Behind what they say in public, they hate the church and democracy, intend to set up a one-party state and rule like the Nazis.

"Now I have had enough. I have to speak out. It was Colonel Grishin who sentenced the old general to die because Uncle Kolya saw through the facade and denounced Komarov. The banker because he too was not fooled. You may not know this, but he used his influence to force the TV stations to cut off the propaganda broadcasts. The Patriarch because he feared the UPF and was about to go public. And the GUVD general because he raided the Dolgoruki mafia who are the paymasters of the UPF. If you don't believe me, check out what I say. It was the Black Guard who mounted those four attacks."

With that he put the phone down, leaving seven Moscow journalists traumatized. When they recovered, they began to check.

Leonid Bernstein was out of the country, but the two commercial television channels quietly leaked that the change in editorial policy had come from the banking consortium to whom they were in hock.

General Nikolayev was dead, but *Izvestia* carried extracts of the earlier interview under the banner headline: "WAS THIS WHY HE DIED?"

The six early-hours raids by the GUVD on the warehouses, arsenals, and casino of the Dolgoruki gang were common knowledge. Only the Patriarch remained cloistered in the Zagorsk Monastery and unable to confirm that he too might be targeted as an enemy of the UPF.

By midafternoon the headquarters dacha of Igor Komarov off the Kiselny Boulevard was under siege. Inside, there was an atmosphere close to panic.

In his own office Boris Kuznetsov was in shirtsleeves, damp patches under each arm, chain-smoking cigarettes he had given up two years earlier and trying to cope with a battery of phones that never stopped ringing.

"No, it is *not* true," he shouted at inquiry after inquiry. "It is a foul lie, a gross libel, and action will be taken in the courts against anyone who gives it further currency. No, there is no link between this party and any mafia gang, financial or otherwise. Mr. Komarov has gone on record time and again as the man who is going to clean up Russia. . . . *What* papers now being investigated by the GUVD? . . . We have nothing to fear. . . . Yes, General Nikolayev did express reservations about our policies, but he was a very old man. His death was tragic but utterly unrelated. . . . You just cannot say that; any comparison between Mr. Komarov and Hitler will be greeted with immediate litigation. . . . *What* senior officer of the Black Guard? . . ."

In his own office Colonel Anatoli Grishin was wrestling with his own problem. As a lifelong officer of the Second Chief Directorate, KGB, it had been his job to hunt down spies. That Monk had caused trouble, massive trouble, he had no doubt. But these new allegations were worse: a senior officer of his own elite, ultraloyal, fanatical Black Guard turned renegade? He had selected every one of them, all six thousand. The senior officers were his personal appointees. One of them a practicing Christian, a wimp with a conscience when the very pinnacle of power was within sight? Impossible.

Yet he recalled reading once of something the Jesuits used to say: Give me the boy until the age of seven and I will give you the man.

Could one of his best men have reverted to the altar boy of years ago? He would have to check. Every single résumé of every senior officer would have to be gone through with a fine-tooth comb.

And what did "senior" mean? How senior? Down two ranks—ten men. Down three ranks, forty men. Down five ranks, almost one hundred. It would be a time-consuming task, and there was no time. In the short term he might have to purge his entire upper echelon, sequester them all in a safe place and forfeit his most experienced commanders. One day, he promised himself, those responsible for this catastrophe would pay, and how they would pay. Starting with Jason Monk. The very thought of the American agent's name caused his knuckles to whiten on the edge of his desk.

Just before five, Boris Kuznetsov secured an interview with Komarov. He had been asking for two hours for a chance to see the man he hero worshiped in order to propose what he felt should be done.

As a student in America Kuznetsov had studied and been deeply impressed by the power of slick and proficient public relations to generate mass support for even the most meretricious nonsense. Apart from his idol Igor Komarov, he worshiped the power of words and the moving image to persuade, delude, convince, and finally overcome all opposition. That the message was a lie was irrelevant.

Like politicians and lawyers, he was a man of words, convinced there was no problem that words could not resolve. The idea that a day might come when the words ran out and ceased to persuade; when other, better words might outmaneuver and trounce his own; when he and his leader might no longer be believed—such a day was unimaginable to Kuznetsov.

Public relations, they had called it in America, the multibillion-dollar industry that could make a talentless oaf a celebrity, a fool a sage, and a base opportunist a statesman. Propaganda, they called it in Russia, but it was the same tool.

With this tool and with Litvinov's brilliant film imagery and studio editing he had helped transform a former engineer with the gift of oratory into a colossus, a man on the threshold of the greatest prize in Russia, the presidency itself.

The Russian media, accustomed to the crude, pedestrian propaganda of their Communist youth, had been credulous babes when presented with the slick, persuasive campaigns he had mounted for Igor Komarov. Now something had gone wrong, badly wrong.

There was another voice, that of a passionate priest, echoing across Russia through the radio and television, media Kuznetsov regarded as his personal fiefdom, urging faith in a greater God and the return of another icon.

Behind the priest was the man on the telephone—he had been told of the campaign of anonymous telephone calls—whispering lies, but oh-so-persuasive lies, into the ears of senior journalists and commentators he thought he knew and owned.

For Boris Kuznetsov the answer still lay in the words of Igor Komarov, words that could not fail to convince, that had never failed.

When he entered the leader's office he was shocked by the transformation. Komarov was behind his desk looking dazed. Spread all over the floor were the daily papers, their headlines blaring accusations upward toward the ceiling. Kuznetsov had already seen them all, the allegations about General Nikolayev, attacks and raids, gangsters and mafia money. No one had ever dared talk about Igor Komarov like that before.

Fortunately, Kuznetsov knew what had to be done. Igor Komarov must speak, and all would be well.

"Mr. President, I really must urge you to give a major press conference tomorrow."

Komarov stared at him for several seconds as if trying to comprehend what he was saying. In his whole political career, and with Kuznetsov's approval, he had avoided press conferences. They were unpredictable. He preferred the staged interview, with presubmitted questions, the set speech, the prepared address, the adoring rally.

"I do not hold press conferences," he snapped.

"Sir, it is the only way to terminate these foul rumors. The media speculation is getting out of hand. I cannot control it anymore. No one could. It is feeding on itself."

"I hate press conferences, Kuznetsov. You know that."

"But you are so good with the press, Mr. President. Reasoned, calm, persuasive. They will listen to you. You alone can denounce the lies and rumors."

"What do the public opinion polls say?"

"National approval for yourself, sir, forty-five percent and falling. From seventy percent eight weeks ago. Zyuganov of the Socialist Union, thirty-three and rising. Markov, the acting president for the Democratic Alliance, twenty-two, rising slightly. That excludes the undecided. I have to say, sir, the past two days could cost another ten percent, maybe more, when the effect filters into the ratings."

"Why should I hold a press conference?"

"It's national coverage, Mr. President. Every major TV station will hang on each word you speak. You know when you speak, no one can resist."

Finally Igor Komarov nodded.

"Arrange it. I will create my address myself."

•   •   •

THE press conference was held in the great banquet hall of the Metropol Hotel at eleven the next morning. Kuznetsov began by welcoming the national and foreign press and lost no time in pointing out that certain allegations of unspeakable foulness had been made over the preceding two days concerning the policies and activities of the Union of Patriotic Forces. It was his privilege, in offering a complete and convincing rebuttal to these ignoble smears to welcome to the podium "the next president of Russia, Igor Komarov."

The UPF leader strode from between the curtains at the rear of the stage and walked to the lectern. He began as he always began, when speaking to rallies of the faithful, by talking about the Great Russia he intended to create once the people had honored him with the presidency. After five minutes he became disconcerted by the silence. Where was the responsive spark? Where was the applause? Where were the cheerleaders? He raised his eyes to some distant clouds and evoked the glorious history of his nation, now in the grip of foreign bankers, profiteers, and criminals. His peroration resounded through the hall, but the hall did not rise to its feet, right hands upraised in the UPF salute. When he stopped the silence continued.

"Perhaps there are questions?" suggested Kuznetsov. A mistake. At least a third of the audience comprised the foreign press. *The New York Times* man spoke fluent Russian, as did those from the

London *Times,* the *Daily Telegraph,* the *Washington Post,* CNN, and most of the rest.

"Mr. Komarov," called out the *Los Angeles Times* correspondent, "I figure you have spent some two hundred million dollars on your campaign so far. That has to be a world record. Where has the money come from?"

Komarov glared at him. Kuznetsov whispered in his ear.

"Public subscriptions from the great people of Russia," he said.

"That's about a year's salary for every man in Russia, sir. Where does it really come from?"

Others joined in. "Is it true you intend to abolish all opposition parties and establish a one-party dictatorship?"

"Do you know why General Nikolayev was murdered just three weeks after he denounced you?"

"Do you deny the Black Guards were behind those assassination attempts two nights ago?"

The cameras and microphones of the state TV and the two commercial networks roamed the room picking up the questions from the impertinent foreigners and the stammered answers.

The man from the *Daily Telegraph,* whose colleague Mark Jefferson had been gunned down the previous July, had also received an anonymous telephone call. He arose and the cameras zeroed in on him.

"Mr. Komarov, have you ever heard of a secret document called the Black Manifesto?"

There was a stunned silence. Neither the Russian media nor the foreigners knew what he was talking about. In reality, neither did he. Igor Komarov, clinging to the lectern and the remains of his self-control, went white.

"What Manifesto?"

Another mistake.

"According to my information, sir, it purports to contain your plans for the creation of a single-party state, the reactivation of the Gulag for your political opponents, rule of the country by two hundred thousand Black Guards, and the invasion of the neighboring republics."

The silence was deafening. Forty correspondents in the hall came from Ukraine, Belarus, Latvia, Lithuania, Estonia, Georgia, and Armenia. Half the Russian press supported the parties destined for abolition, with their hierarchs heading for the camps, accompanied by the press. If the Englishman was right. Everyone stared at Komarov.

That was when the real tumult began. Then he made the third mistake. He lost his temper.

"I will not stand here and listen to any more of this shit!" he screamed, and stalked from the stage, followed by the hapless Kuznetsov.

At the rear of the hall Colonel Grishin stood in the shadow of a hanging curtain and glared at the press with naked hate. Not for long, he promised himself. Not for long.

CHAPTER 19

IN THE SOUTHWESTERN CORNER OF THE CENTRAL ZONE OF MOS-
cow, in a bulge of land formed by a hairpin curve in the Moskva
River, stands the medieval convent of Novodevichi and in the
shadow of its walls the great cemetery.

Twenty acres of land, shaded by pine, birch, lime, and willow,
play host to twenty-two thousand graves where lie the notables of
Russia for two centuries.

The cemetery divides into eleven major gardens. Numbers one
to four cover the nineteenth century, bounded by the walls of the
convent on one side and the central dividing wall on the other.

Five to eight lie between the dividing wall and the perimeter,
beyond which the trucks roar down the Khamovnitchesky Val.
Here lie the great and the bad of the Communist era. Marshals,
politicians, scientists, scholars, writers, and astronauts are to be
found flanking the paths and lanes, their tombstones ranging from
great simplicity to monuments of self-adoring grandiosity.

Gagarin the astronaut, killed flying a prototype while the worse
for vodka, is here, a few yards from the roundheaded stone effigy of
Nikita Khrushchev. Models of airplanes, rockets, and guns testify to
what these men did in life. Other figures stare heroically into obliv-
ion, chests plated in granite medals.

Down the central pathway there is a further wall, penetrated by a
narrow entrance and leading to three smaller gardens, numbers

nine, ten, and eleven. With space at a premium there were hardly any plots left by the winter of 1999, but one had been reserved for General of the Army Nikolai Nikolayev, and here on December 26 his nephew Misha Andreev buried his uncle Kolya.

He tried to make it the way the old man had asked at their last dinner together. There were twenty generals, including the Defense Minister, and one of the two Metropolitan bishops of Moscow officiated.

The whole deal, the old warrior had asked, so the acolytes swung their censers and the aromatic smoke arose in clouds into the bitter air.

The headstone was in the form of a cross, carved in granite, but there was no effigy of the dead man, just his name and beneath it the words *Russky Soldat,* a Russian soldier.

Major General Andreev pronounced the eulogy. He kept it short. Uncle Kolya might have wanted to go to his grave like a Christian at last, but he hated gushing words. When he was done, and while the bishop intoned the parting words, he laid the three magenta ribbons and gold discs of the Hero of the USSR on the coffin. Eight of his own soldiers of the Tamanskaya Division had acted as pallbearers, and they lowered the coffin into the ground. Andreev stood back and saluted. Two ministers and the other eighteen generals did the same.

As they walked back down the central pathway to the entrance and the cortege of waiting cars and limousines, the deputy defense minister, General Butov, put a hand on his shoulder.

"A dreadful thing," he said. "A terrible way to go."

"One day," said Andreev, "I will find them and they will pay."

Butov was clearly embarrassed. He was a political appointee, a desk jockey who had never commanded combat troops.

"Yes, well, I'm sure the militia people are doing their best," he said.

On the pavement the generals solemnly shook his hand, one by one, then climbed into their staff cars and hurried away. Andreev found his own car and drove back to his base.

•   •   •

FIVE miles away, as the winter light faded in the midafternoon, a short priest in cassock and stovepipe hat scurried through the snow and ducked into the onion-domed church on Slavyansky Square. Five minutes later he was joined by Colonel Anatoli Grishin.

"You seemed perturbed," said the colonel quietly.

"I am badly frightened," said the priest.

"Don't be, Father Maxim. There have been reverses, but nothing I cannot take care of. Tell me, why did the Patriarch leave so suddenly?"

"I don't know. On the morning of the twenty-first he received a phone call from Zagorsk. I knew nothing of it. The call was taken by his private secretary. The first thing I knew, I was told to pack a suitcase."

"Why Zagorsk?"

"I found out later. The monastery had invited the preacher Father Gregor to preach the sermon. The Patriarch decided he would like to attend."

"And thus give his personal authority to Gregor and his contemptible message," snapped Grishin. "Without saying a word. Just being there would be enough."

"Anyway, I asked if I would be going too. The secretary said no; His Holiness would take his private secretary and one of the Cossacks as his driver. The two nuns were given the days off to visit relatives."

"You did not inform me, Father."

"How could I know anyone was coming that night?" asked the priest plaintively.

"Go on."

"Well, I had to call the police afterward. The body of the Cossack guard was lying on the upper landing. In the morning I called the monastery and spoke to the secretary. I said there had been armed burglars and a shooting, nothing else. But later the militia changed that. They said the attack had been intended for His Holiness."

"And then?"

"The secretary called me back. He said His Holiness was deeply upset. *Shattered* was the word he used, mainly by the murder of the Cossack guard. Anyway, he stayed with the monks at Zagorsk through the Christmas period and came back yesterday. His principal reason was to officiate at the funeral of the Cossack before the body was returned to his relatives on the Don."

"So he is back. You called me here to tell me *that*?"

"Of course not. It is about the election."

"You have no need to worry about the election, Father Maxim. Despite the damage, the acting president will certainly be eliminated at the first round. In the runoff, Igor Komarov will still triumph over the Communist Zyuganov."

"That's the point, Colonel. This morning His Holiness went to Staraya Ploshad for a private meeting with the president, at his own request. It seems there were two generals of the militia present, and others."

"How do you know?"

"He came back in time for lunch. He took it in his study alone except for his private secretary. I was serving; they took no notice of me. They were discussing the decision that Ivan Markov had finally made."

"And that was?"

Father Maxim Klimovsky was shaking like a leaf. The flame of the candle in his hands fluttered so that its soft light danced across the face of the Virgin and Child on the wall.

"Calm yourself, Father."

"I cannot. Colonel, you must understand my position. I have done all I could to help you, because I believe in Mr. Komarov's vision of the New Russia. But I cannot go on. The attack on the Residence, the meeting of today . . . it is all becoming too dangerous."

He winced as a steely hand gripped his upper arm.

"You are too far involved to pull out now, Father Maxim. You have nowhere else to go. On the one hand you go back to being a waiter at tables, despite the cassock and the holy orders. On the other you await the triumph in twenty-one days of Igor Komarov and myself, and you rise to undreamed-of heights. Now, what did they say at this meeting with the acting president?"

"There won't be an election."

"*What*?"

"Well, yes, there will be an election. But not with Mr. Komarov."

"He wouldn't dare," whispered Grishin. "He would not dare declare Igor Komarov an unfit person. More than half the country supports us."

"It's got beyond that, Colonel. Apparently the generals were insistent. The killing of the old general and the attempts on the banker, the militia man, and most of all His Holiness, seem to have provoked them."

"To what?"

"January first. New Year's Day. They think everyone will have celebrated as usual to such a point that they will be incapable of concerted action."

"What everyone? What action? Explain yourself, man!"

"*Your* everyone. Everyone you command. The action of defending yourselves. They are putting together a force of forty thousand men. The Presidential Guard, the rapid reaction forces of the SOBR and the OMON, some Spetsnaz units, the cream of the Interior Ministry troops based in the city."

"To what end?"

"To arrest you all. Charges of conspiracy against the state. To crush the Black Guard, arrest or destroy them in their barracks."

"They can't. They have no evidence."

"Apparently there is a Black Guard officer prepared to testify. I heard the secretary make the same point, and that was the Patriarch's answer."

Colonel Grishin stood as if he had been hit by an electric charge. Part of his brain told him these gutless freaks could not have the nerve to do any such thing. Another part told him it could be true. Igor Komarov had never deigned to descend into the bearpit of the Duma. He had remained party leader, but not a member, so he had no parliamentary immunity. Neither did he, Anatoli Grishin.

If there was really a senior Black Guard officer prepared to testify, the Moscow State Prosecutor could issue the warrants, at least long enough to hold them in detention until the election.

As an interrogator, Grishin had seen what men were prepared to do when driven by panic; throw themselves from buildings, run in front of trains, charge barbed wire fences.

If the acting president and those around him, his own Praetorian Guard, antigang police generals, militia commanders, had all realized what awaited them if Komarov won, they might indeed be in that state of panic.

"Go back to the residence, Father Maxim," he said at length, "and remember what I said. You are too far gone to seek redemption under the present regime. For you, the UPF has to win. I want to know everything that happens, all that you hear, every development, every meeting, every conference. From now until New Year's Day."

Gratefully the terrified priest scuttled away. Within six hours his aging mother had developed a serious case of pneumonia. He asked for and received from his kindly Patriarch leave of absence until she was recovered. By nightfall he was on the train to Zhitomir. He had done his best, he reasoned. He had done all that was asked of him, and more. But Michael and all his angels would not have kept him in Moscow a moment longer.

That night Jason Monk wrote his last message to the West. Without his computer he wrote it slowly and carefully in block capitals until it covered two sheets of foolscap paper. Then, using a table lamp and the tiny camera bought for him by Umar Gunayev, he photographed both pages several times before burning the sheets and flushing the ashes down the toilet.

In darkness he removed the unexposed film and inserted it into the tiny canister in which it was sold. It was no larger than the top joint of his little finger.

At half-past nine Magomed and his two other bodyguards drove him to the address he gave them. It was a humble dwelling, a detached cottage, or *izba,* far in the southeastern suburbs of Moscow in the district of Nagatino.

The old man who answered the door was unshaven, a wool cardigan wrapped around his thin body. There was no reason for Monk to know that once he had been a revered professor at Moscow University until he had broken with the Communist regime and published a paper for his students that called for democratic government.

That had been long before the reforms. Rehabilitation had come later, too late to matter, and a small state pension with it. At the time, he had been lucky to escape the camps. They had taken his job, of course, and his apartment. He had been reduced to sweeping the streets.

If he survived at all, it was because of a man of his own age who had stood beside him one day in the street, talking in reasonable but English-accented Russian. He never knew Nigel Irvine's name; he just called him *Leeka,* The Fox. Nothing much, really, said the spy from the embassy. Just a helping hand now and again. Small things, little risk. He had suggested the hobby the Russian professor should adopt, and the hundred-dollar bills had kept body and soul together.

That winter's night twenty years later, he stared at the younger man in the door and said, 'Da?'

"I have a tidbit for the Fox," said Monk.

The old man nodded and held out his hand. Monk put the tiny cylinder into his palm, and the man stepped backward and closed the door. Monk turned and walked back to the car.

At midnight little Martti, with the cylinder strapped to one of his legs, was released. He had been brought to Moscow weeks earlier by Mitch and Ciaran on their long drive from Finland, and delivered by Brian Vincent, who could read Russian street maps and find the obscure dwelling.

Martti stood on his ledge for a moment, then spread his wings and rose in spirals high into the freezing night above Moscow. He rose to a thousand feet, where the cold would have reduced a human being to a frostbitten hulk.

By chance one of the InTelCor satellites was beginning its track across the frozen steppes of Russia. True to its instructions, it began to beam its "Are you there, baby?" ciphered message downward to the city, unaware that it had previously destroyed its electronic child.

Outside the capital, the listeners of the FAPSI network scanned their computers for the telltale blip that would mean the foreign agent sought by Colonel Grishin had transmitted, so the triangulators could fix the source of the transmission to a single building.

The satellite drifted away and there was no blip.

Somewhere in his tiny head an impulse told Martti that his home, the place where three years earlier he had hatched as a blind and helpless chick, was to the north. To the north he turned, into the bitter wind, hour after hour through the cold and dark, pulled only by the desire to return home where he belonged.

No one saw him. No one saw him leave the city or cross the coast with the lights of St. Petersburg to his right. He flew on and on with his message, and sixteen hours after leaving Moscow, chilled and exhausted, he fluttered into a loft on the outskirts of Helsinki. Warm hands took the message off his leg and three hours later Sir Nigel Irvine was reading it in London.

He smiled as he saw the text. It had gone as far as it could go. There was one last task for Jason Monk, and then he should go to ground again until he could safely pull out. But even Irvine could not predict quite what the maverick Monk had in mind.

• • •

WHILE Martti flew unseen over their heads, Igor Komarov and Anatoli Grishin sat in conference in the party leader's office. The rest of the small mansion that formed his headquarters was deserted, except for the guards in their room on the ground floor. Outside in the darkness the killer dogs ran free.

Komarov sat behind his desk ashen in the lamplight. Grishin had just finished speaking, reporting to the leader of the Union of Patriotic Forces the news he had learned from the renegade priest.

As he spoke, Komarov had seemed to shrink. The former icy control seeped away, the unhesitating decisiveness appeared to bleed out of him. Grishin knew the phenomenon.

It happened to the most fearsome dictators when suddenly stripped of their power. In 1944, Mussolini, the strutting Duce, had become overnight a shabby, frightened little man on the run.

Business tycoons, when the banks foreclosed, the jet was confiscated, the limousines were impounded, the credit cards withdrawn, the senior executives quit, and the house of cards came tumbling down, actually diminished in size and the old incisiveness became empty bluster.

Grishin knew because he had seen generals and ministers huddled and fearful in his cells, once powerful masters of the *apparat* reduced to waiting for the party's pitiless judgment.

Things were falling apart, the days of words were over. His own hour had come. He had always despised Kuznetsov, spinning his world of words and images, pretending that power came from an official communiqué. Power came from the barrel of a gun in Russia; always had and always would. Ironically, it had taken the man he hated most in all the world, the American scarlet pimpernel, to bring about the present situation, with a UPF president who seemed to have lost his will now almost ready to follow Grishin's advice.

For Anatoli Grishin had no intention of conceding defeat to the militia of acting president Ivan Markov. He could not dispense with Igor Komarov, but he could save his neck and then rise to un-dreamed-of office.

Inside his own world Igor Komarov himself sat like Richard II, maundering over the catastrophe that had overtaken him in such a short time.

At the start of November it had seemed that nothing on earth could prevent his winning the January election. His political organi-zation was twice as efficient as any in the country; his oratory mes-merized the masses. Opinion polls showed he would receive seventy percent of the national vote, enough for a clear win in the first round.

He literally could not understand the transformation, though he could just perceive how, step by step, it had come about.

"It was a mistake to try those four attempts at assassinating our enemies," he said at last.

"With respect, Mr. President, it was tactically sound. Only the foulest luck decreed that three should not be in residence at the time."

Komarov grunted. Bad luck it might be, but the reaction had been worse. Where did the press get the idea he might have been behind it? Who leaked? The media had always hung on his every word; now they were abusing him. The press conference had been a disaster. Those foreigners shouting impudent questions. He had never been subjected to such insolence. Kuznetsov had seen to that. Only private interviews had been allowed, where he had been treated with respect, his views listened to attentively, heads nodding in agreement. Then the young fool had proposed the press confer-ence . . .

"Are you sure of your source, Colonel?"

"Yes, Mr. President."

"You trust him?"

"Certainly not. I trust his appetites. He is venal and corrupt, but he lusts after preferment and the life of a voluptuary, both of which he has been promised. He revealed both visits to the Patriarch by the English spy, and both by the American agent. You read the transcript of the tape recording of the second meeting with Monk, the threats on which I based the decision to silence the opposition permanently."

"But this time . . . would they really have the nerve to strike at us?"

"I do not believe we can discount it. In boxing terms, the gloves are off. Our fool of an acting president knows he cannot win against you, but might against Zyuganov. The generals heading the militia realized just in time what kind of a purge you have in mind for them. Using the allegations of a financial link between the UPF and the mafia, they could cook up charges. Yes, I think they might try."

"If you were they, as a planner, what would you do, Colonel?"

"Exactly the same. When I heard the priest say what the Patriarch discussed while he waited at table, I thought it could not be true. But the more I think it over, the more sense it makes. Dawn of January first is a brilliant time. Who is not hungover from the previous night? What guards are awake? Who can react with speed and decisiveness? Most Russians on New Year's morning cannot even see straight—unless they are kept in a barracks without a drop of vodka. Yes, it makes sense."

"What are you saying? That we are finished? That all we have done was for nothing, that the great vision will never happen, because of a panicky and ambitious politician, a fantasist priest, and some overpromoted policemen?"

Grishin rose and leaned over the desk.

"We have come so far for this? No, Mr. President. The key to success is to know the enemy's intentions. This we do. They leave us no choice but one. Preemptive strike."

"Strike? Against whom?"

"Take Moscow, Mr. President. Take Russia. Both would have been yours in a fortnight. On New Year's Eve our enemies will be celebrating the morrow, their troops locked in barracks until dawn. I can put together a force of eighty thousand men and take Moscow during the night. With Moscow comes Russia."

"Coup d'état?"

"It has happened before, Mr. President. All Russian and European history is a story of men of vision and determination who have seized the moment and taken the state. Mussolini took Rome and all Italy. The Greek colonels took Athens and all Greece. No civil war. Just a fast strike. The defeated flee, their supporters lose their nerve and seek an alliance. By New Year's Day, Russia can be yours."

Komarov thought. He would take the television studios and address the nation. He would claim he had acted to prevent an antipeople conspiracy canceling the election. They would believe him. The generals would be arrested; the colonels would seek promotion by changing to his side.

"Could you do it?"

"Mr. President, everything in this corrupt country is for sale. That is why the Motherland needs Igor Komarov, to scour the pigpen. With money I can buy all the troops I will need. Give me the word and I will put you in the state apartments of the Kremlin at noon of New Year's Day."

Igor Komarov rested his chin on his steepled hands and gazed at the blotter. After several minutes he raised his gaze to meet that of Colonel Grishin.

"Do it," he said.

•   •   •

IF Grishin had been required to organize an armed force to capture the city of Moscow, and to do so starting from scratch in four days, he would never have been able to do it.

But he was not starting from scratch. He had known for months that in the immediate aftermath of Igor Komarov's presidential victory the program for the transfer of all state powers to the UPF would begin.

The political side, the formal abolition of opposition parties, would be for Komarov. His own task would be the subjugation or disarming and disbanding of all the state's armed units.

In preparing for this task, he had already decided which would be his natural allies and which his obvious enemies. Chief among the latter was the Presidential Security Guard, a force of thirty thousand armed men of which six thousand were based inside Moscow and a thousand in the Kremlin itself. Commanded by General Korin, successor to Yeltsin's notorious Alexander Korzhakov, they were all officered by nominees of the late President Cherkassov. They would fight for the legitimacy of the state and against the putsch.

After them came the Interior Ministry with its own army of 150,000 men. Fortunately for Grishin, most of this enormous force was scattered the length and breadth of Russia, with only five thousand in and around the capital. The generals of the Presidium of the

MVD would not be long working out that they would be among the first on the cattle trucks for the Gulag, aware like the Presidentials that there could be no room in the New Russia for them and the Black Guard of Grishin.

Third in line, and a nonnegotiable demand from the Dolgoruki mafia, was the arrest and internment of the two gang-buster divisions, the Federal unit ruled from the MVD's national headquarters at Zhitny Square and the Moscow City unit, the GUVD, run by Major General Petrovsky from Shabolovka Street. Both divisions, and their rapid reaction forces, the OMON and the SOBR, would be in no doubt that the only place for them in Grishin's Russia would be a labor camp or the execution courtyard.

Yet in the cauldron of departmental or private armies that abounded in the collapsing Russia of 1999, Grishin knew he also had natural or purchasable allies. The key to victory was to keep the army unaware, confused, at odds with itself, and finally impotent.

His own immediate forces were his six thousand Black Guards and the twenty thousand teenaged Young Combatants.

The former was an elite force he had created over the years. The officer corps was comprised entirely of battle-trained former special forces, paratroopers, marines, and MVD men, required to prove in savage initiation ceremonies both their ruthlessness and their dedication to the ultraright.

Yet somewhere in the top forty among them must be a traitor. Someone, clearly, had been in touch with the authorities and the media to denounce the four attempted assassinations of December 21 as Black Guard work. The deduction had been too fast to be unprompted.

He had no choice but to detain and isolate those top forty men, and this was done on December 28. Intensive interrogation and the unmasking of the traitor would have to come later. To preserve morale, the junior officers were simply promoted to fill the gaps and told their commanders were away on a training course.

Poring over a large-scale map of the Moscow Oblast, Grishin prepared his battle plan for New Year's Eve. His great advantage was that the streets would be almost empty.

Virtually no work is possible on the afternoon of New Year's Eve as the Muscovites drift away with their stocks of booze to the private homes or group parties where they intend to spend the night.

Darkness comes by half-past three in the afternoon and after that only those desperate to replenish inadequate liquor supplies venture into the freezing night.

Everyone celebrates, including the unfortunate night watchmen and skeleton staffs forbidden to take time off and go home. They bring their own supplies to work.

By six, Grishin calculated, he would have the streets to himself. By six every major ministry and government building would be empty apart from the night staff, and by ten even they and the soldiers still in barracks would be unable to defend themselves.

A first priority, once his attacking forces were inside the city, was to seal Moscow from the outside. This was the job he allocated to the Young Combatants. There were 52 major and secondary roads into Moscow, and to block them all he needed 104 heavy trucks loaded with concrete ballast.

He divided the Young Combatants into the 104 necessary groups, each under the command of an experienced soldier from the Black Guard. The trucks would be acquired by renting them from long-distance haulers or stealing them at gunpoint on the morning of New Year's Eve. At the given hour each pair would be driven into position, moving out from intersections until they were nose-to-nose across every highway, then immobilized.

On every major road into Moscow the border between the Moscow Oblast and the neighboring province is marked by an MVD militia post, a small booth with several bored soldiers and a phone, and a parked armored personnel carrier (APC). On New Year's Eve the APC would be unmanned while the crew celebrated in the hut. In the case of the single highway Grishin needed to enter the city, this post would be suppressed. In the case of all the others, the Young Combatants would drive their blocking trucks to the first intersection inside the city, leaving the militiamen at the border to get drunk as usual, and park the trucks straddling the road. Then the Combatants, two hundred to a group, would mount their ambushes on the city side of the trucks and prevent any relief column from entering Moscow.

Inside the city he needed to take seven targets—five secondary and two primary. As his Black Guard was quartered in five bases out in the countryside, with only a small barracks inside the city to supply Guards for Komarov's dacha, the easiest way would be to drive in on five axes. But to achieve coordination, that would mean a storm of radio traffic. He preferred to bring his whole force in radio silence. He therefore favored one single truck convoy.

His main and headquarters base was to the northeast, so he decided to bring the entire force of six thousand men, fully armed and in their vehicles, to that base on December 30, and invade the city down the main highway that starts as Yaroslavskoye Chaussee and becomes Prospekt Mira—Peace Avenue—as it nears the inner Ring Road.

One of his two primary targets, the great television complex at Ostankino, would lie only a quarter of a mile off that highway and for this he intended to detach two thousand of his six thousand men.

With the remaining four thousand, commanded by himself, he would drive on south, past the Olympic stadium, across the Ring Road, and into the heart of inner Moscow for the greatest prize of all, the Kremlin itself.

Though *Kreml* simply means *fortress* and every ancient city in Russia has its fortress at the heart of what was once the walled town, the Kremlin of Moscow has long been symbolic of supreme power in Russia and the visible possession of that power. The Kremlin had to be his by dawn, its garrison subdued and its radio room unable to call for help, or the pendulum could swing the other way.

His five secondary targets he intended to delegate to the four armed forces he believed he could lock into an alliance even in the short time left to him.

These were the mayor's office on Tverskaya Street, which had a communications room from which appeals could be sent for help; the Interior Ministry on Zhitny Square with its communications network to the MVD's private army scattered across Russia, and the attached OMON barracks next door; the complex of presidential and ministerial buildings on and around Staraya Ploshad; the Khodinka airfield with its GRU barracks, a perfect dropping zone for paratroops if they were called in to help the state; and the parliament building, the Duma.

In 1993, when Boris Yeltsin had turned the guns of his tanks on the Duma to force the rebellious congressmen to come out with their hands up, the building had sustained considerable damage. For

four years the Duma had been transferred to the old Gosplan economic offices on Manege Square, but with the damage repaired the
Russian parliament had gone back to the White House on the river
at the end of Novy Arbat.

The mayor's office, the Duma, and the ministries at Staraya
Ploshad would be empty shells on New Year's Eve, and with the
doors torn down by explosive charges, occupation would be simple
enough. Fighting might erupt around the OMON barracks and the
Khodinka base if the antigang troops or the handful of paratroopers
and army intelligence officers at the old airfield fought back. These
two targets he would give to the special forces units he intended to
buy.

An eighth and obvious target in any putsch would be the Defense
Ministry. This huge gray stone building at Arbatskaya Square would
also be thinly staffed, but at its heart was the communications headquarters that could speak instantly to any Army, Navy, or Air Force
base in Russia. He assigned no troops to storming the place, for he
had special plans for the Defense Ministry.

Natural allies for any extreme right-wing putsch in Russia were
not all that hard to find. Foremost among them was the Federal
Security Service, or FSB. This was the inheritor of his own once
all-powerful Second Chief Directorate, KGB, the vast organization
that kept repression in the USSR at the levels demanded by the
Politburo. Since the arrival of the despised theory called democracy,
its old powers had waned.

The FSB, headquartered at the famous KGB Center on Dzer-
zhinsky Square, now renamed Lubyanka Square, and with the
equally famous and feared Lubyanka jail behind it, was still in charge
of counterespionage and also contained a division devoted to combating organized crime. But the latter was not half as effective as
General Petrovsky's GUVD and had thus not generated the insistent
demands for revenge from the Dolgoruki mafia.

To assist in its labors, FSB commanded two forces of rapid reaction troops, the Alpha Group and the Vympel, Russian for "banner."

These two had once been the two most elite and feared of special
forces units in Russia, sometimes optimistically compared to the
British SAS. What had gone wrong was a question of loyalty.

In 1991 the Defense Minister, Yazov, and the Chairman of the

KGB, Kryuchkov, had mounted a coup against Gorbachev. The coup failed, although it brought Gorbachev down and Yeltsin to preeminence. Originally the Alpha Group had been part of the coup; halfway into the coup it changed its mind, allowing Boris Yeltsin to emerge from the Duma, leap onto a tank, and become a hero before the world. By the time a traumatized Gorbachev had been released from house detention in the Crimea and flown back to Moscow to find his old enemy Yeltsin in charge, question marks about the Alpha Group were hovering in the air. The same applied to Vympel.

By 1999, both groups, heavily armed and hard fighters, were still discredited. But for Grishin they had two advantages. Like many special forces, they had a preponderance of officers and NCOs and few greenhorn privates. The veterans tended, politically, to the extreme right; anti-Semitic, anti–ethnic minority, and antidemocracy. Also, they had not been paid for six months.

Grishin's courtship had been like a siren's song: restoration of the old powers of the KGB, the pampered treatment owed to a true elite, and double salaries, starting the moment of Komarov's coup.

On the night of New Year's Eve, the Vympel troops were assigned to arm up, leave the barracks, proceed to the Khodinka Airfield and army base, and secure both. Alpha Group was given the Interior Ministry and the adjoining OMON barracks, with a detached company taking the SOBR barracks behind Shabolovka Street.

On December 29, Colonel Grishin attended a meeting at the sumptuous dacha outside Moscow maintained by the Dolgoruki mafia. Here he met and addressed the Skhod, the supreme council governing the gang. For him it was a crucial conference.

So far as the mafia was concerned, he had a lot of explaining to do. The raids conducted by General Petrovsky still stung. As paymasters they demanded an explanation. But as Grishin spoke, the mood changed. When he revealed that there had been a plan to declare Igor Komarov an unfit person to participate in the forthcoming elections, alarm took over from aggression. They all had a major stake in his electoral success.

The body blow was Grishin's revelation that this idea had now been superseded; the state intended to arrest Komarov and crush the Black Guards. Within an hour it was the mafiosi who were seeking advice. When he announced his intended solution, they were stunned. Gangsterism, fraud, black market, extortion, narcotics, prostitution, and murder were their specialty, but a coup d'état was high stakes indeed.

"It is only the biggest theft of all, the theft of the republic," said Grishin. "Deny it, and you go back to being hunted by MVD, FSB, all of them. Accept it, and the land is ours."

He used the word *zemlya,* which means the land, the country, the earth, and all that therein is.

At the head of the table the senior of them all, an old *vor v zakone,* a "thief-by-statute" who had been born into the underworld like his father and all his clan, and who among the Dolgoruki was the nearest thing to the Sicilian Don-of-Dons, stared at Grishin for a long while. The others waited. Then he began to nod, his wrinkled cranium rising and falling like an old lizard signaling assent. The last funds were agreed on.

So also was the third armed force Grishin needed. Two hundred of the eight hundred private security firms in Moscow were Dolgoruki fronts. They would provide two thousand men, all fully armed ex-soldiers or KGB hoods, eight hundred to storm, take, and hold the empty White House, home of the Duma, and twelve hundred for the presidential office and attendant ministries grouped on Staraya Ploshad, also empty on New Year's Eve.

•   •   •

ON the same day Jason Monk called Major General Petrovsky. He was still living at the SOBR barracks.

"Yes."

"It's me again. What are you doing?"

"What's that to you?"

"Are you packing?"

"How did you know?"

"All Russians want to spend New Year's Eve with their families."

"Look, my plane leaves in an hour."

"I think you should cancel it. There will be other New Year's Eves."

"What are you talking about, American?"

"Have you seen the morning papers?"

"Some. Why?"

"The latest opinion ratings. The ones taking account of the press revelations about the UPF and Komarov's press conference the other day. They show him at forty percent and dropping."

"So, he loses the election. We get Zyuganov, the neo-Communist instead. What am I supposed to do about it?"

"Do you think Komarov will accept that? I told you once, he's not sane."

"He's going to have to accept it. If he loses in a fortnight, he's lost. That's it."

"That same night, you told me something."

"What?"

"You said, if the Russian state is attacked, the state will defend itself."

"What the hell do you know that I don't?"

"I don't *know* anything. I suspect. Didn't you know suspicion is the Russian specialty?"

Petrovsky stared at the receiver and then at his half-packed suitcase lying on the narrow bunk of the barracks room.

"He wouldn't dare," he said flatly. "No one would dare."

"Yazov and Kryuchkov did."

"That was 1991. Different."

"Only because they made a mess of it. Why not stay in town over the holiday? Just in case."

Major General Petrovsky put down the phone and began to unpack.

●　　●　　●

GRISHIN clinched his last alliance at a meeting in a beer bar on December 30. His interlocutor was a beer-bellied cretin but the nearest thing to the commander of the street gangs of the New Russia Movement.

Despite its portentous name, the NRM was little more than a loose grouping of tattooed, shaven-headed thugs of the ultraright who got their income and pleasure respectively by mugging and Jew-baiting, both, as they were wont to scream at passersby, in the name of Russia.

The block of dollars Grishin had produced lay on the table between them, and the NRM man eyed it eagerly.

"I can get five hundred good lads any time I want," he said. "What's the job?"

"I'll give you five of my own Black Guards. You accept their combat orders or the deal's off."

Combat orders sounded good. Sort of military. The members of the NRM prided themselves on being soldiers of the New Russia, though they had never amalgamated with the UPF. The discipline was not to their liking.

"What's the target?"

"New Year's Eve, between ten and midnight. Storm, take, and hold the mayor's office. And there's a rule. No booze till dawn."

The NRM commander thought it over. Dense he may have been, but he could work out the UPF was going for the big one. About time too. He leaned across the table, his hand closing on the brick of dollars.

"When it's over, we get the kikes."

Grishin smiled.

"My personal gift."

"Done."

They fixed details for the NRM to rendezvous in the gardens of Pushkinskaya Square, three hundred yards up the road from the mansion that housed the government of the city of Moscow. It would not look out of keeping. The square was opposite the principal McDonald's.

In due course, mused Grishin as he was driven away, the Jews of Moscow would indeed be taken care of, but so would the scum of the NRM. It would be amusing to put them in the same trains heading east, all the way to Vorkhuta.

On the morning of December 31, Jason Monk called Major General Petrovsky again. He was in his office at the already half-staffed GUVD headquarters in Shabolovka Street.

"Still at your post?"

"Yes, damn you."

"Does the GUVD run a helicopter?"

"Of course."

"Can it fly in this weather?"

Petrovsky peered out the barred window at the low, lead-gray clouds.

"Not up into that lot. But below it, I suppose."

"Do you know the locations of the camps of Grishin's Black Guard around this city?"

"No, but I can find out. Why?"

"Why don't you take a flight over all of them?"

"Why should I?"

"Well, if they are peace-loving citizens, all the barracks lights should be on, with everyone inside in the warmth, having a noggin before lunch and preparing for an evening of harmless festivities. Take a look. I'll call you back in four hours."

When the callback came, Petrovsky was subdued.

"Four of them appear closed down. His personal camp, northeast of here, is alive like an anthill. Hundreds of trucks being serviced. He seems to have moved the whole force to the one camp."

"Why would he do that, General?"

"You tell me."

"I don't know. But I don't like it. It smacks of a nocturnal exercise."

"On New Year's Eve? Don't be crazy. Every Russian gets drunk on New Year's Eve."

"My point exactly. Every soldier in Moscow will be plastered by midnight. Unless they are ordered to stay sober. Not a popular order, but as I said, there will be other New Year's Eves. Do you know the commanding officer of the OMON regiment?"

"Of course. General Kozlovsky."

"And the commander of the Presidential Security Guard?"

"Yes, General Korin."

"Both now with their families?"

"I suppose so."

"Look, man to man, if the worst should happen, if Komarov should win after all, what will happen to you, your wife, and Tatiana? Worth a night of vigil? Worth a few phone calls?"

When he had put the phone down Jason Monk took a map of Moscow and the surrounding countryside. His fingers roved over the area northeast of the capital. That was where Petrovsky had said the main UPF and Black Guard base was to be found.

From the northeast the main highway was the Yaroslavskoye Chaussee, becoming Prospekt Mira. It was the principal artery and it ran past the Ostankino television complex. Then he picked up the telephone again.

"Umar, my friend. I need a last favor from you. Yes, I swear it's the last. A car with a phone and your number through the night. . . . No, I don't need Magomed and the guys. It would spoil their New Year's Eve party. Just the car and the phone. Oh, and a handgun. If that wouldn't pose too much of a problem."

He listened to the laugh down the phone.

"Any particular kind? Well, now . . ."

He thought back to Castle Forbes.

"You wouldn't be able to get hold of a Swiss Sig Sauer, would you?"

CHAPTER 20

TWO TIME ZONES TO THE WEST OF MOSCOW THE WEATHER WAS quite different, a bright blue sky and the temperature barely two below zero, as the Mechanic moved quietly through the woods toward the manor house.

His preparations for his journey across Europe had been meticulous as always, and he had experienced no problems. He had preferred to drive. Guns and airliners seldom mixed, but a car had many hiding places.

Through Belarus and Poland his Moscow-registered Volvo had attracted no attention and his papers showed he was just a Russian businessman attending a conference in Germany. A search of his car would have revealed nothing further.

In Germany, where the Russian mafia was well established, he exchanged his Volvo for a German-registered Mercedes, and easily acquired the hunting rifle with its hollow-point ammunition and scope sight before pushing further west. Under the new dispensation of the European Community the borders were virtually nonexistent and he passed through in a column of other cars with a bored wave from a single customs officer.

He had acquired a large-scale road map of the area he sought, identified the nearest village to the target and then the manor house itself. Passing through the village he had simply followed the signs to the entrance of the short drive, noted the signboard that confirmed he had the right address, then driven on.

After spending most of the night in a motel fifty miles away, he had driven back before dawn but parked his car two miles away from the manor and walked the rest of the way through the woods, emerging at the edge of the tree line behind the house. As the weak wintry sun rose, he created a lying-up position at the bole of a big beech tree and settled in to wait. From where he sat he could look down at the house and its courtyard from three hundred yards while remaining out of sight behind the tree.

As the landscape came alive, a cock pheasant strutted to within a few yards of him, stared at him angrily, and scurried away. Two gray squirrels played in the beech above his head.

At nine a man emerged into the courtyard. The Mechanic raised his binoculars and adjusted the focus slightly until the figure looked to be ten feet away. It was not his target; a manservant fetched a basket of logs from a shed under the courtyard wall and went back inside.

On one side of the courtyard was a row of stables. Two of the stalls were occupied. The heads of two large horses, a bay and a chestnut, peered over the tops of the half doors. At ten they were rewarded when a girl came out and brought them fresh hay. Then she went back inside.

Just before midday an older man emerged, crossed the courtyard, and patted the horses' muzzles. The Mechanic studied the face in his binoculars and glanced down at the photo in the frosty grass by his side. No mistake.

He raised the hunting rifle and peered through the sight. The tweed jacket filled the circle. The man was facing the horses, back to the hillside. Safety catch off. Hold steady, a slow squeeze.

The crack of the shot echoed across the valley. In the courtyard the man in tweed seemed to be pushed into the stable door. The hole in his back, at the level of the heart, was lost in the pattern of the tweed, and the exit wound was pressed against the white stable door. The knees buckled and the figure slid downward, leaving a smear on the paint. A second shot took away half the head.

The Mechanic rose, slipped the rifle into its sheepskin-lined sleeve, slung it over his shoulder, and began to jog. He moved fast, having memorized the way he had come six hours before, the way back to his car.

Two shots on a winter's morning in the countryside would not be so odd. A farmer shooting rabbit or crow. Then someone would look out of the windows and run across the courtyard. There would be screams, disbelief, attempts to revive; all a waste of time. Then the run back to the house, the phone call to the police, the garbled explanation, the ponderous official inquiries. Eventually a police car would come, eventually roadblocks might be set up.

All too late. In fifteen minutes he was at his car, in twenty minutes moving. Thirty-five minutes after the shots he was on the nearest highway, one car among hundreds. By that time the country policeman had taken a statement and was radioing the nearest city for detectives to be sent.

Sixty minutes after the shots the Mechanic had hefted the gun in its case over the parapet of the bridge he had selected earlier and watched it vanish in the black water. Then he began the long drive home.

•　　•　　•

THE first headlights came just after seven, moving slowly through the dark toward the brightly lit complex of buildings that made up the Ostankino TV center. Jason Monk sat at the wheel of his car, the engine running to charge the heater against the cold.

He was parked just off the Boulevard Akademika Koroleva, on a side road, with the principal office building straight ahead of his windshield across the boulevard and the spire of the transmitting tower behind him. When he saw that this time the lights were not from a single car but a column of trucks, he killed the engine and the telltale plume of exhaust died away.

There were about thirty trucks, but only three drove straight into the parking area of the main building. It was a huge structure, the base five stories high and three hundred yards wide, with two main entrances; an upper superstructure a hundred yards wide with eighteen stories. Normally eight thousand people would work in it, but on New Year's Eve there were fewer than five hundred to ensure the service continued through the night.

Armed men clad in black jumped out of the three parked trucks and ran straight into the two reception areas. Within seconds the frightened lobby staff were lined up against the back wall at gunpoint, clearly visible from the outer darkness. Then Monk watched them ushered away out of sight.

Inside the main building, guided by a terrified porter, the point unit made straight for the switchboard room, surprising the operators while one of their number, a former Telekom technician, disconnected all lines in and out.

One of the Black Guards emerged and signaled with his flashlight to the rest of the convoy, which then rolled forward to fill the parking lot and surround the office building in a defensive ring. Hundreds more Guards poured out and jogged inside.

Though Monk could see only vague shapes in the windows of the upper floors, the Guards according to their plan were fanning out through floor after floor, removing all mobile phones from the terrified night staff and hurling them into canvas carryalls.

To Monk's left there was a smaller secondary building, also part of the TV complex, reserved for accountants, planners, executives, all at home celebrating. It was shuttered in darkness.

Monk reached to the car phone and dialed a number he knew by heart.

"Petrovsky."

"It's me."

"Where are you?"

"Sitting in a very cold car out at Ostankino."

"Well, I'm in a reasonably warm barracks with a thousand young men on the verge of mutiny."

"Reassure them. I'm watching the Black Guards take over the entire TV complex."

There was silence.

"Don't be a bloody fool. You have to be wrong."

"All right. So a thousand armed men in black, arriving in thirty trucks with dipped headlights, were supposed to invade Ostankino and hold the staff at gunpoint. That's what I'm watching from two hundred yards away through my windshield."

"Jesus Christ. He's really doing it!"

"I told you he was mad. Maybe not so crazy. He might win. Is anybody in Moscow sober enough to defend the state tonight?"

"Give me your number, American, and get off the phone."

Monk gave it to him. The forces of law and order would be too busy to start tracing moving cars.

"One last thing, General. They won't interrupt the scheduled programs—not yet. They'll let the recorded stuff go out as usual until they're ready."

"I can see that. I'm watching Channel One right now. It's the Cossack Dance Troupe."

"A recorded show. They're all recorded until the main news. Now, I think you should get on the phone."

But Major General Petrovsky had just disconnected. Although he did not then know it, his barracks would be under attack within sixty minutes.

It was too quiet. Whoever had planned the takeover of Ostankino had planned well. Up and down the boulevard there were blocks of apartment houses, mostly with lights lit, their inhabitants down to shirtsleeves, glasses in hand, watching the same TV that was being hijacked in silence barely yards away.

Monk had spent his time studying the road map of the Ostankino district. To emerge onto the main boulevard now would be asking for trouble. But behind him lay a network of back streets between the housing projects that eventually led southward to the center of the city.

The logical way would have been to cut through to Prospekt Mira, the main road to the center, but he suspected that highway too was no place tonight for Jason Monk. Without putting on his lights, he hung a U-turn in the road, climbed out, crouched, and emptied a magazine of his automatic straight at the trucks and the TV building.

At two hundred yards a handgun sounds like a firecracker, but the bullets carry that distance. Three windows in the building shattered, a truck windshield broke apart, and a lucky shot caught a Black Guard in the ear. One of his companions lost his nerve and sprayed the night with his Kalashnikov assault rifle.

Because of the bitter cold, double-glazed windows are vital in Moscow; with them, and with the television blaring, many residents still heard nothing. But the Kalashnikov shattered three apartment windows and panic-stricken heads began to appear. Several then disappeared to run for their telephones and call the police.

Black Guards were beginning to form up and head toward him. Monk slipped into his car and sped away. He put on no lights, but the guards heard the roar of the engine and fired further bullets after him.

In the MVD headquarters at Zhitny Square the senior officer on duty was the commander of the OMON regiment, General Ivan Koslovsky, who was in his office in the barracks of his three thousand sullen men whose leave he had earlier that day canceled against his better judgment. The man who had persuaded him to do this, speaking from four hundred yards away in Shabolovka Street, was on the phone again and Koslovsky was shouting at him.

"Bloody rubbish. I'm watching the fucking TV right now. Well, who says? What do you mean, you have been informed? Hold on, hold on. . . ."

His other phone was blinking. He snatched the receiver and shouted, "Yes?"

A nervous operator came on the line.

"I'm sorry to trouble you, General, but you seem to be the most senior officer in the building. There's a man on the phone who says he lives at Ostankino and there is shooting in the streets. A bullet smashed his window."

General Koslovsky's tone changed. He spoke clearly and calmly.

"Get every detail from him and call me back."

To the other phone he said:

"Valentin, you could be right. A citizen just phoned that there is shooting out there. I'm going to red alert."

"Me too. By the way, I phoned General Korin earlier. He agreed to keep some presidentials on standby."

"Good thinking. I'll call him."

Eight more calls came through from the Ostankino area concerning firing in the streets, then a more lucid call from an engineer living in a top-floor apartment across the boulevard from the TV center. He was patched through to General Koslovsky.

"I can see it all from here," said the engineer, who like every Russian male had done his military service. "About a thousand men, all armed, a convoy of over twenty trucks. Two APCs facing outward from the parking lot in front. BTR Eighty A's, I think."

Thank God, thought Koslovsky, for an ex-military man. If he had any doubts, they were dispelled. The BTR 80 A is an eight-wheeled armored personnel carrier mounting a 30mm cannon and carrying a commander, driver, gunner, and six-man dismount squad.

If the attackers were dressed in black, they were not army. His OMON teams dressed in black, but they were downstairs. He called his own unit commanders down below.

"Truck up and move out," he ordered. "I want two thousand men out on the streets and a thousand to stay and defend this place."

If any coup d'état was taking place, the attackers would have to neutralize the Interior Ministry and its barracks. Happily the latter was built like a fortress.

Outside, other troops were already on the move, but they were not commanded by Koslovsky. The Alpha Group strike force was closing on the ministry.

Grishin's problem had been timing. Without breaking radio silence until the last minute, he needed to coordinate his attacks. To attack too early could mean the defenders were not well enough into their celebrations; too late and he would lose some of the hours of darkness. He had ordered the Alpha Group to strike at 9:00 P.M.

At 8:30 two thousand OMON commandos left their barracks in trucks and APCs. As soon as they were gone the remainder sealed their fortress and took up defensive positions. At nine they came under fire but for the attackers all element of surprise was gone.

Counterfire raked the streets around the ministry and ripped across Zhitny Square. The Alpha Group soldiers had to take cover and wish they had artillery. But they did not.

"American?"

"Here."

"Where are you now?"

"Trying to stay alive. Heading south from the TV center, avoiding Prospekt Mira."

"There are troops on their way. A thousand of mine and two thousand OMONs."

"May I make a suggestion?"

"If you must."

"Ostankino is only part of it. If you were Grishin, what would you target?"

"MVD, Lubyanka."

"MVD, yes. Lubyanka, no. I don't think he'll have any trouble from his old mates in the Second Chief Directorate."

"You could be right. What else?"

"Surely government headquarters at Staraya Ploshad, and the Duma. For the appearance of legitimacy. And places where resistance might come from. You at the GUVD, the paratroopers at Khodinka Field. And the Defense Ministry. But most of all the Kremlin. He must have the Kremlin."

"That's defended. General Korin has been informed and he is on alert. We don't know how many Grishin has."

"About thirty, maybe forty thousand."

"Christ, we have less than half."

"But better quality. And he has lost fifty percent."

"Which fifty percent?"

"The element of surprise. What about reinforcements?"

"General Korin will be on to the Defense people by now."

Colonel General Sergei Korin, commander of the Presidential Security Force, had reached the barracks inside the Kremlin walls and barred the multidefense Kutafya Gate behind him just before Grishin's main column entered Manege Square. Just past the Kutafya is the bigger Trinity Tower, and inside that, on the right, the barracks of the Presidential Security Guard. General Korin was in his office and on the phone to the Defense Ministry.

"Give me the senior officer on duty," he shouted. There was a pause and a voice he knew came on the line.

"Deputy Defense Minister Butov here."

"Thank God you're there. We have a crisis. There's some kind of a coup going on. Ostankino has gone. The MVD is under attack. There's a column of armored cars and trucks outside the Kremlin. We need help."

"You'll get it. What do you need?"

"Anything. What about the Dzerzhinski?"

He referred to a Special Operations Mechanized Infantry Division, created specifically as an anti–coup d'état defense unit after the putsch of 1991.

"It's at Ryazan. I can have it rolling in an hour, with you in three."

"As soon as possible. What about VDVs?"

He knew there was an elite parachute brigade barely an hour

away by plane, which could drop onto Khodinka Field if the drop zone could be marked out for them.

"You'll get everything I can lay on for you, General. Just hang on."

A team of Black Guards ran forward under covering fire from their own heavy machine guns and reached the shelter of the covered Borovitsky Gate. A shaped charge of plastic explosive was placed on each of the four hinges. As the team ran back, two were cut down by fire from the tops of the walls. Seconds later the charges went off. The twenty-ton wooden doors shuddered as their hinges were torn apart, then teetered and crashed to the ground.

Impervious to the small arms fire, an APC ran up the approach road and into the shelter of the arch. Beyond the wooden doors was a great steel grille. Beyond it, in the parking area where tourists were wont to stroll, a Presidential Guard came into view and tried to aim an antitank at the APC through the bars. Before he could fire, the cannon on the APC took him apart.

Black Guards jumped out of the belly of the carrier and attached further charges to the steel grille. With the attackers back inside, the APC moved out of range until the charges went off and the grille hung drunkenly on a single hinge, then ran forward and knocked it flat.

Despite the fire, the Black Guards began to race into the fortress, outnumbering the Presidentials four to one. The defenders retreated into the various bastions and redoubts that make up the walls of the Kremlin. Others scattered through the seventy-three acres of palaces, armories, cathedrals, gardens, and squares of the Kremlin, and in some places fighting became hand-to-hand. Slowly the Black Guards began to take the upper hand.

·   ·   ·

"JASON, what the hell's going on?"

It was Umar Gunayev on the car phone.

"Grishin is trying to take over Moscow and indeed Russia, my friend."

"Are you all right?"

"So far, yes."

"Where are you?"

"Driving south from Ostankino, trying to avoid Lubyanka Square. Why?"

"One of my men just drove up Tverskaya. There's a great crowd of those New Russia Movement thugs smashing their way into the mayor's residence."

"You know what the NRM think of you and your people?"

"Of course."

"Why not let some of your lads settle the score? This time no one will interfere with you."

An hour later three hundred armed Chechens arrived in Tverskaya Street where the NRM street gangs were rampaging through the seat of the government of the city of Moscow. Across the road the stone statue of Yuri Dolgoruki, founder of Moscow, sat astride his horse and stared with contempt. The door of the city hall was smashed and the entrance wide open.

The Chechens drew their long Caucasian knives, pistols, and mini-Uzis and went inside. Every man remembered the destruction of the Chechen capital of Grozny in 1995 and the rape of Chechnya over the two succeeding years. After the first ten minutes, it was no contest.

The Duma building, the White House, had fallen to the security firm mercenaries with hardly a struggle, since it was occupied only by a few caretakers and night watchmen. But at Staraya Ploshad the thousand SOBR troops were in room-to-room and street-to-street combat with the rest of the men from the Dolgoruki gang's two hundred security companies, and the heavier weapons of the rapid reaction force of the antigang police of Moscow were a match for their opponents' greater numbers.

At Khodinka Airfield the Vympel special forces troops were encountering unexpected resistance from the few paratroops and GRU intelligence officers who, warned just in time, had barricaded themselves inside.

Monk swung into Arbatskaya Square and stopped in amazement. On the eastern side of the triangle the gray granite block of the Defense Ministry stood alone and silent. No Black Guards, no firefight, no sign of entry. Of all the installations a planner of a coup d'état in Moscow or any capital would have to possess, and quickly, the Defense Ministry would be high on the list. Five hundred yards away, down Znamenka Street and across Borovitsky Square, he could hear the crackle of gunfire as the battle for the Kremlin raged.

Why was the Defense Ministry not taken or under siege? From the forest of aerials on its roof the messages must be screaming out across Russia to summon help from the army. He consulted his slim address book and punched a number into his car phone.

In his private quarters two hundred yards inside the main gate at Kobyakova Base, Major General Misha Andreev adjusted his tie and prepared to leave. He often wondered why he put on his uniform to preside over New Year's Eve in the Officers' Club. By morning it would be so badly stained that the whole thing would have to go to the cleaners. When it came to celebrating New Year's Eve, the tank men prided themselves on taking lessons from no one.

The phone rang. It would be his Exec Officer urging him to hurry up, complaining that the lads wanted to get started; first the vodka and the endless toasts, then the food and the champagne for the hour of midnight.

"Coming, coming," he said to the empty room, and reached for the phone.

"General Andreev?" He did not know the voice.

"Yes."

"You don't know me. I was a friend, in a way, of your late uncle."

"Indeed."

"He was a good man."

"I thought so."

"He did what he could. Denouncing Komarov in that interview."

"What are you getting at, whoever you are?"

"Igor Komarov has mounted a coup in Moscow. Tonight. Commanded by his dog, Colonel Grishin. The Black Guards are taking Moscow, and with it Russia."

"Okay, joke's gone on long enough. Get back to your vodka and get off this phone."

"General, if you don't believe me, why not ring anyone you know in central Moscow?"

"Why should I?"

"There's a lot of shooting going on. Half the city can hear it. One last thing. It was the Black Guards who killed Uncle Kolya. On the orders of Colonel Grishin."

Misha Andreev found himself staring at the phone and listening to the buzz from the disconnected line. He was angry. Angry at the intrusion of his privacy on his private line, angry at the insult to his uncle. If anything grave were happening in Moscow, the Defense Ministry would immediately alert army units within a 100-kilometer radius of the capital.

The 200-acre base of Kobyakovo was just 46 kilometers from the Kremlin; he knew because he had once timed it on his car. It was also the home of the unit he was proud to command, the Tamanskaya Division, the elite tank men known as the Taman Guards.

He put the phone back. It rang immediately.

"Come on, Misha, we're waiting to start."

His Exec Officer from the Club.

"Coming, Konni. Just a couple of phone calls to make."

"Well, don't be long or we'll start without you."

He dialed another number.

"Ministry of Defense," said a voice.

"Get me the night-duty officer."

With considerable speed another voice came on the line.

"Who is that?"

"Major General Andreev, Commander Tamanskaya."

"This is Deputy Defense Minister Butov."

"Ah, yes, sorry to disturb you, sir. Is everything all right in Moscow?"

"Certainly. Why not?"

"No reason, Minister. I just heard something . . . odd. I could mobilize in . . ."

"Stay on your base, General. That is an order. All units are confined to base. Get back to the Officers' Club."

"Yes, sir."

He put the phone down again. Deputy Defense Minister? In the switchboard room, at ten o'clock on New Year's Eve? Why the hell wasn't he with his family, or screwing his mistress at some place in the country? He racked his brains for a name, somewhere at the back of his mind, a mate from staff college who had gone on to the intelligence people, the spooks in the GRU. Finally he checked a classified military phone directory and rang.

He heard the buzz for a long time and checked his watch. Ten to eleven. All drunk, of course. The phone at Khodinka Field was answered. Before he could say anything a voice screamed: "Yeah? Hello!"

Behind the voice he heard a chattering sound.

"Who's that?" he asked. "Is Colonel Demidov there?"

"How the fuck should I know?" screamed the voice. "I'm lying on the floor dodging bullets. Are you the Defense Ministry?"

"No."

"Well, look, mate, get onto them and tell them to hurry up with that relief force. We can't hold on much longer."

"What relief force?"

"The Ministry is sending troops from out of town. There's all hell let loose here."

The speaker slammed down the receiver and presumably crawled away.

General Andreev stood with the dead receiver in his hand. No, they're not, he thought, they're not going to send anything.

His orders were formal and absolute. They came from a four-star general and minister in the government. Confined to base. He could obey them and his career remain clean as a whistle.

He stared out across the forty yards of snow-choked gravel toward the brightly lit windows of the Officers' Club, noisy with laughter and good cheer.

But he saw in the snow a tall, straight-backed figure with a small cadet by his side. Whatever they promise you, the tall man said, whatever money, or promotion, or honors they offer you, I don't want you ever to betray these men.

He reached down to the cradle, killed the line, then dialed two figures. His Exec Officer came on the line, backed by roars of laughter.

"Konni, I don't care how many T-Eighties are ready to roll, or how many BTRs, I want everything on this base that can move to be ready to go, and every soldier who can stand, fully armed in one hour."

There was silence for several seconds.

"Boss, is that for real?" asked Konni.

"It's for real, Konni. The Tamanskaya is going to Moscow."

•   •   •

AT one minute after midnight in the year of grace 2000, the first tracks of the first tank of the Taman Guards rolled out of Kobyakova Base and turned toward the Minsk Highway and the gates of the Kremlin.

The narrow country road from the highway to the base was only 3 kilometers long, over which the column of twenty-six T-80 main battle tanks and 41 BTR-80 armored personnel carriers had to proceed in single file and at reduced speed.

Out on the main road, a divided highway, General Andreev gave the order to occupy all lanes and increase to maximum cruise speed. The clouds of the day had broken up into patches and between them the stars were bright and brittle. On either side of the roaring column of tanks the pine woods crackled in the cold. They were cruising at over 60 kilometers. Somewhere up ahead a single driver approached; his lights picked up the mass of gray steel pounding toward him and he drove straight into the woods.

Ten kilometers out of Moscow the column came to the police post marking the border. Inside their steel hut, four militiamen peered above the windowsills, saw the column, and crouched back down, holding each other and their vodka bottles as the hut shuddered from the vibrations.

Andreev was in the leading tank and saw the roadblock trucks first. A number of private cars had approached the roadblocks during the night, waited awhile, then turned and headed back. There was no time for the column to halt.

"Fire at will," said Andreev.

His gunner squinted once and released a single round from the 125mm cannon in the turret. At a range of four hundred yards the shell was still at muzzle velocity when it hit one of the trucks and blew it apart. Beside Andreev's tank his Exec Officer, riding the tank on the other side of the highway, did the same and demolished the other truck. Just beyond the roadblock there was a smattering of small-arms fire from the ambush positions.

Inside the steel cupola on the roof of the turret Andreev's machine gunner raked his side of the road with his 12.7mm heavy machine gun and the firing stopped.

As the column thundered past, the Young Combatants stared in disbelief at the ruin of their roadblock and ambush site, then began to filter away into the night.

Six kilometers later Andreev slowed his column to thirty kilometers an hour and ordered two diversions. He sent five tanks and ten APCs to the right to relieve the garrison being besieged in the barracks at Khodinka Airfield, and, on a hunch, another five tanks and ten carriers to the left, to find their way northeast to secure the Ostankino television complex.

At the Sadovaya Ring Road he ordered his remaining sixteen T-80s and twenty-one APCs to the right as far as Kudrinskaya Square, then left toward the Defense Ministry.

The tanks were now in single file again and reduced their speed to 20 kilometers per hour, their tracks chewing chunks out of the tarmac as they swung into line and headed toward the Kremlin.

In the basement communications room of the Defense Ministry, Deputy Defense Minister Butov heard the rumble above his head and knew there was only one kind of creature in a city at war that can make that kind of thud.

The column pounded through Arbatskaya Square and passed the ministry, pointing now straight toward Borovitsky Square and, on the other side, the walls of the Kremlin. None of the men in the tanks and APCs noticed a car, parked among others, just off the square, or the figure in quilted jacket and boots who left the car and began to trot after them.

In Rosy O'Grady's Pub the Russian capital's Irish contingent was making sure the New Year had been well and truly celebrated, complete with the constant crackle of fireworks coming from the Kremlin down the street and across the square, when the first T-80 growled past the windows.

The Irish cultural attaché lifted his head from his Guinness, glanced out, and remarked to the barman, "Jaysus, Pat, was that a fucking tank?"

In front of the Borovitsky Gate was a parked BTR-80 armored personnel carrier of the Black Guard, its cannon raking the walls on top of which the last of the Presidentials had retreated. For four hours they had fought their way through the grounds of the Kremlin, waiting for reinforcements, unaware that General Korin's remaining troops had been ambushed on the outskirts of the city.

By one in the morning the Black Guards occupied everything but the tops of the walls, 2,235 meters of them and wide enough at the top to march five men abreast. Here the last few hundred of the Presidential Guards were huddled, covering the narrow stone steps from below and denying Grishin's men the final conquest.

From the western side of Borovitsky Square Andreev's lead tank emerged into the open and saw the BTR. At point-blank range a single shell blew the carrier to bits. When the tanks ran over the wreckage, the fragments were hardly larger than hub caps and their tracks flicked them aside.

At four minutes after one, General Andreev's T-80 plunged down the tree-lined approach to the tower and gate, entered the arch with its shattered door and grille, and rolled into the Kremlin.

Like his uncle before him, Andreev disdained to squat beneath a closed turret, peering through the periscope. His turret cover was thrown back and his head and torso were out in the cold, padded helmet and goggles masking his face.

One by one the T-80s rolled past the Great Palace and the pock-marked cathedrals of the Annunciation and the Archangel, pulling past the Czar's Bell into Ivanovskaya Square where once the city crier announced the emperor's decrees.

Two Black Guard carriers tried to take him on. Both were reduced to shards of hot metal.

Beside him the 7.62mm light machine gun and its heavier sister the 12.7 emitted a continuous chatter as the tank's searchlight began to pick up the running figures of the putschists.

There were still over three thousand combat-fit Black Guards investing the Kremlin's seventy-three acres, and it would have been pointless for Andreev's dismount squads to have left their vehicles. Barely two hundred of them would have made small difference on equal terms. But inside their armor, they were not on equal terms.

Grishin had not foreseen armor; he had brought no antitank gunnery. Lighter and nimbler, the Tamanskaya's APCs could penetrate the narrower alleys where the tanks could not go. Out in the open the tanks were waiting with their machine guns, impervious to counterfire.

But the real effect was psychological. To the soldier on foot, the tank is a true monster, its crew peering unseen through armored glass, its machine-gun snouts swiveling to find further helpless targets.

In fifty minutes the Black Guards cracked, breaking cover to run for the sanctuary of churches, palaces, and cathedrals. Some made it; others were caught in the open by the cannon of the BTRs or the machine guns of the tanks.

Elsewhere in the city the separate battles were at different stages. The Alpha Group was close to storming the OMON barracks at the Federal Interior Ministry when one of them caught a scream on his radio from the Kremlin. It was a panic-stricken Black Guard calling for help. But he made the mistake of mentioning the intervention of the T-80s. Word of the tanks flashed through the Alpha Group and they decided enough was enough. This had not gone as Grishin had promised them. He had pledged total surprise, superiority of firepower, and a helpless enemy. None of these had happened. They pulled back and sought to save themselves.

At the City Hall the street gangs of the New Russia Movement had already been taken apart by the Chechens.

In Staraya Ploshad, the OMON troops, supported by General Petrovsky's SOBR men, were beginning to flush the mercenaries from the Dolgoruki mafia's security companies out of the government headquarters.

At Khodinka Airfield the tide was turning. Five tanks and ten BTRs had taken the Vympel Special Assault Group in flank, and the more lightly armed commandos were being pursued through the maze of hangars and warehouses that made up the base.

The Duma was still occupied by the remainder of the privateers from the security firms, but they had nowhere to go and nothing to do but monitor by radio the news from elsewhere. They too heard the scream for help from the Kremlin, recognized the power of the tanks, and began to quit, each man persuading himself that with luck he would never be identified.

Ostankino still belonged to Grishin, but the triumphal announcement destined for the morning news was on hold as the two thousand Black Guards, watching from the windows, saw the tanks move slowly up the boulevard and their own trucks flaming one after another.

The Kremlin is built on a bluff above the river, the slopes of the bluff are studded with trees and shrubs, many of them evergreen. Beneath the western wall lie the Alexandrovsky Gardens. Paths through both sets of trees lead toward the Borovitsky Gate. None of the fighters inside the walls saw the single moving figure coming through the trees toward the open gate, nor did they see him climb the last slope to the ramp and slip inside.

As he emerged from the arch the passing flashlight of one of Andreev's tanks washed across him, but the crew mistook him for one of their own. His quilted jacket resembled their own padded jerkins and his round fur hat looked more like their own headgear than the black steel helmets of Grishin's Guards. Whoever was behind the flashlight presumed he was a tank man from a crippled APC seeking shelter under the arch.

The light flickered over him and went away. As it did so Jason Monk left the arch and ran under the cover of the pine trees to the right of the gate. From the cover of his darkness he watched and waited.

There are nineteen perimeter towers to the Kremlin, but only three have usable gates. Tourists enter and leave by the Borovitsky or the Trinity, troops by the Spassky. Of the three, only one was wide open and he was beside it.

A man deciding to save himself would have to leave the walled enclosure. Come the dawn, the forces of the state would flush out the defeated in hiding, pulling them from every last doorway and vestry, pantry, and cupboard, even down to the secret rooms of the command post beneath the Spassky Gardens. Anyone wishing to stay alive and out of prison would deduce he should leave soon via the only open gate.

Across from where he stood Monk could see the door of the armory, treasure house of a thousand years of Russian history, hanging in splinters where the rear of a turning tank had crushed it. The flickering flames from a burning Black Guard personnel carrier cast a glow over the facade.

The tide of battle moved away from the gate toward the Senate and the arsenal at the northeastern sector of the fortress. The burning vehicle crackled.

Just after two he caught a movement by the wall of the Great Palace, then a man in black came running, doubled over to keep low but moving fast down the facade of the armory. By the burning

APC he paused to look back, checking for pursuit. A tire caught fire and flamed, causing the fleeing man to turn quickly around. By the yellow light Monk saw the face. He had only seen it once before. In a photograph, on a beach at Sapodilla Bay in the Caicos Islands. He stepped from behind his tree.

"Grishin."

The man looked up, peered into the gloom beneath the pines. Then he saw who had called. He was carrying a Kalashnikov, the folded-stock AK-74. Monk saw the barrel come up and stepped behind the fir. There was a chattering burst of fire. Chunks of living wood were torn from the trunk. Then it stopped.

Monk peered round the bole. Grishin had gone. There had been fifty yards between him and the gate, but only ten for Monk. He had not passed.

Just in time Monk saw the muzzle of the AK-74 jutting out of the broken doorway. He stepped back again as bullets tore the tree in front of him. The firing stopped again. Two halves of a magazine, he estimated, and left the tree and ran across the road to flatten himself against the ocher wall of the museum. He had his Sig Sauer against his chest.

Again the barrel of the assault rifle came out of the doorway as the holder sought a target across the road. Unable to see anything, Grishin advanced another foot.

Monk's bullet hit the stock of the AK with enough force to tear it from the colonel's hands. It fell and skittered out onto the pavement, beyond reach. Monk heard running footsteps on the stone floor inside. Seconds later he had left the glow of the burning APC and was crouched in the pitch darkness of the hallway of the Armory.

The museum is on two floors, with nine great halls containing fifty-five showcases. In these are literally billions of dollars' worth of historic artifacts, for such was once the wealth and the power of Russia that everything possessed by the czars, their crowns, thrones, weapons, clothes, right down to horse bridles, were studded with silver, gold, diamonds, emeralds, rubies, sapphires, and pearls.

As his eyes adapted to the darkness, Monk could make out ahead of him the dim shape of the stairs to the upper floor. To his left was the vaulted arch leading to the four halls of the ground floor. From inside he heard a slight bump, as of someone nudging one of the showcases.

Taking a deep breath, Monk threw himself through the arch in a parachute roll, continuing to turn over and over in the darkness until he came up against a wall. As he came through the doorway he half-glimpsed the blue-white flash of muzzle flame and was covered in fragments of glass as a case above his head took the bullet.

The hall was long and narrow, though he could not see it, with long glass cases along both sides and a single display area, also enclosed in glass, in the center. Inside these, waiting again for the bright electric lights and the gawking tourists, were the priceless coronation robes, Russian, Turkish, and Persian, of all the Rurik and Romanov czars. A few square inches of any of them, and the jewels stitched to them, would keep a working man for years.

As the last shard of glass tinkled down, Monk strained his ears and heard at length a gasp as of someone trying not to pant letting out his breath. Taking a triangle of broken plate glass, he lobbed it through the blackness toward the sound.

Glass landed on glass case, there was another wild shot, and the sound of running feet between the echoes of the detonation. Monk rose to a crouch and ran forward, sheltering behind the center display until he realized Grishin had retreated into the next hall and was waiting for him.

Monk advanced to the communicating arch, a second slice of glass in his hand. When he was ready he tossed it far down the hall, then stepped through the arch and immediately sideways behind a cabinet. This time there was no bullet.

With his night vision returned he realized he was in a smaller hall containing jewel- and ivory-studded thrones. Though he did not know it, the coronation throne of Ivan the Terrible was a few feet to his left and that of Boris Godunov just beyond it.

The man ahead of him had clearly been running, for while Monk's breathing after his rest in the trees was measured and even, he could hear somewhere up ahead of him the rasp of the air entering Grishin's lungs.

Reaching up, he tapped the barrel of his automatic high on the glass above him, then pulled his hand down. He saw the flash of a gun muzzle in the darkness and fired quickly back. Above his head more glass broke and Grishin's bullet clipped a shower of brilliants off the diamond throne of Czar Alexei.

Monk's bullet must have been close, for Grishin turned and ran into the next hall which, though Monk did not know it and Grishin must have forgotten, was the last: a cul-de-sac, the hall of the antique carriages.

Hearing the scuttle of feet ahead of him, Monk followed fast, before Grishin could find a new sniping position. He reached the last hall and ducked behind an ornate seventeenth-century four-wheeled carriage embossed with golden fruit. At least the carriages gave shelter, but they also hid Grishin. Each carriage was on a raised dais, cordoned from the public not by glass cases but ropes on vertical stanchions.

He peered out from behind the state coach presented in 1600 by Elizabeth the First of England to Boris Godunov and tried to spot his enemy, but the blackness of the hall was complete and the coaches were only discernible as vague shapes.

As he watched, the clouds outside the tall narrow windows parted, and a single moonbeam filtered through. The windows were burglarproof and double-glazed; it was very dim light.

Yet something gleamed. A tiny point in all that darkness somewhere behind the ornate gilded wheel of the coach of Czaritsa Elizabeta.

Monk tried to remember the teaching of Mr. Sims at Castle Forbes. Two-handed, laddie, and hold it steady. Forget the O.K. Corral—that's fiction.

Monk raised his Sig Sauer two-handed and drew a bead on a spot four inches above the point of light. A slow breath, hold steady, fire.

The bullet went through the spokes of the wheel and hit something behind it. As the echoes drifted away and his ears ceased to ring, he heard the sliding thump of a heavy object hitting the floor.

It could be a ruse. He waited five minutes, then saw that the dim outline on the floor beside the carriage did not move. Slipping from cover to cover behind the antique wooden-framed vehicles, he moved closer until he could see a torso and a head, facedown to the floor. Only then did he approach, gun at the ready, and turn the body over.

Colonel Anatoli Grishin had taken the single bullet just above the left eye. As Mr. Sims would have said, it slows them up a bit. Jason

Monk looked down at the man he hated and felt nothing. It was done because it had to be done.

Pocketing his gun, he stooped, took the dead man's left hand, and pulled something from it.

The small object lay in his palm in the gloom, the raw American silver that had glittered in the moonlight, the luminous turquoise hacked from the hills by a Ute or Navajo. A ring brought from the high country of his own land, given on a park bench to a brave man at Yalta, and torn from the finger of a corpse in a courtyard at Lefortovo Jail.

He pocketed the ring, turned, and walked back to his car. The Battle of Moscow was over.

EPILOGUE

ON THE MORNING OF JANUARY 1 MOSCOW AND ALL RUSSIA AWOKE
to the grim knowledge of what had happened in their capital city.
Television cameras carried the images to every corner of the sprawling land. The nation was subdued by what it saw.

Inside the Kremlin walls there was a scene of devastation. The
facades of the cathedrals of the Assumption, the Annunciation, and
the Archangel were pitted and scarred by bullets. Broken glass glittered against the snow and ice.

Black smears from burning vehicles defaced the exteriors of the
Terem and Facets Palaces and those of the Senate and the Great
Kremlin Palace were torn by machine-gun fire.

Two huddled bodies lay beneath the Czar's Cannon, and the
removal teams carried others out from the arsenal and the Palace of
Congresses where they had taken refuge in the last minutes of life.

Elsewhere the armored personnel carriers and trucks of the Black
Guard smoldered and fumed in the morning light. The flames had
melted tracts of tarmac, which had then re-formed in the cold like
waves of the sea.

The acting president, Ivan Markov, flew back at once from his
vacation home, arriving shortly after midday. In the late afternoon
he received the Patriarch of Moscow and All the Russias in private
audience.

Alexei II made his first and last intervention in the political arena of Moscow. He urged that to continue with plans for a new presidential election on January 16 would be impossible, and that the date should be consecrated to a national referendum on the issue of the restoration of the monarchy.

Ironically, Markov was very susceptible to the idea. For one thing he was no fool. He had been appointed four years earlier to the post of premier by the late President Cherkassov as a skilled administrator, a gray suit with a background in the petroleum industry. But with time he had come to enjoy the power of executive office, even in a system where most of the power lay with the president and much less with the premier.

In the six months since Cherkassov's fatal heart attack he had come to appreciate the panoply of high office even more.

With the Union of Patriotic Forces in ruins from an electoral standpoint, he knew the issue would be between himself and the neo-Communists of the Socialist Union. He also knew he would probably come in second. But a constitutional monarch would, as almost his first act, need to call on an experienced politician and administrator to form a government of national unity. Who better, he reasoned, than himself?

That evening Ivan Markov by presidential decree summoned the deputies of the Duma to return to Moscow for an emergency session.

During January 3, the deputies streamed back across Russia from the farthest corners of Siberia and the northern wastes of Archangel.

The emergency session of the Duma on January 4 was held in the largely undamaged White House. The mood was somber, not least among the deputies of the Union of Patriotic Forces, who were each at pains to tell anyone who would listen that they personally had had no inkling of Igor Komarov's mad act of New Year's Eve.

The session was addressed by acting president Markov, who proposed that the entire nation still be consulted on January 16, but concerning the issue of restoration. As he was not a member of the Duma, he could not formally propose the motion. This was done by the Speaker, a member of Markov's Democratic Alliance Party.

The neo-Communists, seeing presidential power slipping from their grasp, opposed it with their entire voting bloc. But Markov had done his preparatory work well.

The members of the UPF, fearful for their own safety, had been interviewed privately, one by one, on the same morning. The strong impression given to each one of them was that if they supported the acting president, the whole question of the lifting of their parliamentary immunity from arrest could well be dropped. Such a step would mean they could keep their seats.

The Democratic Alliance votes added to those of the Union of Patriotic Forces outweighed the neo-Communists. The motion was carried.

Technically the change was not so difficult to administer. Polling booths were already in place. The sole task was to print and issue a further 105 million ballot papers bearing the simple question and two boxes, one for "Yes" and one for "No."

• • •

ON January 5, in the small northern Russian port of Vyborg a dock security policeman called Pyotr Gromov made his small mark on the footnote of history. Just after dawn he was watching the Swedish freighter *Ingrid B* prepare to leave for Gothenburg.

He was about to turn away and return to his cabin for breakfast when two figures in blue donkey jackets emerged from behind a pile of crates and made for the gangway just as it was to be hauled up. On a hunch he called on them to stop.

The two men had a brief, muttered conversation and then ran for the gangway. Gromov pulled his gun and fired a warning shot in the air. It was the first time he had used it in three years on the docks, and it pleased him mightily to do so. The two seamen stopped.

Their papers revealed both were Swedes. The younger man spoke English, of which Gromov had a few words. But he had worked long enough on the docks to have a better grasp of Swedish. To the older man he snapped: "So what was the hurry?"

The man said not a word. Neither of them had understood him. He reached out and tore off the older man's round fur hat. Something familiar about the face. He had seen it before. The policeman and the fleeing Russian stared at each other. That face . . . on television . . . a podium . . . shouting at the cheering crowd.

"I know you," he said. "You're Igor Komarov."

Komarov and Kuznetsov were arrested and flown back to Moscow. The former leader of the UPF was immediately indicted for high treason and remanded in custody pending trial. He was lodged, ironically, in Lefortovo Jail.

•   •   •

FOR ten days the national debate occupied the newspapers, magazines, airwaves, and TV channels as pundit after pundit intoned his or her opinion.

On the afternoon of Friday, January 14, Father Gregor Rusakov held a revivalist rally in the Olympic Stadium in Moscow. As with Komarov when he had spoken there, his address was carried across the nation, reaching, so the pollsters later estimated, eighty million Russians.

His theme was simple and clear. For seventy years the Russian people had worshiped the twin gods of dialectical materialism and Communism and had been betrayed by both. For fifteen years they had attended at the temple of republican capitalism and seen their hopes traduced. He urged his listeners on the morrow to go back to the God of their fathers, to go to church and pray for guidance.

Foreign observers have long gained the impression that after seventy years of Communist industrialization the Russians must be a mainly city-dwelling people. It is a mistaken assumption. Even by the winter of 1999 over fifty percent of Russians still lived largely unseen and unrecorded in the small towns, villages, and countryside, that vast spread of land from Belarus to Vladivostok, running across six thousand miles and nine time zones.

Within that unseen land are the one hundred thousand parishes that comprise the hundred bishoprics of the Orthodox Church, each with its large or small onion-domed parish church.

It was to these churches that seventy percent of the Russians streamed through the bitter cold on the morning of Sunday, January 16, and from each pulpit the parish priest read out the Patriarchal Letter. Later known as the Great Encyclical, it was probably the most powerful and moving missive Alexei II ever uttered. It had been adopted the previous week in a closed conclave of the Metropolitan bishops, where the voting, though not unanimous, was convincing.

After morning service the Russians went from the churches to the polls. Because of the size of the land and the lack of electronic technology in the rural districts, it took two days to count the votes. Of valid votes cast, the outcome was sixty-five percent in favor, thirty-five percent against.

On January 20 the Duma accepted and endorsed the result, and passed two further motions. One was to extend the interregnum of Ivan Markov for a further period, until March 31. The second was to institute a Constitutional Committee to pass the referendum verdict into law.

On February 20 the acting president and the Duma of All the Russias extended an invitation to a prince resident outside Russia to accept the title and the functions, within a constitutional monarchy, of Czar of All the Russias.

Ten days later a Russian airliner landed after a long flight at Vnukovo Airport, Moscow.

Winter was retreating. The temperature had risen several degrees above zero and the sun shone. From the birch and pine woods behind the small airport reserved for special flights came an odor of damp earth and new beginning.

In front of the terminal Markov led a large delegation containing the Speaker of the Duma, the leaders of all the main parties, the combined Chiefs of Staff, and the Patriarch Alexei.

From the aircraft stepped the man the Duma had invited, the fifty-seven-year-old prince of the English House of Windsor.

•　　•　　•

FAR away in the west, in a former coach house outside the village of Langton Matravers, Sir Nigel Irvine watched the ceremony on television.

In the kitchen Lady Irvine was washing the breakfast dishes, something she always did before Mrs. Moir came in to clean.

"What are you watching, Nigel?" she called as she let the soapy water out of the sink. "You never look at television in the mornings."

"Something going on in Russia, my dear."

It had been, he thought, a close-run thing. He had followed his own principles for the destruction of a richer, stronger, and more numerous adversary by the use of minimum forces, a destruction that could only be accomplished by guile and deception.

His first stage had been to require Jason Monk to create a loose

alliance of those liable to fear or despise Igor Komarov after seeing
the Black Manifesto. In the first category came those destined for
destruction by the Russian Nazi—the Chechens, Jews, and police
who had persecuted Komarov's ally, the Dolgoruki mafia. In the
second came the church and the army, represented by the Patriarch
and the most prestigious living general, Nikolai Nikolayev.

The next task had been to insert an informer into the enemy
camp, not to bring out reliable information but to insert disinformation.

While Monk was still training at Castle Forbes, the spymaster had
made his first unnoticed visit to Moscow to reactivate two longtime low-level sleeper agents he had recruited years earlier. One was
the former Moscow University professor whose homing pigeons
had proved useful in the past.

But when the professor had lost his job for proposing democratic
reforms under the Communists, his son had also lost his high school
place and any chance of going to a university. The young man had
drifted into the church, and after undistinguished sojourns in various parishes had finally been taken on as valet and butler to Patriarch Alexei.

Father Maxim Klimovsky had been authorized to accomplish
four separate betrayals of Irvine and Monk to Colonel Grishin. This
was simply to establish his reliability as an informer for the Black
Guard commander in the heart of the enemy camp.

Twice Irvine and Monk had been allowed to escape before
Grishin appeared, but on the last two occasions that had not been
possible, and they had had to fight their way out.

Irvine's third precept was not to try to persuade his enemy there
was no campaign against him, which would have been impossible,
but to convince him the danger lay somewhere else and, having
been coped with, had therefore ceased to exist.

Following his second visit to the residence, Irvine had been
forced to stay on to give Grishin and his thugs time to raid his room
in his absence, discover his briefcase, and photograph the incrimi-
nating letter.

The letter was a forgery, created in London on real Patriarchate
writing paper and with calligraphy samples of the Patriarch's own
hand, obtained by Father Maxim and handed to Irvine on the previous visit.

In the letter, the Patriarch apparently told his correspondent that he warmly supported the idea of a restoration of the monarch of Russia (which was not true, since he was only considering it), and would urge that the receiver of the letter be the man chosen for the post.

Unfortunately it was addressed to the wrong prince. It bore the name of Prince Semyon, living in his stone farmhouse with his horses and girlfriend in Normandy. Of necessity, he had been deemed expendable.

It was Jason Monk's second visit to the Patriarch that had unleashed stage four—the encouragement to the enemy to overreact violently to a perceived but nonexistent threat. This had been achieved by the tape recording of the supposed conversation between Monk and Alexei II.

Genuine voice samples of the Patriarch had been obtained during Irvine's first visit, because his interpreter Brian Vincent had been wired for sound. Monk had recorded hours of tape in his own voice while at Castle Forbes.

In London a Russian mimic and actor had provided the words that Alexei II apparently spoke on the tape. With computerized sound technology the tape had been created, right down to the stirring of coffee cups. Father Maxim, to whom Irvine had palmed the tape as he passed in the hall, had simply played it from one recorder into the one given him by Grishin.

Everything on the tape was a lie. Major General Petrovsky could not have continued his raids on the Dolgoruki gang because all the knowledge Monk had gleaned from the Chechens about the rival mafia had already been passed to him. Moreover the papers from beneath the casino contained no evidence of Dolgoruki funding of the UPF election campaign.

General Nikolayev had no intention of continuing to denounce Komarov in a series of interviews after New Year's Day. He had said his piece, and once was enough.

Most important, the Patriarch had not the slightest intention of intervening with the acting president to urge that Komarov be declared an unfit person. He had made it quite clear that he would not intervene in politics.

But neither Grishin nor Komarov knew this. Believing they had the opponents' intentions in their grasp and faced a fearful danger, they overreacted badly and launched four assassination attempts. Suspecting they were coming, Monk could warn all four targets. Only one refused to heed the warning. Until the night of December 21, and possibly even later, Komarov could still have won the election with a handsome majority.

After December 21 came stage five. The overreaction was exploited by Monk to broaden the hostility against Komarov from the tiny few who had seen the Black Manifesto into a raging torrent of criticism from the media. Into this exploitation Monk filtered disinformation to the effect that the source for all Komarov's growing discreditation was a senior officer of the Black Guard.

In politics as in so many affairs of men, success breeds success, but failure also generates further failure. As the criticism of Komarov increased, so did the paranoia dormant in all tyrants. Nigel Irvine's final gambit was to play upon that paranoia and hope against hope that the somewhat inadequate vessel of Father Maxim would not let him down.

When the Patriarch returned from Zagorsk, he never went near the acting president. Four days before the New Year, the organs of the Russian state had not a shred of intent to fall upon the Black Guard on New Year's Day and arrest Komarov.

Through Father Maxim, Irvine used the old precept of persuading the enemy that his opponents are far more numerous, powerful, and determined than they really are. Convinced by this second "sting," Komarov decided to strike first. Forewarned by Monk, the Russian state defended itself.

Though not much of a churchgoer, Sir Nigel Irvine had long been an assiduous reader of the Bible, and of all its characters his favorite was the Hebrew warrior Gideon.

As he explained it to Jason Monk in the Highlands of Scotland, Gideon was the first commander of special forces and the first proponent of surprise night attack.

Presented with ten thousand volunteers, Gideon chose only three hundred, the toughest and the best. In his night attack on the Midianites camped in the Valley of Jezreel he used the triple tactics of violent awakening, bright lights, and shattering noise to disorient and panic the larger force.

"What he did, m'dear chap, was to persuade the half-awake Midianites that they were up against an enormous and very dangerous attack. So they lost their nerve and ran."

Not only did they run, but in the darkness they began hacking at each other. By another kind of disinformation, Grishin was persuaded to arrest his own entire high command.

Lady Irvine came in and switched off the TV.

"Come along, Nigel, it's a lovely day and we have to dig in the early potatoes."

The spymaster pulled himself to his feet.

"Of course," he said, "the spring earlies. I'll get my boots."

He hated digging, but he did love Penny Irvine very much.

• • •

IT was just after midday in the Caribbean when the *Foxy Lady* came out of Turtle Cove and headed for the Cut.

Halfway to the reef Arthur Dean swept up alongside in the *Silver Deep*. He had two tourist divers in the stern.

"Hey, Jason, you been away?"

"Yep. Went over to Europe for a spell."

"How was it?"

Monk thought that one over.

"Interesting," he said.

"Good to see you back." Dean glanced into the afterdeck of the *Foxy Lady*. "You don't have a charter?"

"Nope. There are wahoo running ten miles off the Point. I'm going to take some just for me."

Arthur Dean grinned, recognizing the feeling.

"Tight lines, man."

The *Silver Deep* opened her throttle and sped away. The *Foxy Lady* moved through the Cut and Monk felt the thump and surge of the open sea beneath his feet, and the sweet-smelling salted wind on his face.

Pushing on the power he turned the *Foxy Lady* away from the islands and out toward the lonely sea and the sky.